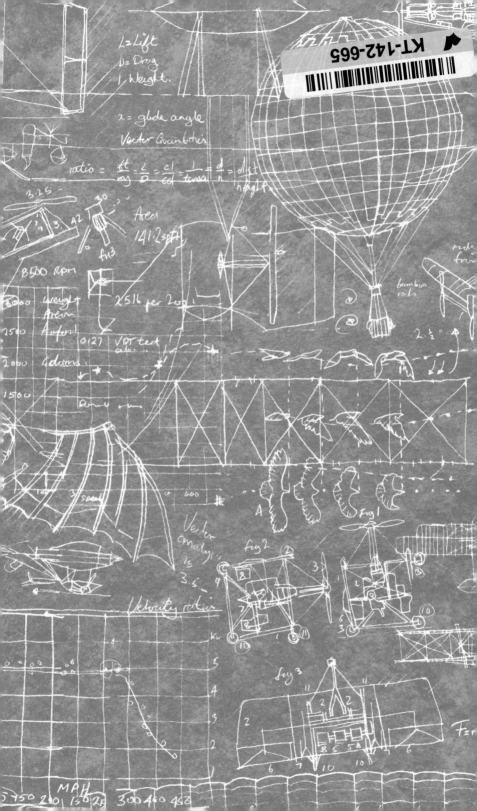

AIRMAN

EOIN COLFER

PUFFIN

PUFFIN BOOKS

Published by the Penguin Group
Penguin Books Ltd, 80 Strand, London WC2R 0RL, England
Penguin Group (USA) Inc., 375 Hudson Street, New York, New York 10014, USA
Penguin Group (Canada), 90 Eglinton Avenue East, Suite 700, Toronto, Ontario, Canada M4P 2Y3
(a division of Pearson Penguin Canada Inc.)
Penguin Ireland, 25 St Stephen's Green, Dublin 2, Ireland (a division of Penguin Books Ltd)
Penguin Group (Australia), 250 Camberwell Road, Camberwell, Victoria 3124, Australia
(a division of Pearson Australia Group Pty Ltd)
Penguin Books India Pvt Ltd, 11 Community Centre, Panchsheel Park, New Delhi – 110 017, India
Penguin Group (NZ), 67 Apollo Drive, Rosedale, North Shore 0632, New Zealand
(a division of Pearson New Zealand Ltd)
Penguin Books (South Africa) (Pty) Ltd, 24 Sturdee Avenue, Rosebank, Johannesburg 2196, South Africa

Penguin Books Ltd, Registered Offices: 80 Strand, London WC2R 0RL, England

puffinbooks.com

First published 2008
1

Text copyright © Eoin Colfer, 2008

The moral right of the author has been asserted

Set in Perpetua by Palimpsest Book Production Limited, Grangemouth, Stirlingshire
Made and printed in England by Clays Ltd, St Ives plc

British Library Cataloguing in Publication Data
A CIP catalogue record for this book is available from the British Library

HARDBACK
ISBN: 978–0–141–38335–4

TRADE PAPERBACK
ISBN: 978–0–141–38336–1

www.greenpenguin.co.uk

For Declan Dempsey

CONTENTS

Part 3: Airman

PROLOGUE

Conor Broekhart was born to fly, or more accurately he was born flying. Though Broekhart's legend is littered with fantastical stories, the tale of his first flight in the summer of 1878 would be the most difficult to believe, had there not been thousands of witnesses. In fact, an account of his birth in a hot-air balloon can be read in the archives of the French newspaper, *Le Petit Journal*, available to all for a small fee at the Librairie Nationale.

Above the article, there is a faded black-and-white photograph. It is remarkably sharp for the period, and was taken by a newspaperman who happened to be in the Trocadéro gardens at the time with his camera.

Captain Declan Broekhart is easily recognizable in the picture, as is his wife, Catherine. He, handsome in his crimson-and-gold Saltee Island Sharpshooters uniform, she shaken but smiling. And there, protected in the crook of his father's elbow, lies baby Conor. Already with a head of blond Broekhart hair and his mother's wide, intelligent brow. No more than ten minutes old and through some trick of the light or photographic mishap, it seems as though Conor's eyes are focused. Impossible of course. But imagine if somehow they had been, then baby Conor's first sight would have been a cloudless French sky flashing by. Little wonder he became what he became.

Paris, summer of 1878

The World Fair was to be the most spectacular ever seen, with over 1,000 exhibitors from every corner of the world.

Captain Declan Broekhart had travelled to France from the Saltee Islands at his king's insistence. Catherine had accompanied him at her own request, as she was the scientist in the family and longed to see for herself the much heralded Galerie des Machines, which showcased inventions promising to make the future a better one. King Nicholas had sent them to Paris, to investigate the possibility of a balloon division for the Saltee Wall.

On the third day of their trip, the pair took a buggy along the Avenue de l'Opéra, to observe the Aeronautical Department's balloon demonstration in the Trocadéro gardens.

'Do you feel that?' asked Catherine. She took her husband's hand, and placed it on her stomach. 'Our son is kicking to be free. He longs to witness these miracles for himself.'

Declan laughed. 'He *or she* will have to wait. The world will still be here in six weeks.'

When the Broekharts arrived at the Trocadéro gardens, they found the Aeronautical Squadron in the shadow of the Statue of Liberty, or rather that of her head. The statue would be presented to the United States when completed, but for now

Lady Liberty's head alone was being showcased. The copper structure dwarfed most of the fair's other exhibits and it was amazing to imagine how colossal the assembled statue would be when it finally stood guard over New York City's harbour.

The Aeronautical Squadron had inflated a dirigible balloon on a patch of lawn, and was politely holding the crowd back with a velvet rope. Declan Broekhart approached the soldier on sentry duty and handed him his sealed letter of introduction from the French ambassador to the Saltee Islands. Within minutes they were joined by the squadron's captain, Victor Vigny.

Vigny was lithe and tanned with a crooked nose and a crown of jet-black hair that stood erect on his scalp like the head of a yard brush.

'*Bonjour*, Captain Broekhart,' he said, removing one white glove and shaking the Saltee Island officer's hand warmly. 'We have been expecting you.' The Frenchman bowed deeply. 'And this must be Madame Broekhart.' Vigny checked the letter in mock confusion. 'But, *madame*, nowhere here does it say how beautiful you are.'

The Frenchman's smile was so charming that the Broekharts could not take offence.

'Well, Captain,' said Vigny, sweeping back his arm dramatically to introduce his balloon. 'I give you *Le Soleil*, the Sun. What do you think of her?'

The dirigible was undeniably magnificent. An elongated golden envelope swaying gently over its leather-bound basket. But Declan Broekhart was not interested in decoration, he was interested in specification.

'A bit more *pointed* than others I've seen,' he noted.

'*Aérodynamique*,' corrected Vigny. 'She glides across the sky like her namesake.'

Catherine unhooked herself from her husband's arm.

'A cotton-silk blend,' she said, craning her head back to squint at the balloon. 'And twin screws on the basket. A neat piece of work. How fast does she travel?'

Vigny was surprised to hear such technical observations from a female, but he disguised his shock with a few rapid blinks, then smoothly delivered his answer.

'Ten miles an hour. With the help of God and a fair wind.'

Catherine peeled back a corner of leather, revealing the woven basket underneath.

'Wicker and willow,' she said. 'Makes a nice cushion.'

Vigny was enchanted. 'Yes. *Absolument*. This basket will last for five hundred hours in the sky. French baskets are the best in the world.'

'*Très bien*,' said Catherine.

She hoisted her petticoats and climbed the wooden steps to the basket, displaying remarkable agility for a woman eight months' pregnant. Both men stepped forward to object, but Catherine did not give them time to speak.

'I dare say I know more about the science of aeronautics than both of you. And I really don't think I have crossed the Celtic Sea to stand in a glorified field while my husband experiences one of the wonders of the world.'

Catherine was perfectly calm as she made this statement, but only a dullard could have missed the steel in her voice.

Declan sighed. 'Very well, Catherine. If Captain Vigny permits it.'

Vigny's only answer was a Gallic shrug that said, *Permit it? I pity the man who tries to stand in this woman's way.*

Catherine smiled.

'Very well, it is settled. Shall we cast off?'

Le Soleil loosed its anchors shortly before three that afternoon, quickly climbing to a height of a few hundred feet.

'We are in heaven,' sighed Catherine, clutching her husband's hand tightly.

The young couple looked upwards into the belly of the balloon itself. The silk was set shimmering by the breeze and sparkling by the sun. Golden waves billowed across its surface, rumbling like distant thunder.

Below them the Trocadéro gardens were emerald lakes, with Lady Liberty's head breaching the surface like a Titan of legend.

Vigny fed a small steam engine, sending power to the twin propellers. Fortunately, the prevailing wind snatched the smoke away from the basket.

'Impressive, *non*?' shouted the Frenchman above the engine's racket. 'How many are you thinking of ordering?'

Declan pretended not to be impressed. 'Perhaps none. I don't know if those little propellers would have any effect against an ocean wind.'

Vigny was about to argue the merits of his steam-powered dirigible when a sharp flat crack echoed across the skies. It was a noise familiar to both soldiers.

'Gunshot,' said Vigny, peering towards the ground.

'Rifle,' said Declan Broekhart grimly. As captain of the Saltee Sharpshooters he knew the sound well. 'Long range. Maybe a Sharps. See, there.'

A plume of grey-blue smoke rose into the sky from the western border of the gardens.

'Gun smoke,' noted Vigny. 'One cannot help wondering who the target might be.'

'No need to wonder, *monsieur*,' said Catherine, her voice shaking. 'Look above you. The balloon.'

Both men searched the golden envelope for a puncture. Both found one. The bullet had entered through the lower starboard quadrant and exited through the upper port section.

'Why are we not dead?' wondered Declan.

'The bullet was not enough to ignite the hydrogen,' explained Vigny. 'An incendiary shell would have done so.'

Catherine was badly shaken. For the first time in her short life, mortality was at hand, and not just her own. By stepping into the balloon's basket she had put her child's life at risk. She folded her arms across her stomach.

'We must descend. Quickly. Before the envelope rips.'

In the fraught minutes that were to follow, Vigny proved his skill as an aeronaut. He perched on the basket's lip, gripping a stanchion in one hand and the gas-release line in the other. With a tap of his boot he pushed the tiller wide. *Le Soleil* swung in a gentle arc. Vigny intended to set her down inside the velvet rope.

Declan Broekhart stayed at his wife's side. Strong and stubborn as Catherine was, the gunshot had shocked her system. This had the effect of bringing forward her child's due time. The body realized that it was in mortal danger, so the best chance for the baby was in the wide world.

A spasm of pain buckled Catherine's knees. She collapsed backwards, cradling her stomach.

'Our son is coming,' she gasped. 'He refuses to wait.'

Vigny almost fell off his perch. '*Mon Dieu.* But, *madame*, this is impossible. I cannot allow it on my ship. I do not even know if this is good luck or bad luck. I will have to check the aeronaut's manual. It would not surprise me if we had to sacrifice an albatross.'

It was Vigny's habit to chatter wittily when anxious. Wit in times of danger was, in his opinion, very cavalier. This did not stop him performing his duties. He guided the dirigible expertly towards the chosen landing spot, compensating for the leaks with expert tugs on the gas line.

On the basket's cramped floor, Catherine struggled to deliver her child. Her leg shot out involuntarily as the pain hit. The stroke was a lucky one, catching her husband on the shin and snapping him out of his near panic.

'What can I do, Catherine?' he asked, keeping his voice steady, his tone light, as though giving birth in a falling balloon was the most natural thing in the world.

'Hold me steady,' replied Catherine through gritted teeth. 'And give me your weight to push against.'

Declan did as he was told, calling over his shoulder to Vigny.

'Steady. Keep her steady, man.'

'Talk to the Almighty,' retorted Vigny. 'He is sending the gusts of wind, not I.'

They were in reasonably good order. The envelope was damaged, but holding her integrity. The Broekharts huddled on the floor, engrossed in the business of bringing life to the world.

They would have made it. Vigny was already imagining the first sip of the champagne he planned to order the moment his feet touched solid ground, when the air was split with a brace of gunshots. Both bullets pierced the balloon, and this time their effect was more severe. One passed straight through as its predecessor had, but the second clipped a seam, sending a rip racing to the crown of the balloon. Air and gas screamed from the distressed dirigible like a company of banshees.

Vigny pitched forward into the basket, bouncing off Declan Broekhart's broad back. They were in God's hands now. With the envelope so grievously ruptured, the Frenchman could not claim a single degree of control over the balloon's path. They dropped rapidly, the deflating envelope flapping above them.

Catherine and Declan ignored their own fates, concentrating on their child's.

'I see the baby,' said Declan, shouting into the wind. 'Almost there, my darling.'

Catherine Broekhart held back the despair clamouring in her mind and pushed her baby into the world. He arrived without a cry, reaching out to grip his father's finger.

'A boy,' he said. 'My strong son.'

Catherine gave herself not a minute to recover from her brief labour. She leaned forward and grasped her husband's lapel.

'You cannot let him die, sir.' It was an order, plain and simple.

Vigny swaddled the newborn in his blue Aeronautical Squadron jacket.

'We can but pray,' he said.

Declan Broekhart climbed to his feet, taking in the literal gravity of their situation at a glance. The basket was in virtual freefall now, slicing east directly towards Lady Liberty's head. Any considerable impact would surely result in the baby's death, and he had been forbidden to allow that. But how to avoid it?

Fortune saved them, at least temporarily. The envelope spent its last breath, then impaled itself on the third and fourth rays of Liberty's crown. The material ripped, bunched and jammed between the rays, halting the basket's murderous descent.

'Providence,' breathed Captain Broekhart. 'We are spared.'

The basket swung like a pendulum, grazing the lower curve of Lady Liberty's cheek with each pass. The copper bust rang, attracting gawkers like church worshippers. Catherine held on to her baby son, absorbing the impact as best she could. The envelope's threads popped with cracks like gunfire.

'The balloon will not hold,' said Vigny. 'We are still twenty feet up.'

Declan nodded. 'We need to lash her to the statue.' He grabbed Le Soleil's anchors, tossing one to Vigny. 'A case of the finest red wine if you make the shot.'

Vigny tested the anchor's weight. 'Champagne, if you don't mind.'

Both men threw their anchors high between the last two rays of Lady Liberty's crown. Their aim was true and the anchors bumped the statue's ringlets, then slid back down, raising sparks as the metal surfaces cracked together. The anchors bit on both sides of the crown and stuck fast. Declan and Vigny quickly pulled a loop of rope through the basket's bow and stern rings, cinching them tight.

Not a moment too soon. With the screech of a seabird, the balloon material ripped itself free of the statue's crown, dropping the basket a further stomach-lurching yard until the anchor ropes took the strain. The ropes groaned, stretched and held.

'My basket is now a cradle for your baby,' panted Vigny, and then, 'Champagne. A case. The sooner the better.'

Declan squatted below the basket's rim, tugging the Frenchman's cuff until he too bent low.

'Your hunter may have more bullets to spend,' he said.

'True,' agreed Victor Vigny. 'But I think he will have fled. We no longer present such an enormous target, and by now the *gendarmes* will be on his trail. I imagine it was an anarchist. They have been making threats.'

In the Trocadéro gardens, the entire crowd had pooled below the basket. They had come to the World Fair expecting spectacle, but here was high adventure. The Aeronautical Squadron leaned long ladders against the wicker basket to rescue *Le Soleil*'s stranded passengers. Catherine climbed down first, aided by the gallant Captain Vigny. Then came the proud father, cradling the miraculous baby in his arms. People gasped and surged forward. *A child. There had been no child in the basket when it took flight.* It was as if the world had never before seen a baby.

Born in the sky. Imagine it. A child of wonder.

Ladies and gentlemen elbowed each other shamelessly, longing for a glimpse of his cherubic face.

Look, the eyes are open. His hair is almost white. Perhaps the altitude?

Someone popped the cork on a bottle of champagne, and an Italian count passed around Cuban cigars. It was as if the entire assembly were celebrating the baby's survival. Vigny snagged the bottle, quaffing deeply.

'Perfect,' he sighed, passing it to Declan Broekhart.

'He is a charmed boy. What will you call him?'

Broekhart grinned, deliriously happy.

'I thought perhaps Engel. He came from the skies, after all. And our family name is Flemish.'

'No, Declan,' said Catherine, stroking her son's white-blond hair. 'Though he is an angel, he has my father's brow. Conor is his name.'

'Conor?' said Declan, in mock protest. 'Irish from your family. Flemish from mine. The boy is a mongrel.'

Vigny lit two cigars, passing one to the proud father. 'Now is not the time to argue, *mon ami*.'

Declan nodded. 'It never is. Conor he shall be called. A strong name.'

Vigny bonged a knuckle on Lady Liberty's chin. 'Whatever he is called, this boy is indebted to Liberty.'

This was the second omen of the day. Conor Broekhart would eventually pay his debt to liberty. The first omen was, of course, the airborne birth. Perhaps he would have been a sky pilot even without *Le Soleil*, or perhaps something was awakened in him that day. An obsession with the sky that would consume Conor Broekhart's life, and the lives of everyone around him.

And so a few days after Conor's famous birth, Captain Declan Broekhart and his family sailed from France back to the tiny sovereign state of the Saltee Islands off the Irish coast.

The Saltee Islands had been ruled by the Trudeau family since 1171 when England's King Henry II had given them to Raymond Trudeau, a powerful and ambitious knight. It was a cruel joke as the Saltee Islands were little more than gull-infested rocks. By placing Trudeau in charge of the Saltee Islands, Henry fulfilled his contract of granting his knight an Irish estate, but also made it clear what happened to overly ambitious knights.

When Raymond Trudeau objected to the king's grant, Henry delivered the often-quoted *Trudeau Admonishment*.

'You disagree with an appointee of God Himself,' Henry is recorded as saying. 'Perhaps Monsieur Trudeau considers *himself* above his king. Perhaps Monsieur Trudeau considers himself fit for royal office. So be it. You shall take the Saltee Islands with my blessing, but not as baron. You are their king. King Raymond the First. I will demand neither tithe nor tribute from you or your descendants in perpetuity and, as an added reward, you may wear your crown to my court. Whatever you may find on those most bountiful isles is yours to keep.'

Trudeau could do nothing but bow and stammer his thanks, bitter though the words were. This was a terrible insult, as there was nothing to be found on the Saltee Islands but sea birds and their droppings, and little grew there thanks to the showers of sea spray that coated both islands during rough tides, giving nothing to the Saltees but their name.

But Raymond Trudeau's fortune was not as bleak as it seemed. Following his effective banishment to the Saltee Islands, a strange glowing cave was discovered by one of his men who was burning gulls from their perches. The cave was a glacial deposit of diamonds. The largest mine ever discovered, and the only mine in Europe. Henry had ordained Raymond Trudeau king of the most valuable estate in the world.

Seven hundred years later and the Trudeau family were still in power in spite of over a dozen invasion attempts from English, Irish and even pirate armies. The famous Saltee walls held fast against cannon, shot and ram, and the celebrated Saltee Sharpshooters were trained to shave the whiskers off a pirate a mile away. There were only two industries on the Saltees. Diamonds and defence.

The Saltee prison was packed to bursting with the foulest dregs of murdering humanity that Ireland and Great Britain had to offer. They worked the diamond mine until they had served their time or died. Most died. A sentence on Little Saltee was a death sentence. Nobody really cared. The Saltees had been making many people rich for centuries, and none of those many people wanted the status quo to change.

Nevertheless change was afoot. Now, there was a new king on the Saltee throne, an American, King Nicholas the First, or *Good King Nick* as he was known in an increasing number of households. Barely six months in power and already King Nicholas had drastically improved the quality of life for his 3,000 subjects, abolishing taxes and building a modern drainage system, that ran through the town of Promontory Fort on Great Saltee's northern tip.

When the royal yacht, *Razorbill*, pulled into Saltee Harbour at dawn after a three-day voyage from France, King Nicholas himself was there to meet her. Truth be told, he did not much look like the other kings of the day, a youthful thirty-seven, dressed in stout hunting leathers and a flat cap. His sideburns were trimmed back, and hair cut military style close to the skull. His face was tanned, with a tic-tac-toe pattern of faded scars on his forehead from a close call with a landmine. A stranger might assume Nicholas to be the king's gamekeeper, but never the king. There was no pomp or circumstance about the man, and he lived as plainly as one could in a stately palace. Nicholas had served as a skirmisher and a balloonist during the American Civil War, and it was said that he slept on the window seat in his royal chamber because the bed was too soft.

Nicholas was a new breed of European king. One who was determined to use whatever power he had to improve the quality of life for as many people as possible. Good King Nick. Declan Broekhart loved him like a brother.

Declan hitched the yacht's bowline, then leaped on to the jetty to greet his monarch.

'Your Majesty,' he said, bowing slightly.

King Nicholas returned the bow, then punched his friend on the shoulder.

'Declan! What kept you? I read about your miraculous airborne baby before I see him. I can only pray that he has inherited his mother's features.'

While the men shared a chuckle, Catherine stepped on to the gangplank, holding her precious bundle wrapped in a blanket.

'Catherine,' said Nicholas, taking her arm. 'Shouldn't you be resting?'

'I had my fill of rest on-board.' Catherine pulled little Conor's blanket down past his chin. 'Now, your newest subject would like to meet his king.'

Nicholas peered into the swaddling clothes, finding a baby's face in the shadows. He was a little disconcerted to find the child's eyes focused and seemingly taking his measure.

'Ah,' he said, rearing back slightly. 'So . . . alert.'

'Yes,' said Catherine proudly. 'He has his father's sharpshooter eyes.'

But King Nicholas saw more.

'Perhaps. But he has the Broekhart chin too. Stubborn to a fault. Your brow though, Catherine. A scientist perhaps, like his mother.' He tickled baby Conor's chin. 'We need scientists. There's a new world coming our way from America and Europe too. The Saltees won't stay independent unless we have something to offer the world, and the diamond mine on Little Saltee won't last forever. Scientists, that's what we need here.' King Nicholas tugged on riding gloves. 'Teach him well, Catherine.'

'I will, Your Majesty.'

'And take him up to the palace. Introduce him to Isabella.'

'I'll take him up after breakfast,' promised Catherine.

Nicholas smiled sadly. 'Isabella's mother would have had a gift ready and wrapped. The perfect gift.' The king stood silently for a moment, remembering his wife, then roused himself. 'And now, Declan, sorry to drag you away, but apparently some opium smugglers have dug themselves into Lady Walker's Cave. Right under our noses.'

'I'll take care of it, Majesty. Perhaps you would escort Catherine to our quarters?'

'Nice try, Captain,' grinned Nicholas, clapping his hands, 'hoping to keep me out of harm's way.' The king was excited again, the old soldier in him relishing the chase. Unlike most old soldiers, he did not relish the kill. These smugglers would be sent to work the diamond mine on the prison island of Little Saltee, but not harmed unless it was unavoidable.

'Come now, we have dawn light and low tide. Criminals do not like to get up early, so we should catch them napping.'

The king touched his cap to Catherine, then strode off down the jetty towards a small company of Saltee cavalry on horseback. It was, in fact, the entire Saltee Army mounted division. A dozen expert horsemen on Irish stallions. Two of the horses were without riders.

Declan was anxious to stay with his wife, but more anxious to be about his work.

'I must go, Catherine. The king will injure himself swinging into those caves.'

'You go, Declan. Keep him safe; the islands need Good King Nick.'

Captain Broekhart kissed his wife and baby, then followed King Nicholas to where the cavalry waited, horses carving spiralled shavings from the jetty planks with their hooves.

'Your father, the hero,' Catherine told baby Conor, waving his tiny hand towards Declan. 'Now, let's go home and make ready to meet a little princess. Would you like to meet a princess, my stubborn scientist?'

Conor gurgled. It seemed as though he would.

PART 1:

BROEKHART

CHAPTER 1:

THE PRINCESS AND THE PIRATE

Conor Broekhart was a remarkable boy, a fact that became evident very early in his idyllic childhood. Nature is usually grudging with her gifts, dispensing them sparingly, but she favoured Conor with everything she had to offer. It seemed as though all the talents of his ancestors had been bestowed upon him. Intelligence, strong features and grace.

Conor was fortunate in his situation too. He was born into an affluent community, where the values of equality and justice were actually being applied, on the surface at least. He grew up with a strong belief in right and wrong, which was not muddied by poverty or violence. It was straightforward for the young boy. Right was Great Saltee, wrong was Little Saltee.

It is an easy matter now, to pluck some events from Conor's early years and say, *There it is. The boy who became the man. We should have seen it.* But hindsight is an unreliable science and, in truth, there was perhaps a single incident during Conor's early days at the palace that hinted at his potential.

The incident in question occurred when Conor was nine years old and roaming the serving corridors that snaked behind the walls of the castle chapel and main building. His partner on these excursions was the Princess Isabella, one year his senior and always the more adventurous of the two.

Isabella and Conor were rarely seen without each other, and often so daubed with mud, blood and nothing good that the boy was barely distinguishable from the princess.

On this particular summer afternoon, they had exhausted the fun to be had tracking an unused chimney to its source and had decided to launch a surprise pirate attack on the king's apartment.

'You can be Captain Crow,' said little Conor, licking some soot from round his mouth, 'and I can be the cabin boy that stuck an axe in his head.'

Isabella was a pretty thing, with elfin face and round brown eyes, but at that moment she looked more like a sweep's urchin than a princess.

'No, Conor. You are Captain Crow, and I am the princess hostage.'

'There is no princess hostage,' declared Conor firmly, worried that Isabella was once again about to mould the legend to suit herself. In previous games, she had included a unicorn and a fairy that were definitely not part of the original story.

'Of course there is,' said Isabella belligerently. 'There is because I say there is, and I am an actual princess, whereas *you* were born in a balloon.'

Isabella intended this as an insult, but to Conor being born in a balloon was about the finest place to be born.

'Thank you,' he said, grinning.

'That's not a good thing,' squealed Isabella. 'Doctor John says that your lungs were probably crushed by the alti-tood.'

'My lungs're better than yours. See!' And Conor hooted

at the sky to show just how healthy his lungs were.

'Very well,' said Isabella, impressed. 'But I am still the princess hostage. And you should remember that I can have you executed if you displease me.'

Conor was not unduly concerned about Isabella having him executed as she ordered him hung at least a dozen times a day and it hadn't happened yet. He was more worried that Isabella was not turning out to be as good a playmate as he had hoped. Basically he wanted someone who would play the games he fancied playing, which generally involved flying paper gliders or eating insects. But lately Isabella had been veering towards dressing-up and kissing, and she would only explore chimneys if Conor agreed to pretend they were the legendary lovers Diarmuid and Gráinne, escaping from Fionn's castle.

Needless to say, Conor had no wish to be a legendary lover. Legendary lovers rarely flew anywhere, and hardly ever ate insects.

'Very well,' he moaned. 'You are the princess hostage.'

'Excellent, Captain,' Isabella said sweetly. 'Now, you may drag me to my father's chamber and demand ransom.'

'Drag?' said Conor hopefully.

'Play drag, not real drag, or I shall have you hung.'

Conor thought, with remarkable wit for a nine-year-old, that if he had actually been hung every time Isabella ordered it, his neck would be longer than a Serengeti giraffe's.

'Play drag, then. Can I kill anyone we meet?'

'Absolutely anyone. Not Papa, though, until after I see how sad he is.'

Absolutely anyone.

That's something, thought Conor, swishing his wooden sword, thinking how it cut the air like a gull's wing.

Just like a wing.

The pair proceeded across the barbican, she *oohing* and he *arring*, drawing fond but also wary looks from those they passed. The palace's only resident children were well liked, not at all spoilt, and mannerly enough when their parents were nearby, but they were also light-fingered and would pilfer whatever they fancied on their daily quests.

A certain Italian gold-leaf artisan had recently turned from the cherub he was coating one afternoon to find his brush and tray of gold wafers missing. The gold turned up later coated on the wings of a week-dead seagull that *someone* had tried to fly from the Wall battlements.

They crossed the bridge into the main keep, which housed the king's residence, office and meeting rooms. And this would generally have been where the pair would be met with a good-natured challenge from the sentry. But the king himself had just leaned out of the window and sent the fellow running to catch the Wexford boat and put ten shillings on a horse he fancied in the Curracloe beach races. The palace had a telephone system, but there were no wires to the shore as yet, and the booking agents on the mainland refused to take bets over the semaphore.

For two minutes only, much to the princess's and the pirate's delight, the main keep was unguarded. They strode in as though they owned the castle.

'Of course, in real life, I *do* own the castle,' confided

Isabella, never missing a chance to remind Conor of her exalted position.

'Arrrr,' said Conor, and meant it.

The spiral staircase passed three floors, all packed with cleaning staff, lawyers, scientists and civil servants, but through a combination of low infant cunning and luck the pair managed to pass the lower floors to the king's own entrance: impressive oak double doors with half of the Saltee flag and motto carved into each one. *Vallo Parietis* read the words. *Defend the Wall.* The flag was a crest bisected vertically into crimson and gold sections with a white blocked tower stamped in the centre.

The door was slightly ajar.

'It's open,' said Conor.

'It's open, hostage princess,' Isabella reminded him.

'Sorry, hostage princess. Let's see what treasure lies inside.'

'I'm not supposed to, Conor.'

'Pirate Captain Crow,' said Conor, slipping through the gap in the door.

As usual, Nicholas's apartment was littered with the remains of a dozen experiments. There was a cannibalized dynamo on the hearthrug, copper-wiring strands protruding from its belly.

'That's a sea creature and those are its guts,' said Conor, with relish.

'Oh, you foul pirate,' said Isabella.

'Stop your smiling then if I'm a foul pirate. Hostages are supposed to weep and wail.'

In the fireplace itself were jars of mercury and experimental fuels. Nicholas refused to allow his staff to move them downstairs. Too volatile, he explained. Anyway, the fire would only go up the chimney.

Conor pointed to the jars. 'Bottles of poison. Squeezed from a dragon's bum. One sniff and you 'vaporate.'

This sounded very possible, and Isabella wasn't sure whether to believe it or not.

On the chaise longue were buckets of fertilizer, a couple gently steaming.

'Also from a dragon's bum,' intoned Conor wisely.

Isabella tried to keep her scream behind her lips, so it shot out of her nose instead.

'It's fert'lizer,' said Conor, taking pity on her. 'For making plants grow on the island.'

Isabella scowled at him. 'You're being hanged at sundown. That's a princess's promise.'

The apartment was a land of twinklings and shinings for a couple of unsupervised children. A stars-and-stripes banner was draped round the shoulders of a stuffed black bear in the corner. A collection of prisms and lenses glinted from a wooden box closed with a cap at one end, and books old and new were piled high like the columns of a ruined temple.

Conor wandered between these columns of knowledge, almost touching everything, but holding back, knowing somehow that another man's dreams should not be disturbed.

Suddenly he froze. There was something he should do. The chance may never come again.

'I must capture the flag,' he breathed. 'That's what a pirate captain is supposed to do. Go to the roof, so I can capture the flag and gloat.'

'Capture the flag and goat?'

'Gloat.'

Isabella stood hands on hips. 'It's pronounced goooaaat, idiot.'

'You're supposed to be a princess. Insulting your subjects is not very princessy.'

Isabella was unrepentant. 'Princesses do what they want – anyway we don't have a goat on the roof.'

Conor did not waste his time arguing. There was no winning an argument with someone who could have you executed. He ran to the roof door, swishing his sword at imaginary troops. This door, too, was open. Incredible good fortune. On the hundred previous occasions he and Isabella had ambushed King Nicholas, every door in the palace had been locked, and they had been warned by stern-faced parents never to venture on to the roof alone. It was a long way down.

Conor thought about it.

Parents? Flag?

Parents? Flag?

'Some pirate you are,' sniffed Isabella. 'Standing around there scratching yourself with a toy sword.'

Flag, then.

'Arrr. I go for the flag, hostage princess.' And then in his own voice, 'Don't touch any of the experiments, Isabella. 'Specially the bottles. Papa says that one day the king is going to blow the lot of us to hell and back with his concoctions, so they must be dangerous.'

Conor went up the stairs fast, before his nerve could fail him. It wasn't far, perhaps a dozen steps to the open air. He emerged from the confines of the turret stairwell on to a stone rooftop. From dark to light in half a second. The effect was breathtaking, azure sky with clouds close enough to touch.

I was born in a place like this, thought Conor

You are a special child, his mother told him at least once a day. *You were born in the sky, and there will always be a place for you there.*

Conor believed that this was true. He had always felt happiest in high places, where others feared to go.

Conor climbed on top of the parapet, holding tight to the flagpole. The world twirled round him, orange sun hanging over Kilmore Quay like a beacon. Sea glittering below him, more silver than blue, and the sky calling to him as though he actually were a bird. For a moment he was bewitched by the scene, then the corner of the flag crept into his vision.

Arrr, he thought. *Yon be the flag. Pride of the Saltees.*

The flag stood perfectly rectangular, crimson and gold with its tower so white it glowed, held rigid by a bamboo frame so that the islands' emblem would stand proud no matter what the weather. It struck Conor that he was actually standing on top of the very tower depicted by the flag.

This may have caused a tug of patriotic pride in an older

islander, but to a nine-year-old all it meant was that his picture should be included on the flag.

I will draw myself on after I steal the flag, he decided.

Isabella emerged on to the rooftop, blinking against the sudden light.

'Come down from the parapet, Conor. We're playing pirates, not bird boy.'

Conor was aghast. 'And leave the flag? Don't you understand? I will be a famous pirate, more famous than Barbarossa himself.'

'That wall is old, Conor.'

'Pirate Captain Crow, remember.'

'That wall is old, *Conor*. It could fall down. Remember the slates came off the chapel during the storm last year?'

'What about the flag?'

'Forget the flag and forget the goat. I'm hungry, so come down before I have you hanged.'

Conor stamped down off the wall, sulking now. He was about to challenge Isabella, say that she could go ahead and have him hanged for all he cared, *and* she was a rotten hostage. Whoever heard of a hostage *giving* the orders. She should learn to weep and wail properly instead of threatening to execute him a hundred times a day.

He was about to say all of this, when there came a dull thump from below that shook the blocks beneath their feet. A cloud of purple smoke oomphed through the doorway, as though someone had cleared a tuba.

Conor had a suspicion bordering on certainty.

'Did you touch something?' he asked Isabella.

Isabella was haughty even in the face of disaster. 'I am the princess of this palace, so I am quite entitled to touch whatever I wish.'

The tower shook again. This time the smoke was green and it was accompanied by a foul smell.

'What did you touch, Isabella?'

The princess of the palace turned as green as the smoke.

'I may have removed the cap from the wooden box. The one with the pretty lenses.'

'Oh,' said Conor. 'That could be trouble.'

King Nicholas had explained the lens box to Conor once, delighted to find that the boy's passion for learning equalled his own.

The lenses are arranged in a very specific order, he had said, squatting low so that his own eye appeared monstrous through the first lens. *So when I remove the cap, and light comes in one end, it's concentrated by successive lenses until it can set paper alight at the other. With this little gadget it might be possible to start a fire from a distance. The ultimate safe fuse.*

Conor remembered thinking at the time that you could leave the box by the window and have it light the fire for you each morning, a chore that he was none too fond of.

And now Isabella had removed the cap.

'Did you move the box?'

'Mind your tone, commoner!'

Commoner? Isabella must really be terrified.

'Isabella?'

'I possibly placed it on the table, by the window to see the colours passing through.'

Obviously the device had caught the afternoon light, releasing the power of the lenses into the king's laboratory, filled with the fertilizer, jugs of fuel and various explosive materials. The concentrated light had obviously landed on something combustible.

'We have to go,' said Conor, all thoughts of Captain Crow forgotten. He was no stranger to the power of explosives. His father was in charge of the Wall defence and had brought Conor along on a trip to collapse a smugglers' cave. It was a birthday treat, but also a lesson to stay away from anything that went boom. The cave wall had collapsed like toy bricks swatted by a toddler.

The tower shook again, several floor blocks rattled in their housings, then dropped into the apartment below. Orange and blue flames surged through the holes, and the snap and grind of breaking glass and twisting metal frightened the two children.

'Up on the wall,' said Conor urgently. 'The floor is falling.'

For once, Isabella did not argue. She accepted Conor's hand and followed him to the lip of the parapet.

'The floor is a foot thick,' he explained, shouting over the roar of the flames. 'The parapet is four feet thick. It won't break.'

The explosions went off below like cannon fire, each one issuing different odours, different colour smoke. The fumes were noxious, and Conor presumed his own face was as green as Isabella's.

It doesn't matter if the parapet holds, he realized. *The flames will get us long before then.*

To Isabella and Conor it felt as though the entire world shook. The stairwell spewed forth flame and smoke as though a dragon lurked below, and from the courtyard came the screams of islanders, as chunks of the tower crashed down from above.

I need to get us out of this place, thought Conor. *No one else can save us, not even Father.*

There was no way to walk down, not through the inferno below. There was only one way down, and that was to fly.

King Nicholas was down the corridor, in the privy, when his daughter blew up his apartment. He was admiring the new Royal Doulton wash-out toilet he had recently had plumbed into his own bathroom. Nicholas had considered installing them throughout the palace, but there were rumours of a new flush toilet on the horizon and it would be a pity to be one step behind progress.

We must embrace progress, be at the forefront of it, or the Saltees will be drowned by a tidal wave of innovation.

When the first explosion rattled the tower, Nicholas briefly thought that his own personal plumbing could be responsible for the din, but realized that not even the bottle of home-brewed ale that he had consumed with Declan Broekhart the previous evening could result in such a disturbance.

They were under attack then? Unlikely, unless a ship had managed to approach undetected on a clear summer's afternoon.

A thought struck him.

Could he have left the cap off the lens box? If so much as a spark took flight in that room ...

King Nicholas finished his royal business and yanked the door open, quickly closing it again as a roiling cloud of smoke and flame invaded the bathroom, searing his lungs. His apartment was destroyed, no doubt about it. Luckily there was no one in his rooms or above them, so the tower's other occupants should easily escape.

Not the king, though. King Nicholas the Stupid is trapped by his own mouldering experiments.

There was a window, of course. Nicholas was a great believer in the benefits of good ventilation. He was a devotee of meditation too, but this was hardly the time for it.

The king stuffed a towel under the door, to stop a draught inviting the fire in, and flung the window wide. Glass and brickwork tumbled past his open window, and the entire structure shuddered as another explosion shook the tower. Nicholas poked his head out for a sideways peek just in time to see a plume of multicoloured smoke expelled from his lounge.

There go the fuel jars.

Below, the courtyard was in chaos. The fire division, to their credit, had already hauled the pump wagon to the base of the tower, and were cranking up some water pressure. If there was one thing they had plenty of on the Saltees, it was water. On any other day, the salt sea spray would have doused the fire, but today in spite of a stiff breeze, the sea was as flat as a polished mirror.

One man stood near the base of the tower. He cut a jaunty figure in his French aviator's jacket and feathered cap. At his feet lay a large leather valise, and he seemed quite amused by the entire exploding tower situation.

Nicholas recognized him immediately, and called down.

'Victor Vigny. You came?'

The man beamed, a startlingly white smile from the centre of his tanned face.

'I came,' he shouted in the French accent you would expect from one in such attire. 'And a good thing I did, Nick. It seems like you still haven't learned to keep a safe laboratory.'

Another explosion. Blue smoke and a shudder that rattled the tower to its foundations. The king ducked out of sight, then reappeared in the window.

'Very well, Victor. Banter over and done. Time to get me down from here. Any of that famous Vigny ingenuity make it across the Atlantic?'

Victor Vigny grunted, then cast an eye around the courtyard. The fire wagon had a ladder hooked on its flank, a rope too. Neither was long enough to reach the king.

'Who designed this thing?' he muttered, hefting the coiled rope on to his shoulder. 'Tall towers and short ladders. Just goes to show, there are idiots everywhere.'

'What are you doing?' asked a member of the fire brigade. 'Who said you could take that?'

Vigny jerked a thumb skywards. 'Him.'

The fireman frowned. 'God?'

The Frenchman winced. Idiots *everywhere*. 'Not quite so lofty, *mon ami*.'

The fireman glanced upwards, catching sight of the king in the window.

'Do what he says,' roared Nicholas. 'That man has saved my life in the past, and I trust him to do it again.'

'Yes, Your Majesty. I am at your . . . at his service.'

Victor pointed at the ladder. 'Lean that against the wall, below the window.'

'It won't reach,' said the fireman, eager to say something intelligent.

'Just do it, *monsieur*. Your king is getting a little hot under the collar.'

The fireman grabbed a comrade and together they propped the ladder against the tower. Victor Vigny was halfway up before the stiles hit the wall.

The tower transmitted its vibrations into the rungs, and Victor knew that it wouldn't be long before it blew its top, like a plugged cannon. The king's apartment and everything above it would soon be no more than dust and memories.

He quickly reached the top of the ladder and, threading his legs through the rungs, he slid the rope off his shoulder and down his arm.

'Nimble, ain't he?' commented the fireman to his partner. 'But as I intelligently said, that there ladder don't reach.'

The debris was showering down now, lumps, shards and entire granite blocks. There was no avoiding it for the three men working at the ladder. They bore the blows with hunched shoulders and grunts.

'Lean it back,' Victor called down, sweat dripping from his face. He tore his feathered cap off as it caught fire, revealing the shock of spiked hair that had earned him the nickname La Brosse. 'You owe me a hat, Nicholas. I've had that one since New Orleans.'

The firemen took the weight of ladder and Parisian, pulling him three feet back from the tower wall. Victor Vigny took half a dozen coils in his hand and sent them spinning upwards. He had judged the coils accurately, landing the spliced end directly in King Nicholas's hand.

'Tie her off strong now, and be quick about it.'

Victor cinched the rope to the top rung, and then slid down the stiles as fast as he could without stripping the skin from his palms.

'Ladder don't reach,' the fireman pointed out, while Victor plunged his hands into the nearest fire bucket.

'I know that, *monsieur*. But the ladder reaches the rope, and the rope reaches the king.'

'Ah,' said the fireman.

'Now stand back. If I know your king, that tower has more explosives in it than a similarly sized cannon. I believe we may be about to shoot down the moon.'

The fire brigade gave up. They couldn't pump enough pressure to reach the blaze, and even if they could that fire was all sorts of colours and pouring water on it could just make it angry.

So they stood back out of the spitting castle's range,

waiting to see if the last male Trudeau in the line could save himself from death by fire or fall.

Inside the bathroom, King Nicholas put his Royal Doulton toilet through its most rigorous test. True, the toilet had been constructed to bear the weight of a hefty adult, but possibly not one swinging from a rope tied to its piping. With a dripping towel draped over his forehead, the king put four loops around the evacuation pipe and a few hitches on the end.

I really hope that pipe does not burst. Being burned alive is bad enough, without being found covered in waste.

The bathroom's stout wooden door was cracking with heat, as though soldiers battered from without. The steel bands buckled, sending rivets pinging around the room like ricocheting bullets.

Nicholas struggled on, wiping his eyes with the towel, inching towards the dim yellow triangle that must be the window. There was no thinning of the smoke, just a faint glow in its centre.

Just follow the rope, he told himself. *It's not difficult. Move forward and don't let go of the rope.*

Nicholas tumbled through the window, remembering to hold on to the rope. He juddered to a halt at the end of its slack, like a condemned man on a gibbet.

'Quit your dossing, Nick!' hollered Victor Vigny. 'Get yourself down. One hand after the other. Even a simpleton like this fireman here could manage it.'

'I could indeed!' shouted the fireman, deciding he would worry about the insult later, if at all.

Below the plume of smoke, King Nicholas could breath again. Each successive gasp of fresh air drove the toxins from his system and returned strength to his limbs.

'Come down, man! I didn't travel from New York City to watch you swing.'

Nicholas grinned, his teeth a flash of white. 'I almost died, Victor. Some sympathy would be nice.' These simple sentences were a considerable effort, and each phrase was punctuated by a fit of coughing.

'That's it now,' said Vigny. 'The old Nick. Down you come.'

The king came down slowly, his journey interrupted by several explosions. Once his feet had found purchase on the top rung, Nicholas descended quickly. There were other lives at stake here after all, and if he got Victor killed because of his own monumental carelessness, the Frenchman would plague him from the afterlife.

Victor had him by the elbows before his boots touched the cobbles, whisking the king away to the relative safety of the keep. They watched from behind an open gorge tower as the king's ladder was seared and blackened.

'What the devil was in there?' asked Victor.

The king's throat whistled with each laboured breath. 'Some gunpowder. Fireworks. A couple of jars of experimental fuel, Swedish blasting oil. Fuse tape. We have been using the old grain store beneath as a temporary armoury. And, of course, fertilizer.'

'Fertilizer?'

'Fertilizer is important on the Saltees, Victor. It's the

future.' He remembered something. 'Isabella. I must show her that I am unharmed. She must see for herself.' He cast his gaze around the courtyard. 'I don't see her. I don't . . . Of course. Someone has taken her to safety. She is safe, isn't she, Victor?'

Victor Vigny did not meet his friend's gaze, his eyes were directed instead over the king's shoulder at the tower's parapet wall. There were two somethings in the midst of the smoke and flame. Two *someones*. A boy and a girl. Perhaps nine or ten years of age.

'*Mon Dieu*,' breathed the Frenchman. '*Mon Dieu*.'

The turret roof was completely gone now apart from ragged blocks round the walls, as though the dragon had grown and now occupied the entire tower. Through swathes of smoke and flame, Conor could see crumbling masonry and falling beams.

A thick column of smoke coughed from the tower, which had effectively become a chimney, drawing air from below to feed the fire. The smoke rose like a giant gnarled tree, black against the summer sky.

Isabella was not in the least hysterical, instead an eerie calm had descended over her, and she stood on the parapet, eyes glazed as though she were half asleep and uncertain of the reality of the situation.

The only way down is to fly, thought Conor. It had long been his dream to fly once more, but these were not the perfect conditions.

He had almost flown on his fifth birthday when the

Broekharts had gone on a day trip to Hook Head in Ireland to see the famous lighthouse. Conor's present had been a large kite in the Saltee colours. They set it loose on a windswept seaside pasture and a sudden gust had lifted Conor to the tips of his toes, and would have dragged him out to sea, had his father not grabbed his elbow.

Kite. Saltee colours. The flag.

On the parapet, Conor pounced on the flagpole, pulling at the knots holding the bamboo frame. The knots twisted in his hands, pulled by the wind that flapped the flag in its frame.

'Help me, Isabella,' he cried. 'We must untie the flag.'

'Forget the flag, Captain Crow,' said Isabella dully. 'Leave the goat too. I don't like goats. Sneaky little beards.'

Conor struggled on with the knots. The ropes were thicker than his slim fingers, but they were brittle from the heat and fell apart quickly. With one momentous wrench, he pulled the flapping flag out of the wind, wrestling it to the parapet. It bucked and cracked under him like a magic carpet, but Conor kept it secure with his own body.

He could barely see Isabella now. She was like a ghost in the smoke. He tried to call her, but smoke went down his throat faster than words could come up. He retched and *arrked* like a seal, flapping his arms at the princess. She ignored him, deciding instead to lie down on the parapet and wait for her father.

Conor fumbled with his belt buckle, pulling the leather strip out from the loops of his trousers' waistband. Then he rolled on to his back, and passed the belt behind the flag's bamboo diagonals.

This is an insane plan. You are not a pirate on some fantastic adventure.

This wasn't a plan, there was no time for plans. This was a desperate act.

In the melee of smoke, explosions and jets of flame, Conor struggled to his feet, keeping the flag's tip low, hiding it from the wind.

Not yet. Not yet.

He almost stumbled over Isabella. She seemed to be asleep. There was no reaction when his fingers pulled at her face.

Dead. Is she dead?

The nine-year-old boy felt tears flow over his cheeks, and was ashamed. He needed to be strong for the princess. Be a hero like his papa.

What would Captain Declan Broekhart do?

Conor imagined his father's face in front of him.

Try something, Conor. Use that big brain your mother is always talking about. Build your flying machine.

Not a machine, Papa. There is no mechanism. This is a kite.

Flame was climbing the parapet wall, blackening the stone with its fiery licks. Crossbeams, carpets, files and furniture tumbled into the hungry fire, feeding it.

Conor lifted the princess, dragging his friend upright.

'What?' she said grumpily. Then the smoke filled her windpipe and any words dissolved into a coughing fit.

Conor stood straight, feeling the massive flag flap and crackle in the wind.

'It's like a big kite, Isabella,' he rasped, words like glass in his throat. 'I will hold you round the waist, like this, and then we move to . . .'

Conor never finished his instructions, because a further explosion, funnelled by the tower caused a massive updraught, plucking the two children from the parapet and sending the flag spinning into open air like a giant autumn leaf.

The circumstances were unique. Had they jumped, as was Conor's plan, they would not have had enough height for the flag to slow their descent. But the updraught caught in their makeshift kite and spun them up another hundred feet, and took them out over the sea. They hung there, in the sky, at the plateau of the air tunnel. Weightless. Sky above and sea below.

I am flying, thought Conor Broekhart. *I remember this.*

Then the flying finished and the falling started, and though it was drastically slowed by the flag, it seemed devilishly swift. Sights dissolved into a kaleidoscope of fractured blues and silvers.

The flag caught a low breeze and flipped. Conor watched the clouds swirl above him, stretching to creamy streams. And all the time he held on to Isabella so tightly his fingers ached.

He was crying and laughing and he knew it would be painful when they hit the water.

They crashed into the ocean. It was painful.

When he saw his daughter on the parapet, King Nicholas had tried to scramble up the tower like a dog climbing out of a well. In seconds his nails were torn and fingers bloody.

Victor Vigny had dragged him away from the wall.

'Wait, Nick. This is not over yet. Wait. The boy . . . he's . . .'

Nicholas's eyes were wild and anguished. 'What? He's what?'

'You have to see it. Come now. We need a boat, in case the wind takes them.'

'A boat? A boat? What are you saying?'

'Come, Nick. Come.'

Nicholas howled and dropped to his knees as his daughter flew into the air.

Victor watched, amazed. This boy. He was special, whoever he was. Maybe nine, no more than ten. What ingenuity.

The explosion took them high, Victor watched their trajectory and then set off for the pier at a run, dragging the king behind him.

'The flag could drown them,' he puffed. 'The frame will collapse and the flag will wrap around them both.'

The king had recovered himself and soon outstripped the others through a trader's gate and down to the jetty. There were already half a dozen boats on their way to the fallen flag. The first to reach them was a small quay punt, sculled across the wave tops by two muscled fishermen. A line of slower vessels trailed behind them to the pier.

'Alive?' Nicholas roared, but the distance was too great. 'Are they alive?'

The flag was pulled from the sea and wet bundles rolled

from it. Victor caught the king and gripped his shoulder tight.

The little punt spun in a tight circle and the fishermen pulled for shore, their oars kicking spume from the water. The news travelled faster than they could, passed from one boat to the next. The words, inaudible at first, became clearer with each fresh call.

'Alive. Alive. Both of them.'

Nicholas sank to his knees and thanked God. Victor smiled first, and then began to clap with delight.

'I came to teach the princess,' he shouted to no one in particular. 'But I will teach that boy too, or perhaps he will teach me.'

CHAPTER 2:

LA BROSSE

Conor Broekhart was quite the hero for a time. It seemed as though everyone on the island visited him at the castle infirmary to listen to the tale of his improvised glider, and to knock for luck on the gypsum cast on his broken leg.

Isabella came every day, and often brought her father, King Nicholas. On one of these visits he brought his sword.

'I didn't want to jump off the tower,' Conor objected. 'I couldn't think of another way.'

'No, no,' said Nicholas. 'This is the Trudeau ceremonial sword. I am making you a peer.'

'You are making me appear?' said Conor doubtfully. 'Is this a magical trick?'

Nicholas smiled. 'In a way. One touch of this sword and you become Sir Conor Broekhart. Your father then becomes Lord Broekhart; of course your mother will become Lady Broekhart.'

Conor was still a little worried about the crusader's blade five inches from his nose.

'I don't have to kiss that, do I?'

'No, just touch the blade. Even one finger will do. We will have a proper ceremony when you are well.'

Conor ran a finger along the shining blade. It sang under his touch.

Nicholas put the sword aside. 'Arise, Sir Conor. Not straight away, of course. Take your time. When you are well, I have a new teacher for you. A very special man who worked with me when I flew balloons. I think that you, of all people, will really like him.'

Balloons!

As far as Conor was concerned the king could keep his peerage, so long as he could fly balloons.

'I am feeling much better, Your Majesty. Perhaps I could meet this man today.'

'Steady on, Sir Conor,' laughed the king. 'I will ask him to drop by tomorrow. He has a few drawings you might like to look at. Something about heavier-than-air flying machines.'

'Thank you, Your Majesty. I look forward to it.'

The king chuckled, ruffling Conor's hair.

'You saved my daughter, Conor. You saved her from my carelessness and her own tinkering fingers. I will never forget that. Never.' He winked. 'And neither will she.'

The king left, leaving his daughter behind. She had not spoken for the entire meeting, indeed she had not said much to Conor since the accident. But today some of the old light was back in her brown eyes.

'Sirrrrr Conor,' she said rolling the title around in her mouth like a hard sweet. 'It's going to be more difficult to have you hanged now.'

'Thank you, Isabella.'

The princess leaned in to knock on his cast.

'No, Sir Conor Broekhart. Thank you.'

*

Someone else came to see Conor that day, late in the evening when the nurse had shooed his mother home. The infirmary was deserted save for the night nurse who sat at her station at the end of the corridor. She drew a curtain round Conor's bed and left a light on so that he could read his book.

Conor leafed through George Cayley's *On Ariel Navigation*, which theorized that a fixed-wing aircraft with some form of engine and a ruddered tail could possibly carry a man through the air.

Heavy reading for a nine-year-old. In truth Conor skipped more words than he knew, but with each pass he understood more.

Engine and tail, he thought. *Better than a flying flag at any rate.* And fell asleep dreaming of a shining sword wrapped in a flag, sinking in Saint George's Channel.

He awoke to the sound of a boot heel scraping on stone, and the heavy sigh of a large man. A sigh so guttural that it was almost a growl. This was a sound to make a boy decide to pretend that he was still asleep. Conor opened his eyes the merest slit, careful to keep his breathing deep and regular.

There was a man in his bedside chair, his massive frame swathed in shadows. By the red cross on his breast he saw it was one of the Holy Cross Guard. Marshall Bonvilain himself.

Conor's breath hitched, and he covered it with a small moan, as though plagued by night terrors.

What could Bonvilain want here? At this hour?

Sir Hugo was the direct descendant of Percy Bonvilain

who had served under the first Trudeau king seven centuries before. Historically the Bonvilain's were high commanders of the Saltee Army and were also given leave to assemble their own Holy Cross Guard, which at one time was used to conduct raids to the mainland or hired out to European kings as professional soldiers. The current Bonvilain was the last in the line and the most powerful. In fact, Sir Hugo would have been declared prime minister some years earlier when King Hector died, had not a genealogist discovered Nicholas Trudeau eking out a living as an aeronaut in the United States.

Sir Hugo was an unusual combination of warrior and wit. He had the bulk of a lifelong soldier, but also the ability to present devastating argument in a surprisingly mellow voice.

If that Saltee fellow don't cut you one way, he does it t'other, Benjamin Disraeli reportedly said of the marshall.

Conor had once heard his father say that Bonvilain's only weakness was his burning distrust of other nations, especially France. The marshall had once heard a rumour of the existence of a French army of spies, La Légion Noire, whose mission was to gather intelligence on Saltee defences. Bonvilain spent thousands of guineas hunting members of the fictitious group.

Bonvilain's breath was deep and regular as though he were resting; only a gloved finger tapping his knee betrayed that he was awake.

'Asleep, boy?' he said suddenly, his voice all honey and menace. 'Or maybe awake, feigning sleep.'

Conor held his silence, shutting his eyes tight – suddenly, without reason, terrified.

Bonvilain hunched forward on his chair. 'I never really took notice of you before now, little Broekhart. The first time, you were a baby. But this time, this time it could fairly be said that you . . . saved someone who should be dead. Broekharts. Always Broekharts.'

Conor heard leather stretch and creak, as Hugo Bonvilain clenched a gloved fist.

'So I wanted to see you. I like to know the faces of my . . . of my king's friends.'

Conor could smell the marshall's cologne, feel his breath.

'But I have said too much already, boy. You need peace and quiet to recuperate from your miraculous escape. Truly miraculous. But remember that I am watching you, very closely. The knights are watching you.'

Bonvilain stood in a rustle of the Holy Cross sheath he wore over his suit.

'Very well, young Broekhart, time for me to go. Perhaps I was never here. Perhaps you are dreaming. It might be better for you if you were.'

The curtain round his bed swished as the marshall took his leave.

Conor dared to open his eyes after a moment to find Bonvilain's face an inch from his own.

'Ah, awake after all. Capital. I forgot to knock the cast. I could certainly benefit from some of your luck.'

Conor lay rigid and silent as the marshall hoisted his

broken leg uncomfortably high, then administered two sharp raps on the gypsum cast.

'Let us hope you don't give away all of that wondrous luck, young Broekhart. You might be needing it.'

Bonvilain winked, and was gone, the curtain rippling behind him like a ghost.

Perhaps it was a dream after all. Just a nightmare.

But the dull pain from Bonvilain's hoisting still throbbed in his leg. Conor Broekhart slept little for the rest of the night.

Of the billion and a half of people on Earth, there were perhaps five hundred that could have helped Conor achieve his potential as a pilot of the skies. One of these was King Nicholas Trudeau and another was Victor Vigny. That these three should be brought together at such a time of industrious invention was little short of miraculous.

The race for flight is littered with such fortuitous groupings. William Samuel Henson and John Stringfellow, Joseph Louis Gay-Lussac and Jean Baptiste Biot, and of course Charles Green and the astronomer Spencer Rush. The Wright brothers can hardly be included in this category, as it was almost inevitable that they would meet, sleeping as they did in the same bed chamber.

Conor had long known of King Nicholas's interest in ballooning, after all it had been his livelihood for many years. Conor and Isabella had spent many nights by the fireside in Nicholas's apartment enthralled by the king's dramatic tellings of his airborne adventures. Victor Vigny was a familiar figure in these stories. He was generally presented as small in stature, broad of accent, timid and inevitably in need of rescue by King Nicholas.

The Victor Vigny that Conor met on his first day of instruction did not tally with King Nicholas's description. He was neither tiny nor timid, and according to castle talk, it was Victor Vigny who had rescued the king.

The day after his release from the infirmary, Conor limped into Victor's quarters on the second storey of the main building. This particular apartment had always been set aside for visiting royalty, but now the Parisian seemed firmly ensconced. The walls were covered with charts, and celestial models hung from the ceiling. A skeleton in the corner wore a scorched feathered cap and a scimitar was clutched in his bony grip. There were more swords in a rack, arranged from light to heavy. Foil, sabre, broadsword.

The man himself was on the balcony, stripped to the waist, performing some kind of exercise. He was a tall muscled man, and seemed by his movements not in the least timid.

Conor thought he would watch a while before interrupting. The Parisian's movements were slow and precise. Fluid and controlled. Conor had the impression that this particular discipline was more difficult than it looked.

'It's not polite to spy,' said Victor, without turning, his accent not so broad but definitely French. 'You are not a spy, are you?'

'I am not spying,' said Conor. 'I am learning.'

Vigny straightened, then adopted a new position, knees bent, arms stretched to the side.

'That is a very good answer,' he said, grinning. 'Come out here.'

Conor limped to the balcony.

'This is called t'ai chi. Practised since the fourteenth century in China. I learned it from a juggler on the fair circuit. That man claimed to be a hundred and twenty years old. A regimen for mind and body. It will be our first lesson every day. Followed by Okinawan Karate and then fencing. After breakfast we open the books. Science, mathematics, history and fiction. Mostly in the area of aeronautics, which happens to be my passion, *jeune homme*. Yours too, I'll wager, judging by your kite-flying exploits.'

Karate and aeronautics. These did not sound like traditional occupations for a princess.

'Will Isabella be coming?'

'Not until eleven. She has needlepoint, etiquette and heraldry until then, though she may occasionally join us for fencing. So, for four hours every day, we can learn how to fight and how to fly.'

Conor smiled. *Fighting and flying.* His last teacher had started the day with Latin and poetry. Sometimes Latin poetry. Fighting and flying sounded much more enjoyable.

'Now, how does the leg feel?' asked Victor, pulling on a shirt.

'Broken,' said Conor.

'Ah, not only a flyer but a joker. No doubt you'll be spouting witticisms as your glider plunges into the side of a mountain.'

Glider? thought Conor. *I am to have a glider. And something about a mountain?*

Victor took a step back, folded his arms and took measure of his pupil. 'You have potential,' he said at last. 'A slim build. The best for an airman. Most people don't realize that flying a balloon takes a degree of athleticism, quick reactions and so forth. I imagine piloting an engine-driven heavier-than-air flying machine will take much more.'

Conor's heart thumped in his chest.

A flying machine?

'And you have brains. Your tower rescue proved that. More brains than that king of yours. Stocking a laboratory with explosives. He's been doing that for years you know; it was only a matter of time. As for your personality, Princess Isabella says that you are not the most odious person in the castle, and coming from a female that is high praise indeed, Sir Conor.'

Conor winced. His title still sounded outrageous to him. If it were never used again, he would be happier. Though he had noticed today that cook gave him a toffee apple for no particular reason. And curtsied too. *Curtsied?* This was the same cook who had battered his backside with a floury rolling pin not two weeks before.

'So, are you ready to learn, lad?'

Conor nodded. 'Yes, sir. More than ready, eager.'

'Good,' said Victor. 'Excellent. Now, hobble this way. I have some unguents that should help that leg of yours on its way to soundness. And exercises too, for the toes.'

All of this sounded far-fetched, but no more so than an engine-driven, heavier-than-air flying machine. It was the age of discovery and Conor was prepared to believe anything.

Victor pulled a ceramic jar from a high shelf. The lid was waxed canvas, tied on with reeds. When the cover came off, the smell was like nothing or nowhere Conor had ever smelled or been.

'An African man from the Sahara – had a camel act – taught me how to make this.' He took a dollop on two fingers and smeared it where the cast met Conor's leg, below the knee. 'Let it seep down under the cast. Smells like Beelzebub's backside, but, when the gypsum comes off, the bad leg will be better than the good one.'

The unguent sent Conor's skin tingling. Hot and cold at the same time.

'If we are scientists,' he said, keeping his tone respectful, 'why do we need to fight?'

Victor Vigny sealed the pot, thinking about his answer. 'I fully expect, Conor Broekhart, that between the two of us, we will learn to fly, and when that day comes, when we reveal our wondrous machine, someone will come to steal it from us. It has happened to me before. I built a glider from willow and silk: beautiful. She made the air sing when she passed. I flew a monkey over a hundred feet. For six weeks I was the toast of the fair. Tent full every night.'

Conor could see the glider in his mind. A monkey. Fabulous.

'What happened?'

'There was a Russian knife thrower. He came around to my wagon one night, with half a dozen friends. They burned my glider to ashes, and gave me a few licks to send me on my way. Threatened, you see, by progress. When the choices are a flying monkey or a knife thrower, who would pick the knife thrower?'

'The knife thrower's mother perhaps.'

Victor ran his fingers through his black hair to ensure it was appropriately erect. 'Maybe, funny *jeune homme*. But then again, the females love a nice monkey. Many's the mother would ignore her own kin for the chance to gawk at an airborne simian. The point being that, when the knife throwers come, you must be prepared.'

Conor thought about Marshall Bonvilain's visit.

Let us hope you don't give away all of that wondrous luck, young Broekhart. You might be needing it.

'Where do we start?' he asked.

Victor plucked a slim blade from the rack. 'We start at the heart of swordplay,' he said, slicing the air till it whistled. 'With the foil.'

And so work began.

In later, darker times, when Conor Broekhart, alone and disheartened, remembered the life that was his, the handful of years with Victor Vigny always stood out as the happiest.

They studied martial arts, pugilism and weapons.

'The first true fencing master to leave us an actual method of arms was Achille Marozzo,' Victor told his pupil. 'His

Opera Nova is now your bible. Read it until it becomes a part of you. When that one is ragged, then we move back in time to Filippo Vadi.'

They spent hours on training mats putting the masters' theories into practice.

'First you learn to hold a sword. Think of it as a conductor's baton. Used properly, there is not an untrained man in the world who can stand against you.'

With buttoned swords, Conor learned to thrust, parry, feint, double and riposte. He lost pints of liquid each morning in sweat, then replaced them with a jug of Victor's foul-tasting Oriental tea.

His first weapon was a short foil, but as his wrists grew stronger he progressed to épée, sabre and rapier. Victor sawed the cast off Conor's leg a month early, but forced him to wear a soaked bandage instead that turned his leg yellow, along with all his bed linen.

'More circus tricks?' Conor had asked.

'No,' replied the Frenchman. 'An American friend of mine is a miracle worker with poultices and pots. Actually Nick has sent for him. I will tell you more when he has finished his work.' And would say no more on the subject.

Victor had little time for anything heavier than a cutlass.

'No broadsword, unless you plan to go on a crusade, and even then look what happened to the crusaders. While they were hefting their broadswords, Saladin was sticking his scimitar into their armpits.'

The Frenchman introduced Conor to escapology.

'Scientists are the enemies of tradition,' he said, dumping a box of assorted handcuffs on the table. 'And tradition owns all the prisons.'

And so, more hours were spent picking locks and chewing knots. Conor found the t'ai chi most valuable when he was tied to a chair with a tantalizing apple shining at him from the table. He was now able to reach parts of his own body that previously he could not have located with a backscratcher and mirror.

Victor was a great believer in the right man for the job.

'You need to talk to your father about guns,' he told Conor. 'Nick tells me that Declan Broekhart is the finest shot he has ever seen, and we spent a summer with Wild Bill Hickok in Abilene, so that's high praise.'

Declan was delighted to help with his son's education, and began taking Conor on Wall patrol, and down to the shooting range with a duffel bag of arms. He shot Colts, Remingtons, Vetterli-Vitalis, Spencers, Winchesters and a dozen other models. Conor was a quick study, and a natural marksman.

'For your fourteenth birthday you shall have your own Sharps,' his father promised him. 'By then we should know what would suit your shoulder. I would give you one for your next, but your mother says ten is too young.'

The only weapon Victor did give Conor a few pointers on was his prized Colt Peacemaker, which Wild Bill himself had given him.

'He invited me to come to Deadwood with him,' he told Conor. 'But it was not the right career choice for an aeronaut.

Prospectors tend to shoot down balloons. Also I am too handsome for a prospecting town.'

All of these physical lessons were fine, but what Conor really yearned for was a mental challenge. Victor had promised him that they would build a flying machine, and the Frenchman did not disappoint. The ability to defend oneself was a necessity, but the race for flight was an obsession.

'And it is a race, *jeune homme*,' he told Conor, one morning as they stretched silk over a balsa wing frame. The wood had been part of a special shipment from Peru. 'Many of the world's greatest inventors and adventurers have turned their attention to this problem. Man will fly; it is inevitable. More than twenty years ago, Cayley's triplane glider carried a passenger. Wenham and Browning have built a wind tunnel to study drag. Alphonse Pénaud was so certain of his designs that he drew up plans for retractable landing gear. Retractable! The race is on, Conor, make no mistake, and we must be first past the finishing line. Fortunately, the king supports our efforts, so we will not want for funds. Nicholas knows what the power of flight would mean to the Saltees. The islands would no longer be cut off from the world. Diamonds could be transported without threat from bandits. Medicines could be flown in from Europe. Flown in, Conor.'

Conor did think about this. He thought of nothing else. Any free minutes he had were taken up with sketching plans or building models. He forgot all about pirate games and insect eating.

Sometimes his father despaired. 'Wouldn't you like to

make a friend? Perhaps play in the mud, get yourself dirty?'

But Conor's mother was delighted that their son had inherited her own love of science. 'Our boy is a scientist, Declan,' she would say as she helped him to cover a wing, or carve a propeller. 'The race for flight will hardly be won in the mud.'

Conor made a lampshade for the light in his room. A paper screen painstakingly decorated with depictions of da Vinci's flapping-wing device, a Montgolfier balloon and Kaufman's theoretical flying steam engine. Heat from the bulb rotated the shade at night, and Conor would lie in bed watching projections of these fabulous machines drift across his ceiling.

One day, he would think dreamily. *One day*.

CHAPTER 3:

ISABELLA

Conor was fourteen by the time the teacher and pupil were convinced that manned flight was within their grasp. They had built a hundred models, and several life-size gliders, all of which had ended up stamped to pieces and piled on to the bonfire. Their efforts fuelled not only the fire but the island tavern conversation. There was general agreement that the Frenchman was a lunatic, and it seemed as though the Broekhart boy was going the same way. Still, it was a nice diversion of an evening to go watch a grown man jump off a high wall flapping his paper wings. And still the king footed the bill. Bringing in experimental engines from Germany, special wood from South America.

Magic wood, sniggered the tavern wits. *Brimmin' with fairy dust.*

Not that the Saltee islanders complained overmuch about how Good King Nick spent his diamonds. Even if he wasted the odd pouch on a French birdman, life on the Saltees was better than it had been for generations. There was work for all who wanted it. And schooling too, with scholarships to Dublin and London for the bright sparks who didn't fancy working for a living. The infirmary was well stocked with instruments to poke and prod at a person's organs. If you can scream, then yer alive, as the saying goes. The sewage pipes were working, carrying all the waste out to sea, which meant sickness was down. Rats were a thing of the past, on Great Saltee at least, and Bonvilain's Holy Cross Knights were held on a tighter leash. There was no more of the random beating or imprisonment without trial that the marshall, God bless him, was so fond of. There were grants available for home improvements, and plans for telephone wires between Great Saltee, Little Saltee and even mainland Ireland. So no one was too upset if the king wished to indulge himself in a little scientific tomfoolery. It wasn't as if the Frenchman was ever going to fly. A man in a bird suit is still a man.

Weight and wingspan were Conor and Victor's main problems. How can something float on air if it is heavier than air? By forcing air over the wings quickly enough to generate lift, which negates the force of gravity. To generate lift you need big wings, which are heavy. If you use small wings, they must be flapped with a machine, which is heavy. Every solution presents a dozen problems.

In spite of more than three years of failures, Victor believed their method was correct.

'We must learn control, before we fly with an engine. Gliding is the first step. Lilienthal is our model.'

The German aviator Otto Lilienthal had flown over twenty-five yards in his glider, the *Derwitzer*. He was Victor and Conor's latest hero.

La Brosse never lost hope for more than five minutes. These minutes were usually spent stamping on the latest failed prototype. After that, it was back to the schoolroom and more plans.

Finally, Conor built a model that his teacher approved of. The student held his breath, while the master studied his work.

'You know that this can never fly.'

'Of course,' said Conor. 'The airman is an essential part of the ship. His movement steers it. He pushes the horizontal rudder left, the ship banks right.'

'So we can't test your model.'

'No. Not unless you know an extremely intelligent monkey.'

Victor smiled. 'I seem to remember talking about flying monkeys once before. At any rate, monkeys are intelligent enough stay on the earth, where they belong.'

'What does that make us?' wondered Conor.

Victor picked up the model, swishing it through the air, feeling the craft's urge to fly. 'It makes us visionaries, *jeune homme*. A monkey glances up and sees a banana, and that's as far as he looks. A visionary looks up and sees the moon.'

Conor smirked. 'Which resembles a big banana.'

'Oho!' said Victor. 'You would mock me? Your teacher? For such impudence you must pay.'

The Frenchman tossed the model on to a cushion and made a run for the sword rack. Conor was there before him, drawing out his favourite foil, which also happened to be Victor's favourite.

'Oh, black card, *monsieur*,' said Victor, selecting a slightly shorter épée for himself. 'Taking a man's blade. How long will you hold on to it, I wonder.'

Conor backed over to the training mat, never taking his eyes from his teacher.

'*En garde!*' shouted Victor, and attacked.

In the early years, when the sport was new to Conor, the Frenchman would call instructions as they fenced.

Thrust, parry, riposte. Footwork. Move your feet, you lead-footed islander. Again, here comes my thrust, so parry. Feet, Conor, feet.

No instructions any more. Now the Frenchman struggled to stay in the fight. There were no pulled thrusts or forgiving slaps with the side of a blade. This was as war.

They battled the length and breath of the chamber, even moving out to the balcony.

He is a veritable devil, thought Victor. *Not a bead of sweat on his brow. Only fourteen and already he outstrips me. But the old dog has a few tricks in him yet.*

'That is the best model you have built,' panted Victor. *Riposte and counter riposte.*

Conor did not reply. Never lose concentration. If your opponent makes jokes about your mother, bat them aside as you would a clumsy lunge. Insults will only make you bleed if you allow them into your heart.

'I think you should name this one,' commented the Frenchman. *Parry on the foible, backwards glide and riposte.*

Victor's swipe knocked a bonsai tree from his terrace; below a donkey snorted his complaint.

Victor is desperate, thought Conor. *I have him. Finally.* He leaped from his leading foot, attempting a fleche attack, which the Frenchman barely managed to parry.

Victor fell back on his left foot, but kept the tip of his blade centred.

'I think you should call her the *Isabella*,' he said.

The name distracted Conor for barely a second, but this was ample time for Victor to breach his defence. The teacher quickly dropped low, thrusting his sword upwards for an easy passata-sotto. Had not the blades been buttoned, Conor's heart would have been pierced from below the ribs.

'*Touché*,' said Victor gratefully, resting for a moment on one knee.

Groaning, he hoisted himself erect then returned to the cool shade of his chamber.

Conor followed dully, moments later sliding the foil into its leather sleeve on the rail.

'Why would you say that?' he asked quietly.

Victor shrugged. 'Does it matter? You dropped your guard. Our friend, the flying monkey, could have defeated you.'

Conor did not appreciate the humour. If anything he seemed irritated by it.

'It was a low trick, Victor.'

'I am still alive, so it was a *good* trick. You, on the other hand, have a ruptured heart.'

Conor retrieved his model from its nesting place, plucking lint from the tail.

'Oh, don't sulk, please,' begged Victor, with much melodrama. 'You are allowed to love a princess. It is every young man's duty to fall head over heels with a princess. You are lucky enough to actually have one to hand.'

'Love . . . a princess,' spluttered Conor. 'What? I really don't know . . .'

Victor poured himself a glass of water. 'What an effective denial, *jeune homme*. But don't feel bad; I regularly reduce people to unintelligible stammers. It's a Gallic gift. The Italians have it also.'

His student was so nonplussed that eventually the Frenchman showed some mercy.

'I am sorry, Conor *jeune homme*. I knew you had the glad eye, but I didn't realize how glad. Arrow in the heart, is it?'

Conor's only reply was a small nod, the barest dip of his chin. He sat on the divan, straightening his model's rudder, blowing gently on the wings.

Victor sat beside him. 'Why, then, do you wear the expression of a man on the gallows steps? You love a princess, and she doesn't openly despise you. Celebrate, *jeune homme*. Live your life. Young love is common, but that doesn't mean it isn't precious.'

Conor longed to talk on this subject. It was something he had been playing close to his chest for quite a while now. If it had not been for the gliders, he would have gone insane thinking about it.

Victor read his pupil's mood and kept silent. He noticed, not for the first time, that Conor was more man than boy now physically. He was tall for his age and strong, his countenance was generally serious and his co-ordination was excellent thanks to the fencing. Combined, these traits gave him the appearance of an older youth. Emotionally, though,

Conor was very much a boy. He was a well of feelings, full to the brim, ready to spill over.

'Isabella is my oldest friend,' Conor began slowly. 'I have only three friends my own age. And she is the oldest. Mother says I met her before I was even a week old.'

'That's young, *vraiment*,' said Victor. 'I remember the hour of your birth well. We all had a lucky escape.'

'Have you seen the photograph? From the French newspaper. I look like an old man searching for his teeth.'

'I hate to be the bearer of bad news, *jeune homme*, but your looks have not improved much.'

The banter relaxed Conor and he continued to air thoughts that he had never shared before. 'I don't know if she is beautiful or not – I suppose she is. I like her face, that's all I know. Sometimes I don't need to see her; I just hear her behind me and I forget every thought in my head. For God's sake, Victor, I am fourteen now, not twelve. I have no time for babbling foolishness.'

'Don't be so hasty,' said Victor. 'There's always time for babbling.'

'It happened at her last birthday. So, I gave her a present, as usual. And when she unwrapped it, I could see she was disappointed. She had hoped for something different.'

'What did you give the princess? I don't recall.'

'A spring-loaded glider. You remember? The single-wing design.'

'Ah, yes. Just what every princess hopes for.'

Conor was desolate. 'I know. She hated it. No doubt she flew it straight into Saint George's Channel. I began to think about it. About Isabella. And what could be wrong. I realized that a glider was not a good present for a young lady. Isabella has become a young lady, and I cannot stop thinking about her.'

Victor stretched until his shoulders cracked. 'You are lucky, *jeune homme*, to have me here this day. For I am an expert in all areas of instruction, including the women-folk.'

Conor was doubtful. 'Which explains why you are a bachelor in his forties.'

'I choose to be a bachelor,' said the Frenchman, wagging a finger. 'There are plenty of ladies who would gladly tether Victor Vigny to their gatepost given the chance. If I had a drop of champagne for every heart I've broken, I would have had a full magnum before now.'

'Can you, then, offer any sincere advice with no mention of a flying monkey?'

'Very well, Conor Broekhart. Listen and be amazed.' Victor leaned forward, elbows on knees as though about to present a great academic treatise. 'The reason, I suspect, why Isabella was disappointed with the glider was that she expected something special.'

'Is that the best you can do?' said Conor.

'She expected something special from you,' continued Victor unabated, 'because you have become a young man, and she a young woman.'

Conor did not understand what exactly was being said. 'This is all biology, Victor. I know this.'

'No, *imbecile*. She noticed you as a young man before you

noticed her as a young lady. She had hoped for your enlightenment in time for her birthday; the glider said otherwise.'

'And so she thought . . .'

'Isabella thought that you still saw her as a childhood friend.'

'But I don't, not any more.'

'She doesn't know that. How would she know it, through mental projection?'

Conor cradled his head. 'This is so confusing. Flying machines are easier.'

'Welcome to the rest of your life, *jeune homme*. This is how things are. But let me conclude my lecture on an optimistic note. If Isabella had not wanted something special from you, specifically you, she would not have been disappointed. Do you see?'

Confusion was writ large on Conor's features. 'No. It's as clear as mud.'

'I myself gave her a very dull book, and she was delighted. But from you she wanted more than a present, she wanted a token.'

'Mud, mud. Barrels of mud.'

Victor slapped his own forehead. 'The boy is a dunderhead. She wished a token of affection *from* you, because she has affection *for* you.'

A smile spread across Conor's face.

'Do you think so?'

'Good God! I see ivory. The first today. Where is the royal photographer?'

The smile winked out like a capped lamp. 'You're right, I think. It makes sense.'

'So if it makes sense, why once more the face of doom?'

'The original reason, which I had forgotten for a moment. Prince Christian of Denmark has requested tea with Isabella. It is the first stage of a royal courtship. Isabella has agreed to receive him today. This very afternoon.'

'Oh. Not to worry. I doubt this Prince Christian can overturn fourteen years of friendship in an afternoon.'

'Yes, but he is a *prince*.'

'And you, sir, are a Sir. Anyway, Nicholas is a thoroughly modern king. Isabella will marry the man, or flying monkey, that she loves.'

'Do you really think so?'

'I do. It is like the old fairy tale. The boy saves the princess, they fall in love. He invents a flying machine along with his dashing teacher of course. They get married and name their firstborn after the aforementioned dashing teacher.'

Conor frowned. 'I don't recall that fairy tale from nursery.'

'Trust me, it's a classic. Let Isabella have her tea. I doubt very much that an engagement will be announced. Next week we begin work on a plan of action. Perhaps it's time for Shakespeare.'

Conor thumped his knee. This was progress.

'Damn next week. We can work now. I could have a sonnet ready by this evening.'

Victor stood, pacing the length of his study, which also served as a lounge and classroom.

'First, mind your language. You are fourteen and inside the walls of a palace, not to mention in the company of a genius. Second, I have work to do this afternoon. Important work. There is a man I must visit. And tomorrow morning, I have some imports to check in our new laboratory.'

Conor transferred his thoughts from one obsession to another.

'Imports in our new laboratory. You spend almost every evening in this laboratory. When can I see it, Victor? Tell me.'

The Frenchman raised a warning hand.

Wait, the gesture said. *And be quiet.*

He closed the doors to the balcony, then checked that no one listened behind the door.

'Let me ask you something,' he said to his intrigued student. 'These romantic feelings you've been having. Why haven't you talked to your father?'

Conor frowned. 'I would. We are close, but this past year he has been preoccupied. The Knights of the Holy Cross grow stronger. There have been several incidents of violence against citizens and visitors. The knights openly flout the king's wishes. Father worries for the king's safety.'

'He is right to worry,' confided Victor. 'Bonvilain's men grown bolder by the day. The Marshall was almost prime minister, and believes there may still be a chance of obtaining that exalted office. The king has plans for a parliament, but not one that will be presided over by the knights. Serious political machinations are afoot on both sides. It is a time for caution and secrecy.'

'Is this tied to the man you must meet? And the new laboratory?'

'Yes. To both. The man risks his life to send news of Bonvilain's hold over the prison authorities.'

'And the laboratory?'

Victor knelt before Conor, gripping his shoulders. 'It is almost ready, Conor. Finally. The renovation is finished, not that you would know from the outside. And the equipment has arrived to build our flying machine.'

Conor's heart thumped against his ribs. 'Everything?'

'Yes. Everything we asked for and more. Nicholas doubled the order, and asked for anything else he could think of. A veritable Aladdin's cave of wonders for two airmen like us. Six engines. Five crates of balsa. Silk and cotton by the roll, cable, pneumatic rubber tyres, Conor. Expensive but worth it. Two pairs of dashing goggles, the latest precision tools. Everything we need to build a workshop like nowhere on earth, and thanks to a generous grant from Nick, we have an old Martello tower outside Kilmore in which to build it. A place where Bonvilain won't be looking over our shoulders. We shall have our own wind tunnel, *jeune homme*. Think of it.'

Flying machines were already taking off in Conor's mind. 'When can I see it?'

'Soon,' Victor promised. 'Soon. Only two people on the islands know about our equipment. Three now including you. To others it is simply a hugely expensive collection of mismatches. An idiot's shopping list locked inside a ruin.'

'But why the secrecy?'

'You do not yet understand the magnitude of what we attempt. When we succeed; the Saltee Islands will be the toast of the civilized world and King Nicholas will be the man who taught the world to fly. His position secure for as long as he lives. Until then, he is a crackpot king selfishly emptying the Saltee coffers. We are a stick to beat him with. This consignment is huge. It must be kept secret until we are ready. Until then, we can pretend that our trips are educational.'

Conor understood, but his excitement made him reckless. 'Curse Bonvilain. He holds back science.'

'Not for long,' said Victor soothingly. 'Very well, I will sneak you across on the ferry next weekend. You can peruse our new engines.'

'Next weekend. Good.'

'We can read some Shakespeare on the boat.'

Conor's face was blank. 'Shakespeare, I . . .' Then he remembered and jumped to his feet. 'Oh. Isabella will be at tea now. I must talk to her directly afterwards. What time is it?'

The Frenchman ignored the carriage clock on his mantle, consulting instead the sundial on his balcony.

'I would say, perhaps a quarter past five.'

'How could you know that?' asked Conor in disbelief. 'You can't see the sun today, not through all those clouds.'

Victor winked. 'Other men may not see the sun, *jeune homme*. But I am a visionary.'

*

Conor's head buzzed with new information as he crossed the keep towards the Broekhart apartments. The day was grey, with dull light falling on the granite walls, rendering them close to black. There was nothing to distract him from his thoughts of invention and romance.

Victor was right. Isabella sat beside him every day for Latin, French, mathematics and now Shakespeare. He would have his chance. And what better way to impress a girl than by building a flying machine for her? A real aeroplane, not a toy. He would name it the *Isabella*, if Victor agreed, and how could a dashing romantic such as the famous La Brosse stand in the way of young love?

Conor crossed the inner courtyard, the intensity of his thoughts hurrying him along. He ignored neighbours and failed to notice friends, but rather than think him rude these people smiled.

Look at young Broekhart with his head in the skies. No surprise there — was he not born in the clouds?

A pig crossed his path, and Conor bumped into its filthy flank.

'Sorry, Princess,' blurted Conor, his thoughts mixing with reality.

The drover scratched his chin. 'Who are you calling Princess? Me or the pig?'

Conor apologized twice, once to the pig and again to its owner, before hurriedly continuing across the yard, this time with his eyes focused on the here and now.

'Porkchop says she's free on Wednesday,' the drover called after him, much to the amusement of anyone within earshot.

Conor took himself and his burning cheeks round the nearest corner, which was not the way he wished to go, but at least he was out of the drover's sight.

He rested against the wall for a moment, until his scarlet embarrassment faded, ignoring the passing traffic of militia, civil servants and merchants. A couple of Bonvilain's knights stumbled by, obviously drunk, plucking whatever they wished from the market stalls. No payment was offered and none asked for.

Conor heard an unfamiliar sing-song accent waft through an open scullery window.

'. . . so very handsome,' the voice said. 'Gretchen, you know that little German princess, with those ears and the estates, she would kill, *kill*, to have afternoon tea with Prince Christian. But he is with the choosing your Isabella. She should be honoured. If you to ask me, he will making all the talking today. He will not the coming back. Christian does not like the boating, with the big waves and sick making.'

Christian would do all his talking today.

Conor came close to panicking in the street. He felt sure that the struggle to keep such powerful emotions under control must surely have resulted in some disfigurement of his forehead.

I must talk to Isabella now.

He would go to the princess. Tell her that the spring-loaded glider had been a bad idea. He would gather some flowers, and wrap them in paper, and on the paper a poem.

Pathetic. That sounds pathetic even to me, and it was my idea. I am no poet. If Isabella likes me, it is not for my poetry.

He would go to her, and be himself. Just remind her of his existence before Prince Christian charmed her off to Denmark. Maybe tell a joke. One of Victor's.

What's happening to me? he asked himself.

Conor had always thought that the most powerful emotion he would ever experience was the thrill of scientific discovery. To do something that no one in the history of the world had done. What could compare to that?

But then he began to see Isabella through different eyes. He noticed how she brightened the classroom with her jokes and attitude, and even her constant insults and threats of torture seemed somehow endearing. He realized that her brown eyes could make everything else in a room disappear. He wished the mornings away until she appeared in the classroom.

I must talk with her. Even my flying machines will not get me to Denmark!

The princess's rooms were below the king's in the rebuilt main tower. There was a sentry on the Wall above the tower door. Conor knew him as one of his father's favourites in spite of his relaxed attitude to authority.

That Bates will be the death of me and himself, Declan often complained. *I don't know which is sharper, his aim or his tongue.*

Conor saluted him. 'Corporal Bates, nice evening.'

'Really? Not if you're up on a wall with an ocean breeze blowing up your trouser leg it isn't.'

'I suppose. I was just making conversation. I'm really here to –'

'See Isabella, as usual. You have that big lovestruck gombeen head on you again. Go on up there before the Denmarkian fellow steals her away on his hobby horse.'

If Conor had been really listening, the *hobby horse* comment might have made him pause.

'It's Danish and do you think he can steal her away? Have you heard anything?'

Bates stared at Conor as though he were mad, then smiled slowly. 'Oh, I think he has a good chance. Strapping lad like him. And the way he eats up all his dinner. Very commendable. I'd get up there if I were you.'

'Should I wait here while you announce me?'

'No, no,' said Bates. 'You go on up. I'm sure the princess would love to see you.'

Not exactly procedure, but Bates's cavalier disregard for protocol was legend.

'Very well, I will go. Thank you, Corporal Bates.'

Bates saluted merrily. 'You are so welcome, young Broekhart. But don't thank me now; just make sure I get an invitation to the wedding.'

Conor hurried up the staircase and he was panting by the time he reached the princess's floor. The stairway opened to an arched vestibule with four glowing electric globes, a spectacular Norman medieval tapestry and a cherub fountain, which generated more noise from its two pumps than it did water. The vestibule was deserted, apart from Conor who steadied himself against the wall wishing he wasn't sweating and covered in mud.

Of all the days to be wrestling pigs and running up stairs.

From behind Isabella's door came peals of delighted laughter. Conor knew that laugh well. Isabella saved that particular laugh for special occasions. Birthdays, christenings, May Day. Pleasant surprises.

I have to go in there, to hell with the consequences.

Conor drew himself up, pasted his hair down with a licked hand and barged into the private apartment of a royal princess.

Isabella was kneeling at her small gilded reception table, hands dripping red.

'Isabella!' shouted Conor. 'You're bleeding.'

'It's just paint,' said Isabella, calmly. 'Conor, what are you doing here?'

There was a little well-dressed boy at the table.

'This funny man is smelling of the poo poo,' said the boy, pointing a finger dripping in green paint.

Conor suddenly felt ill.

Oh my god. Little child. Paint. Eats all his dinner.

Isabella's face was stern. 'Yes, funny man, explain the poo poo smell to Prince Christian.'

'*This* is Prince Christian?'

'Yes, he is painting a masterpiece for me, using only his fingers.'

'And also the paint,' the prince pointed out.

Isabella nodded. 'Thank you, Christian, you are so clever. Now, Conor, explain the odd smell.'

'There was a pig in the courtyard,' said Conor weakly. 'Porkchop, I think her name was. We bumped into each other.'

Christian clapped his hands in delight, splattering paint over himself.

'The funny man does not have money for the horse, so he is riding the pig.'

Conor did not rise to the jibe. He deserved it and more.

I must look like a halfwit, he thought. *Straight from fencing and pig wrestling.*

Isabella cleared her throat. 'Ahem, Sir Conor. Could you, in the minute left of your life before I have you executed, explain what you are doing here?'

Now that he *was* here, Conor was not sure what to say, but he did know that it should be something true. Something meaningful.

'Firstly, Your Highnesses, apologies for the intrusion. Isabella, I had something . . . I *have* something I need to say to you . . .'

Isabella had not heard that tone from Conor before. Not once in fourteen years.

'Yes, Conor,' she said, the mischievous twinkle absent now.

'About your birthday . . .'

'My birthday is not for a while yet.'

'Not this birthday, last birthday.'

'What about my last birthday?'

There was a stillness then, silence even below in the courtyard as if the entire world was waiting for Conor's answer.

'That spring-loaded glider . . .'

'You don't want it back, do you? Because the window was open and I . . .'

'No. No, I don't want it back. I just felt I should tell you that it was the wrong gift to give you. I hope you were expecting something different. Special.'

'A spring-loaded glider is very, very special,' said Prince Christian seriously. 'If the princess is not the wanting it?'

Isabella held Conor's gaze for a few seconds, seemingly dazed, then blinked twice.

'Very well, Prince Christian, I think teatime is over. I hope you enjoyed your tea and cakes and the lemonade.'

Prince Christian was not eager to leave. 'Yes, the lemonade was pleasing. I was wondering may I have the vodka?'

'No, Christian,' said Isabella brightly. 'You are only seven years old.'

'A brandy then?'

'Absolutely not.'

'Yes, but in my country it is the custom.'

'Oh really. Let's ask your nanny, shall we?'

Isabella pulled a bell cord on the wall, and seconds later a Danish nanny arrived, gliding into the room like a carriage on rails. The lady was not smiling, and looked as though she rarely did.

She took one look at Prince Christian and rolled up her sleeves.

'I am the baby prince washing now,' she said, grabbing Christian by the forearm.

'Let go of me, servant,' squealed Christian, struggling vainly. 'I am your master.'

The nanny scowled. 'That's quite enough of the master–servant talk, Christian. Be a good little prince and Nanny will make you wienerbrød for supper.'

Immediately mollified, the little prince was led from the apartment, trailing blobs of paint behind him.

Isabella wordlessly disappeared into her washroom, and Conor heard water being poured.

She's washing off the paint, he thought. *Should I stay now? Or should I go? When she left the room, was that a dismissal?*

Things had suddenly changed. They had always been equal before, now he was worrying about her every feeling, her every footstep.

I should go. We can talk later.

No. Stay. Definitely stay. Victor would not run away. If I go now, we will be back to confusion tomorrow.

'Who are you talking to, Conor?'

Conor was about to protest that he had not been talking, when he noticed that his lips were already moving.

'Oh, I was just thinking aloud. When I am nervous, I sometimes . . .'

Isabella smiled kindly. 'You really are a scatterfool, aren't you, Sir Conor?'

Conor relaxed. She was teasing him. Familiar ground.

'I am sorry, Princess. Will you have me garrotted?'

'I prefer hanging, as you well know.'

Conor took a deep breath and bared his soul. He did it quickly, like jumping into the ocean, to get the pain over with.

'I came because you told me this tea was part of a royal courtship.'

Isabella had the grace to blush. 'I may have said so. I was teasing.'

'I see that now. Too late to save me from embarrassment.'

'Christian's father has business here. I am doing my royal duty, that's all. No courtship.'

'None.'

Conor's shoulders slumped. At least now, he did not feel like a participant in some kind of race.

'So you built up your courage, and came charging up here to declare your love?'

'Well I . . .'

Do not panic. Do not panic.

'Something like that.'

Isabella moved to the balcony and stood leaning on the carved balustrade, dark hair flowing down her back, white fingers on the stone. Beyond and below, the Wall lights were popping on like a regiment of orderly fireflies.

I should speak now, while she is turned away. It will be easier without her eyes on me.

'Isabella, things are . . . Things are changing for us . . . between us. And that's good. That's as it should be. Natural. It's only natural that things change.' Conor groaned inwardly, this was not going very well.

Say what you want to say.

'What I *want* to say is that perhaps our days of climbing

chimneys are over, although I like climbing chimneys, but perhaps there are new things to do. To share. Without the company of Danish princes.'

Isabella turned to him, and her mocking smile was not as steady as it usually was.

'Conor, you are such a scientist. Is there not a shorter, more concise way, to say all of this?'

Conor frowned. 'Perhaps there is. I would have to do a few experiments. I am new to this and I feel clumsy.'

Isabella made a show of pouring some lemonade from a jug. 'I am the same, Conor. Sometimes I feel as though we have made our own world here, and I have no wish to leave. Everything is perfect. Now, it is perfect.'

Conor smiled tentatively, coming back to himself. 'So, I am not to be executed.'

'Not today, Sir Conor,' the princess said, handing him the glass. 'After all, you rescued the princess from the tower. There is only one way for that fairy tale to end.'

Conor choked on a mouthful of lemonade, spraying his pig-dung-stained trousers.

'An interesting combination of smells,' commented Isabella.

'Pardon me, Princess,' said Conor. 'I am amazed by your friendly reception. I imagined myself trussed up by Danish guards by now.'

Isabella turned her brown eyes full on him. 'Conor, I could search the world for another swashbuckling scientist, but I doubt if I would find one like you.' The princess realized that she had said a little too much, and felt compelled to add, 'Even if you are a lanky-limbed, overbrained oaf.'

Conor accepted the first half of the compliment with a smile, and the second half with a grimace.

'I feel exactly the same,' he said. 'Apart from the scientist, lanky-oaf part. You know what I am trying to say.'

'Yes, Sir Conor,' said Isabella, teasing him with his title again. 'I do.'

CHAPTER 4:

TREASON AND PLOT

Conor did not return home after his meeting with Isabella; he was too elated. He felt as though his heart were half its previous mass. Somehow, against all the laws of science, just sharing his thoughts with the princess seemed to make him lighter. So even though he was already late, Conor decided to preserve the feeling by passing an hour alone in his favourite hideaway. Somewhere he had not been for several months.

More times than he could remember, Conor's parents had forbidden him to climb the keep turret. In general, he respected their wishes, but every boy has some secret transgression that he cannot surrender. For Conor, it was his perch high in the eaves below the north-east turret. This was the place where he felt closest to his nature, where he felt that the race for flight could actually be won by a boy and his teacher.

But this evening he was not thinking about heavier-than-air flying machines as he squeezed out through a medieval murder hole, and clambered along the ivy to the wooden trestles that had been put in after the chemical fire in Nicholas's apartment. Tonight he was thinking about Isabella. Nothing specific. Just contented, warm thoughts. As soon as his back rested on the tower's familiar mouldings, Conor felt a familiar peace settle over him. He was surprised to find the spot a tight squeeze. Soon, he would outgrow this hiding place, and he would have to find another high spot to dream of flight.

Conor sat, watching the sun set over the ocean, sharing the view with the dozen or so gulls that hoped against hope that someone would leave an open barrel of fish inside the curtain wall. Across the bay he could see a large fire somewhere in Kilmore, and the beam from the Hook Head lighthouse already cast its cone of light across Saint George's Channel. It was a beautiful early summer night and presently the narrow patch of water between the Saltees glimmered with moonshine as though bridged.

Directly below his feet, a team of guards were running a cannon drill. And on the Great Saltee Wall, Conor was sure he could see his father striding between watch posts, dark cloak flapping behind him.

He was not tempted to call out. Better to delay his next punishment for this offence as long as possible.

Conor, I could search the world for another swashbuckling scientist, but I doubt if I would find one like you.

He smiled at the echo of the words in his mind.

Conor's thoughts were interrupted by a regular scraping along the stone inside the tower. Feet on the steps. In all his climbs to this lofty spot, the only footsteps Conor had ever heard on those steps besides his own were his father's coming to fetch him down. Declan Broekhart was fifty feet below on the Wall, and so it could not be him.

Conor twisted slightly in his cramped position, so that

he could hang back on a creeper and peep in through the murder hole's leaded glass. The wind caught his hair as he leaned from shelter, and he had a sudden powerful recollection of how he used to adopt this same position as a younger boy.

I would pretend to fly. I remember that.

Conor smiled at the memory.

Soon, there will be no need to pretend. Victor and I will design the machine, and I will fly it past Isabella's window.

A figure moved inside the turret. Conor saw a shadow first, made jumpy by a jarred lamp, then the dark shape of the lantern held low to light the steps only. Shards of light flickered across the deep folds of cloth and face. The colour red sprang to life under the light. A red cross. Then a heavy brow and glittering eyes. Bonvilain.

Conor stayed still as a gargoyle. Bonvilain had almost inhuman perception. He could spot a seal's head in stormy seas. The marshall would have good reason not to approve of Conor's loitering so close to the king's offices, and could justifiably shoot him as a traitor.

I will sit without breathing or stirring, until the marshall is well gone. Then home quickly.

The sight of Bonvilain's sharply shadowed features had quite sucked the joy from the evening. That would have been the end of the day's adventures, had not something else gleamed in the lamplight. Something that Conor knew well. A long-barrelled revolver, with a band of pearl grip poking from below Bonvilain's fingers.

It was, without the shadow of a doubt, Victor's Colt Peacemaker. This was extremely curious. Why would Marshall Bonvilain be prowling the serving passages of the castle with Victor's pistol?

You're making a mistake. That can't be Victor's gun.

But it was. Conor's keen eye had picked out enough detail to know he was not mistaken. He had studied the gun countless times, breath fogging the glass case.

There must be a thousand explanations for this. Just because you do not know the reason, doesn't mean there isn't one.

It was true and sensible, but Conor was a boy and a scientist, the most curious breed of human alive, and he could no more turn away from this than a convict could ignore an open door. If Bonvilain had Victor's gun, then his teacher should know about it, and know why. His teacher had long suspected that the marshall was not to be trusted and here could be the proof.

Conor waited several moments, until the last light of Bonvilain's lantern danced past and darkness had closed behind the marshall, then swung himself monkeylike to the sill built into the murder hole, an action that would have had his parents clutching their hearts in shock.

Had the window creaked on his way to the murder hole? He couldn't remember as it hadn't been of vital importance at the time. Conor tested it with a gentle prod. No creaking, just a slight rasp of dust in the hinges. Safe enough, surely.

He slipped inside, arms first, walking along the floor with his hands until his feet dropped to the floor behind him.

Conor crouched on the uneven granite, listening. The sound of his own breath hitting the stone seemed enormous. Bonvilain would hear it surely.

But no. The marshall's footsteps continued at their previous pace and Conor could see faint flickers from the lamp ahead. He turned his face to the light, and followed Bonvilain up the spiral staircase on all fours, feeling his way, staying low.

This passage led to the serving door in King Nicholas's own apartment, which was bolted shut and guarded whenever the king was in residence, but when Conor slid his head round the corner, the door was unguarded and wide open. No guard meant no king. And if King Nicholas was not in his apartments, why would Bonvilain be skulking around up here, armed with another man's pistol?

A myriad reasons. There are things that you do not know. For example, King Nicholas may have asked for the gun so that he could have a replica made for Victor, to complete the set. A birthday present.

Unlikely, but possible.

Conor crept through the doorway, quiet as the curious breed of tailless Manx cat that had taken hold on the island. The light ahead was dim, but steady. Bonvilain was still. Had he heard something or was he listening to something? Waiting or spying?

Conor's stomach twinged. He should go back now. Really. Interfering in the marshall's business was a serious business. Bonvilain was never reluctant to cry traitor, and good men had been gaoled for less.

But the revolver. Victor's revolver.

Half a dozen steps more, Conor promised his prudent half. *I will peek round the next bend, then retire. Little or no risk.*

Not exactly true, but Conor proceeded nonetheless, searching out every step with probing fingers before mounting it. He hugged the floor and wall, seeking the darkest shadows and inched his face around the final twist in the stairs.

Bonvilain was half a dozen steps above; the lantern rested at his feet, casting sharp triangles of light upwards. His face appeared demonic in this light, but it was just the angle. Surely.

Suddenly Bonvilain's head turned towards Conor's position, and he had to fight every instinct not to stand up and flee. He was invisible, cloaked by the dark. After a long breathless moment, Conor realized that the marshall's main intention was not to cast his eyes down the stairway, but to move his ear closer to the wall. He was listening to something. Or, more likely, someone.

And another detail, in his left hand a dark lump. Light glinted on a chiselled edge and Conor saw that Bonvilain held a brick. He had removed a small brick from the wall and was eavesdropping on whoever was in the king's apartment.

Words floated down the stairwell, and because of the turret's acoustics they were as clear to Conor as they doubtless were to Bonvilain himself.

The king's voice. And Victor's. So the marshall spied on his own king.

Conor closed his eyes and strained his ears, trying to make sense of what he heard, when what he should have been doing was running just as fast as his young legs would carry him. Running to fetch his father.

Inside the king's apartment, Victor Vigny was seated in one of a pair of Louis XV armchairs by the fireplace. The main door crashed open and in bounded King Nicholas, balancing two frosted tankards on a tray. With great pomp and much bowing Nicholas I presented Victor with a cold glass of beer.

'That is fantastic,' said Victor after a deep swig. 'Colder than the backside of a polar bear. The refrigerator is working well, I see.'

Nicholas sat and took a drink from his own glass. 'Perfectly, though the ammonia is a little dangerous. Those Germans need to find a new gas.'

'Someone will,' said Victor, wiping away a foam moustache. 'That's progress.'

'Can you imagine the benefits of reliable refrigeration?'

'You mean beyond cold beer?' joked Victor.

Nicholas rose to pace the floor, the subject of progress never failing to excite him.

'We can trade with the United States. Fresh produce. And we can export too.'

'Diamonds don't need freezing,' quipped Victor.

'Other things. The Plantago. And we can freeze produce out of season, in a giant warehouse. Strawberries and salmon all year.'

ARTEMIS FOWL

EOIN COLFER

AND THE TIME PARADOX

NEW AUGUST 2008

Victor was suddenly serious. 'You, my good friend, have bigger fish to worry about.'

'What have you heard?' asked Nicholas, sitting once more.

Victor sighed. 'It is as bad as you feared, and worse. My man on Little Saltee tells me that Bonvilain works the prisoners to death. As far as he can tell, many of the inmates are guilty of nothing more than vagrancy. We can't prove it yet, but by my count at least half of the diamonds go missing between the mine and the treasury.'

'Dammit,' swore Nicholas, hurling his glass into the fireplace. 'Bonvilain is a plague. A blight on the Saltees. He treats the islands as his personal property. I must be rid of him.'

Victor nodded towards the fireplace. 'A fine beginning. Crystal in the grate should have the marshall quaking in his boots.'

The king's eyes flashed fire for a moment, but then he settled, and looked towards the grate, perhaps regretting the loss of a cold beer.

'How long have we been together, Victor?'

'If I answer this, will a speech be next?'

'Oh, I am missing my beer now.'

Victor relented. 'Twenty years, Nick. Every fair in the blessed United States, and now the top of this fine castle.'

'All that time and what have we achieved? Victor, we can help people here. Not just a few shillings to the needy, actually help. Make things better forever. It's all in the machines. We

can build them. Look at young Conor Broekhart. Have you
ever seen a mind like that?'

'I know it,' said Victor with a touch of pride. 'Isabella
knows it too.'

Nicholas smiled. 'Poor Conor.'

'I think poor Conor has no idea of the hoops Isabella will
trot him through.'

The king could not stay happy long. 'Damn him! Damn
Bonvilain. He is a tyrant. I am the king, am I not? I will be
rid of him.'

'Careful, Nicholas. Sir Hugo has the army on his side.
Declan Broekhart is the only one who could sway them.
The men look up to him. We should invite him to one of
our talks.'

The king nodded. 'Very well. Tonight. I cannot wait
another day. I will see Bonvilain in prison before the month
is out. The future will only wait for so long. This island is
trapped in the Middle Ages because of that man. His guards
are murderous thugs and his justice is self-serving and
vicious. After seven hundred years, the alliance between
the Trudeau and Bonvilain families is about to come to
an end.'

'I'll drink to that,' said Victor, tipping back the rest of his
beer.

Bonvilain came through the serving door with the Colt
already extended, walking with confident measured strides.
There was no overblown villain's preamble, Sir Hugo had

been in too many life-or-death situations for that. He allowed himself one sentence only.

'Victor Vigny, you have killed the king.'

Both Frenchman and monarch reacted quickly, neither bothering with protestations or pleadings. There was murder in Bonvilain's eyes, not a single doubt about that. Victor hurled his body across the room to shield his friend, while Nicholas's right hand dropped to the Smith and Wesson revolver that he always wore slung low on his hip in the American style.

Victor, the younger man, almost achieved his goal, but no matter how quick the man, the gun is quicker. Bonvilain fired and the bullet clipped the webbing between the Frenchman's outstretched thumb and index finger, which deflected the bullet slightly, but not enough to save the king. Nicholas fell back in his chair and was dead before the Smith and Wesson dropped from his fingers.

Bonvilain grunted, satisfied, then picked up the king's gun and turned it on Victor Vigny, who lay on the hearth rug, blood streaming from his hand.

'You almost made the distance,' said Bonvilain admiringly. 'Commendable effort.'

Victor looked into the marshall's eyes and knew his own life was over.

'So, I am the murderer?' he said.

'Yes. You shot the king with your own gun. There is a test they are developing in Scotland Yard that can match the bullet to the gun. I shall have an expert shipped over. I have also employed a Dutch handwriting expert to forge letters from you to the French government detailing the Saltee defences. I ask you, do these sound like the actions of a man who has trapped the islands in the Middle Ages?'

'Nobody will believe that I killed the king,' protested Victor. 'He was like a brother to me.'

Bonvilain shrugged. 'Not many knew that. You were his secret spy, remember? Spying on me. Now, to business. I am sure you have a dirk in your boot, or a Derringer in your beard, or some other spy trickery, so fare thee well, Victor Vigny. Tell your master that the alliance between the Trudeau and Bonvilain families continues a while longer.'

'You will never stop us all,' cried Victor, valiantly jumping to his feet, a dirk in his hand, pulled from some fold of clothing.

Bonvilain tutted, shooting Victor four times in the chest. A little excessive perhaps, but he was understandably upset – after all, the king had been murdered.

A thought struck him.

Stop us all. What had Vigny meant by that? Were there more spies on the islands?

'Or were you toying with me, Frenchman?' he asked squatting down and curling Victor's fingers around the grip of his own Colt Peacemaker. 'Leaving a few doubts behind to prey on my mind?'

The main door opened and a sentry entered.

'Am I supposed to come in yet?' he asked.

'Yes, yes,' said Bonvilain, irritated that it had been necessary to involve a sentry. He would have to be disposed of at the earliest opportunity. 'You see what has happened here? You heard the gunshots and came in. They shot each other, simple as that. You don't need to offer any opinions. You say what you saw.'

The sentry nodded slowly, though this was not the first time he'd heard these simple instructions.

'I say what I saw. Yes, Marshall. And you won't kill me?'

'Of course not, Muldoon. You wear the red cross. I don't kill my own guards.'

Muldoon was obviously relieved. 'Good news for me. Thank you, Marshall. I appreciate being allowed to continue with my worthless life.'

Bonvilain was struggling not to end Muldoon's worthless life immediately. 'You should probably go and raise the alarm.'

Muldoon bobbed his head. 'Yes, Marshall. Absolutely. But who is that boy behind you, sir?'

Bonvilain blinked. 'Excuse me?'

Conor was a sharp young man, and it hadn't taken him long to realize what was happening. Apparently Victor was not just the royal tutor, he was also a spy for King Nicholas. Bonvilain must have listened to this conspiracy blossom from his spot behind the wall, and intended to put an end to it, before it put an end to him.

But why Victor's gun?

His teacher's own voice chided him.

For goodness' sake, boy. Is it not obvious?

Conor paled in the darkness.

Of course. Victor's weapon. Victor's crime.

When Bonvilain went through the door, Conor had already formulated a rudimentary plan. He would rush through two paces behind shouting a warning. Victor should react quickly and disarm Bonvilain without undue difficulty.

He was on his feet and halfway up the stretch of stairs, when the first shot rang out.

So quickly? So quickly? Who had taken the bullet? Perhaps King Nicholas had fired first and all was well. Only one shot, after all. One shot for one man.

Conor kept moving, but carefully now. He did not want to be shot for a traitor by his king or teacher. They would be nervous, on the lookout for Bonvilain's men, and there was no need for a warning now. It was too late, one way or the other.

The boy eased into the doorway, squinting against the sudden lamplight. His eyes adjusted in time for him to witness Victor shot down as he rushed Bonvilain. He froze, speechless, as his eyes took in the tableau of horror before him. The king, dead. Victor too. Horribly. And Bonvilain grinning and talking to himself like a madman. Now he was placing Victor's gun in the Parisian's hand. These events were nightmarish. Too brisk to be true. They skimmed the surface of reality like skipped stones on a flat sea.

A knock on the door, and in comes a sentry. Conor recognized him from his corridor-roaming with Isabella. A dullard, in the watch because of some relation. But a subject, nonetheless, and so should be warned.

Conor was a breath from shouting when the sentry began

to converse with Bonvilain. The man was a part of things! Bonvilain would escape completely. The king would be dead and Victor's memory blackened. It was unbearable.

This plot must be stopped. Bonvilain could not be allowed close to Isabella. Conor stooped low, creeping to Victor's side, using the furniture as cover. The Parisian lay on his side, as though comfortably asleep. His eyes were wide with surprise and blood bubbled on his lips. Dead. Dead.

Conor fought the tears. What would Victor have him do? What would his father have him do? Stop this conspiracy. He had training aplenty to do it and there was a loaded gun inches from his fingers.

Then Victor's eyes blinked and found focus. The Frenchman lived for a stolen moment.

'Don't do it, boy,' he whispered, showing a remarkable grasp of the situation. 'The Martello tower in Kilmore. Find it and burn it. Bonvilain must never learn our secrets. The eagle has the key. Go now. Go.'

Conor nodded, the tears coming freely, dripping from his nose and chin.

Martello tower. Kilmore. Burn it. Go now.

He might have left then and avoided years of heartache, had not the Parisian rattled out his final breath.

Dead. Again.

Conor was stunned. To lose his friend and mentor twice in as many minutes. They would never fly together now.

They would never fly.

The Broekhart in him took over, pushing down the scientist. Victor had been trying to protect him, but there was no need;

Conor was trained in all the weapons of combat, including Oriental and Indian, had they been available.

Conor prised the Colt from Victor's hands. The pearl handle against his palm brought both confidence and sadness. This was a gun he had twirled a thousand times while Victor chided him for a show-off.

He twirled it again to settle himself, then popped out the cylinder, checking the load. Five shots left. Plenty for some wounding. Conor came to his feet, the tears on his face drying quickly.

The sentry saw him first.

'But who is that boy behind you, sir?' he said dully.

Bonvilain turned slowly, already pulling a sad face.

'Ah, young Broekhart,' he said, as though Conor was expected. 'A terrible tragedy.'

Conor aimed the Colt at Bonvilain's chest, a large enough target. 'I heard everything, Marshall. I saw you shoot Victor.'

Bonvilain dropped the act. His face was once again its sharp self. Angles and shadows.

'No one will believe you.'

'Some will,' said Conor. 'My father will.'

The marshall considered this. 'You know, I think you might be right. I suppose that means I must kill you too, unless you kill me.'

'I could do it. And that oaf too,' said Conor, cocking the Colt.

'I am sure you could, theoretically, but the time for theory is over. This is not the practice field, Conor; we are at war now.'

'Stand where you are, Marshall. Someone heard the shots. They will be coming.'

'Not through these walls. No one is coming.'

It was true and Conor knew it. Victor had told him that one night he and Nicholas were testing fireworks in the grate and not a soul in the palace had heard.

'You, soldier. Put down your rifle and sit on the chair.'

The sentry did not appreciate being ordered about by a fourteen-year-old boy, but then again the boy seemed very familiar with the weapon in his fist.

'This chair? There's blood on it.'

'No, idiot. That chair. By the wall.'

The sentry laid his weapon on the stone floor, shuffling across to a stool by the wall.

'This is a stool,' he mumbled. 'You said chair.'

Bonvilain took a sneaky step forward, hoping that Conor was distracted by the sentry's inanities. Not so.

'Don't move, traitor. Murderer.'

Bonvilain smiled. His teeth were glossy, like yellow pearls.

'Now, Conor, I will explain to you what I am about to do. I intend, and this is a promise, to take a leisurely walk across the space between us and then choke the life from your body. The only way you can stop this coming to pass is to shoot me. Remember, this is war – no school today.'

'Stay where you are!' shouted Conor, but the marshall was already on his way. Five steps divided them. Four now.

'Take your shot, boy. Soon I will be too close and it will be difficult to get a bullet past my hands.'

I chose badly, Conor realized. *I should have fled down the passage and fetched my father.*

He had never shot a person. Never wanted to.

I want to build a flying machine. With Victor.

But Victor was dead. Murdered by Bonvilain.

'I am upon you,' said the marshall.

Conor shot him twice, under his outstretched arms in the upper chest.

I had to do it. He gave me no choice.

Bonvilain's steps faltered slightly, but he kept coming. He was purple in the forehead, but the light in his eyes never wavered.

'And now,' he said batting the gun from Conor's fingers, 'to choke the life from your body. As promised.'

Conor was lifted from the floor, his arms and legs flapping, battering ineffectively against the marshall's flanks, which seemed to jingle when struck.

'I am a Templar, boy,' said Bonvilain. 'Have you never heard of us? We like to wear chain mail going into war. Chain mail. I have a vest on at the moment just in case things did not play out as I planned. Prudence is never wasted, as we see here today.'

This revelation did not matter much to Conor now. All he knew was that Bonvilain still lived. He had been shot, but lived.

'You hold him, Marshall!' said the sentry, reclaiming his rifle. 'Hold him still and I will shoot him.'

'No!' shouted the marshall, imagining the indignity of an epitaph that included the phrase *accidentally shot while strangling a youth*.

'You prefer to do it yourself,' said the sentry, sulking slightly.

Bonvilain thought as he strangled. He held in his hands, literally, the solution to his Captain Broekhart difficulty. Victor Vigny had been right: Declan Broekhart was his only real opposition in the Saltee Army. Surely there was a way to win the captain's loyalty from this situation. And if it required a little manipulation, was that not his speciality?

An idea poked from the depths of Bonvilain's brain, like the head of a sly serpent from a swamp. What if the rebel Victor Vigny had not acted alone. *What if* he had an accomplice, the sentry for example. The sentry was certainly expendable.

Bonvilain felt a shiver run up his spine. He was on the verge of brilliance, he could feel it. For Bonvilain, it was moments like these that made life tolerable. Moments that presented him with a challenge worthy of his specific talents.

'You there, idiot,' he said to the sentry. 'Open the window.'

'That one?' said the sentry, though there was but one window in the apartment.

'Yes,' said Bonvilain innocently. 'The one overlooking the cliffs.'

*

Conor awoke from near strangulation in a damp windowless cell, where he languished for hours. His solitude was interrupted periodically by a brace of guards who stomped with considerable gusto on his slim frame. On their final visit, the pair stripped him of his clothing and bundled him into a Saltee Army uniform.

As yer own clothes stink of blood and fear.

Conor wondered about this briefly through his pain. Why a soldier's uniform? Before his addled brain could reach any conclusion, the beatings recommenced, backhanded blows across the face. One eye closed and he felt the blood flow down his nose. The guards propped something soft on his head. A towel perhaps? To staunch the flow of blood maybe? It seemed unusually compassionate.

There were more confusing meddlings with his person. One swabbed his cheeks with what smelled like gunpowder. The other scratched on his arm with an ink pen. It went on for what seemed like hours.

When the guards were satisfied with their arrangements, the fatter of the pair clamped a set of manacles on Conor's wrists and a lunatic box over his head, pulling the head cage's leather mouth strap tight until it forced Conor's teeth apart, ratcheting back between his jaws. The only noises he could make now were groans and grunts.

The cell itself was a ten-foot block of hell, and Conor could not credit that such a place existed on Great Saltee.

The walls and floor were granite. Hewn from the island itself. No bricks or mortar, just solid rock. There was no escape from here. Water trickled through grooves worn by centuries of erosion. Conor did not waste a second thirsting for it. The combination of lunatic box and manacles meant that he could not pass anything through the metal grille to his mouth. In any case, the grooves themselves were flaked by salt. Sea water.

They left him for an age, wallowing in his misery. The king was dead. Isabella's father murdered by Bonvilain. Victor was gone too. In the blink of an eye, his mentor and friend cruelly killed. And what was to become of Conor himself? Surely Bonvilain would not leave breath in the body of a witness. Conor felt the weight of the cage upon his head, the gall of manacles chafing his wrists and the threat of his impending murder heavy on his heart.

The metal slab of door swung, dragging on the hinges. A tallow yellow light filled the room with a sickly glow, and in that glow stood the unmistakable silhouette of Sir Hugo Bonvilain. The king's marshall and murderer. Because of this man, Isabella was an orphan.

Rage took hold of Conor's body, filling his limbs with strength. He lurched to his feet, arms outstretched towards Bonvilain.

The sight cheered Bonvilain tremendously. The man actually whistled as he grasped the lunatic box's grille, stuffing his thick fingers between the bars. He stepped to the side and casually swung Conor into the wall, wincing at the clang and clatter.

'I used your own *momentum* against you,' he said, as though school were in session. 'Basic training. *Basic*. If one of my men made that mistake I'd have him flogged. Didn't that French dandy teach you anything?'

Bonvilain squatted, propping Conor against the rough damp wall.

'A great day, isn't it? Historic. The king is gone, apparently assassinated by rebels. Do you know what that means?'

Conor could not reply even if he wanted to. If it had not been for the pain, this would all seem like a cruel dream. A night terror.

Bonvilain rattled the lunatic box, to make sure he had Conor's attention.

'Hello? Young Broekhart. Still with us?'

Conor tried to spit at his captor, but all he could do was gag.

'Good. Alive for now. Anyway, about the king being dead, let me *tell* you what it means. It means an end to these ridiculous reforms. Money for the people. The people? Unwashed, uneducated rabble. No more money for *the people*, you can bet the blood in your veins on that.'

Everything King Nicholas has done will be undone, thought Conor dully. *All for nothing.*

'Isabella becomes queen. A puppet queen, but a queen nonetheless. And can you guess what her obsession will become?'

Of course. It was so obvious that a boy could see it, even in Conor's dazed state.

'I see by your eyes that you *can* guess. She will dedicate her life to stamping out the rebels. It will consume her; I will make sure of it. There will be no end to the number of rebels I will unearth. Any merchant who refuses to pay my tax. Any youth with a grudge. All rebels. All hanged. I am closer now to being king, than any Bonvilain has ever been.'

This statement hung between them, heavy with centuries of treason. Creak of manacle chains and drip of water.

Bonvilain yanked Conor's head as close as the bars would allow, and unhooked the box's mouth strap.

'Before he died your teacher said that I would never stop them all. Was Victor Vigny working with the French aeronauts? Or La Légion Noire – the Black Legion?'

Conor's lip was swollen from one punch or another and his jaws were shot with pain, but he managed to speak.

'There is no Black Legion. You will destroy the Saltees fighting an imaginary enemy.'

'Let me tell you something, little man,' snarled the marshall. 'If it weren't for the Bonvilains, these islands would be nothing more than rocks in the ocean. Nothing but salt and bird droppings. We have nursemaided the Trudeaus for centuries. But no more. These islands are mine now. I will milk them dry and Queen Isabella stays alive so long as she does not interfere with that plan.' Bonvilain rattled Conor's cage. 'I am interested to hear what you think of this plan, young Broekhart.'

'Why tell me, murderer? I am not your priest.'

Bonvilain shook the lunatic box, as though it were a mystery gift.

'Not my priest. Very good, I will miss our exchanges. I

tell you, little Broekhart, because these are the very moments that make life worth living. I am at my best in the thick of action. Stabbing, shooting and plotting. I enjoy it. I exult in it. For centuries, the Bonvilains have been behind the throne, steering it with their machinations. But never anything like this.'

Bonvilain was almost dazed by happiness. Everything he had planned for was now within reach.

'And you, my little meddler, have transformed a good plan into a perfect one. It's your father, you see. He is a great soldier – I can admit it. A wonderful soldier. He inspires great loyalty among the men. I was planning to remove him, and weather the storm. But now the rebel Victor Vigny and you, his indoctrinated student, have killed the king. Your father is honour bound to protect the new queen with every breath in his body. And because I will promise to keep his son's name out of the investigation, Declan Broekhart will owe me his reputation, and so you have made him loyal to me. For that, I thank you.' Bonvilain leaned closer, his face stretched in pantomime sadness. 'But I have to tell you that he hates you now and so will Isabella when I tell her my version of tonight's events. Your father, I would go so far as to say, would kill you himself, if I would allow it. But that's family business and none of mine. I should let him tell you himself.'

And with that Bonvilain hooked up the lunatic box's bridle and threaded the manacle chain through a ring on the wall. He stood, his knees cracking, his huge frame filling the cell, his broad scarred brow suddenly thoughtful.

'You would think I suffer, with all the people I have killed, the hundreds of lives I have destroyed. Should demons not visit me at night? Should I not be tormented by guilt? Sometimes, I lie still in my bed and wait for judgement, but it never arrives.'

Bonvilain shrugged. 'Then again, why should it? Perhaps I am a good man. After all, Socrates said: *There is only one good, knowledge, and one evil, ignorance.* So, as I am not ignorant, I must be good.' He winked. 'Do you think that argument will fool Saint Peter?'

Conor realized at that moment that Bonvilain was, in a very dangerous way, completely mad.

Bonvilain came back to the moment. 'Anyway, let us continue the philosophical discussion some other time. Why don't I fetch your father? I fancy he has a few words for his errant son.'

Bonvilain strode jauntily from the cell whistling a Strauss waltz, conducting with an index finger.

Conor was left on the floor, neck aching from the weight of his cage. But in spite of the pain, there was now a spark of hope. His father would see through this charade surely. Declan Broekhart was nobody's fool and would not leave his son to wallow in a filthy cell. In minutes, Conor felt certain, he would be free to expose Bonvilain as a murderer.

Bonvilain had not even bothered to close the cell door. A moment later, he shepherded Declan Broekhart into the room. Conor had never seen his father so distressed. Declan's back, usually ramrod straight, was hunched and shuddering and he held on to Bonvilain like an old man leaning on his nurse. The face was the worst thing. It was dragged down by grief: eyes, mouth and wrinkles running like candle wax.

'Here he is,' said Bonvilain softly, with great compassion. 'This is he. Just a few seconds.'

Conor inched along the wall, straightening himself.

Father, he tried to say. *Father, help me.* But all that emerged from between his swollen, hampered lips were thin groans.

Declan Broekhart loomed over him, tears dripping from his chin.

'Because of you,' he whispered. 'Because of you . . .'

Then he lunged at Conor, reaching not to embrace, but to kill. Bonvilain was ready for it. He restrained Declan Broekhart with strong arms.

'Now, Declan. Be strong. For Catherine. And for young Isabella. We all need you. The Saltees need you.'

As he said this, Hugo Bonvilain peered over Broekhart's shoulder and winked merrily.

This combination of grief and lunacy were like physical blows to young Conor. He recoiled from his father, drawing his knees to his chin.

What was happening? Was the world mad?

Declan Broekhart gathered himself, dragging a sleeve across his brow.

'Very well, Hugo,' he said haltingly. 'I am composed now. You were right. That wretch is nothing to me. Nothing. His death would not restore anything. Little Saltee can deal with him. Let us leave here; my wife needs me.'

Wretch? His father was calling him a wretch.

'Of course, Captain Broekhart. Declan. Of course.'

And so Bonvilain led him out. Two soldiers together, comrades in grief.

What? What is this? Declan? Little Saltee?

Conor used the last of his strength to moan around his mouth strap, calling his father back. And his father did turn back, if only for a moment. If only to deliver a few final withering remarks. He vented these words with his eyes closed, as if to even look at his son was more than he could bear.

'Your foul actions have taken my king from me,' he said. 'And worse, much worse – because of what you have done this day, I have no son. My son is gone, and this . . .' Declan Broekhart paused to struggle with his rage, eventually calming himself. 'My son is gone, and *you* remain. A word of warning, traitor. If I ever see you again, it will be on the day I kill you.'

These were words that no man should hear from another, but from father to son they were indescribably harsh. Conor Broekhart felt as though he was indeed broken-hearted, as his name suggested. He could do nothing but raise his manacled hands to the lunatic box's grille and tug repeatedly, jerking his injured head until the pain drove those hateful words from his head.

'Insane,' said Bonvilain sadly, leading Declan Broekhart from the cell. 'But then, he would have to be, to do what he did.'

As they left the cell, Bonvilain could barely maintain his show of grief. The waiting guards were ready to draw cutlasses, but Bonvilain shook his head slightly. His manipulation had worked so Declan Broekhart would live for now.

'Take the captain back to his carriage,' he instructed the guards. 'I will watch the prisoner myself.'

Declan grasped Bonvilain's wrist. 'You have been a friend today, Hugo. We have had our fiery moments in the past, but that is behind us. I will not forget your speedy apprehension of the traitor. And I trust he will pay for his part in the king's murder, and for what he did to Conor. My son.'

Broekhart's face cracked in grief once more.

How weak the man is, thought Bonvilain. *There is no need for such hysterics.*

'Of course, Declan. He shall pay. You can count on it.'

They parted with a handshake and Broekhart half walked, half stumbled along the length of the stone corridor. Bonvilain returned to Conor's cell, to where the wretched boy lay unconscious. A tiny fly in the master spider's web.

Bonvilain knelt beside him. He found himself feeling a touch sorry for young Conor.

It's natural, not weakness, he told himself. *I am human after all.*

It was incredible, really, how easily the entire thing had been accomplished. Allow the king to set up his meeting with Victor, then blame the Parisian for Nicholas's murder. Conor Broekhart had been a delightful bonus, a way to keep the father loyal. Admittedly he had toyed with them both a little, but that was the skill of it. His god-given talent to manipulate people.

The final part of the plan had only occurred to him after Conor had surprised him in the king's apartment. Following his near strangulation, the boy's face had been so swollen that he was barely recognizable. Even his own mother wouldn't know him. Bonvilain had ordered the youth to be dressed as a soldier, a ratty old ball wig arranged on his head and his chin coated with gunpowder stubble. The final trick was to have one of his sergeants, a gifted man with pen and ink, to draw a quick copy of the regimental tattoo on Conor's forearm. A small touch, but enough to make an impression. With the blood, shadows, wig and uniform, it was unlikely that Broekhart would know his own son. Especially if he had just been informed that *his* son had been wrestled out of the king's window, trying to defend Nicholas, and that this prisoner was one of the traitorous soldiers involved in the plan. A sentry's corpse had already been found at the base of the Wall, Conor's dead body must have been swept south by the currents.

Of course, if Declan Broekhart had recognized his son, then Bonvilain himself would have immediately slit his throat. Conor could have taken the blame for that too. A busy day for the boy. Regicide in the afternoon, patricide in the evening.

But now, thanks to Bonvilain's little games, Declan Broekhart thought his son was dead and Conor thought his father despised him for being a traitor. Sir Hugo had utter control over the Broekhart family and should Declan ever turn against him, then Conor could be resurrected and used to blackmail his father. Unswerving loyalty in return for his son's life. Bonvilain knew that toying with Conor was unnecessary and cruel, but that was the fun of it. His own brazen audacity thrilled him.

Bonvilain clapped his hands gently three times.

Bravo, maestro. Bravo.

I love this, thought Bonvilain. *I* exult *in it*.

PART 2:

FINN

CHAPTER 5:

LITTLE SALTEE

The following evening Conor Broekhart was roughly bundled into a shallow-draught steamboat and shipped off to Little Saltee. He was the only prisoner on deck, and was forced to share the aft cage with two pigs and a goat. There were two guards on the grubby steamboat, and the most senior was eager to share his own importance with Conor.

'I don't normally ferry prisoners,' explained the man, an Irishman, aiming a kick at the cage door to make sure Conor was listening. 'Only the warden insisted I ship your bones personally. Myself, as it were, the order came direct from Marshall Bonvilain. So, what's a body to do? Turn down Bonvilain? I doubt it, sonny. Not unless you want to spend the afternoon shaking hands with your maker.'

Conor was not interested in chatter. He was as lost in this day as a chick wet from the egg. On the surface, things were the same. He recognized Little Saltee's shape to the north, but it seemed a dreadful place now even at a distance. Yesterday he had looked upon the island as the seat of justice. *Only yesterday?* Could it be? How much had happened in one day.

The ferry's broad hull hammered the waves, raising a salty mist that the boat steamed through. The spray unfurled across the gunwales, drenching the cage's occupants. Not one of them flinched. For a moment Conor felt only blessedly cool, then the salt sank into his wounds causing him to cry out.

His cry seemed to please his escort. 'Ah! Still alive are we, Mister Conor Finn?'

Mister Conor Finn?

Conor wasn't surprised. Bonvilain would not wish his prisoner's real name known. So he was to be Conor Finn.

'Conor Finn,' continued the guard. 'Friend to smugglers and first-class lunatic. Turf head. Scatterfool. You won't be enjoying it in our mad wing. Not in the slightest.'

Conor Finn. Smuggler and lunatic.

Bonvilain was taking no chances. Even if there were someone to talk with. Who would believe a smuggler and a lunatic?

'No, Little Saltee is not a place for mirth. No maypoles nor circus antics. Especially not for Conor Finn. Bonvilain says to take special care of you in the mad wing. And if Bonvilain says it, then Arthur Billtoe does it.'

Conor squinted through puffy eyelids, taking a serious look at this guard. The man was not unlike a lithograph Victor had once shown him of the *Pongo Abelii* or Sumatran orang-utan. His pugnacious features were ringed with a thick fringe of dirty brown and grey hair, the same hair that ran in rivulets into the neck of his ruffled pirate's shirt. He wore thigh boots on squat powerful legs and silver rings adorned his fingers. At another time, Conor might have poked fun at this man's swashbuckling rig. But now, his appearance was frightening. How could someone so removed from reality be trusted to perform a guard's duties?

Still, there existed somewhere a spark of the old Conor. The Conor from yesterday.

'Nice boots, Captain,' he mumbled.

Billtoe was not angry, not a bit of it. He smiled, revealing half a dozen plug-stained teeth.

'Oh, we shall have some sport with you, my lad. You have no idea. I dress how I fancy, and I do what I fancy. In my corner of Little Saltee, Arthur Billtoe is king.'

The king is dead, thought Conor, leaning back against the animals in his cage. *I saw him dead.*

The animals were bony and shivering and almost as miserable as Conor himself.

The steamer swung round the tip of Galgee Rock and on to a crescent beach below Little Saltee's turreted gate. The sun was setting between gun ports and cast a red light across the sand. Crabs scuttled in rock pools fighting for scraps, and a funnel of gulls inland marked the gaol's kitchen just as surely as any flag. Billtoe opened the cage carelessly, hauling Conor out by his manacle's chain while his partner secured the bowline.

'Here we are, Mister Conor Finn. I should warn you: men don't much like soldiers on Little Saltee. Be you soldier or be you not, you're wearing the trousers.'

For the first time, Conor regretted his height. He could easily pass for enlisting age, though there was no beard on his chin.

I wish I could fly, he thought, gazing longingly into the morning sky. *Leave this nightmare behind. Fly home to . . .*

But he could never fly home. No more lessons with Victor. No more models of gliders and airships. No more fencing with Isabella. And his father had sworn to kill him on sight; a promise was infinitely more painful than the act itself would be. A large part of Conor wished his father had made good on his promise immediately.

Billtoe tumbled Conor over the gunwale on to a low wooden jetty, into the restraining arms of the second guard.

'Let's get the fleas off him, Mister Pike,' he said. 'Feed him some slop, and get him ready for the mine.'

Arthur Billtoe dug a plug of chewing tobacco from his pocket, stuffing it between bottom teeth and lip.

'We're soldier boy's family now, so let's send him off to work with a Little Saltee kiss. A nice long one.'

The guards urged Conor along the slipway with prods from their rifle butts. As they passed into the prison proper, Conor noticed that the curtain wall was at least twelve feet thick and built of solid granite. Hundreds of years ago, Raymond Trudeau had ordered the prison built from the rock dug from the island itself. As the walls went up, the prison went down. There were cave-ins and floods and prisoners died, but prisoners dying had never been enough to stop the mining, until King Nicholas took the throne. Now that Bonvilain was in charge, inmate safety would hardly be high on the agenda.

The guards bustled him beneath a portcullis, its black iron teeth clanking with every wave shudder. They emerged into a wide courtyard overlooked by salt-blasted crenellations and at least a dozen sharpshooters.

In one corner of the courtyard was a sunken pool, which had been roughly walled. The pool was six feet by six. The depth was made unclear by the clouds of algae and slime lurking below the surface. The water stank of stagnation and rot.

'In you pop,' said Billtoe cheerily, a second before heaving Conor over the lip with a forearm.

'Kill anything, those mites will,' Conor heard him say in the fraction of a moment before the murky water closed over him, and his manacles dragged him to the spongy bed.

Conor tensed every sinew and muscle, expecting more saltwater pain, but instead the water soothed his cuts. Fresh water. Something else too. Natural anaesthetic in the weeds perhaps. Before Conor could appreciate this unforeseen bliss, the clouds in the pool moved towards him purposefully. They were alive! Conor was on the point of opening his mouth to yell out, when his good sense prevailed. He was underwater. Opening his mouth would mean inviting these microscopic characters into his gut. He sucked his lips between his teeth, sealing them tight, and fought the manacle's weight so that he could pinch his nostrils closed. His ears would have to fend for themselves.

The mites went to work on Conor's person, scraping his skin with their infinitesimal teeth. To Conor this seemed like macabre torture, but to his person these mites were a boon.

Plant spores, agitated by the mites, disinfected his wounds, which the mites cleaned by eating all traces of infection. They chipped off blood and scab, diving deep into gashes, chewing back to the bare wound. They ate loose hair and dirt, even gnawing the fake regimental tattoo on the boy's forearm. The only things they ignored were the dots of gunpowder on Conor's jowls, but those were sluiced off by the currents created by his own thrashings.

Conor didn't believe the guards would let him drown. Bonvilain would not deliver him to this place so that he could be murdered in the courtyard. Nevertheless, the nibbling mites pushed him to the brink of despair and had the guards not gaffed his chain and lugged him from the pool, he would have opened his mouth and accepted flooded lungs rather than endure another second of mites scouring his skin.

Conor lay gasping on the rough flagstones, their ridges hard against his forehead. There were mites on him still. He could feel their vibrations on his eyebrows and in his ears, their buzzing on his skin.

'Get them off,' he begged his captors, hating himself for doing it. 'Please.'

The guards did so, chuckling, with buckets of salt water lined up for the purpose. The salt sting traced burning lines along his body like sections of the barbed wire King Nicholas had imported from Texas. But even this sting was preferable to a million mites' teeth.

Billtoe swiped the seat of Conor's trousers with his boot.

'Up you get, Conor Finn. Move now if you want a bed,

otherwise it's sleep in the open. Makes ño difference to me, but they're cranking the bell in the pipe tomorrow and you need all your energy for the bell.'

This talk of pipes and bells was gibberish to Conor. A church orchestra perhaps? Conor doubted that there would be anything as spiritually uplifting as church music in this place. He stood slowly, head to one side, dislodging the last of the mites.

'What were those creatures?' he asked, his voice strange in his own clogged ears.

'Feeder mites,' answered Billtoe. 'Freshwater parasites. It takes real care to breed those little beauties. This is the only pool of 'em outside of Australia, thanks to Wandering Heck. We heat it special.'

Conor minded this little lesson closely. Victor had told him never to disregard information. Information was what saved lives, not ignorant heroics. And yet all the information inside Victor's head, hadn't managed to save his own life. Wandering Heck's proper title was King Hector II, the king of the Saltees before Nicholas. King Hector had been far more interested in exploring other continents than running his own country, a fact that must have suited Marshall Bonvilain.

Conor stood, allowing his arms to sag low, so the ground could bear the weight of his chain. Something hissed near his left eye. A heated hiss. Conor was too beaten down by the day to react. Otherwise he could have delayed the inevitable until a few more guards were summoned. As it was, a single guard was more than sufficient to hold him against the wall. Arthur Billtoe pinned his left hand to the stone with a red-hot cattle brand.

'A Little Saltee kiss,' said Billtoe. 'Hope you enjoy it.'

Conor stared at it incredulously for a moment, watching the water boil off, smelling the scorched reek of his own flesh. There was no pain. But it was coming, and there was no way on earth to avoid it.

I want to fly away from this place, thought Conor. *I need to fly away.*

The pain arrived, and Conor Broekhart flew away, but only in his tired mind.

CHAPTER 6:

IN THE MIDDLE OF WYNTER

Morning arrived early on Little Saltee, heralded by a single cannon shot aimed towards the mainland. The shot was a Saltee tradition that had been missed only twice in the six hundred years since King Raymond II had inaugurated the custom. Once in AD 1348 when an outbreak of plague wiped out half the population in less than a month, and then again in the Middle Ages when Eusebius Crow's pirate fleet had all but overrun Great Saltee. The single cannon shot served both to awaken the prisoners and to remind Irish smugglers, brigands or even government forces that the Saltee forces were vigilant and ready to repel all attackers.

Conor Broekhart awoke on a wooden pallet to the sound of cannon echo. He had slept deeply in spite of all that had happened. His body needed time without interruption to repair itself and so had granted him a night of dreamless sleep. Numerous pains assaulted his senses, but the most urgent sang from his left hand.

A Little Saltee kiss.

So it was all real, then. The king's assassination. The orphaning of dear Isabella, and his own father's threats of murder.

All real.

Wincing, Conor raised his hand to inspect the wound, and

was surprised to find it covered with a neat bandage. Green fluid oozed through the material's border.

'Do you like that dressing, boy?' said a voice. 'The green muck is *Plantago lanceolata*. I put some on your face too. Cost me my last plug of tobacco from one of the guards.'

Conor squinted across the cell's gloom. A pair of long, thin legs poked from the shadows. A skinny wrist was draped over one knee, long fingers tapping imaginary piano keys.

'You did this?' asked Conor. 'The dressing? I have . . . I had a friend who was good with medicines.'

'As a young man, I rode with the Missouri Ruffians for a year during the Civil War,' continued the man, his accent American. 'I learned a little about medicine. Of course, when *they* learned that I was a Yankee spy, Jesse James himself took a poker to my skull. I suppose he thought I'd seen enough.'

'Thank you, sir. I was not expecting kindness in this place.'

'And you won't see much,' granted the Yankee. 'But what you *do* see shines like a diamond in a bucket of coal. Naturally, we lunatics are the kindest of the bunch.'

Conor was momentarily puzzled. *We lunatics?*

Then he remembered that Bonvilain had declared him insane. A turf head, scatterfool.

The American was still talking. 'Of course, *technically*, I am an invalid, not a lunatic, but we are all lumped together here on Little Saltee. Lunatics, invalids, violent cases.' He stood slowly, extending a hand. 'Allow me to introduce myself. My name is Linus Wynter. With a Y. In the middle of

Wynter, you understand. You will be seeing a lot of me, but I won't be seeing much of you, I'm afraid.'

Wynter emerged from the shadows like a stack of brooms falling from a closet. A tall gangle of a man, over fifty, clothed in the ragged remnants of a once-fine evening suit. Like Conor, he wore a bandage. But his was tied across the sockets where his eyes had been. Jesse James had done a thorough job with his poker, the scars of which ran in purple welts across Wynter's high brow.

Wynter tugged on the bandage. 'I used to wear an opera mask when I played. Very melodramatic. Very *Dickens*.'

Conor shook Linus Wynter's hand as firmly as he could manage.

'Conor . . . Finn. That is my name now.'

Wynter nodded, his prominent nose and Adam's apple sending angular shadows dancing across his face and neck. 'Good. A new name. In Little Saltee it is better to become a different person. The old *Conor* is dead and gone. A man needs a new sensibility to survive here. Even a very young man.'

Conor flexed his fingers. Pain scraped his tendons, but everything functioned as it should. He examined his prison cell without enthusiasm. It was as rough and ready as his previous cell with one small barred and glassed window and a couple of wooden pallets.

Something Wynter had said struck him belatedly.

Even a very young man?

Conor waved his hand before Wynter's eyes. 'How can you tell my age? Have your other senses compensated?'

'Yes, they have, so if you could lower your hand. But I know all about you, young Conor Broekhart or Conor Finn, because you were fevered in the night and kept me awake with your babblings. The king? He is truly dead, then?'

Tears welled on Conor's eyelids. Hearing a stranger say the words aloud had the effect of planting Bonvilain's deed in the real world.

'Yes. I saw him dead.'

Wynter sighed long and mournfully, running his fingers through fine greying hair. 'That is indeed grave news. More than you know. Bonvilain will drag these islands back to the dark ages.'

'You know Bonvilain?'

'I know a lot about the affairs of the Saltees.' Wynter seemed about to elaborate, his mouth open for the next word, when he paused, cocking his head to one side in the manner of a deer that senses nearby hunters. 'Time for histories this evening. Over dinner perhaps.' He leaned forward, fingers scrabbling through the air like spiders until they settled on Conor's shoulders.

'Now listen to me, Conor Finn,' he said with some urgency. 'The guard approaches. They will try to break you today. Watch carefully for trouble. A sly blade. A plank across the shins. Come through this day intact, and tonight I shall teach you how to survive this hell. There is an end to it, and we shall see it, believe me.'

'Break me?' said Conor. 'Why?'

'It is the way here. A broken man, or even boy, is not

likely to upset production. And on Little Saltee production is the real king, not Arthur Billtoe.'

Conor pictured the monkey pirate who had ferried him to the prison. It was unlikely that Billtoe would lift a bejewelled finger to protect Conor.

'What can I do?'

'Work hard,' replied Wynter. 'And trust neither man nor beast. Especially a sheep.'

Before Linus Wynter could explain this unexpected remark, the door's heavy bolt scraped through its rings with an almost musical sound.

'Top C,' said Wynter dreamily. 'Every morning. Wonderful.'

This was a noise that Conor would yearn for over the months to come, a noise he heard in his dreams. The latch's release signified liberation from his dank cell, but also served as a reminder that the liberation was temporary. Social diarists record that survivors of Little Saltee often suffered from insomnia unless their bedchamber doors were fitted with rusted bolts.

Arthur Billtoe peeped round the door, wearing the cheery expression of a kindly uncle waking his nephew for a plunge in the swimming hole. His hair was slicked back with a smear of grease and thick stubble poked through his skin like nails driven from the inside.

'Ready for the pipe are you, Conor Finn?' he said, jingling a set of handcuffs.

Wynter's fingers gripped tight, like coal tongs. 'Mouth

shut. Work hard. Mind the sheep. And don't cross Mister Billtoe.'

Billtoe entered the cell, clapping the cuffs round Conor's wrists. 'Oh yes, never cross me, little soldier. You lay one finger on me and you will be strapped to a low ring at high tide. And as for the sheep. Wise words from the blind man. Sheep are not for stewing here on Little Saltee.'

All this talk of sheep was strange and ominous. Conor guessed that he had a surprise coming, and not the jolly kind.

Traditionally in hostelries and even in prisons around the globe, breakfast is served before a shovel is lifted. Not so on Little Saltee. Here the morning meal was used as an incentive to work harder. No diamonds, no bread. It was a straightforward equation that had proved effective for centuries. Conor had expected a detour to a mess hall, but instead was led directly to the diamond mine, or the pipe, as the prison's occupants called it.

Billtoe explained Little Saltee's routine on the way.

'Salts with a tum full of grub are inclined to be satisfied and dopey,' he said, chewing on a hank of bread, which he stored in his pocket between bites.

To Conor, who hadn't tasted a morsel in twenty-four hours, this was yet another form of torture. His hunger pangs were soon subdued by Billtoe's revolting habit of half-swallowing each mouthful, then regurgitating it to relish the taste once more. Each regurgitation was accompanied by a convulsion that ran along Billtoe's spine like a flicked rope.

Though Conor was repulsed, he knew his hunger would soon return, gnawing on the lining of his stomach, as if his body had turned on itself in desperation. He was distracted from his hunger by the peal of a church bell in the distance. This was something of a mystery in such a godforsaken place.

Billtoe seemed cheered by the sound.

'Say your prayers, boy,' he cackled.

The guard jabbed his rifle butt into Conor's spine, pushing him along a cobbled passageway lit by torches and dawn glow from roof portholes. The surf crashed against the granite wall on their left, which was half-natural half-hewn as though the island was growing through the structure. Each wave crash shook the entire corridor and set a hundred rivulets pulsing through mortar as crumbly as cheese.

'Below sea level, we are,' explained Billtoe, as though Conor needed telling. 'A while back the prison and the mine were two separate things. But the Trudeaus' greed and the inmates' labour drew them together. The prison basement was heading that way and eventually the two met up. Just a matter of bashing through a wall. It was fortunate for us guards in the mad wing. Now there's no need for us to venture out in the elements – we let the lunatics work the pipe. Half the time they don't even know it's dangerous and most of them will work until their hands bleed if you tell 'em that's what Mummy would want.'

This exposition was delivered in a cheery tone that belied Billtoe's cruel nature. If it had not been for the gun butt in his back and the burning Saltee kiss on his hand, Conor might have believed the guard a decent man.

They passed along a maze of corridors, dotted with strong doors and collapsing arches. The entire prison basement seemed in danger of imminent cave-in.

'Looks like the whole place is coming down, don't it?' said Billtoe, reading Conor's expression. 'It's been looking like that since I got here. Doubtless this pit will outlive you. Though you being a Salt, that's not much of a boast.'

Salt. Conor had heard the term before. This was what Little Saltee inmates were called. Forever branded as such by the *S* on their hands. He was a Salt now.

They emerged from the corridor into an open area, which may have been a pantry in previous centuries. The walls were smeared with faded spice marks and flour swabs. The central flags had been excavated and ladders thrown down to the area below. Roughly a score more guards stood around, tooled with standard rifles but also more personal weapons. Conor spotted Indian blades, whips, dirks, cutlasses, American six-shooters, blackjacks and even one samurai sword. The Saltee tradition of hiring mercenaries had left its mark on local weaponry. The guards lounged about, smoking, chewing and spitting. They feigned easiness, but Conor noted that every last man of them had a fist on some weapon or other. This was a dangerous place to be, and it didn't do to forget it.

The ladders dropped down to open water. Deep, black

and ridged with whatever light could find it. More guards were ranged about the cave walls below, keeping their boots above the water line. Several convicts wrestled with a scaffolding rig, taking the weight of a huge brass bell which swung pendulously in the confined space, knocking stone splinters from the cave wall where it struck and sending huge cathedral bongs booming through the upper level.

'Welcome to the pipe,' said Billtoe, spitting bread-crumbs.

Conor knew something of the island's geology from Victor's teachings and quickly realized what was happening here. The Saltee diamond pipe was brewed in the gullet of a volcano on the other side of the world, sliced off by a glacier and deposited off the Irish coast. This meant that someday the diamond supply would run out, especially considering the constant and eager mining by the Trudeau family. This was not the first time underwater mining had been used to bolster diamond supplies, but King Nicholas had banned the practice within six months of his coronation. This brass bell was a diving bell, from the belly of which prisoners could chip rough diamonds from the underwater section of the pipe. King Nicholas's decrees were being overturned before his body was cold. Bonvilain had clearly been plotting for long bitter years.

'That bell is ancient,' Conor said, almost to himself. 'It must be a hundred years old.'

Billtoe shrugged theatrically, then unlocked Conor's handcuffs. 'That fact doesn't bother me, being that I'm not the one going down in it, thank God. A man could get hurt and worse, as you will find out this fine morning. Down you go.'

Another shove from Billtoe's rifle butt sent Conor stumbling towards a broad ladder poking from the cave's shadows. The ladder beams jabbed him in the chest, preventing a tumble into the hole, and the end of a very short mining career.

'One coming down,' Billtoe shouted.

The senior guard scowled up through the gloom. Conor recognized him as Billtoe's partner of the previous evening. His main distinguishing features were a seeming lack of any hair and a pinched stance, which made him seem almost hunchbacked.

'We don't need another, Arthur,' he cried. 'Full complement, we have. Even if a few croak it in the bell.'

Billtoe took Conor by the scruff, urging him on to the ladder. 'That's enough out of you, Pike. This is Marshall Bonvilain's special boy, remember? He needs to be looked after.'

Pike's expression changed from wheedling to leering. 'Ah, the special boy. The little prince. Send him down. I have a few rams waiting to bump horns with him.'

Sheep again. What could it mean?

Billtoe stepped on Conor's fingers, forcing him down a rung. 'Down you go, Conor Finn. Don't make me break your fingers. These are good boots and Salt blood would ruin 'em on me.'

There was a curious, expectant silence as Conor climbed down into the pit. He could feel the temperature drop with every rung, until the cold of the water crept from its surface like an invisible cowl draping itself heavily on Conor's shoulders. He was really scared during those moments. Almost too petrified to move, but gravity tugged at his bones, helping him on his way.

The mad-wing convicts were a motley lot, favouring the stony-stare, slack-jawed demeanour. They glared at Conor with loathing and fear and the threat of harm hung heavy in the salty air. For long moments, the only sounds were the creaking ladder and the gentle slap of water on rock.

Finally Conor arrived on the surface, feeling like an enemy flag under the hammering gaze of so many hostiles. Billtoe stepped down behind him and pointed at the diving bell.

'That there is Flora. You know what she is, Salt?'

Conor mumbled his reply. 'She's a diving bell.'

'No, turf head. She's a . . .' Billtoe was frustrated to have his information stolen. He poked Conor in the chest with a rigid finger. 'Yes, she *is* a diving bell. And because you know all about it you can be first into her. Flora has been out of service for several years, but I'm sure all is well with her fittings.'

Conor forced himself to study the bell, though all he wanted to do was clasp his knees in a quiet corner and cry for the bad luck that had cursed him. The bell seemed sound enough, though deeply gouged by stone in several places. She was suspended by a network of chains that hitched to an iron hoop dangling over its prow. The hoop in turn fed half a dozen more chains to the scaffolding above. The chains seemed as ancient as the bell, with several rust-dappled links shedding flakes as they swung. A cracked rubber hose poked from the top of the bell, snaking upwards to a hand-cranked bellows affair, which Conor presumed to be an ancient air pump. The pump was being cranked by two inmates. One was racked with consumptive coughing fits and the other paused regularly to spit tobacco phlegm on to the rocks. Not the ideal pair for the job. Conor would not rely on either to supply enough oxygen to fuel the lungs of a small dog.

Billtoe stepped well back and called out his command to a guard above.

'Lower her down. Do not break the hose or the warden will tan all our hides.'

The diving bell descended in fits, according to the strength of the inmates bearing the strain and the clumsy coiling of chains on the previous use. Some of the links had fused in tangled knots and now popped free sending the diving bell lurching and swinging. The cavern walls resounded with irregular clangs and bongs, causing anyone with free hands to cover their ears.

'Hell's bells, man!' Billtoe called up to his comrade. 'It sounds like drunk day in Saint Christopher's in here.'

Saint Christopher had been adopted by the Trudeaus as the Saltees' patron saint. The church on Great Saltee bore his name.

'It ain't my fault, Billtoe,' retorted the guard. 'She's coming, ain't she. Mind I don't land her on your head.'

It was said only in jest, but Billtoe stepped aside smartish just the same. Flora swung lower, like a skittish baby monkey on a rope, until eventually she splashed into the black water, sending wave rings rushing to the rocks.

'Every day,' sighed Billtoe, mopping his brow with a kerchief. 'We have to go through this blasted rigmarole every day from this out.' He turned his attention and annoyance to the prisoners at the pumps.

'Crank! You apron-tugging, turnip-brained scatterfools.'

'Yes, boss,' they mumbled, and set to pumping the bellows, sending air through the rubber hose and into the bell itself. The hose wriggled and flipped as the air inflated it slightly.

The bell sank slowly into the sea, emitting a curious shivering hum as the water caressed its surface.

Billtoe elbowed Conor. 'You hear that, soldier boy? We call that the *siren's song*. Because it's the last sound many of you Salts hear. Lord, I had forgotten how soothing it was.'

A band of glass with rubber seals was set into the diving bell's dome. The window was covered with a scree of algae and filth that made it impossible to see through.

Billtoe followed Conor's gaze. 'Yes, pity about that port. Filthy as a beggar's britches. We won't be seeing much of what goes on in there today. I do hope and pray there are no unfortunate accidents.'

Conor had little doubt that whatever was coming would be unfortunate for him, but it would be no accident. Billtoe meant to break him in the bell. This whole affair was becoming nightmarish. He recoiled from the guard as he would from a brandished torch.

'What are you twitching for, boy?' asked Billtoe. 'Crazed so soon? You'd best be keeping your wits about you in the bell.'

Surprisingly, these were bordering on words of wisdom

from the prison guard. They were meant as a warning and Conor took them as one. Whatever his problems, he'd best forget them until he was safe in his cell. Linus Wynter would help him to survive this hellhole, but only if he lived long enough to see him again. While Conor did not believe that the traitor Bonvilain wished him dead, perhaps there was a kind of sheep that did not follow orders so well.

'What do I need to do?' he asked Billtoe, best to be as prepared as possible.

Billtoe was happy to deliver a lecture. 'We lower Flora on to the pipe, then you goes down with your partner and chip off diamonds. Simple as bread pudding.' He barked at an inmate loitering at the waterline. 'You, fish bait. Give him your belt.'

The man placed a protective hand on his belt. 'But, boss. I been polishing these tools for years. Got 'em from my dad.'

Billtoe tapped his head, as though there was water lodged in his ears.

'What's this chattering? I hear the chattering of a dead man. Must be leaking through his punctured neck.'

Two seconds later, the leather belt was in Conor's hands. Billtoe ran through the tools.

'You got your pick hammer for breaking down the rock. Hammer the rock, then pick out the diamonds, which will resembled nothing more than glassy marbles. Don't worry about breaking the diamonds, you won't be able to, because they're the . . .'

'Hardest substance in nature,' said Conor automatically.

'Hardest substance in nature,' continued Billtoe, then scowled. He reached over and cuffed Conor on the temple. 'Don't be supplying me with information that I am supplying to you. That is a very annoying trait, which I would relish beating out of you.'

Conor nodded, ignoring the pain in his head, just as he was ignoring the other pains.

'This here,' said Billtoe proudly, pointing to a little trident tool, 'is a Devil's Fork. Invented on this very island by one Arthur Billtoe over twenty years ago. Got me a job for life, this little beauty did. Plus Marshall Bonvilain himself granted me a house on Great Saltee. It's tele . . . tele . . .'

'Telescopic,' said Conor, thinking that if Billtoe could not even pronounce the word telescopic, it was unlikely that he had invented a telescopic tool. More likely he had stolen the idea from an inmate.

'Exactly, telescopic. On the tip of me tongue, it was.'

Billtoe slipped the fork from its holder and twisted a few rings, extending the tool from eight inches to three feet.

'Now, yer can wriggle this little beauty into cracks and spear any stones what has fallen down there. Amazing, eh?'

Conor knew enough to nod, though an extendable fork was hardly amazing in anyone's book. It was practical though, and canny, and proved that Bonvilain knew a good idea when he saw one.

'So all you have to do, Salt, is swim down there into the bell and dig out as many diamonds as you can until your swing is over. Stash them in your net and bring them back up. Simple as bread pudding. Naturally we search all the divers, and if we find any stones outside of that net, then I find the biggest bull of a guard on the island and have him flog the thievery out of you. Straight enough for you, little soldier?'

Conor nodded, wondering how close the pipe was to open sea.

Once more, Billtoe displayed a disturbing ability to anticipate Conor's very thoughts.

'Of course, you may decide to swim for it. The lure of freedom may be too strong for you. Feel free to give it your best. You may even make it – mind you, you'd be the first, and bigger men than you have tried. We still get bodies washing up in the cave, decades after they went in. And do you know something? They all look the same way. Dead.'

Conor cinched the belt round his waist, drawing it tight to the last hole. He could figure no escape from this task. In Greek mythology when the heroes were faced with daunting trials, they went about them with stoic determination and emerged victorious. Conor could not muster an ounce of determination for this trial; all he felt was a weight of exhaustion. And even if he did emerge victorious, his only reward would be more of the same tomorrow, and the day after that.

Billtoe encouraged him with a friendly wink and a jaunty tapping of his fingers upon the pistol stock at his waist. Conor set foot in the water and the cold gripped him in its icy fist, squeezing the life from his toes. An involuntary gasp escaped his lips, causing much laughter from the assembled men.

Conor took a moment to become used to the water

temperature, casting a quick eye around the cave, wondering if there were a single person who would come to his aid. Every gaze he crossed was hostile. These were rugged men in evil surroundings, with little time to waste on sympathy. Conor realized that were it not for their uniforms, it would be impossible to separate the guards from the inmates. He was alone in this endeavour. Fourteen and alone. This was one of the few occasions in Conor's life when his father was not there to provide guidance. And if Declan Broekhart *had* been there, perhaps he would have laughed along with the rest of them. It was an unbearable thought.

Though he was without doubt on his own, there was something in Conor Broekhart that would not allow him to give in. His mother's brain and his father's spirit were strong in his heart. He would endure somehow, and survive. If Conor could return to his cell still breathing, then the American, Linus Wynter, could teach him a lesson or two about Little Saltee.

Push it all from your mind, he told himself. *Forget your family, the king, Isabella. Forget them all. Just live to think on them another day.*

This was easier conceived than achieved, but Conor did the best he could, concentrating on the scene before him, shutting away his torment. He stepped off the rocky ledge, sinking fast into the cold, dark waters of Little Saltee.

For a moment the cold was absolute and it seemed as though nothing could ever be any colder. Conor thrashed his limbs, not from fear but to generate some heat. He had often swum on the Saltee beaches before, but the waters he was in now had never been blessed with sun. There was nothing to raise the temperature a few degrees.

Conor opened his eyes, peering through the liquid gloom. Below him, he spied a blob of orange, like a fading sun in the grip of black space.

The bell.

It is not so far down, he told himself. *A chap would have to be a pretty poor swimmer not to make that distance. Ten kicks at most.*

Conor duck dived, cupping his hands to better scoop the water. He had always been a good swimmer and immediately the orange blob assumed its proper bell shape and he could make out the texture of its surface. This tiny success comforted him somewhat.

I am not helpless. I can still do things.

The bell swung gently two feet above the cave bed, air bubbles leaked like pearl strings from a dozen tiny breaches. Conor hooked his fingers under its curved rim and wriggled inside. His efforts were rewarded by air, not by any means sweet or fresh but air nonetheless. Conor filled his lungs to capacity, ignoring the rubbery smell and the oily film that instantly coated his nose and throat.

The water rose six inches into the bell, and the surface below Conor's feet was uneven, slick and treacherous. This was not an ideal working environment. The bell itself had a diameter of barely ten feet, and swung in irregular arcs with the current, butting Conor in the shoulder and elbow. He hunched his shoulders as far as possible, protecting his head. The light was murky and wavering.

Conor peered upwards through the porthole but could make out nothing more distinct than vague wavering silhouettes. Perhaps men? Perhaps rocks? It was impossible to tell. But then one of the silhouettes detached itself from the group.

Conor watched with a dread colder than sea water as the figure leaped into the ocean, shattering its surface into a jigsaw of silver crescents. The sound of the splash carried through the bell's air hole. Another sound carried too; laughter, wafting through the pipe like ghost mirth. Dark, vicious, threatening laughter.

Conor choked down absolute terror.

Survive. You can do things. Survive.

Then something flashed past. A pale limb. Thick and muscled, swatting at the water. And on the forearm drawn with bold punctures, visible even through a sheen of scum, a tattoo of a horned ram.

A sheep, thought Conor. *Sheep are not for stewing here on Little Saltee.*

The figure disappeared from view, pulling itself down the bell curve. Hands slapped at the brass, setting off a cacophony of shuddering clangs inside the bell's skirt. The clangs reverberated around the diving bell until Conor prayed for silence. Surely his ears were bleeding. Then four thick fingers curled under the bell's rim, shimmering white in the water.

Each finger was tattooed with a single letter. Even upside down it didn't take a scholar to read what the letters promised.

P. A. I. N.

Conor didn't doubt it for a second.

A huge man dragged himself along the seabed, mindless of the sharp rocks scraping his flesh. When he stood inside the bell, a dozen red rivulets ran down his torso. It suddenly seemed to Conor that there was not enough air left to breath. He backed away until the diving bell's cold metal moulded the curve of his spine.

The man's size was doubtless exaggerated by the confined space, but still he seemed a giant to Conor. He spread his arms wide, tinkling his fingers on the brass bell as though it were a grand piano. The sweet sound was hardly appropriate for the situation. Whatever this man intended to do, he seemed to be in no hurry to complete his mission. He stretched this way and that, cracking neck and knuckles all the while wearing an expression of serene contentment. Conor read many things into that half smile. A confidence in his brutish abilities, the memories of past violence and the anticipation of the job at hand.

The man smiled, a yellow tobacco grimace, but then his expression drooped as he realized Conor's age.

'Hell's bells, you're nothing but a boy. What did you do? Lie about your age to get a ticket for the army? Are you that desperate to patrol a wall? There ain't even a war on.'

'You're a sheep,' said Conor numbly. 'Sheep are not for stewing here on Little Saltee.'

The man stroked his tattoo fondly. 'There are those that call us sheep, but our name proper is the Battering Rams.

That being our favourite method of doing the big job.'

Conor understood the sheep references now. The Battering Rams were a notorious gang of London Irish who were involved in smuggling in ports from London to Boston and whose other main source of income was from hiring out thugs. It would seem that this particular ram had been gainfully employed.

'Ah well,' continued the man. 'I've been paid now, and I don't like to disappoint my employers, so you'll have to take your licks, boy or not.'

'Are you going to kill me?' asked Conor. The man's smell filled the bell, clogging the confined space. Sweat, blood, tobacco and stale breath.

The man rolled his shirt open, revealing a list tattooed on his chest. 'I *could* kill you, and my employer would still be in credit, because he paid me three pounds.'

Conor read the words on the man's pale flesh:

Punching – 2 shillings
Both eyes blacked – 4 shillings
Nose and jaw broke – 10 shillings
Jacked out (knocked out with a black jack) –
    15 shillings
Ear chewed off – same as previous
Leg or arm broke – 19 shillings
Shot in leg – 25 shillings
Stab – Same as previous
Doing the Big Job – 3 pounds and up

The man buttoned his shirt.

'He paid me the full three pounds, but said I was to spread it out. Keep punching on a daily basis until he was out of credit. That's a fair whack of punching, but you being such a slip of a whelp, I reckon one belt a day should do it. Maybe, if the task is becoming tiresome after a few weeks, I may chew your ear off just to finish it.'

Conor was finding it difficult to believe what he was hearing. The man had such a professional manner, as though he were a roofer quoting for a slate job.

'What will you do if your prices go up?'

The man frowned. 'You mean the tattoo? I never thought of that. I suppose I'll have to have it writ over. There's a little Galway geezer what is good with the needles. Anyway, see yer tomorrow . . .'

'What?' said Conor, but before his teeth had closed over the final consonant, the man's huge fist had already begun its arc, swinging towards Conor's head like a cannonball. The last things Conor saw were the letters P. A. I. N., but he remained conscious for long enough to hear the Battering Ram sing this savage ditty:

> 'We stabs 'em,
> We fights 'em,
> Cripples 'em,
> Bites 'em.
> No rules for our mayhem.
> You pay us, we slays 'em.
> If you're in a corner,

> With welshers or scams.
> Pay us a visit,
> The Battering Rams.'

And then the whole world was wet and Conor gladly allowed himself to be tugged away by the currents.

Maybe this time I won't wake up, he thought. *I need never wake up again.*

But wake up he did, many hours later with Linus Wynter bending over him, green paste dripping from his fingers.

'More Plantago, I fear,' he explained. 'This is becoming a habit.'

Conor closed his eyes again, fearful that he would cry. He kept himself still for long minutes, breathing quiet breaths through his nose. He could feel the cold muck on his temple, where the giant had struck him, and more on his hand where the brand still scalded.

There must be an end to this? How long could a mind endure such torture and stay whole?

'You have been asleep for nearly twelve hours. I saved your rations for you. Have some water at least.'

Water. The very word had the power to awaken Conor fully. His throat felt flaked with thirst.

Man's primary instinct is to survive, Victor had once told him. *And he will endure almost anything to follow his instincts.*

'Water,' croaked the boy, raising his head, until the Plantago juice ran down his forehead.

Wynter held a rough earthenware cup to Conor's lips,

dribbling water down his throat. To Conor, the drink tasted like life itself, and soon he felt strong enough to hold the cup. He sat slowly, sighing gratefully for the simple pleasure of slaking his thirst.

'And now you should eat,' said Wynter. 'Keep your body strong. A fever in here could kill you.'

Conor laughed, a feeble shuddering. As though fever would ever have the chance to kill him. The Battering Ram had almost three pounds' worth of beatings to dole out, and it was hardly likely that Conor could survive those.

Wynter pressed a shallow bowl into Conor's hand.

'Whatever happened to you, and whatever is going to happen, you will not have a prayer without strength in your limbs.'

Conor relented, picking a chunk of cold meat from the bowl of stew. Even when hot, Conor doubted that the meal could ever have been called appetizing. The meat was tough, with a wide band of fat and hard burn ridges along each side. But meat was strength, and strength was what he would need to go back in the bell with a mad ram.

'Now,' said Wynter, 'tell me what happened today. They brought you back here on a plank. For a moment I couldn't even find a heartbeat.'

Conor chewed on a lump of meat. The fat was slick and rubbery between his teeth.

'They put me in a diving bell with one of those Battering Rams.'

'Describe him,' instructed Wynter.

'Big man. Enormous. Tattoos all over. P. A. I. N. on his knuckles and –'

'A price list on his chest,' completed Conor's cellmate. 'That's Otto Malarkey. The top ram. That animal has beaten more men than he can count. And he can count well enough, especially when there's coin involved.'

'He's been paid coin aplenty to keep handing out daily beatings. This is how they will break me.'

'A simple but effective plan,' admitted Wynter. 'Set the big man beating the little man. That tactic worked on everyone, even Napoleon.'

Conor took a drink of water. Now that his senses were returning, he could taste the saltpetre in it. 'There must be something I can do.'

Wynter thought on it, fixing the bandage across his eyes with long pianist's fingers.

'This problem is more important than all the daily vexations I had planned to educate you on this evening. Malarkey must be dealt with if you are to survive, young Conor.'

'Yes, but how?'

'You need to rest. Lie flat and think on your strengths. Draw on everything you have ever been taught. Tease out every violent daydream you have ever nursed in your darkest hours. You must have talents: you are a tall boy and strong.'

'And if I do have talents, what then?' insisted Conor.

'Another simple plan,' whispered Wynter. 'Older even than the first. When you see Malarkey next, you must immediately kill him.'

Kill him.

'I can't. I could never —'

Wynter smiled kindly. 'You are a good lad, Conor. Kind. Killing is hateful to you, and the thought that *you* could ever take a life is a terrible one.'

'Yes. I am not the kind of . . .'

Wynter raised a conductor's finger. 'We are *all* that kind of person. Survival is the most basic instinct. But, you are sensitive, I can tell, so I will help you along the road to murder. Since my eyes were taken from me, I have become adept at recreating images in my head. I can see the concert halls of my youth. Time and concentration fill the spaces until the picture is complete. Every velvet-covered chair, every footlight, every gilded cherub.' For a long moment, Wynter was lost in his own colourful past, then the sounds and smells of Little Saltee shattered his mental image. 'What I need you to do is close your eyes and picture the man who sent you here. Use your hatred of him to awaken the killer instinct.'

Conor did not need to concentrate for long. Bonvilain's face sprang into his mind's eye, complete with hateful eyes and derisory sneer.

'And now, Conor, tell me, do you think you can kill?'

Conor considered everything Bonvilain had done to the Broekhart family.

'Yes,' he said. 'I can kill.'

Linus Wynter smiled sadly.

'We all can,' he said. 'God save our souls.'

CHAPTER 7:

THE DEVIL'S FORK

In the door opposite Conor Broekhart's bunk there was a small rectangular window. Perhaps three times in every hour a guard passed by bearing a torch. Flickering orange light poured into the gloom of their cell, casting a vague dancing flame on Conor's hand when he raised it to examine his Saltee kiss. There, already crusted in scab, a cursive *S*. He was branded now, forever a criminal.

A kind of peace had descended on Conor. Events were simply so monumental that he could not deal with them, and that brought a kind of freedom. There was nothing to do but concentrate on Otto Malarkey, the deadly Battering Ram who so cheerfully swatted his prey around the diving bell.

Must he be killed? Is there no other way?

There was not, he concluded. Sadly it was either Otto Malarkey or himself. And though Conor had never been puffed by self-importance, he sincerely believed that he had more to offer the human race than the murderous Malarkey. At the very least, he would try to avoid killing any *more* of his fellow man.

But how to kill Malarkey? How?

What skills had he learned from Victor? The foil, of course, had always been his greatest success. He had the strength of a fencing master in his wrists. And the agility of a youth in his limbs. But how to combine the two?

I don't even have a foil, or anything like one.

But then Conor remembered the tool belt that had been cinched about his waist. Perhaps that was not strictly true. Perhaps Arthur Billtoe had unwittingly come to his rescue.

The following day's routine was the same as the previous one's. Shortly after the single cannon-shot salute, Billtoe appeared at the cell door, a fresh slab of grease taming his locks. That morning he appeared to have shaved sections of his face, leaving the rest sprouting black, silver and ginger bristle.

'Ready for round two with Malarkey?' he asked, rifle held before him in case Conor should prove resistant to the idea of being hammered around a diving bell by a Battering Ram.

Conor stood painfully, the stiffness of various mistreatments binding his bones.

'I am not ready, Mister Billtoe, but I don't suppose that makes a shadow of difference.'

Billtoe chortled, fishing the handcuffs from his belt. 'You are right, lad. You have hit the badger on the nut. Not one shade of difference. Let's be having you, and why not order a big pot of Plantago stew from Mister Wynter, if he could *see* his way clear to mixing it up.'

Linus did not react to the goading, just held his face in a grim aspect. Conor took this as a reminder of what had to be done. Today he became a killer, or else a corpse.

*

The route to the pipe was the same, but on this morning there was a commotion behind the cell doors. Inmates roared taunts and slapped the wood with the flats of their hands.

'Moon madness,' explained Billtoe. 'She was hanging in the sky last night like a silver shilling. Always gets the lunatics riled up.'

A nugget of information popped into Conor's mind. 'That's what the word means. Moonstruck, from the Latin *lunaticus.*'

Billtoe propelled Conor along the corridor with a boot in the small of his back. 'Don't keep giving me information. It makes me feel stupid and feeling stupid irritates me.'

'A familiar feeling, I'll bet,' muttered Conor.

Billtoe could not be certain whether or not he was being insulted, he tapped Conor with his boot again, just to be on the safe side. 'Talk clever to Malarkey. He loves a lippy mark, just adds to his enthusiasm.'

Malarkey's name doused Conor's wit, and his despair was clear on his face.

'That's right,' cackled Billtoe. 'Stick that in one of your lesson books. Go on, write it down. Not so generous with the information now, are you?'

The diving bell was already below water when they arrived at the pipe, its tip poking through the surface. The blurred shapes of two inmates were visible through the porthole, hacking agitatedly at the rock below their feet. Guards chose pumpers from a gang of prisoners corralled into a wooden pen on the storeroom level, changing them often to keep the air flowing.

'The pipe never sleeps,' said Billtoe. 'Not now that Good King Nick is gone. All day every day pulling angel tears out of the earth. And do we see a penny? We do not.'

Conor noted the guard's bitterness. It could prove to be useful information, if he remained on this earth long enough to make use of it.

'There are compensations though. Sport like this, for example,' said Billtoe unlocking Conor's handcuffs. 'Not that we can see what's going on between prisoners *inside* Flora. Not clearly, you understand.'

So that was it. Nobody knew anything, because nobody could see anything.

Billtoe called to Pike, the gang boss.

'Here, switch them up. Time for Malarkey to earn his few shillings.'

He handed Conor a tool belt.

'In case you are conscious for long enough to find a few stones.'

Pike pulled the cork bung from the bell's air tube and hollered the order down. Moments later, two drenched convicts popped from the choppy water, to be briskly elbowed aside and frisked for concealed diamonds. It was a thorough searching that would have uncovered anything larger than a single blood drop.

Conor climbed down the ladder, eyeing the cave for Malarkey. The Battering Ram was easily spotted, reclining on a clump of rocks that bluntly resembled a throne. He threw a mock punch Conor's way, no doubt expecting today's performance to be a repeat of yesterday's.

Not this time, sheep, thought Conor. *This is the final show. The curtain comes down this morning.*

Conor set both feet on the rock and headed directly for the shoreline. He did not wait for instruction from Pike. Conversation was the last thing he wanted now. Words would simply be a distraction. Before diving into the salty water, he patted the belt at his waist, to make sure the Devil's Fork was in its holder. Without this simple tool, he would have little chance of overcoming Malarkey.

The water closed around him and Conor's fingers sought out handholds on the diving bell, pulling himself along its curve until he found the rim. Once inside, the bell's terrible confined space nearly quashed his will, and Conor was forced to draw several deep breaths before he could even force himself to stand.

Follow your instinct, he told himself. *Allow it to consume you.*

From the air hole, he heard a splash followed by whoops and cheers. Malarkey was on the way. The Battering Rams spurred on their champion, though none were expecting much of a contest. Displaced water waves shook the bell, sending up a rich hum within its curves.

I must act quickly. Be ready.

Conor glanced upwards. Malarkey had paused at the porthole to further torture his victim. He knocked the glass, grinning broadly, though his yellow teeth were lost in the porthole's scum sheen.

The instant Malarkey's face disappeared from view, Conor set to work. He quickly extended the mining tripod to its full length, tightening the rings so that the tool would not easily collapse. The tripod was roughly the same as a youth's practice foil, but terribly balanced with the weight entirely towards the tip. Still, a makeshift foil was infinitely better than nothing.

Conor filled his left hand with the wet diamond pouch from his belt, and scrunched it into a soggy sphere. He was as prepared now as he could be, and yet this entire sequence of events had a tinge of unreality about it. Unbelievable things were happening at a terrific rate.

Like many boys his age, Conor had often imagined going into combat. This was nothing like his daydreams. In Conor's fantasies, heroic soldiers faced off against each other on windswept battlefields to the sounds of drums and bugles. There was nothing heroic about this reality. A cramped space, the stink of oil, sweat and fear, and the sickness in the pit of his gullet at the thought of having to kill another human, however vile the man might be. It was as his father had always said: war was never noble.

A pale, water-wavering slab of arm crept under the bell rim. The temptation was strong to stab it with the trident, but that would be foolish. He would sacrifice the element of surprise for a gain of only a tiny wound. Malarkey would retreat, gather himself, then return with grim determination.

Conor held back, bending his knees, getting ready to spring. Malarkey lurched under the rim, appearing in spurts, face up, his long strands of fine hair fanning about his head like seaweed. He was smiling still, streams of air bubbles leaking between his teeth. Once his feet had cleared the rim, Malarkey flipped carelessly on to all fours and breached the water like a walrus.

Conor's breath came fast. Strike now, or the moment was past and he had his two shilling's worth coming.

Malarkey began to rise, and while he was still bent almost double, Conor used the knobs of the big man's spine as a step ladder and climbed on to his shoulders. It was a precarious position, and could last barely a moment. A moment was ample to stuff his wadded diamond pouch squarely into the air duct, stoppering it.

Malarkey shrugged him off, still smiling. He was bemused in fact.

'What yer trying to accomplish, soldier boy? Flight? Even an eagle would be bested by a ram in here.'

'I blocked the air,' said Conor coldly. 'We have two minutes to escape.'

This last fact was a barefaced lie, but not one that would be weighing on Conor's conscience. There was air enough in here for half an hour at least, but with any luck Malarkey would not know that.

For once luck ran Conor's way and the jaunty expression slid from Malarkey's face like greased steak from a pan as he noticed the pipe's blockage.

'You blasted numbskull,' he shouted, the bell vibrating sympathetically with his words. 'Do yer want to kill us both?'

Conor held the makeshift foil behind his back.

'No. Not both of us.'

Malarkey's expression changed to the peeve of a kindly schoolmaster who has finally been exasperated beyond the limits of his patience.

'I did you quick yesterday, soldier boy. A single punch and *that's* a talent. Today, I'm going to be taking my sweet time, and not minding so much about bruises or bones.'

'That's right, sheep,' said Conor. 'Keep talking, waste the air.'

Malarkey reached out, grabbing Conor by the throat.

'Now you pop yourself back up on my shoulders and pull out that plug and I might strike you once, but charge for two.'

It was obvious from his tone that Malarkey thought this a great kindness.

Conor pulled out the trident so quickly it whistled.

'The plug is staying in,' he said, thrusting the tiny fork heads into Malarkey's leg.

The Battering Ram dropped Conor, yelping like a kicked mutt. He reared back, striking his head a sound bong against the bell. The impact crossed his eyes and set his ears ringing.

Conor used the moment to settle his stance: knees bent, makeshift foil extended and left arm cocked behind him.

Attack now! his good sense urged. *No time for sportsmanship.*

But this was not sportsmanship. Conor wanted Malarkey to realize what was happening to him. The hired thug must never be able to convince himself that Conor had triumphed through luck. And so he waited until Malarkey's vision cleared, then spoke, two words only.

'*En garde.*'

Malarkey growled.

'You think those words scare me? You think I haven't heard them from a score of prissy officer types what are now no more than bones in their uniforms?'

Malarkey spread his arms wide, advancing through the water. '*En garde* it is then, soldier boy.'

Conor could almost hear Victor's voice.

Wait for the move. Wait for him to commit.

The wait was not a long one. Malarkey swung in with the same haymaker that he had landed the day before. Conor found that it was not so lightning fast when you were waiting for it.

Conor used a simple *attaque au fer*, which sets up an offensive by deflecting the opponent's blade, though in truth he was deflecting himself more so than Malarkey's arm, which he was addressing as a military-type broadsword.

Now. Facing Malarkey's flank, he slashed down three times, the fork blurred with speed, like a golden fan. Three red stripes appeared on the band of flesh between Malarkey's shirt and trousers' band.

These strikes were for pain.

Malarkey yelped once more, then howled lustily as the pain settled to a steady burn. Conor threw his shoulder into the man's buttocks, not the most pleasant place to be even for a second, but it did have the effect of clanging

Malarkey into the bell curve. His forehead collided with the brass, setting the bell ringing once more.

Now, to the rear, Conor thrust deeply through the water and above Malarkey's heel, feeling the tines puncture the tough flesh.

That strike was for immobility.

Malarkey collapsed like a wall under cannon shot, filling the bell with spray. The Battering Ram continued to howl, demented with pain and anger. Conor felt his resolve falter.

'Kill you,' sobbed Malarkey. 'I will skin the flesh from your frame.'

Conor's resolve was firm once more.

He laid several flat strikes around Malarkey's back and shoulders, forcing him deeper into the sea. With his free hand he shoved straight-fingered jabs into the man's kidneys, causing him to reflexively inhale half a gallon of water. A trick adapted from karate.

Malarkey was effectively helpless. Wallowing in the shallow water, blinded by pain and salt. An infant with a mean disposition could kill him.

Conor leaned back against the bell curve, panting. His hatred for Malarkey had disappeared as quickly as it had flared up. And yet, this issue of a bounty must be solved today. Was Linus Wynter right? Must he kill this man?

Malarkey rolled on to his back and lay there sobbing, his face inches above the surface, wavelets from his own thrashings slopping water down his gullet.

Conor placed a soldier's boot on the man's neck,

contemptuously knocking aside Malarkey's weak grabs.

'You see now what I can do?' he hissed, surprised at the venom in his own voice.

Malarkey could not answer. Even if there had not been a boot at his throat, he was beyond words.

Stop talking. Kill him!

Conor jammed the trident deep into the folds of flesh beneath Malarkey's chin. One more push and the tines would pierce the skin and sever an artery.

'This is no lucky accident. I can kill you easy as a Sunday chicken.'

Malarkey's eyes suddenly focused. The thought of visiting the afterlife helps to concentrate the mind.

'Do you understand that, Mister Battering Ram? I could kill you.'

Do it. Stop your jabbering.

Conor tightened his grip on the fork, the muscles along his arm tensed. Three drops of blood pooled round the trident heads.

One last push and his tormentor would torment him no more.

'Please,' said Malarkey, the word gurgling in his throat.

A bead of sweat trickled into Conor's eye. Water lapped at the bell curve, humming gently.

'Please, spare me,' said the mighty Battering Ram.

I can't do it. I have no wish to kill this man.

Conor realized that he was not a killer and this filled him with warm relief, because it showed that he had not lost himself entirely in spite of all he had endured. He hadn't been raised to gain the upper hand through murder, not if there were other avenues.

There must be another way. A more intelligent way.

Conor chewed on his problem without relieving the fork's pressure on Malarkey's neck. The Battering Ram must be made an ally. This struggle could not go on day after day. He quickly cobbled together a possible way out, for both of them.

'Listen to me, sheep,' said Conor, twisting the trident. 'I am going to float out of this bell, just like yesterday.'

Otto Malarkey's brow creased. 'But I –'

'Quiet!' shouted Conor, with an authority he hadn't known he possessed. 'Listen to me now. We are hatching a plan, you and I. We will come down here every day, and you will supposedly give me my two shillings' worth. That way, you can still be king of the sheep. The big ram. In reality we will have ourselves a quiet talk, and you can help me to survive in here.'

Concentration was not easy for Malarkey in his distressed state, but he did think of something.

'What about my foot? I can't walk.'

A problem, true. Water dripped from the bell curve, spattering them both with indoor rain. Conor wracked his brain for a solution.

'After I leave. Wait an hour, perhaps two, then make a great commotion on climbing out of the bell. Thrash around underwater and say the bell trapped you. Blame your ankle injury on Flora. It is a painful wound, but not serious. I missed the Achilles tendon, luckily for you. Strap it tight, and stay off it for a few hours. You will be solid as an oak tomorrow.'

Malarkey was growing brave again; Conor could see it in the squint of his eye. He had his breath now, and fancied his chances. Any moment he would make a lunge for his young tormentor, then Conor would be forced to kill him. This newfound courage must be nipped in the bud. Conor lashed him once on each forearm, temporarily deadening the nerves.

'Is it more stripes you want? Are you too mutton-headed for life? Accept my proposition, sheep, and you can live with your honour intact. If not, you can suffer defeat at the hands of a boy.'

It seemed as though the prospect of defeat was worse than that of death. Malarkey gritted his teeth, nodding, unable to meet Conor's eye.

'I have your word?'

Victor had once told him that the city gang members had developed a curious sense of honour, almost echoing that of the Samurai Bushido code.

'Yes, blast you, my word on it.'

Conor grinned coldly, a mechanism he would come to rely on in desperate situations.

'I will trust you on it. No need for a handshake.'

It was a cruel joke. Malarkey's arms were dead at his side like two slabs of butchered beef.

'Very well, then, sheep. We have an agreement. Be warned, if you try trickery tomorrow, I will not be so merciful, or silent.'

Conor twisted the rings on his trident, collapsing it.

'No need to get up, I'll see myself out.'

Conor was surprised at his own comment. A second malicious joke in as many minutes. It was not like him to sneer at someone whatever the circumstances, but perhaps Little Saltee was moulding him into a different person. The kind that might possibly survive.

Conor filled his lungs to slide under the rim. Before salt water clouded his vision, he saw a final frustration dropped upon Malarkey: the wadded diamond pouch fell from the air hole, plopping directly on to the man's face.

Malarkey cursed long and filthily, but his words were muffled by the sopping bag. A bag that he was unable to reach up and brush away.

CHAPTER 8:

CONOR FINN

Billtoe and Pike carried Conor back to his cell on a plank and they were careless in their work. Conor endured several bumps and jolts, which almost made up for Malarkey's neglected two shillings' worth.

Thinking him unconscious, they chattered on about the state of the islands.

'Bonvilain will strip this place of anything within a million years of becoming a diamond,' said Pike. 'I'd feel a tot of pity for the Salts, if they weren't lower than barnacles.'

'Barnacles,' agreed Billtoe. 'But at least barnacles don't give you lip. And you don't put yourself in for a visit to the warden's office if you happen to stamp on a barnacle.'

They two-stepped the plank round an awkward corner, scraping Conor's elbow along the wall.

'I'd say you could stamp on all the prisoners you like, now that Good King Nick is knocking at the pearlies. Bonvilain never minded before.'

'True for you, Pikey,' Billtoe laughed, following it with a regurgitating hurk. 'Good times are here, that is until Isabella comes of age. Possibly she's one for the people, like her father. I hear worrying good things about her.'

'Ah yes, Princess Isabella,' said Pike. 'I wouldn't be concerning yourself on that score. She won't wear the crown till her seventeenth birthday and that's two years away. I would bet my Sunday boots that something tragic will happen to our little princess after that if she starts queering things for the marshall.'

It took all Conor's resolve not to grab Billtoe's weapon and make a bid for freedom right then, but Conor Finn dying on a cold prison floor would do little to help Isabella. He needed to bide his time and wait for an opportunity.

The guards reached Conor's cell and simply raised one end of the plank, sliding him through the doorway. He tumbled to the wall and lay there, limbs splayed and moaning. The moans were real.

Pike and Billtoe stood framed by the doorway.

'You know something, Pikey,' said Billtoe, scratching an itch on his collarbone. 'Maybe I'm getting old and soft, but I've taken a liking to young Conor Finn.'

Pike was more than surprised. *Liking* prisoners was not Billtoe's form.

'Really?'

'No,' said Billtoe, shutting the cell door. 'Not really.'

Conor lay still until the guards' footsteps faded first to echoes then silence. Another minute for safety, then he crawled upon his bunk hiding his face with a forearm, though he was alone in the cell. The shaking began suddenly, racking his entire body from toe to crown, as though he had grasped a wire of the electric, like a labourer he had seen working in Coronation Square, all those years ago. On another island, in another life.

There was simply too much to think about. Father, Mother, King Nicholas, Isabella. His own plight in this prison. Bonvilain, the Battering Rams, Billtoe and Pike. Images of these friends and foes passed through his mind, branding him with more pain than a Little Saltee kiss.

Mother and Father taking him to Hook Head to fly his paper kite. King Nicholas's stories of the American Civil War and why he fought in it. Bonvilain's face, features set in a permanent sneer. Otto Malarkey, fear of death in his dark eyes.

Too much. Too much.

Conor gritted his teeth and imagined himself flying until the shaking stopped.

Pike booted Linus Wynter back into the cell some hours later, just as Conor was finishing his first meal of the day.

'I put yours on the flat stone by the window,' he said to the gangly American. 'It's the warmest spot in here. You sit, I'll get it.'

Wynter tutted, heading straight for the flat stone. 'No need. I know where the griddle is. I have been here almost a year, young Conor.' He bent down and tinkled the air with two fingers until he found the bowl. 'But, thank you, that was very thoughtful.'

Wynter perched on his bed, selecting a lump of gristle, dripping with grease. 'Oh Lord, it's hardly the Savoy, is it. I spent a night there in eighty-nine. Fabulous. Full electric lighting, a bath in every suite. And the water closets – I dream of the water closets.'

'We've had electric lighting since eighty-seven on Great Saltee,' said Conor. 'King Nicholas says that we have to embrace change.' Conor's face fell. 'King Nicholas *said* that.'

Wynter did not comment, chewing the fatty lump in his mouth thoroughly, lest it choke him on the way down.

'So, young Finn, are we going to swap water-closet stories all evening, or are you going to tell me of your adventures in the bell?'

'I let Malarkey live,' said Conor. 'But I thrashed him soundly and he knows I can do it again. Next time I won't keep quiet about it, and we'll see how long he survives as head ram after that.'

Wynter froze, a dripping gobbet of meat halfway to his mouth.

'Hell's bells, boy. If I could look at you admiringly, I would. Nick was right about you.'

'Nick? King Nicholas? You knew the king?'

'We met in Missouri. He was in the balloon corps. Actually, he *was* the balloon corps. He towed two raggedy hot-air rigs around to various battle sites. Our paths crossed at Petersburg in sixty-five. I wasn't much use to anyone back then, having had my eyes poked out by the teenage Jesse James. And Nick was just about tolerated by the generals, so we struck up a friendship. He taught me how to tie knots and fill ballast bags. Even took me up a few times. I had no idea that he was royalty; of course, neither did he.'

Conor had always been a fast thinker. 'It can't be coincidence that you're here.'

Wynter cocked his head to one side, listening carefully.

'No, Conor, it's no coincidence. Nick sent me here to spy for him.'

'You're a spy? You shouldn't tell me this. I could be anyone. Another spy sent in to find you out.'

'You could be, but you're not. I have heard of you before from Victor Vigny. He visited me here days ago and took my news to the king. The pretext was that I had stolen from him. Such cloak and dagger.' Wynter reached out long fingers until he found Conor's shoulder. 'King Nicholas thought of you as a son. Victor said you were his greatest hope for the future. You're no spy.'

Conor felt a twinge of sadness. He had thought of the king almost as a second father.

An awful truth struck him. 'But now, Mister Wynter, you are truly imprisoned here with the rest of us.'

Wynter sighed. 'It would seem so. I can hardly tell Mister Billtoe that I am actually a professional spy posing as a vagrant musician.'

'I suppose not,' Conor agreed. 'Who were you spying on?'

Again, Linus Wynter listened before replying. 'Marshall Bonvilain. Nicholas had come to suspect Bonvilain of treason in many areas, but especially on Little Saltee. Bonvilain was running it like his own personal slave camp. Prison reforms were implemented only when Nicholas or his envoys came to visit. The king needed a man on the inside, and who better to spy on a music-loving warden than a blind musician. Nobody would suspect a man who cannot spy anything of *being* a spy.'

'I see,' said Conor.

Wynter grinned. 'Do you really? What's it like.'

Conor smiled, his first in days. The smile was a twinkle in the gloom and did not last long.

'I don't think I can make it through this, Mister Wynter. I am not strong enough.'

'Nonsense,' snapped Wynter. 'You showed courage today, and ingenuity. Anyone who can thrash that brute Malarkey can certainly find the strength to survive Little Saltee.'

Conor nodded. There were people in worse straits than him. At least he had youth and strength on his side.

'Tell me, Mister Wynter, how do you go about your business?'

'What business is that?' said Wynter innocently.

'The business of being a spy, of course.'

Wynter pulled a convincing horrified face. 'Spying? Me? But, you foolish boy, I am blind, which is the same as brainless and only slightly better than dead. Why, you could plant me at the piano in the warden's office, and he would go about his business exactly as though I wasn't even there.'

'But now there is no one to report to?'

'Precisely. A while back, Nicholas requested my temporary release to play in his orchestra. I gave him my first report then. There was another due tomorrow. I would surmise that I shan't be delivering that report, or any more.'

Conor felt a sudden kinship for this tall American.

'We are together, then.'

'Until one of us is released. And when I say *released*, I mean it in the Little Saltee sense. Occasionally an inmate disappears and the guards tell us he has been released.'

'Dead then.'

'I would guess. Murder is the most expeditious way to prevent overcrowding. I pray that we fortunate two are never released.'

Conor was surprised. 'Fortunate? A curious choice of words.'

Wynter wagged a reed-like, knuckle-knobbed finger. 'Not at all. We are two like-minded, civilized men. Just think who we might have drawn as cellmates.'

Conor's memory flashed on Malarkey's features, shaped by the violence of his life.

'You are right, Mister Wynter. We are indeed fortunate.'

Wynter raised an imaginary glass of champagne.

'Your health,' he said.

'Your health,' rejoined Conor, and then, 'Clink.'

The cell itself was a study in the Spartan, not much more than a hole in the island. There was one window high in the wall, of letterbox size. The light admitted by this portal was weak and watery, without the strength to cut through more than a few feet of shadow.

The walls themselves were expertly hewn with barely a need for mortar, which was just as well as the surface mortar had long since crumbled, allowing various fungi to spread themselves across the joins. Conor estimated the dimensions to be twelve feet by fourteen. Hardly enough for two tall men to spend their confinement in comfort. Then again, comfort was hardly the issue.

As he lay on his hard cot that evening, Conor dreamed of his family. Eventually his thoughts grew so painful that a small pathetic cry crept through his lips.

Linus Wynter did not comment, he merely shifted in his bed to show that he had heard and was awake for conversation if needed.

'You said that you would instruct me,' whispered Conor. 'Tell me how to survive in this place.'

Wynter turned on his back, clasped his hands on his chest and sighed.

'What you must do, what we both must do now, is so terribly difficult that it is close to impossible. Only the most determined can achieve it.'

Conor felt that he could indeed do the close to impossible if it meant that he would survive Little Saltee. 'What, Mister Wynter? Tell me. I need some relief.'

'Very well, Conor. There are two parts to this scheme. The first has the sound of an easy task, but, believe me, it is not. You must forget your old life. It is dead and gone. Dreaming of family and friends will plunge you into a dark hell of despair. So build a wall round your memories and become a new person.'

'I don't know if I can . . .' began Conor.

'You are Conor Finn now!' hissed Wynter. 'You must believe it. You are Conor Finn, seventeen-year-old army corporal, smuggler and swordsman. Conor Finn will survive Little Saltee. Conor Broekhart's body may survive, but his spirit will be crushed as surely as though Bonvilain clamped it in a vice.'

'Conor Finn,' said Conor haltingly. 'I am Conor Finn.'

'You are a killer. You are young and slim, true, but ruthless with your blade — arm as strong as a steel band. You prefer your own company, and will brook no insult. Not so much as a dirty look. You have killed before. Your first when you were fifteen, a grog head who dipped your pocket. This is all the truth.'

'It's true,' murmured Conor. 'All true.'

'You have no family,' continued Wynter. 'No one to love, or to love you.'

'No one . . .' said Conor, but the words were hard to utter. 'No one loves me.'

Wynter paused, tilting his head, hearing Conor's distress. 'This is the way it must be. In here, love will rot your brain. I know this to be true. I had a wife once, lovely Aishwarya. Dreams of her fuelled my days during my five years in a Bengal prison. This was enough to sustain me for a while, but then my love turned to suspicion. And finally to hate. When I heard that she had died of typhoid, the guilt nearly killed me. I *would* have died if they hadn't kicked me out.' Wynter was quiet for as long as it took him to relive those horrible times.

'Love must die in here, Conor; it is the only way. Once you open your heart . . .'

'Love must die,' said Conor, storing images of his parents in a padlocked chest at the back of his mind.

'But something must take its place,' said Wynter in a stronger voice. 'An obsession to fire your enthusiasm. A reason to live, if you like. I myself have music. I keep an opera on the broiler inside my head and in other places. Amadeus himself would weep. My music is never far from my thoughts. It is my fondest wish to have it performed in Salzburg. One day, young Conor. One day. My opera keeps me alive, you see.' Wynter slipped two fingers under his eye bandage, massaging his ruined sockets. 'I see music like you see colours. Each instrument is a stroke of the brush. The gold of the strings. The deep blue of the bassoon. Even as I trot out pompous marches for the warden on his rickety piano – that sound board is not even spruce – I am dreaming of my opera.'

Wynter's lips murmured across the phrases of his beloved music.

'And what about you, Conor?' he asked after several bars. 'Do you have a dream? Something that fills your mind with hope but never pain?'

The answer came quickly to Conor.

I want to fly.

'Yes,' he said. 'I have a dream.'

The night arrived though it made little difference to the light in Conor's cell. There was a slight thickening of the dirty darkness but that was all. They were trapped in a limbo of gloom, with only food and work to instruct them as to the time of day. Conor lay on his cot wrestling with thoughts of his family, which he was not supposed to be thinking. Shrugging off one's old self was not as simple as discarding a dirty shirt. Memories popped up unbidden, clamouring to be examined. Mister Wynter was right: this *was* the most difficult thing he had ever had to do. Conor could feel the sweat coating his face like a wet flannel and the voice of his mother seemed as real to him as the cell walls.

How could you do it, my son? How could you betray us all?

Conor bit his knuckle until the voice faded. He needed distraction, and proof that this new-life strategy was effective.

'Mister Wynter,' he whispered, 'are you asleep?'

Cloth rustled on the other cot, then Linus answered, 'No, Conor Finn. I am awake. Sometimes I think that I never truly sleep. One eye on the real world, so to speak. The legacy of a lifetime's spying. Are you having trouble burying Conor Broekhart?'

Conor laughed bitterly. 'Trouble. It is impossible, Mister Wynter.'

'No, not impossible, but devilish hard. It took me months to forget my real self. To become this rakish, devil-may-care playboy. Even talking to you about this is opening a chink in the door to my previous self.'

'Sorry,' said Conor. 'Tell me of your dream, then. The opera.'

Wynter sat up. 'Really? You would like to hear my music?'

'Yes. Perhaps your music will give me enthusiasm for my own project.'

Wynter was suddenly stuttering. 'V-very well, Conor. But you are the first person ever . . . That is, we are hardly in the correct environment. The acoustics in here are of the worst kind; even the human voice will be mangled by these close quarters.'

Conor smiled in the dark. 'I am a kind audience, Mister Wynter. My only request is that your music be to a higher standard than your spying.'

'Ahh,' said Wynter, beating his breast with a fist. 'A critic. Of all the cellmates I could have chosen.' But the joke had calmed him and he began his performance in confident tones.

'Our story is entitled *The Soldier's Return*. Imagine, if you will, the great state of New York. The Civil War has ended and the men of the One Hundred and Thirty-Seventh Infantry have returned to their homes in Binghamton. It is a time of mixed emotions, great joy and deep sorrow. For these men and their families, nothing can ever be the same again . . .'

And following this sparsest of introductions, Linus Wynter launched into his overture.

It was a grand number, but not pretentious, switching between moods. From delirious joy and relief, to unfathomable sorrow.

It could have been comical. A blind man playing all the parts of an orchestra for a frightened boy. But somehow it was not. Conor felt himself lost in the music and the story sprang up around him as he listened.

It was a sad yet triumphant tale, with fine arias and soaring marches and Conor clung to it for a while, but by and by the story faded, leaving the music alone. But music must have pictures to go with it, and in Conor's mind the pictures were of a flying machine. Heavier than air, yet soaring among the clouds, with Conor himself guiding the rudder. It could be done, and he would be the one to do it.

I will do it, he thought. *I will fly and Conor Finn will survive Little Saltee.*

The third day. Billtoe arrived after the cannon, looking as though he had been dragged to work through the sewers. This, Conor was beginning to realize, was his standard appearance.

Wynter sniffed the air on hearing the hinges.

'Ah, Guard Billtoe. Right on time.'

Billtoe flicked a chicken bone he had been sucking at the blind prisoner. 'Here, Wynter, boil yourself some soup. And you, Conor Finn, look lively. The pipe waits. Maybe today we'll get some work out of you, if you're not too occupied with the unconscious floating.'

Conor sat in his bed, feeling the itch of salt and dirt on his back.

'On my way, Mister Billtoe.'

He trudged to the door, searching his heart for a spark of enthusiasm for anything. Linus Wynter provided it with a farewell and a tilt of the head that served as a wink.

'Until this evening then, Conor *Finn*.'

Conor could not help but smile. Being part of a secret is a great source of strength.

'Until this evening, when the *soldier returns*.'

Wynter's face broke into a broad smile, wrinkles stretching the scars that ringed each eye like rays from the sun.

'I await *The Soldier's Return* then.'

Billtoe scowled, uncomfortable with anything more than abject depression from the convicts.

'Quit with the conversation and out the door with you, Finn.'

Conor Finn left the dank cell, leaving Conor Broekhart further behind with every step.

Malarkey was already in the bell when Conor swam under. The huge convict was squeezing water from his long hair like a washerwoman wringing towels.

'Salt makes the hair brittle,' he explained, glancing at Conor under the crook of a raised elbow. 'If a man favours the long styles, he has to get as much out as he can. Sometimes I think it's wasted work, as no one on this blinking rock gives my hair a second glance.'

Conor was not sure how to react to this genial gent who had replaced yesterday's hired brute.

'Ah . . . My mother recommends oil for brittle hair.'

Malarkey sighed. 'Yes, oil. Where to get it, though; there's the puzzle I have wrestled with for a decade.'

The man was serious, Conor realized. This was important to him.

'Billtoe seems to have a ready supply. The man's head is as greased as a wrestling pole.'

'Billtoe!' spat Malarkey. 'That snake. I wouldn't please him with a plea.'

Conor had a thought. 'Well then, I have noticed that our daily stew is loaded with some form of cooking oil. A small pool collects in the bowl. I dare say it would do you more good on your head than in your stomach.'

Malarkey was thunderstruck. 'God almighty, you are correct, soldier boy. There it was every day, three times a day, staring me in the mush, and me looking for oil. That's good advice.'

'And free,' Conor added. 'Though you may smell like stew.'

'What matter?' said Malarkey. 'My hair will shine bright enough for a Piccadilly stroll.'

Conor shook the water from his own hair. He must, he thought, with the shaking and the caked dirt, bear more than a passing resemblance to a vagabond mutt. It was time to look to his appearance. Perhaps Otto Malarkey was the man to quiz on hygiene.

Malarkey finished with his hair and threw his head back.

'Now,' he said, in a more serious tone. 'We have unfinished business.'

Conor tensed. Was it time for another row? Some students needed more than one pass at a lesson before the information took hold. He placed a hand on the butt of the Devil's Fork in his belt.

'What business is that? More paid beatings?'

'No, soldier boy, no!' said Malarkey hurriedly. 'Your solution to that affair is a sound one. We fake the entire thing for a fortnight. You keep mum and that is that. Saves my knuckles and your head, best all round. A pity I didn't think of it before now. I could have saved myself the pain of arthritis. Between the aching joints and brittle hair, this place will be the death of me.'

Conor relaxed somewhat, but left his hand on the fork. 'I knew a cook on Great Saltee who suffered from arthritis. She always swore that willow bark is good for joint pain, if you can get it.'

Malarkey nodded. 'Willow bark?'

'Grind it into your stew, or simply suck on a piece. Though it is hard on the stomach.'

'No worries on that score. I could digest a live bear with barely a twinge.'

Conor frowned. 'So then, what is this *business*?'

'I talked to Pike,' said Malarkey, hiking a thumb at the bell porthole. 'We decided that it would be best to do a little work before I knock you senseless. So, I thought we might dig around a bit, find a few stones then take our ease for a while. Following that, I drag you on out of here and no one is any the wiser. How does that sound, for a plan?'

Conor was about to agree, but then thought on his new identity. Conor Finn was a young devil, and would not be satisfied without profit.

'It's a passable plan. Most of the elements are there, but what of the three pounds you were paid to beat me?'

Malarkey was ready for this line. 'One for you, two for me.'

'I prefer the other way around.'

'I have a proposition,' said Malarkey. 'We go straight down the middle, if you teach me how to use that fork the way you do. Proper fencing is a powerful tool. I could earn some real money, nail me a few officers.'

It was clear in Malarkey's face that he was eager for this arrangement.

'And can you keep the Battering Rams from slipping a blade between my ribs?' asked Conor.

Otto Malarkey shrugged back his long hair. 'There's only one way to guarantee that.' He rolled up his sleeve, revealing the horned-ram tattoo. 'You must take the ink. Only members of the brotherhood are safe. I'll stand for you, if you teach me fencing. I could say you took the beatings and have Irish blood in you, though your accent is well-bred Saltee. A Kilmore mum maybe? I think that you're below army age, but that don't matter to the Battering Rams. If you're big enough to hold a pistol, you're big enough to fire one.'

Joining the Rams was a sticking point. Conor Broekhart would never take up with a criminal gang, but then again Conor Finn would.

'I'll take your ink, but I won't pay any dues nor swear an oath.'

Malarkey laughed. 'Oath! The only oaths we have in the Rams are foul ones. As for dues, the fencing lessons will do enough.'

Conor rubbed his bicep where the tattoo would sit. 'Very well, Otto Malarkey, we have an agreement. I expect the money tomorrow.'

'Not tomorrow,' said Malarkey. 'From now on you will be searched every day. Wait until you carry the ram on your arm, then certain guards have hazy allegiances. Their search will be less thorough, for the right price, of course.'

Already Malarkey was proving useful. It could well be that the man's idle chatter would be a fair trade for a few fencing lessons.

'Very well, Malarkey, after the tattoo is dry. Until then we fence and dig. First fencing, while the mind is sharp.'

Conor extended his trident, flicking his left arm up behind him.

Malarkey mimicked the stance.

'So, Conor Finn, you'll teach me everything you know?'

'Not everything,' said Conor, smiling tightly. 'If I did that, then *you* could kill *me*.'

Billtoe waited until Conor supposedly regained consciousness before leading him back to his cell through the subterranean hallways of Little Saltee. For the first time since his arrival, Conor took careful account of his surroundings, counting each step, noting each door and window.

This section of the prison had a bowed look, as if the entire wing had dropped a floor since its construction. Walls leaned in overhead and the floor sank like a drain. Stone arches had lost their soffits or keystones and stood crookedly, like the efforts of a child's building blocks. The walls were dotted with pitch patches where water had wormed its way through the cracks. Dozens more rivulets had yet to be filled. A gurgling saltwater stream ran down the centre of the collapsed floor.

'Pretty, ain't it,' said Billtoe, taking note of Conor's roving eye. 'This place could flood at any second, they say. Of course *they* have been saying that since long before I put on the uniform. If I was you, I'd try to escape this hellhole. That's always good for a giggle. You should see what desperate men are willing to try. Jumping off the wall is a favourite. The crabs never go hungry on Little Saltee. Tunnelling is another one. Tunnelling! I ask you. Where does these turf heads think they are? The middle of a meadow? We got barely a spoonful of clay on this island, and yet we have these gaol-crazed prisoners spending every waking minute sniffing out a vein. I tell you straight, little soldier, if you *do* find some earth on Little Saltee, then you should plant yourself some vegetables.'

Conor knew not to interrupt. After all, in a previous existence he had learned that information saved lives, and there was a wealth of information to be gathered about this place. Luckily Guard Billtoe seemed eager to dish it just as fast as he could get it out of his flapping mouth.

He pushed Conor down a corridor, a full step lower than the rest. The floor ran off at a gentle gradient, water actually flowing under some of the doors.

'Home again, fiddle dee dee,' sang Billtoe. 'The lunatic wing. We got all sorts here. Deaf, dumb, blind. One legged, one armed. Fellas what have got a bump on the noggin. Every class of lunatic you care to mention. We got one fellow who doesn't do words. Just numbers. All blooming day numbers. Tens and hundreds, thousands even. Like a blooming banker he is. Don't even know his name, so we call him Numbers — clever, eh?'

Conor stored that nugget. A numbers man could be useful if his counting meant something. There were calculations in any plan.

They arrived at Conor's cell door. Conor noticed the steel hinges and heavy locks.

Billtoe turned a key in the lock. 'Big door, ain't it? These doors are about the only thing we keep repaired around here.' He winked at Conor. 'Couldn't have you simpletons running around during the night, spooking each other with your crying for Mummy and counting and such. I like it better when you stay in your cell and howl.' Billtoe wiped an imaginary tear from his cheek. 'It sounds like a choir of angels. Helps me sleep during my time on the island.'

The man was an animal. Base and foul. In a just world he would be the prisoner and Conor a free man. The door swung open, helped along by the slant of the wall.

'In you go, Salt. Enjoy being on your lonesome.'

Conor was halfway down the ramped floor before the words registered. He turned, but the door was already closing.

'On my lonesome? Where is Mister Wynter?'

Billtoe spoke through a shrinking slice of light between door and frame. 'Wynter? That cheeky blind beggar? Why, he's been released. Solitary for you from here on out, the marshall's orders.'

Conor felt his weight pulling him to the floor, and was on his knees before he could stop himself.

Murder is the most expeditious way to prevent overcrowding, Linus had said. *I pray that we fortunate two are never released.*

'You've killed him,' breathed Conor.

But he was talking to a closed door.

CHAPTER 9:

LIGHT AT THE END

This latest disaster had Conor huddled at the back of the cell, sobbing like a baby. He was alone now. Friendship could have brightened time spent even here. But now there was no one. He crawled as far back as he could into the room, and was dully surprised to find the room extended deeper into the rock than he had believed. Behind Wynter's cot was a deep alcove with roughly the dimensions of four stacked coffins. This he could tell by touch alone as not a glimmer of light extended to the black hole.

He lay there for hours, feeling his determination sliding away like weed sluiced from a slipway. The new identity he had created for himself dissolved, bringing poor desperate Conor Broekhart to the surface.

So he stayed, wrapped in nothing but self-pity, wallowing in dreams of family all night long. Useless, futile dreams. Conor could well have perished in the next few days, dead from a broken heart, if not for one little ray of light.

In the early hours, Conor woke to see a red line flickering on the opposite wall. For a long sleepy moment this line puzzled him, resembling nothing more than a ghostly number one, wavering gently. Was this a message of some kind? Could his cell be haunted? Then he awakened fully and realized that the line was, of course, a shaft of sunlight. But from where?

For distraction's sake, Conor decided to investigate. It took no more than a moment for him to find that a narrow fissure along the seam between two blocks of the alcove extended to the outside world and was allowing weakened light to filter through. Conor tapped the left block with a fingernail and was surprised to find that it budged, scraping against its neighbours. He prodded more forcefully and the block wobbled on its base, dislodging caked muck. The block itself cracked, for it was not a true block, merely a husk of dried mud. Conor wiggled one finger along the side of the false block and popped it from its hole. A wedge of sunlight blasted him in the eyes, blinding him for several seconds. Not that it was light of any great brightness, but it was the first direct light Conor had seen in many hours.

Conor closed his eyes, but did not turn away. The heat on his face was wonderful, like a gift straight from the hand of God. He thumped at adjoining blocks, checking for more counterfeits. But there were none. The rest of the wall was solid as a mountain. One hole only, the size of his two fists.

He squatted there for a while feeling the light warm his skin, watching it trace the veins in his eyelids, until at last he felt prepared enough to open his eyes. He was not disappointed with what he saw, because he had not allowed himself to feel any hope. This hole was a devilish small one, and deep too, encased by four feet of solid rock, with barely a napkin's worth of sky at its end. Only a rat could escape through this tunnel, perhaps a largish one would struggle. And even if by some miracle he managed to mimic Doctor Redmond, the famous escape artist, and wiggle through this narrow pipe, where would he go? The ocean would swallow him up quicker than a whale swallowing a minnow. If he managed to steal a boat, the sharpshooters on the walls would pick him off for sport. No one had ever escaped from Little Saltee. Not one single person in hundreds of years.

So, accept this light as a small secret gift, and nothing more, Conor told himself. *Allow it to heat your face and wipe your mind clean of pain, if even for a moment.*

Conor sagged back against the compartment wall, relishing the meagre warmth. Who had made this fake block? he wondered. And what had caused the hole? There were any number of answers to both questions, and no way of confirming one of them.

The prison walls possibly sagged an inch, concentrating vectors of force at this point, pulverizing the block. Or perhaps successive generations of inmates scraped away with primitive tools. Saltwater erosion, or rainwater. Though that was unlikely in less than a millennium. A combination of all these factors, most likely, and a dozen more besides.

Conor studied the clay block, which had hidden this treasure of light. It was chipped, but intact. It would certainly serve to hide the hole for his tenancy. But he would not hide the opening just yet; Billtoe would not arrive for a short time. Until then he would enjoy the dawn like scores of convicts before him. The devil take his troubles.

Water. A mug of water would be nice.

Conor closed his eyes again, but images of his parents tormented him so he opened them again, and for a long moment thought he was dreaming or insane. What was happening, should not, could not be happening. The wall of this hidden alcove was aglow, and not just with sunlight, with a strange ghostly green glow. Not the entire wall, just lines and dots. Familiar characters. Conor realized that he was staring at music. The walls and roof of this tiny alcove were covered in music.

Mister Wynter had said: 'I keep an opera on the broiler inside my head and in other places.'

The other place was back here in a secret alcove. He would have shared that fact, had they not killed him.

Conor ran his fingers along a series of notes, up and down they went like a mountain range.

What was this glow? How was it possible?

Victor's ghost tormented him.

Come on, dimwit. We studied this. Basic geology. And you call yourself a man for the new century.

Of course. It was luminous coral. It only grew in certain specific conditions, which must have been freakishly mimicked by this damp, close environment.

Conor scraped away a thin layer of mud to reveal the rough plates of luminous coral below. This part of the cell was living coral, fed by the constant drip of salt water. It must have grown up through the rock over the centuries and was activated by the sunlight. What a marvel. He had not expected to find marvels here.

There were other marks too, fainter than the musical

notes. In older hands and quainter language. Conor found the diary of Zachary Cord, a confessed poisoner. And also a rambling curse scratched by one Tom Burly, damning the seventeenth-century warden for a hater of justice. Conor had no trouble accepting that as truth.

So this was how Linus had kept himself sane during his hours of solitude. He had recorded his music on the only surface available to him – a mud-covered crypt – without ever knowing his parchment was luminous. It brought tears to Conor's eyes when he reached the final notes and the word *Fin*, engraved with considerable flourish. Linus Wynter had managed to finish his life's work before being 'released'.

It was a noble tradition, this recording, and one that Conor suddenly knew he intended to continue. He would commit his own ideas to the walls of this tiny alcove. In fact, the mere notion set his heart beating faster. To have a canvas on which to diagram his designs was more than he had hoped for.

He scrabbled around Linus Wynter's bunk until he found what he had known must be there. His most recent stylus. It was hidden under a leg of his cot. The chicken bone Billtoe had tossed earlier, one end ground to a point. Perfect.

Conor scrambled into the alcove, lying flat on his back. He would begin on the ceiling, and he would sketch only until the cannon fired.

With confident strokes, Conor Finn etched his first model into the damp mud, allowing the luminous green coral to shine through a moment later. It was something he had been working on with Victor. A glider with a rudder and adjustable wings for lateral balance.

On the wall the diagram was static, but it Conor's mind it soared like a bird. *A free bird.*

CHAPTER 10:

UNLUCKY FOURTEENTH

1894. Two Years Later

Arthur Billtoe took one last chew on a wad of tobacco, then spat a mouthful of juice towards the hole in the floor. The stringy wad missed its target, landing square on the toe of his own boot.

'Sorry,' said the guard, then realizing he apologized only to himself, cast an eye around in the hope that no one had overheard, or they might think him simple and lock him away with the scatterfools.

No one *had* overheard except Pike, and that hardly mattered as Pike was only half a step removed from idiocy himself. In any case, Billtoe decided to cover up his blurted apology.

'Sorry,' he repeated, but louder this time. 'It's sorry I am for the poor lunatic Salts inside Flora this night.'

The prison guards stood in the subterranean pantry overlooking the dive hole. Below them, Flora was submerged ten fathoms in dark Saltee waters. The seas outside were rough and the tunnel to open water had become something of a blow-hole, rattling the diving bell with each bellow of bubbles from its spout. With every impact a flurry of peals rose through the chamber.

'Sorry indeed,' continued Billtoe. 'They'd best move sharpish or Flora will remove a limb or two.'

Pike did not believe for a second that Billtoe was actually concerned for a prisoner, any more than he would be concerned for a blade of grass. But it didn't do to contradict Arthur Billtoe if you were further down the prison ladder than he was, or he would set you working Christmas Eve on the mad wing.

'Don't you waste your legendary compassion, Arthur,' said Pike, rubbing his hairless head.

Billtoe glanced sharply at his comrade. Was that wit? No, surely not from a man who thought that electricity was a gift from the fairies.

'No, worry not. It's Finn and Malarkey on the night shift.'

Billtoe nodded. Finn and Malarkey. Those two were the best pair of miners ever to work the bell. Young Finn was the brains of the pair no doubt, but whatever he pointed to, Malarkey would dig up with the strength of a giant.

And to think, two years ago when Conor Finn arrived on Little Saltee, he'd been little more than a scrap of a boy destined for a stitched-up canvas bag and a burial at sea. Now he was a force in the Battering Rams and one of the main sources of income for Billtoe himself.

Billtoe cleared his throat. 'I'll be searching Finn and Malarkey myself, Pike.'

Pike winked slyly. 'As is your habit, Arthur.'

Billtoe ignored the insolence. It wouldn't do to get into an argument about private diamond stashes, but he silently resolved to mark Pike down for supervision of the sewage works. It was bad enough that Pike's comments were bordering on insolent, but Billtoe had also heard whispers that Pike was selling information to the Kilmore arm of the Battering Rams without cutting in his old friend Arthur Billtoe.

Billtoe leaned over the edge, peering down into the lamp-lit abyss. The bell glowed and shimmered in the dark waters, humming with every stroke of the current. Through the filthy porthole he could see vague movements and shadows. Finn and Malarkey mining, he presumed.

Best of luck, Salts. Bring back a goose egg for Uncle Arthur.

Billtoe spat a second wad of chewed tobacco, and this time it sailed into the hole, landing on the bell's rubber air hose.

'Hmmm,' he grunted proudly, winking at Pike. Then he strode to the ladder, trying to project an air of incorruptibility. He wanted to be on the rocks when Finn and Malarkey surfaced.

'Here, Arthur,' Pike called after him. 'You're walking funny. Was it that herring?'

Billtoe scowled. He would have to do something about Pike. 'No, you hunchbacked, hairless son of a circus oddity. I am being incorruptible.'

'That would have been my second guess,' said Pike, who like many dullards had a streak of sharp wit in him.

Conor Finn and Otto Malarkey fought like demons inside the diving bell. Their makeshift swords sang as they cut the air and sparked along each other's shafts. Both men perspired freely, breathing so deeply that the water level rose at their feet. They were sucking in air faster than the pump could supply it.

'Your *balestra* is clumsy,' panted Conor. 'More grace, Otto. You are not a hog in a pen.'

Malarkey smiled tightly. 'Hogs are dangerous animals, Conor. If you are not careful, they can run you through.'

And with that, he abandoned the rules of fencing, dropping his blade and charging his opponent, arms spread.

Conor reacted quickly, dropping to his stomach and rolling underwater, knocking Malarkey's legs from under him. The big man went down heavily, clanging his temple against the bell curve on his way down. By the time he recovered his bearings, Conor had his trident jammed under his chins.

'Your hair looks well,' said Conor. 'A healthy shine.'

Malarkey preened. 'You're not the only one to notice. I've been eating the oily fish, as you suggested. It's costing me a fortune in bribes and I hate the stuff, but with results like this I will suffer the taste.'

Conor helped Malarkey to his feet. 'You need to practise the *balestra*. It is a dancer's leap, not a drunken stumble. But, apart from that, your progress is good.'

Malarkey rubbed his head. 'Yours too. That was a neat little roll just then. The king of the tinkers couldn't have done it sweeter. I have never seen a fighter like you, Conor. There's the sword which is mostly Spanish, but with some French. Then the proper pugilism that I would class as

English. But there's the chopping and kicking too, which I have a notion is Oriental. I saw a fellow once in the West End, gave a demonstration of that chopping and kicking. Broke a plank with his foot. At the time I thought it was trickery, but now I am glad I didn't call him on it.'

An image of Victor flashed behind Conor's eyes. He snuffed it out brutally.

'I have picked up a few things in my travels,' he said.

Malarkey huffed. 'Typical Conor Finn. Most people in here are desperate for someone to listen to their story. Telling it to the walls they are. Not Conor Finn. Two years you've been instructing me, and I have learned no more than a dozen useless facts about you in that time. The most obvious being that your beard is multicoloured.'

Conor bent at the knees, examining his burgeoning beard in the water. As far as he could tell, there were strands of blond, red and even a few greys in the sparse growth. Surely grey was unusual in the beard of a sixteen-year-old boy. No matter. It gave him the appearance of someone perhaps five years older.

He had changed utterly in the past two years. Gone was the gangly skinny youth who sobbed his way through his first night of imprisonment, and in his place was a tall, muscled, flinty young man who commanded respect from inmates and guards alike. People may not like him, or seek his company, but neither would they toss insults his way or interfere with his business.

'You should shave that beard,' commented Malarkey. 'All

your lovely hair, then that ratty beard. People only notice the beard, you know.'

Conor straightened. His blond hair was pulled back with a thong, so that it did not interfere with his work. It had darkened a few shades since he last walked in the sunlight.

'I am not as concerned with grooming as you, Otto. I *am* concerned with business. Tell me, how is our hoard?'

'It grows,' said Malarkey. 'Seven bags buried we have now. All in the salsa beds.'

Conor smiled, satisfied. Billtoe had ordered the Suaeda salsa beds planted on Conor's own advice. The plants grew like weeds, were saline resistant and provided cheap meals for the convicts. This meant a few pounds a month for Billtoe to steal from the food funds. Of course, prisoners had to be allowed to tend the beds, which was when Malarkey and his Rams buried their stolen diamonds.

'Not that they do us much good in the earth,' continued Malarkey. 'Unless a diamond bush sprouts, and even then Billtoe would strip it bare.'

'Trust me, Otto,' said Conor. 'I don't intend being here forever. Somehow I will get our stones and send your share to your brother, Zeb. I promise you that, my friend.'

Otto clasped his shoulders. 'The Rams have certain funds, but with riches on that scale my brother could bribe my way out of here. I could be a free man. I could stroll through Hyde Park with my magnificent hair.'

'I will succeed, my friend. Or die in the attempt. If you are not free in a year, it is because I am dead.'

Malarkey did not waste his breath asking Conor for details of his plan. Conor Finn laid out his cards sparingly. Another subject then: 'Badger Byrne has not paid his due yet,' he said. 'How's about I issue a few taps?'

'No more violence, remember. Anyway, Badger has been laid up with shingles, I hear. Let him rest a while.'

Otto Malarkey pursed his lips in frustration. 'Rest, Conor? Rest? Always the same response with you. I haven't dished out a beating since you took the ink.'

Conor rubbed the Battering Ram tattoo on his upper arm. 'That's hardly true, Otto. You near drove MacKenna into open water.'

'True,' admitted Malarkey, grinning. 'But he's a guard. And English too.'

'All great strategists know when to use force and when to use reason. Alexander of Macedonia, Napoleon.'

Malarkey laughed outright. 'Oh aye, little Boney was a great one for the reason. Just ask anyone that was at Waterloo.'

'The point is that we have seven bags now, where we had none before. Seven bags. A tidy fortune.'

'It might as well be seven bags of clay,' scoffed Malarkey. 'Until your plan succeeds. I don't know how you're going to do it. Even the guards have not managed to smuggle diamonds from Little Saltee. A man would need wings.'

Conor glanced sharply at Malarkey. Could he know something? *No*, he thought. *Just a turn of phrase.*

'Yes,' he said. 'A man would indeed need wings.'

*

Billtoe was waiting for them at the shoreline, up to his ankles in water just in case another guard would beat him to the search.

'Right you two lemon-sucking scurvy dodgers. Stand away from each other and raise your arms.'

Conor fought the urge to strike this pathetic grafter. To assault Billtoe would surely satisfy him briefly, but it would just as surely lead to a beating that would leave him near dead and incapacitated. He could not afford to be incapacitated now, not when things were going so well with the design. Not with the coronation so close.

Billtoe began his search, making a great show of being thorough.

'You'll get nothing past me, Finn. Not so much as a bubble of seaweed. No, sir. Arthur Billtoe knows all your tricks.'

The man was as good as advertising his intentions. *Protesting too much.*

Presently, he happened across the small stone in the leg of Conor's much repaired army breeches. Without a word, he flicked the diamond up his own sleeve. This was his payment for a lax search.

'Any news?' Conor asked, while Billtoe moved on to Malarkey.

Billtoe laughed. 'You Salts are devils for news, aren't you? The most mud-boring happening is like a golden nugget to you.'

'More like a diamond,' said Conor.

Billtoe's hands froze on Malarkey's shoulders. 'Is that insolence, soldier boy? Did I hear insolence?'

Conor hung his head. 'No, sir, Mister Billtoe. I was trying to be humorous. Friendly, like. I misjudged the moment, I think now.'

'I think that too,' said Billtoe, frowning, but his expression improved when he came across the stone in Otto's shirt pocket. 'Then again, nothing wrong with a bit of humour. We're all men after all. Wouldn't want you to think that we guards didn't have hearts in our chests.'

'Yes, Mister Billtoe. I will work on my delivery, perhaps.'

'You do that,' said Billtoe. 'Now let me *deliver* some news.' He paused. 'Did you see that? You said *delivery* then I repeated it in *my* sentence. Now that's delivery. Pay attention, Finn, you could learn something.'

Only in prison, thought Conor, *could such a bore be tolerated.*

'I shall keep my ears open and my mouth closed, Mister Billtoe.'

'Good man, Finn. You're learning, if slowly.'

A year ago, Billtoe would have punctuated this lesson with a dig from his rifle butt, but he hesitated these days before striking Finn. It did not do to unnecessarily antagonize the Battering Rams, and Conor Finn himself was not a young man you wanted snapping on you. He cut a fearsome figure, except for the beard, which could do with some foliage.

'Anyway. My nugget of news. Queen Victoria of Great Britain has declared a wish to attend Princess Isabella's coronation. She will not come on the fourteenth, because she believes the number to be unlucky, having lost a grandson on that date. So the coronation has been moved forward two weeks to the first of the month, though Isabella will be still sixteen. We will see your balloons then. Or should I say, *my* balloon.'

Conor's practised composure almost slipped away from him, to reveal internal turmoil.

The first. He was not ready. Everything was not in place.

'The first?' he blurted. 'The first you say, Mister Billtoe.'

Billtoe cackled and spat. 'Yes, the first, Finn. Did you not receive your invitation? I keep mine with me at all times, tucked into my velvet cummerbund.'

Billtoe's tasteless chuckles died in his throat as he noticed Conor's expression. Fearsome was the best word to describe it. And while the prisoner made no aggressive move, Billtoe decided that it was best not to prod him any more. He made a silent decision that Conor Finn would have to spend a few days in his cell alone, to learn some humility, Ram or no Ram.

The guard relieved Conor and Malarkey of their diamond nets, ushering them towards the ladder. He thrust his fingers among the dozen or so wet stones in each net. The rough diamonds were like glazed eyes, slipping and clanking. Billtoe could tell it was mostly dross. The best was in his sleeve.

'Traps shut now, both of you. Climb on out and thank God that I didn't decide to shoot you for no good reason. You are alive today because of Billtoe, never forget that.'

Malarkey rolled his eyes. 'Yes, Mister Billtoe. We thank God for it.'

They climbed from the pit and into the pantry. The entire

room was in constant vibration from tidal shock, and scores of water jets spurted and drooped with each pulse of water. Every day for the past two years, it had seemed to Conor as though the subterranean mine must surely collapse. Every day he had longed to work above sea level with the so-called normal inmates, but his requests were refused.

Orders from the palace, Billtoe had told him. *If Bonvilain wants you underground, then that's where you stay.*

In all his time on the island, Conor had only been allowed outside once to supervise the planting of the salsa garden. On that day, the salt-blasted surface of Little Saltee had seemed like a paradise.

Conor winked a farewell to Otto Malarkey as Pike took the Battering Ram to his cell. Billtoe led him away from the main building to the mad wing's main door. As with all the wings, there were no keys to this door, just a heavy vertical bolt which was winched from the next floor up. Billtoe rang the bell, then doffed his hat and showed his face to the guard above.

'The right place for you, Billtoe,' called the guard, though the spy hole, then hoisted the bolt.

'Every day,' muttered Billtoe, flinging the door wide. 'Every blooming day, the same comment.'

Conor waited until they were deep into the mad wing's slowly collapsing corridor, before speaking. His arrangements with Billtoe must be kept secret.

'Have my sheets arrived?'

This cheered Billtoe immediately. He had forgotten the sheets.

'Ah, yes. His majesty's extra sheets. Today or tomorrow, I am not sure. What's your hurry?'

Conor strove to look shamefaced. 'I cannot sleep, Mister Billtoe. My mind has convinced my body that if I had sheets, as though I were a boy in my mother's house, then maybe a day's rest would be mine.'

Billtoe nodded at one of the chimney flues dotting the wall. 'Maybe we should stuff you up the chimney. The ghosts could sing you a lullaby.'

The flues ran in complicated routes behind the prison walls, once a network of hot air, now sealed tight by stone and mortar, but still Salts scrambled up, given the chance, only to lose themselves in the twists and turns, one stone corner looking much like another.

'Anyway, sheets is against regulations,' Billtoe said, holding out his empty hand, though he had already been paid.

Conor clasped the hand, passing on the rough diamond he had been keeping for himself. 'I know, Mister Billtoe. You're a saint. With a few hours' sleep behind me I will work doubly hard for you.'

Billtoe squinted craftily. 'More than double. Treble.'

Conor bowed his head. 'Treble, then.'

'And I need more ideas,' pressed Billtoe. 'Like the salsa and the balloons.'

'I will set my brain on it. With some sleep, I feel certain the blood will flow more freely. I have a notion for a twelve-shot revolver.'

'I don't know about that,' said Billtoe frowning. 'It's one

thing to allow prisoners to dig in a garden or draw a balloon, but playacting with firearms . . .'

Conor shrugged. 'Think on it, Mister Billtoe. There's a lot of coin in arms. We could be partners upon my release.'

Greed shone in Billtoe's eyes like yellow fever. Partners? Not likely. If Finn's twelve-shot revolver worked, then it would be Arthur Billtoe's notion. Bed sheets were a small price to pay.

'Partners it is. I'll get those sheets down to you next shift.'

'Silk,' Conor reminded him. 'They must be silk. I had silk as a child.'

Billtoe balked, then checked himself. A twelve-shot revolver. His name would go down in history with Colt and Remington.

'Very well, Finn. But I warn you, these balloons of yours better work on the day. If they do not, you will suffer.'

If my balloons don't work, I will do more than suffer, thought Conor. *I will die.*

During his internment on Little Saltee, Conor had managed to barter for a few basic comforts. A bucket of mortar sat on a stone and was used to patch the weeping walls. A sewing kit to repair his worn uniform was wrapped in leather and hung from a peg. He had even managed to secure a straw mattress for his bed. Linus Wynter's cot had been converted to a table where he could study the few texts that Billtoe had deemed harmless, and work on the plans for his approved schemes, such as the salsa garden and the coronation balloons.

In fact the salsa garden had not been Conor's idea. Victor had talked of it during one of their horticultural lessons. The Parisian had even written to King Nicholas about introducing the vegetable to the Saltees. The advantages of such a plot were threefold he explained. It would allow the prisoners outdoors for some exercise, it would teach them a valuable skill and the salsa itself would add a much needed vegetable to prison meals.

It was a harmless idea, presented by Conor to gain Billtoe's trust. There were no disadvantages and no possibility of escape or injury. No one had ever died from vegetable assault. Coronation balloons were Conor's next suggestion. Billtoe had seized eagerly on the idea, puffed with the success of the salsa garden. In Billtoe's mind, the coronation balloons were his ticket to promotion, in fact they were Conor Finn's ticket to freedom.

There were several major obstacles standing between Conor and escape to the mainland. There were locks, of course, and the doors around them, and the walls in which the doors were embedded, and the guards on duty outside these walls. But the main difficulty was the island itself. Even if an inmate could pass through the prison walls like a spectre, there were still over two miles of ocean between him and the Irish village of Kilmore Quay.

This particular stretch of ocean was notoriously unsafe, with riptides and currents that lurked beneath the surface like malignant agents of Poseidon. So many vessels had been lost in this patch of Saint George's Channel that the British Navy painted it red on their charts. And even if the seas did not do for an escapee, the famous Saltee Sharpshooters would put a few air holes in the back of his head. So swimming for the shore was not a realistic option. No, the only way to escape Little Saltee was to fly, and that was where Conor's coronation balloons came in.

It would be a spectacular addition to the coronation celebrations, he had told Billtoe one night on their walk to the pipe, *if the Saltee Sharpshooters could pick hot-air balloons from the night sky. What a display of marksmanship.*

Billtoe was not convinced.

Shooting balloons. He sniffed. *A child's trick.*

Conor was expecting this response.

But what if the balloons were loaded with Chinese fireworks, he said. *And, when struck, would light up the night sky with a string of spectacular explosions.*

Billtoe stopped sniffing. *Spectacular explosions, eh?*

This is a brand-new invention, Conor continued. *This has never been seen before. Marshall Bonvilain would be extremely impressed.*

Impressing the marshall is a good thing, mused Billtoe.

Billtoe's Balloons, people will call them. By next year they will be launching them in London, Paris, the next World Fair.

The guard's eyes glazed over, lost in dreams of his own fame and fortune. Then he snapped back.

It would never be allowed. Prisoners working with gunpowder. Impossible.

I don't need to work with gunpowder, said Conor soothingly.

All I need is paper and ink to design the balloons. Have them made up on Great Saltee if you like, but make sure they are tied to our walls for an impressive shot.

Billtoe nodded slowly. *All you need is paper and ink?*

And perhaps a day above ground as a reward. One day a week, that's all I ask.

Now Billtoe felt as though the upper hand was his.

Ah, so that's it. You would have me defy Marshall Bonvilain himself.

One day. A night-time stroll even. I need to breathe the air, Mister Billtoe. These balloons could make you rich. You will be famous.

Billtoe tucked a chew of tobacco under his lip, taking several moments to mull it over.

I will give you the paper and ink, and I will have a single balloon manufactured on Great Saltee, at my expense. If a test is successful, then you shall have your day outside after the coronation. If not, then I will strip your cell of anything resembling a comfort and the next time sunlight falls on your eyes you will be too dead to appreciate it.

The test had been successful, spectacularly so, and Bonvilain immediately approved the manufacture of several fireworks balloons in a small workshop on Great Saltee. The marshall was always eager to demonstrate the island's sophistication to visiting dignitaries, and fireworks balloons would serve both as a delightful show of innovation and a chilling reminder of the Sharpshooters' prowess.

The marshall jovially assured Guard Billtoe that the balloons would indeed bear his name, if they exploded successfully on the night. Not only that but he would receive a commendation and a generous pension for his efforts. In truth, Billtoe had never seen the marshall so happy. He even hinted that Billtoe could well be sent to various foreign capitals for balloon demonstrations. Billtoe came away from this audience glowing, and well disposed towards Conor Finn.

The exploding balloons were clever contraptions, and Bonvilain did not believe for a second that the idea was Billtoe's, but the test was such a dazzling success that he did not care who his guard had cut the notion from. It worked and neither the British nor the French had it.

Each pyrotechnical balloon was a simple sealed hydrogen balloon coated with phosphorous paint. Inside the balloon there was a pack of fireworks and a short fuse. All the marksman had to do was nail the centre of the glowing balloon with a nitroglycerine bullet, and the hydrogen would ignite, setting off the fuse to the fireworks' pack.

For Queen Victoria's entertainment, Bonvilain's sharpshooters would pop these balloons from a distance of almost a mile. It would be a spectacular finale to the coronation celebrations.

Conor had not shared this idea with Billtoe out of a patriotic desire to excite the coronation audience. If everything proceeded according to his plan, then one of the balloons would bear an extra cargo. A human cargo.

But now, because of Queen Victoria's superstition, the coronation was being moved forward and he was not ready.

The vital silk sheets were still in a linen closet on Great Saltee. His plans were incomplete. To be thwarted now, having plotted for months, would be a cruel blow.

Conor crawled to the niche behind what he still thought of as Wynter's bed, popping out the false brick. Crimson sun rays flooded the space, sinking into the coral, which drank the light in and converted it to green energy. He had long ago traded his day job for the night shift to allow him more daylight with his plans.

In less than a minute, the entire cell glowed with a thousand calculations, schematics and blueprints. A treasure trove of science brought to life by nature. The walls bore dozens of sketches of balloons, gliders and heavier-than-air flying machines. These scratched pictures represented two years of obsessive study. All previous diaries had been written over, except the final four bars of Linus Wynter's opera, and the word *Fin*.

For the first few months, dreams of the machines themselves had been enough to fuel Conor through the long lonely hours, but a man cannot stay in the air forever, even in his dreams. And so a purpose for his flying machines was needed. A place to land.

Conor Broekhart would have flown to his parents, to Isabella, but in two years they hadn't once questioned Bonvilain's version of events. If they had, surely he would have received a visit or a message. Isabella could have saved him. She could have waved a royal finger and had him pardoned or banished if their young love had meant a thing to her. Obviously it had not. He was deserted and despised.

Young Conor felt these things as certainly as he felt the cold rock under his feet. And so his heart hardened and selflessness was suborned by selfishness.

Conor Finn took over and Conor Broekhart was displaced. And where Broekhart had nobility, Finn had self-interest. He would make himself rich by stealing from the people who had stolen his life. The Saltee Islands would pay for the past two years. A diamond per day. And once he had money enough, he would buy Otto's freedom, then book passage to America and begin his life anew. This was his plan, and it kept him alive just as surely as his heartbeat.

And so, how to escape? By land, sea or air? There was no land, the sea was treacherous, so that left the air. He must fly out of here, or if not fly then at least fall slowly. An idea was born, but one that was to take more than a year of planning and manipulation.

Suddenly the coronation was shifted and his schemes shattered like broken mirrors, and there were only days to put the pieces together.

Conor lay on the uneven ground, salt water darkening his clothes, studying his plans. He must memorize the designs now, and then destroy them. These plans would be valuable to any army in the world, but especially to Bonvilain. And the greatest torment that Conor could ever endure was the notion that he had somehow aided Marshall Hugo Bonvilain.

He traced each line with his forefinger. Every plane, every twist of propeller, each line and rudder, the arrows that denoted airflow, even the fanciful clouds that his artistic side had almost unconsciously etched. As soon as a glider, balloon or aeroplane was committed to memory, he smeared mud across the design, patting it into every groove.

By sunset, these amazing plans existed only inside the head of Conor Finn.

Billtoe arrived thirty minutes late that evening, swathed from head to toe in silken sheets.

'Catch a goo at me,' he warbled. 'I'm the emperor of Rome, I am. Arthur Billtoe Caesar.'

Conor was waiting by the door, and was dismayed to see Billtoe's boot heel catching on the hem of one sheet. He had enough stitching to do without repairing rips too.

'My sheets,' he said, in strangled tones.

Billtoe stopped his tomfoolery. Inmate Finn had that look on his face again. The fearsome one.

'Here you are,' he said, suddenly eager to be out of this tiny room. 'And while you're sleeping on 'em, dream about that twelve-shot revolver, partner.'

Partner, thought Conor doubtfully. *As if Arthur Billtoe would ever accept a prisoner as partner.*

Conor caught the thrown sheets, laying them carefully on his bed.

'Thank you, Mister Billtoe. These mean the world to me. These and my walks on the outside.'

Billtoe wagged a finger. 'After the coronation, soldier boy. *After.*'

'Of course,' said Conor contritely. 'After.' He took a timid step forward. 'I was hoping to have the revolver designs ready for the coronation. Perhaps if I didn't have to work for the next few nights . . .'

Billtoe backed out of the cell. 'Don't even ask, soldier boy. This is starting to sound like a relationship. As though we *do* things for each other. Favours and such. Well, it ain't a relationship. Not of the friendly type at any rate. You do whatever you can to stop me slitting your throat in the night. That's all there is to it.'

Conor knew better than to wheedle. Once Billtoe was set in his path, trying to change his course would only send him trundling along it faster.

'I am sorry, Mister Billtoe. Of course you are absolutely correct. There's work that needs doing.'

Conor thrust out his hands for the handcuffs, as he had every day for the past two years. And just as *he* had been doing for the past two years, Arthur Billtoe ratcheted them on tight enough to pinch. Other guards stopped cuffing their charges after the first while, but not Billtoe. Care only took seconds, but it could keep a person alive for years. Billtoe had no intention of ending his days with his head stove in by some fisheye-sucking inmate who had lost the will to live and replaced it with the desire to commit murder.

'That's right, Salt. Those diamonds aren't going to just pop out of the ground and jump into the royal treasury themselves, now are they?'

Conor winced as the steel bit into his flesh.

Two more days, he thought to himself, doing his utmost to hide his hatred of Billtoe behind a mask of compliance. *Two more days, then I can begin to collect my diamonds.*

Billtoe was thinking too.

This one is not broke. He stands broke, but his eyes are burning. I will have to keep an eye on Mister Conor Finn.

Conor Finn was important to Billtoe, and it was not just for the clever notions, and the calm he seemed to have generated in the ranks of the Battering Rams. He was important because every so often Marshall Bonvilain enquired after the young man's health. There was a story somewhere in soldier boy's past but Billtoe had no desire to find out the specifics. It wasn't healthy to have the marshall wondering how good a man was at keeping his mouth shut. He might decide that the man in question would hold his silence better on the bottom of the ocean with only the crabs to know the contents of his brain.

Billtoe shuddered. Sometimes his mind conjured the most gruesome images. Perhaps they were memories seeping from Little Saltee's walls.

'Look lively, Salt. There's more'n you to be seen to, and only Billtoe to see to 'em.'

With a last regretful glance at the precious sheets on his bed, Conor followed Billtoe through the doorway and into the flooded corridor. There was a spring tide that day and salt water ran along grooves eroded into the mortar. Conor swore he saw an eel wriggling through the tiny torrent. This entire wing was a death trap, and had been for centuries. When he had first arrived, there were signs of King Nicholas's planned renovations: scaffolds, ladders and such. But these had all disappeared within days of the king's death.

No. Not simply death, thought *Conor. Murder. His life was stolen, as mine was stolen from me.*

But soon he would steal it back.

The following days were a blur of feverish toil. By night, Conor mined the pipe, sucking down the bell's greasy air almost as fast as the pump team could send it through the vent. By day he worked on his sheets, stitching with lengths of thread he had bartered for, and cutting with a sharp stone whetted on the cell walls. There were twelve panels to be cut, hemmed and stitched. The silk was not as tightly woven as he would have liked, but there was nothing to be done about that now. It would have to do. The work was flawed, Conor knew that, but how could he be exact with poor light, improvised materials and no experience? He was most likely stitching a shroud for himself, but even the idea of a quick death held more comfort than a lifetime in this cell.

On the evening before the coronation, Conor almost gave himself away. Run ragged by stitching and mining, he began to behave like the lunatic he was supposed to be. When Billtoe collected him for his shift, Conor's face hung from his skull like a wet cloth and his lips flapped in a dull mumble.

He is breaking, thought Billtoe satisfied. *It was the sheets that did it. Sometimes reminders of home are too potent to bear. The work will go quickly now; he will be desperate to please me.*

The guard clapped on the handcuffs and led the way down the flooded corridor. He enquired on Conor's progress regarding the revolver, but all he heard in reply was a burble of counting.

Billtoe stopped suddenly, wavelets scurrying from his boot heels.

'What's that you're saying? Numbers is it? A count of some sort?'

Conor barely managed to avoid shunting his keeper. He had been making a count. A vital and secret one. He realized that one slip of the lip could be disastrous to his plan.

'A nursery rhyme, Mister Billtoe,' he mumbled, flushed. 'Nothing more.'

Billtoe looked him square in the face.

'You're red as a boiled lobster, soldier boy. Are you up to some scheming? Some numbers' plan?'

Conor hung his head. 'Just embarrassed. Those sheets set me thinking of my mother. Of the rhymes she used to recite for me.'

Billtoe laughed. Perhaps Conor Finn was not as fearsome as supposed. Then again, he had seen bigger men than him with Mummy's handkerchief clutched in one hand and a bloody dagger in the other.

'Come to your senses,' he advised the prisoner. 'A diving bell is no place for daydreamers. You're away with the birds.'

Nearly, thought Conor. *Very nearly.*

The final day whirled past. For months, time had mocked him, prolonging itself elastically. Each second a yawning chasm. But now there was not time enough to squeeze in the day's work. To Conor, it seemed to take an age simply to thread a needle. His fine mind was fuzzy with fear. Twice he sewed sections of his contraption upside down, and was forced to pick out the stitches. Sweat dripped constantly from his brow, speckling the silk sheets.

This is ridiculous. I am a scientist. Look upon this as an experiment.

It was no use. He could not calm himself. The spectre of failure tapped his shoulder in time with the water dripping from the ceiling. There would be other plans certainly, he already had the bones of half a dozen. Some more convoluted, some less so. He had designed a diving helmet, like a miniature bell, which should contain enough air to get him to open water, after that he could manually inflate a pig's bladder and swim to shore by night. To amass the materials for that plan would take five years, at the very least.

Five more years. Unbearable.

Conor redoubled his efforts, blinking the fog from his eyes, pressing his fingertips together until the shake subsided. The coronation was tonight, he must be ready.

CHAPTER 11:

TO THE QUEEN HER CROWN

The Saltee islanders were preparing for celebration. The British royal yacht, HMY *Victoria and Albert II*, a 360-foot paddle steamer, lolled regally in Fulmar Bay with the waves of Saint George's Channel tipping her gently like the fingers of a child on a rubber balloon. The queen herself was happily ensconced in one of the palace's sumptuous apartments. Her diary records that: *I find the air of industry in this miniature kingdom wonderfully exhilarating. Looking down from my balcony window at the commerce far below, one almost feels as though one has arrived in Swift's Lilliput.*

Almost every patch of Great Saltee's 200 acres had been appropriated for the celebrations. The South Summit was festooned with clusters of pikes decorated with crimson and gold flags. The streets of Promontory Fort were painted in the same coloured stripes. Every man with a hammer was banging in nails, and every man without one was hanging bunting from those nails. Even the weather gods were proving benevolent on the day, pouring down sunshine on the little principality, setting the waves dancing with sparkles. The southern cliffs lost some of their gloom, fringed in beards of white spume.

It seemed to the gentlemen of the world's press as though the kingdom of the Saltees was an oasis of calm amid the political consternation of Europe. They sat in seaside taverns in Fulmar Bay, boiling up their gullets with traditional spicy gull pancakes and cooling them off again with tankards of Irish stout. No journalists were permitted on Little Saltee, and none had been invited who might press the matter.

On the surface, happiness and contentment abounded, but as in many things the surface gave a treacherous reading. Many were unhappy in the kingdom. Taxes had been reintroduced, and heavy tithes on imports. Public services were so skimped on that they were almost non-existent, and residency had been granted to an assorted bunch of motley characters who were then spivved up and handed commissions in the Saltee Army, the best barracks too. Common scarred veterans most of them, landing on the port with clanking sacks of weapons. Bonvilain was filling his ranks with mercenaries and turning away raw recruits. Building his own private army many said, though the marshall claimed that he was merely protecting the princess from revolutionaries.

Captain Declan Broekhart would, once upon a time, have objected vehemently to Bonvilain's politics, but now he was too besieged by his own demons. Catherine Broekhart too was haunted by sadness, though she concealed it for the sake of their eighteen-month-old baby son, Sean.

Declan was consumed and ravaged by grief. He wore it like a coat. It was more a part of him now than his eyes and ears. It took his hunger and his strength. It ate away his girth and his stature. Declan Broekhart had grown old before his time.

Often Catherine would encourage him to fight his way clear of his dark mood.

'We have another son now, Declan. Young Sean needs his father.'

His answer was always a variation on the following:

'I am no father. Conor died at *my* post, doing *my* duty. My life is gone. Spent. I am a dead man still breathing.'

Declan Broekhart shunned close contact, eager for punishment. He grew tight-lipped and short-fused. He returned to his duties at the palace, but his manner had changed. Where before he had inspired devotion, now men obeyed him through fear. Declan worked his men hard, chastising honest soldiers who had been at his side for years. No dereliction of duty was left unpunished, however slight. Declan prowled the Great Saltee Wall at night, clothed entirely in black, searching for an inattentive sentry. He demoted soldiers, docked their pay and on one occasion had a watchman dismissed for nodding off in the guard hut.

This last was three days before the coronation, when Declan was at his most tense. When the news trickled through to him that the punished watchman was worn out with newborn twins and a wife still in her bed, Catherine believed her husband might come to his senses, but instead Declan Broekhart turned a degree colder.

Little Sean cried from the bedroom, his midday sleep disturbed.

Catherine wiped her eyes, so the baby would see her happy. 'Do you think Conor would want this?' she said, making one last attempt. 'Do you think he looks down from a hero's heaven and rejoices at what his father has become?'

Declan cracked, but he did not break. 'And what have I become, Catherine? Am I not still a man who fulfils his duties to the best of his abilities?'

Catherine's eyes blazed through the last of her tears. 'Those of *Captain* Broekhart, certainly. But *Declan* Broekhart, husband and father? As you say yourself, those duties have been neglected for some time now.'

With these harsh words Catherine left her husband to his brooding. When he was certain that she could no longer see him, Declan Broekhart clasped his hands on either side of his head, as though he could squeeze out the pain.

Declan had never recovered from Conor's supposed death, and perhaps he never would have, had two events not occurred one after the other on the day of Isabella's coronation. Alone, these events might not have been enough to raise him from his stupor, but together they complemented one another, shaking the lethargy from Declan Broekhart's bones.

The first was a simple thing. Common and quick, the kind of family happening that would not usually qualify as an event. But for Declan something in those few seconds warmed his heart and set him on the road to recovery. Later he would often wonder whether Catherine had engineered this little incident, or for that matter, the second one too. He questioned her often, but she would neither admit nor deny anything.

What happened was this. Little Sean came waddling from his room, unsteady on chubby legs. When Conor had been that age, Declan called his legs *fat sausages* and they rolled on the rug like a dog and its pup, but he hardly noticed Sean, leaving the rearing to Catherine.

'Papa,' said the infant, slightly disappointed that his mother was not to be seen. Papa ignored him. Papa was not a source of food or entertainment, and so little Sean toddled on towards the open bay window. The balcony was beyond, and then a low wrought-iron railing. Hardly enough to contain an inquisitive boy.

'Catherine,' called Declan, but his wife did not appear. Sean skirted a chair, teetering briefly to starboard, then on towards the window.

'Catherine. The boy. He's near the window.'

Still, no sign of or reply from Catherine, and now little Sean was at the sill itself, a pudgy foot raised to step over.

Declan had no choice but to act. With a grunt of annoyance he took the two strides necessary to reach the child. Not such a momentous undertaking, unless you consider that this was perhaps the fifth time that Declan Broekhart had set hands on his son. And at that exact moment the boy turned, pivoting on the ball of his heel, the way only the very young can, and Declan's fingers grazed Sean's cheek. Their eyes met and the boy reached up, tugging Declan's bottom lip.

The contact was magical. Declan felt a jolt run through his heart, as for the first time he saw Sean as himself and not a shadow of his dead brother.

'Oh, my son,' he said, hoisting him up and drawing him close. 'You must keep away from the window; it is dangerous. Stay here with me.'

Declan was halfway back to life. Perhaps he would have continued the journey in fits and jumps, an occasional shared smile, the odd bedtime story, but then there came a knocking on the front door. A series of raps, actually. Regal raps.

Before Declan had the chance to register the sounds, the door burst open and one of his own men stepped across the threshold, holding the door wide for Princess Isabella.

Declan was caught tenderly embracing his son, a most un-Broekhart-like action. He frowned twice, once for the soldier: a warning to keep this sight to himself. A second frown for Princess Isabella, who was clothed in full coronation robes. A vision in gold and crimson silk and satin, more beautiful than even her father could have dreamed. What could she be doing here? On this of all days?

Isabella opened her mouth to speak. The princess had her entreaty prepared. Declan had requested Wall duty for the ceremony, but she had needed him at her side, today of all days. She missed Conor and her father more than ever, and the only way she could get through the ceremony was if the man who she considered a *second* father was restored to her. And not simply in body, but in spirit. Today Declan Broekhart must remember the man he had been.

Quite a fine speech; obviously the girl would make a fine queen. However, no one heard the words, for the moment Isabella laid eyes on Declan cradling his son, her posture slumped from queen to girl and she flung herself at his chest weeping. Declan Broekhart had little option but to wrap his free arm around the weeping princess.

'There, there,' he said uncertainly. 'Now, now.'

'I need you,' sobbed Isabella. 'By my side. Always.'

Declan felt tears gather on his own eyelids. 'Of course, Majesty.'

Isabella thumped his broad chest with her delicate fist.

'I need *you*, Declan. *You.*'

'Yes, Isabella,' said Declan gruffly. 'By your side. Always.'

Catherine Broekhart stepped in from the balcony where she had been waiting, and joined the embrace. The guard at the door was tempted, but decided against it.

The coronation was a wordy affair, with clergy and velvet and enough Latin chanting to keep a monastery going for a few decades. It was all a bit of a blur to Declan Broekhart who installed himself behind his queen on the altar, so he could be there to smile encouragingly when she looked for him, which she did often.

Shortly after the papal nuncio lowered the crown, Declan noticed his wife's dress.

'A new dress?' he whispered. 'I thought we weren't coming?'

Catherine smiled archly. 'Yes, you did think that, didn't you.'

Declan felt a glow in his chest that he recognized as cautious happiness. It was a bittersweet emotion without Conor there at his shoulder.

They rode in the royal coach back from Saint Christopher's towards Promontory Fort, though in truth the town now covered almost every square foot of the island. As the population increased, houses grew up instead of out and were shoehorned into any available space. The higgledy-piggledy town reminded Declan of the Giant's Causeway, a chaotic honeycomb of basalt columns in the north of Ireland. Though these columns were marked by doors and windows and striped by the traditional bold house colours of the Saltee Islands. As for the islanders, it seemed they were all on the street along with half of Ireland, cheering themselves hoarse for the beautiful young queen.

The coach was shared with Marshall Bonvilain in full ceremonial uniform including a Knights of the Holy Cross toga worn loosely over it all. The Saltee Templars were the only branch to have survived Pope Clement V's fourteenth-century purge. Even the Vatican had been unwilling to risk disrupting the diamond supply.

Bonvilain took advantage of the new queen's distraction to lean across and whisper to Declan.

'How are you, Declan? I'm surprised to see you here.'

'As am I, Hugo,' replied Declan. 'I hadn't planned to come, but I am happy to find my plans changed.'

Bonvilain smiled. 'I am happy too. It does the men good to see your face. Keeps them alert. Nice work dismissing that sentry by the way. Sleeping sentries is just the opening the rebels need. One chink in the wall and they're in. And I needn't tell you the heartache they can cause.'

Declan nodded tightly, but in truth Bonvilain's speech seemed a little hollow on this day. There had been little rebel activity for many months, and some of the marshall's arrests had been made on the flimsiest of evidence.

Bonvilain noticed the captain's expression.

'You disagree, Declan? Surely not. After all the Broekharts have endured?'

Declan felt his wife's fingers close around his. He gazed past Isabella's shining face, through the window, over the heads of a hundred islanders and into the blue haze of sea and sky.

'I don't disagree, Marshall. I just need to think about something else today. My wife, and my queen, they need me. For today at least.'

'Of course,' said Bonvilain, his tone gracious, but his eyes were hard and his teeth were gritted behind his lips.

Broekhart recovers, he thought. *His scruples are already returning. How long before the dog bites his master?*

Hugo Bonvilain waved a gloved hand at the cheering citizens on the roadside.

Better not to take the chance. Perhaps it is time for a little blackmail. Declan Broekhart could not bear to lose his elder son a second time.

Little Saltee

Conor was ready for flight. His sewing was done. A double seam would have been better but there was not a strand of thread left. The device was as sound as it would ever be.

The sounds of revelries drifted across from the Great Saltee Wall. Singing, cheering, stamping of feet. A great coming together. A thousand faces flushed in the glow of the wall lamps. Conor imagined the crowds lined a dozen deep waiting for the great show of fireworks. It seemed as though the very prison walls shook, though a stretch of ocean separated prisoners from the party.

The buzz of coronation excitement had communicated itself through the prison, and many of the prisoners hooted through their windows or dragged tin cups across their barred windows.

Surprisingly perhaps, most of the inmates showed monarchist leanings in spite of their incarceration at Her Majesty's pleasure. A ragged chorus of 'Defend the Wall', the Saltee national anthem, bounced off the walls and under Conor's cell door.

He found himself humming along. It was strange to hear the words *King Nicholas* already replaced by *Queen Isabella*.

How could you believe Bonvilain's lies? Why did you not send for me, Isabella?

Confusion bred heat in his forehead and Conor felt the strength of it cloud his brain. His senses piled on top of one another. Sight, touch, smell. Grime in the wrinkles of his forehead. The cell door seemed to shake in its housing. Sweat, damp and worse from his cell. He closed his eyes, breathing deeply through his nose. One of Victor's tricks, brought back from the Orient.

Breathe in cold air, clear the mind.

Conor pushed thoughts of Isabella aside. Time now to concentrate. Billtoe's steps were on the flagstones outside. One last time through the checklist.

Mud on his back?

Yes. He could feel it crusting inside his collar. At last, a use for the damp wall. There is always a use for everything, Victor had told him. Even pain.

The device secured?

Conor reached round under his loose jacket, tugging at the rectangular pack concealed on his chest. The ropes groaned at his pull, but they were homemade and imperfect. Woven from raggy ends and cut-offs. Spliced together and daubed with candle wax.

The cuff peg?

Concealed in his palm. A jagged ivory cone, measured by pressing the cuffs' ratchet hard into his palm when Billtoe was removing them. The cuff peg was an old escapologist's trick, and would only work on a set of single-lock cuffs with some play in the bolts, but Billtoe's cuffs were old enough to have belonged to Moses, and Conor had been yanking at the bolts for half a year now. There was enough play. When Billtoe slapped the cuffs on, Conor would quickly plug the hole with the ivory peg. The ratchet would be deflected while appearing to close.

Mud, devices, pegs! This plan was lunacy.

And as such could never be anticipated. Conor stepped on his uncertainty with a harsh boot. There was not the time now. His plan would liberate him, or kill him, and both were preferable to more long years in this hell pit.

Billtoe's key clanked into the ancient lock, turning with some effort. The guard shouldered the door open, complaining as usual, but with one cautious hand on his pistol.

'An angel is what I am, sticking it out with you clods, when a man like me would be welcomed into any discerning society in the world. I could be a prince, you know, Finn. An emperor, darn it. But here I stays, so that you can tell me my twelve-shot revolver is not ready yet.'

'It is ready,' blurted Conor, playing the excited, eager-to-please prisoner. 'I have the plan here.'

Billtoe was canny enough to be suspicious. Lesser brains would have lost the run of themselves and the price of their distraction would be a stove-in skull, but Arthur Billtoe's prime instinct was self-preservation.

'Where, exactly now, would that plan be? I won't be doing any bending over, or fumbling in shadows.'

'No. Lying on the table. Shall I hand it to you?'

Billtoe cogitated. Coughing up a lump of recently swallowed rations for a re-chew.

'No, soldier boy. How's about I cuff you as per usual, then have a little look-see at the plan myself.'

Conor extended his hands, happy to comply. 'Do I get my walks, Mister Billtoe? You promised I would.'

Billtoe smiled as he clamped on the cuffs, one eye on the table.

'It's your beard that has me grinning. A pathetic shrub. It ain't ready for growing yet. You ought to trim it back, thicken it up. The Rams ain't going to be ordered to by some runt with a bare gorse on his chin. And we'll talk about *walks* after I have a good study of this drawing.'

Billtoe plucked the page from the table with two grubby fine-boned fingers.

'You know, I've been talking to a few mates. Apparently there's a German makes twelve-shot revolvers.' He spat a stream of tobacco juice on the flags, to show his displeasure.

'But small calibre,' argued Conor. 'To accommodate the bullets. With this design the cylinder is actually a screw, so the bullets can be as big as you wish, and the weight is spread out more efficiently so it will work for rifles too.'

The design was preposterous and utterly unworkable, but looked pretty on paper.

'I don't know,' grumbled Billtoe. 'A screw, you say?'

'Have one made. Like the balloons. Do a test.'

Billtoe folded the page roughly, stuffing it into a pocket.

'That I will, Master Finn. And if this turns out to be a scatterfool's daydream, the next time you see daylight will be on the day I toss you from the south wall.'

Conor nodded glumly, hoping his excitement did not shine from his forehead like the Hook Head lighthouse.

Billtoe had made a mistake. In his eagerness to see the revolver plan, he hadn't noticed Conor's sleight of hand, plugging the Bell and Bolton handcuffs, diverting the ratchet to one side. His hands were free, but it was not yet time to make use of this.

'This is no daydream, Mister Billtoe. This is our future. You can register the patent, then perhaps pay a few bribes to get me out of here.'

Billtoe feigned great indignance. 'Bribes! Bribes, you say. I am deeply offended.'

Conor swallowed, a man holding his nerve. 'Let's speak plain, Mister Billtoe. I am in this hole for life, unless you can pull me out of it. I'm not expecting freedom right away . . .'

Billtoe chuckled. 'I am relieved to hear it. *The pressure is on*, says I to meself. *Immediate freedom or no deal*. But you're not expecting freedom, so there's a worry lifted.'

'But I would dearly love a cell on the surface. Or near it. Maybe a mate to share with. Malarkey would be suitable, I think.'

'I bet he would. Lovely and cosy, all Rams together. No wheedling now, Finn. First I have the model made, and when it doesn't explode in my face, then we parley.'

'But, Mister —'

Billtoe held up a flat hand.

'No. Not a word more, soldier boy. Your balloons have not taken flight yet. I may be coming for you in the morning with a Fenian pike.'

Conor hung his head in defeat, in reality hoping he had not overplayed his role. The entire revolver notion was merely misdirection, any magician's meat and potatoes. Fill Billtoe's mind with notions so that he would be less attuned to what was unfolding in front of his eyes.

'Now, let's be off to work. Well, work for you. I'm off topside to supervise your . . . *my* . . . coronation balloons.'

Conor sidled past Billtoe, through the doorway, careful to keep his mud-caked back on the guard's blind side. His plan was a house of cards, a *citadel* of cards. One unlucky glance could bring the entire structure down.

No time for that now. Begin your count.

His count. Another largely theoretical card in the citadel. Conor had long since discovered that there was a blind spot in the corridor between his cell door and the diving-bell wing. One of the mad wing's occupants had been in front of him six months previously on the walk to the warden's weekly speech. The man was tiny with a disproportionately large head, especially the forehead, which sat atop his eyebrows like a porcelain slug. It was the man Billtoe had called Numbers, because inside his strange head, everything was reduced to mathematics, the purest science. He would spout long streams of digits, and then laugh as though he were watching cabaret in Paris.

On that morning, half a year ago, Conor had watched the man lope down the line before him, muttering his numbers, measuring his steps.

Fourteen was the last in his list.

Then Numbers took a sideways hop, and disappeared.

No. Not disappeared, but certainly not as visible. There, in sudden black shadows, shaking with mirth at his own joke. A joke that could see him hanged.

Numbers held his position until Pike noticed him missing, then hopped from his hiding place.

'Fourteen,' he exclaimed in a screeching shriek. 'Fourteen, eighty-five, one half.'

Pike did not get the joke, proceeding to cuff Numbers round the ear hole several times.

There were no more demonstrations from Numbers, but Conor learned quickly. He had seen the trick once and set about dissecting it.

How do you unravel a magician's secret?

Start at the reveal and work backwards.

There was a natural blind spot in the corridor, something

magicians and escapologists created artificially on stage with lights, drapes or mirrors. A tiny spot of isolated darkness, surrounded by stimuli that drew the eye. A patch of near invisibility. It would not stand up to any scrutiny, but for a second in frenzied circumstances it would do.

For the next few weeks, Conor watched the space and analysed the numbers.

Fourteen, eighty-five, one half.

It was no deep code. Numbers had taken fourteen steps from his cell door along the path, then hopped half a step, eighty-five degrees to the right. Into the belly of the blind spot. Conor simply added the five steps necessary to find the spot for himself.

Once there, he was amazed by how obvious it was. Overlapping layers of shadow, untouched by torchlight, further shaded by a slipped cornice stone, with a spume of spilled crimson paint on the flagstones a foot to the left. A cylinder of blackness that would take no more than a heartbeat to pass through. But, once inside, it formed a cloak of near invisibility that could be enhanced by further misdirection.

Billtoe walked beside him, muttering about his lack of respect for his superiors.

Twelve.

'And the warden? Don't talk to me about the warden. That man makes decisions that boggle the mind. Too much time in the Indian sun if you ask me. Blooming Calcutta fried his mind.'

Fifteen.

'The money the man wastes. The cash money. It makes my

heart sick. I fair feel ill just talking about it, even to a Salt.'

Nineteen.

Billtoe clicked his fingers at Conor, meaning stop where you are.

Now comes the vital moment. All strands converge. Live or die on this instant.

Billtoe stepped to the wing door, tinging the bell with his fingernail. No response for a long moment, then a familiar mocking voice from the spy hole above.

'Ah, Billtoe. Is it out, you want? From the mad wing? Are you certain sure that's the right direction?'

Billtoe's posture stiffened. A dozen times a day he had to endure this ribbing.

'Can you not simply open a bolt, Murphy? Turn the wheel and lift the bolt, that is all I require from you.'

'Sure I know it's all you require, Arthur. The rest is free, a little daily gift. I am the funny fairy, dropping little lumps of humour on your head.'

Six feet up, the wheel was turned and bolt lifted. The door to the mad wing swung open.

'If I could put in words how much I hate that man,' muttered Billtoe, turning. 'Then Shakespeare himself could kiss my . . .'

The final word of Billtoe's sentence turned to dust in his dry throat because his prisoner had disappeared. Vanished into the air.

Not my prisoner, thought Arthur Billtoe. *Marshall Bonvilain's. I am a dead man.*

*

While Billtoe stood glaring skywards into the spy hole, Conor found himself rooted to the spot. He had imagined this moment so often that it seemed unreal to him now, as though it could never really materialize. In his mind's eye he saw himself confidently putting his plan into action, but the flesh-and-bone Conor Finn stayed where he was. One and a half steps to the left of the corridor's blind spot.

Then Billtoe began his turn, and Conor's life to come flashed before him. Five more decades under night and water until his skin was leeched of all colour and his eyes were those of a tunnel rat.

Act! he told himself. *It is a good plan.*

And so he acted in an exhaustively practised series of movements. Conor took a pace and a half to his right, spun round so his muddied back faced Billtoe and tossed his open handcuffs into the grate of the nearest sealed chimney. The rattle drew Billtoe's eyes away from the blind spot.

'Stupid boy,' he groaned. 'He's gone up the spouts.'

The guard hurried past Conor, who huddled camouflaged in his hiding place, his brown jacket blending effectively with the corridor walls. Billtoe kicked the grate angrily, then bent low to holler up the chimney.

'Come down from there, halfwit. They are sealed, all of 'em. The only thing you'll find up the spouts are the mouldering remains of other scatterfools.'

There was no response, but Billtoe imagined he heard a rustle.

'Aha!' he shouted. 'Your clumsiness betrays you. Down now, Finn, or I will discharge my weapon. Do not doubt it.'

Conor moved like a prowling cat, stealing sideways to the open wing door. He must not reveal himself. This plan would only succeed if nobody worked out that he was gone. To be spotted now would mean a brief chase and a long time recovering from whatever beating the guards decided to dish out. He edged beneath the spy hole, searching for a face. There was none, just the tip of a boot and the lower curve of a cauldron stomach.

Conor slipped across the door saddle, and the closeness of freedom sent him light-headed. He almost bolted for the outer door. Almost. But one stumble now could kill him. It was so close, tantalizing. Only a dark wedge of stained wood separated him from the outside world.

The door opened and two guards strolled through, sharing a snide sniggering joke.

I will have to kill them, decided Conor. *It will be easily done. Snag the first's dagger and gut them both. I can make a run for the balloons.*

He flexed his fingers slowly, getting ready for the lunge, but it wasn't necessary. The guards simply did not see him; they turned towards the mining wing without once pointing an eyeball his way.

I could have murdered them, realized Conor. *I was ready to strike.*

Even this thought could not delay him for long. Little Saltee guards were not to be seen as normal people. They were cruel gaolers, who would gladly toss him from the highest turret into the maws of the sharks that patrolled the waste pipes.

Conor moved quickly, feeling that his store of good fortune was depleting rapidly, and slipped through the outer doorway as soon as the guards had rounded the corner. He found himself at the foot of a narrow stairway with a rectangular patch of starred night at its end. Twelve steps from open air.

This was the blurred section of his plan. From here to the balloons was unknown territory. He had some memory of his admission to the prison, and Malarkey had educated him in the set-up as much as he could, but prisoners did not climb these stairs, neither did they patrol the wall. He must trust to his wits, and whatever luck was left in the bottom of the barrel.

I will surely fail if I stay here, he thought, mounting the steps two at a time.

Salty air washed over him as he emerged into the darkness, and its tang almost made him cry. Of course there had been air in his cell, but this was pure and fresh, untainted by the smell of offal and sweat.

I had forgotten how sweet the sea air is. Bonvilain took this from me.

He was two steps below ground level now. A low stone wall shielding him from the main courtyard. It seemed smaller than he remembered, barely more than a walled yard. Two aproned butchers worked on a hanging pig carcass on the diagonal corner. They sliced fatty strips of meat from the haunches, rinsing them thoroughly in a water bucket, pushing their thumbs into the folds of flesh, rivulets of blood dripping from their elbows. Conor found himself lost in the image, a sight that he had missed without knowing it. Honest labour. Life and death.

An explosion boomed overhead and swathes of multicoloured sparks rained from the sky. Conor ducked low, then saw that the explosion was of his own design. They were igniting the coronation balloons.

Too early. Too early. It is not yet fully dark.

One of the butchers swore from shock, then caught himself, made a joke of it.

'Good thing that pig is dead. The fright would have done for him.'

The second, a smaller man, pulled the kerchief from across his nose.

'To hell with this, Tom. I'm going up on the walls. I don't care what the warden says.'

The other butcher, Tom, pulled down his own kerchief. 'You know what? You're right. The lass is our queen too. Let the warden eat half an hour past due. It's not as if he hasn't got enough lard stored away to be getting on with.'

The butchers shared a laugh and hung their aprons on a fence post.

A second balloon exploded, releasing a swarm of dancing golden sparks.

'Oh, the Saltee Sharpshooters are earning their pay tonight. Look lively now.'

The butchers left their work, skipping sharply up steep stone steps to the crenellated battlements above, leaving the courtyard deserted apart from the prisoner concealing himself in the stairwell. A third balloon exploded, casting stark shadows from the wall, lighting night like a photographer's phosphorous flash.

Three gone, thought Conor. *Three already. Too early.*

He scrambled up into the courtyard, improvising a plan as he went. All the months of plotting fell apart in front of his eyes. Timing was everything, and it was all wrong. He skirted the walls, casting furtive glances to the battlements. There were a few soldiers, but most would be on the far side, enjoying the spectacle. And the lee of the wall was made all the darker by the shocks of light from the fireworks. Anyone who had looked directly at them would be without night vision for several moments.

This is all wrong, thought Conor, snatching a butcher's apron from the fence post. *I am supposed to have at least an hour to figure out how the balloons are tied. Billtoe thinks I have bolted up the chimney, so no one will be searching for me out of doors. I should not be harried in this way.*

But harried he was, and there was little point wasting seconds rebelling against it. Every second wasted could see another nitroglycerine bullet on the way to its target.

Conor found a bloody kerchief in the apron's pocket and tied it across his nose, then took another second to thrust his hands and forearms into the pig's belly, greasing them with blood and gore. A butcher now, to his fingertips.

The nearest stairwell was the one recently mounted by the butchers, so Conor ignored it, boldly crossing to the western wall. He ambled slowly, imitating butcher Tom's bow-legged gait.

He was not challenged. Nobody saw, or nobody knew.

There was a wooden gate at the foot of the stairway, but it was fastened with a simple latch, more to stop it flapping than with a mind for security. Conor pushed through, and up the stairs with him, boots crunching on sand and salt.

A guard stood above, his heels half moons on the top step, rocking gently with the brass music drifting across from Great Saltee. Conor had no choice but to disturb him, edging past with muttered apologies.

'God, you're dripping blood, Tom,' said the guard. 'This is a coronation not a battlefield. Don't let the warden smell you on the upper level stinking like that. He has a delicate stomach, though you wouldn't know it from the size of him.'

Conor faked a convincing enough chuckle, then threaded his way through the throng of guards and staff piled on to the battlements. There were women here too, dressed in coronation finery. All the fashions of the day, Conor supposed, outrageous bodices and leg-of-mutton sleeves.

There are too many people. The warden was throwing a party. Best seats in the islands. This was not a part of my calculations. The wall should be clear for safety reasons. I told Billtoe. I told him.

The Little Saltee parapet walkway was ten feet wide, with a chest-high open gorge wall on the ocean side, and a sheer drop to the main bailey on the other. A rope had been strung along between posts to stop the drunken gentry from stumbling to their deaths. Conor recognized several guards serving drinks, dressed as prisoners in immaculate blue serge overalls. Obviously the warden was hoping to discredit the rumours of unChristian treatment of the inmates. These prisoners were so well treated that they could be trusted to pass out champagne and plates of hors d'oeuvres. There was not a nook or gap without a clay brazier stuck in it, baking skewers of shrimp and lobster for the guests to pluck at. Nowhere for an escaping prisoner to crouch and catch his breath.

Conor wiped the fine mist of salt spray from his face. The mist. He had forgotten that too. How could an islander forget the mist? One more thing on Bonvilain's account. Worth a few diamonds surely, if Conor had the luck of the devil and managed to cast himself off from this cursed island.

Another balloon exploded, followed a second later by a dozen interlaced swirls of crimson and gold sparks. The Saltee colours. Very amusing for the watching crowd. The sparks flitted to earth in showers casting their light on the waters below, some held their energy until a wave folded over them, like a child catching a star.

A few sparks had the audacity to land on the wall, singeing expensive silk dresses. A great tragedy indeed.

I told him, thought Conor, not unhappy with this development. *It is not safe here.*

A genteel panic spread through the audience. Champagne glasses were tossed into the sea along with seafood platters, as moneyed folk hurried to the various stairways, preferring not to be set afire by low-flying fireworks.

Pandemonium. Good.

Conor moved against the tide towards the next balloon, reaching for the stout rope fastening it to a brass ring on the battlements. Across the sound Great Saltee was a riot of lights and music. Brass-band tunes thumped across the water, echoing on itself, arriving in waves. There were so many torches and lanterns that the entire island seemed to be ablaze.

His fingers grazed the rope and a second later felt it slacken as the balloon exploded.

Conor swore and quickened his pace. Only six balloons left. He barged through the assembly, caring nothing for angry looks. If any of these gentlemen wished to fight a duel over a rough shouldering, he would have to oblige them another time.

Shouts and protests followed him down the path. He was attracting attention but there was no helping it.

It was a race now. Conor versus the Saltee Sharpshooters. He could only hope that his own father was not holding a rifle as Declan Broekhart rarely missed.

The next balloon detonated, the concussion seeming to shake the very island.

Overloaded that one. Surely.

There were four balloons aloft now and a fifth anchored on the quay wall under a tarpaulin. The moving target. The flying balloons glowed bright like the moons of some distant planet. They bobbed in the wind, difficult shots.

Not difficult enough, two more exploded in quick succession. Conor could hear the applause from Great Saltee. A grand affair indeed.

He made a decision. No time to rein in the flying balloons, he must go for the earthbound. It would be watched by a guard, but that must be risked. It was his last chance in this night of botched plans.

His way was clear now, so Conor ran, butcher's apron flapping around his legs, the smell of pig blood hot in his nostrils. A guard blocked his way, not intentionally; he was simply there on duty. Conor thought to barge him from the wall, but at the last second changed his mind and ran him into the battlements instead. A sore head was preferable to a crushed skull.

The wall was more or less deserted. High society can move at a pretty pace when their fine garments are under attack. All that stood between Conor and the last balloon was a courtesy rope and another guard who was actually sucking on a lit pipe.

A lit pipe beside a hydrogen balloon.

'Hello!' called Conor. 'You there! Guard.'

The guard stood, eyes round with a natural doziness.

'Sir. Yessir. What can I . . . Who do you be?'

Conor leaped the rope with no slowing of his pace. His boots clicked on the uneven cobbles as he hurried towards the guard. The quay wall ran a hundred yards into Saint George's Channel, acting as a breakwater and a semaphore station.

'You are smoking, man!' shouted Conor, in a voice of authority. 'There is hydrogen in that balloon.'

The guard paled, and then yelped as another balloon burst into multicoloured flames. The rope sagged slowly to earth like a beheaded snake.

'I . . . I didn't know . . .' he stammered, tossing his pipe away as though it would bite him. 'I never thought . . .'

Conor cuffed the man roughly, knocking off his hat.

'Idiot. Buffoon. I smell a leak. And you have put sparks on the ground.'

More stammering from the guard, but not one protest that hydrogen was an odourless gas.

'I must . . . I must . . . run away,' he said, tossing his rifle aside, so that the bayonet raked the cobbles, throwing up more sparks.

'Dolt,' said Conor.

'I didn't even want the bayonet,' whined the guard. 'It's ceremonial.'

'We must cut the balloon loose,' said Conor.

'You do it. I will commend you for a medal.'

And with that the guard launched himself into space, legs running through the air until they found purchase on a group of rich gawkers in the keep below. The lot of them went down in a pile like skittles.

Conor was alone with the balloon for the moment, but already there were more astute guards mounting the steps, perhaps wondering why a butcher was handing out orders. Conor twisted the bayonet from the rifle, no time to struggle with knots now. He pulled back the greasy tarpaulin to find a glowing balloon encased in a fishing net and tethered to several lobster pots.

Conor held the balloon with his left hand, sawing at the ropes with his right, careful not to puncture the balloon itself.

'Tom,' called a voice to his rear. 'What are you playing at, Tom? That's the entire show's climax, that is.'

'She's ruptured,' shouted Conor. 'And the fuse has caught a spark. I can hear it buzzing. Stand back.'

So, like prudent guards who were paid less than your average street hawker, they stood back for a few moments, but then nothing much happened except a butcher hacking at ropes.

'Eh, Tom. There's a two-second fuse on those yokes. You shouldn't be much more than a smear of butcher-coloured mush on the walls by now.'

'Oh my God,' shouted Conor over his shoulder, seeking to spread alarm. 'God help us all.'

Pike was one of the guards, and he was all too aware that Billtoe would lump him with responsibility for the balloon, and so forged past the others up the steps.

'Stop what you're doing, butcher,' he called, in a voice quavering with fear and forced courage. 'Cease or I will spill your innards on the stones.' He hoped the word *cease* would lend him more authority than he possessed.

The last strand of the last rope pinged and the balloon lurched towards the heavens, almost yanking Conor's left arm from his socket. He would have let go, had he not tangled the arm in the netting up to the elbow.

'Help me,' he shouted, knowing they could never reach him in time. 'Save me, please.'

Pike thought about shooting the balloon down, but decided against it for two reasons. If his bullet did ignite the fireworks he could kill himself and the several daring minor European royals who had wanted a closer view of the spectacle. Death by whizz-bang was not a pleasant way to go. And even if he survived the fireworks, Billtoe would use his head for a boot polisher.

Better to take a shot and miss completely. He hoisted his rifle, taking careless aim.

'You've had your warning, butcher!' he yelled, pulling the trigger.

Unfortunately Pike was a terrible shot, and his deliberate miss took the heel from Conor's boot.

'Halfwit,' shouted Conor, then a gust of easterly wind caught the balloon and snatched him away.

The guards watched him go, slack-jawed and befuddled. It was obvious what had happened, but how exactly? And why? Did the man steal the balloon or did the balloon make off with the man?

Pike was struck by the strange beauty of the scene.

'Look at that,' he sighed. 'Just like the fairy wot caught hold of the moon.'

And then, on remembering Billtoe, 'Stupid butcher.'

Great Saltee

The Saltee islanders were genuinely happy. Now that Good King Nick's girl had taken her place on the throne, things could go back to the way they had been. Queen Isabella would set matters straight. She was a good girl, a kind girl – had she not demonstrated it a hundred times? Shipping supplies to the Irish poor. Sending the palace masons into town to work on village houses. That girl remembered the name of everyone she met, and would often visit the hospital to welcome new babies to the island.

It was true that Isabella had faded since her father's assassination. Losing Conor Broekhart had compounded her pain. No father and no shoulder to cry on. But now her grieving was done and Captain Declan Broekhart was by her side, proud as punch, for the entire island to see.

This was a day for celebration, no doubt about it. The only one wearing a sour expression was that old goat Bonvilain, but he hadn't smiled in public since Chancellor Bismarck tripped over the church steps on a state visit in the late seventies.

Isabella was queen now and Captain Broekhart was himself again. Soon there would be no more taxes, and no more innocents hauled off to Little Saltee on trumped-up charges. No more mercenaries landing on the docks with their rattling haversacks and cruel eyes.

The coronation ceremony had proceeded without a hitch. Isabella's insistence that the dinner seating be rearranged to accommodate the Broekharts had ruffled a few noble feathers, but the young monarch would not be put off. Declan and Catherine had sat on her left for the entire day, with Queen Victoria on the right. Marshall Bonvilain had been forced to shuffle down two seats at the first table and was not best pleased. Not that he cared a jot where he sat, but Catherine Broekhart had been whispering into Isabella's ear for the entire day, and he had never liked that woman. Too political for her own good.

Bonvilain sulked through the meal, complaining that the wine was tepid and the soup too salty. The lobster shell, he declared, was far too brittle.

Even Sultan Arif, a Turkish mercenary who had been with Bonvilain for more than fifteen years and risen to the position of captain, raised an eyebrow at this.

'A Templar concerned for the state of his lobster?' he said. 'You have been at court too long, Marshall.'

Bonvilain calmed himself. Sultan was the closest thing he had to a friend, though he would have him murdered without remorse if it ever became necessary. Arif was the only man in the kingdom brave enough to speak plainly.

'It's not just the lobster,' he said, nodding towards Declan Broekhart.

'Ah, yes. The lapdog remembers that he is actually a guard dog.'

'Exactly,' said Bonvilain, happy with Sultan's imagery.

Sultan tossed a stripped chicken bone on to his plate. 'In Turkey, if a guard dog turns on its master, then we simply slit the beast's stomach.'

Bonvilain smiled at the idea. 'You can always cheer me up, Captain. But this particular dog is very popular, as is his mistress. We must consider this problem carefully.'

Sultan nodded. 'But don't rule out my solution.'

Bonvilain stood, as a toast was proposed to the new queen.

'No,' he whispered to Sultan Arif. 'I never rule out stomach slitting.'

Sultan smiled, but his eyes were cold. Every season, he

promised himself that he would leave this madman and return to Ushak. In fact, Bonvilain was barely a man any more. He was the devil. And sooner or later the devil destroyed everything in his reach. It was his nature.

After the coronation dinner, the official celebrations began, though for the 3,000 Saltee islanders and more than 6,000 visitors, the celebrations had been in full swing since the moment the papal nuncio laid the ermine-trimmed crown on Isabella's head.

There was a strong army presence on the street. No one below the rank of lieutenant had been given leave to enjoy the coronation. In fact, Bonvilain had borrowed a company from the English General, Eustace Fitzmorris, stationed in Dublin, and paid handsomely for the privilege. An extra 130 troops with instructions not to tolerate verbal abuse or public drunkenness and to keep a special eye out for Frenchmen acting suspiciously.

There was a carnival atmosphere as Queens Isabella and Victoria mounted the dais outside the palace at Promontory Fort. The citizens congregated in Promontory Square, and listened raptly as the new queen delivered her first royal address.

Bonvilain could not fail to notice that she squeezed Catherine Broekhart's hand for courage throughout.

Sultan leaned in to comment. 'A fine speech,' he said. 'I especially liked the phrases *tax revision* and *political amnesty.*'

Bonvilain made no reply. He was beginning to wonder if he had miscalculated by allowing Isabella to live. He *had* supposed she would be easily manipulated, and until now she had been. Also, he needed an undisputed heir on the throne. It would be most inconvenient if a dozen or so gold-digging pretenders landed at Saltee Harbour with a family tree rolled up under their arms, and their own agenda for the Saltee diamonds. Great Britain and of course France would be delighted to see political uncertainty in the Saltees — it could be just the excuse they needed to step in and support a new order. This was Bonvilain's kingdom, but he needed a figurehead to keep him in power.

No, Hugo Bonvilain decided. Isabella needed to live, at least until she provided an heir to rule after her. Then there would be an unfortunate accident. In the royal yacht perhaps.

Sultan spoke again. 'Ah, you're smiling. In public too.'

'Thinking pleasant thoughts,' said Bonvilain, waving a jolly wave down the line at Declan Broekhart.

Declan Broekhart was on the verge of enjoying himself, though every time a smile tugged at his lips, it was accompanied by a twinge of guilt as he remembered his dead son.

What were you doing in the palace, Conor? How could I have put you in that man's care?

It was still difficult to believe how easily Victor Vigny had fooled them all. Catherine had refused to believe that Vigny was a spy and assassin, until a search of his quarters revealed a trunk of weapons and poisons, detailed plans of the Saltee defences and a letter from an unnamed author threatening to kill Vigny's family unless he obeyed his orders.

Catherine saw her husband's eyes cloud over, and realized she was losing him to memories.

'Isn't this fabulous, Declan,' she said, stroking her husband's hand. 'Isabella is queen. A great day for the islands.'

'Hmm,' said Declan. 'Those English soldiers are a disgrace. Ruffians, every last one of them. I wouldn't be surprised if Fitzmorris cleaned out his prisons. Look at them, unshaven, slouching ne'er-do-wells.'

'Your sharpshooters look well enough.'

'Yes, they do,' said Declan, proud in spite of himself.

A dozen of his men stood on the Great Saltee Wall across the square, level with the top step of the dais. They were buffed, brushed and smart in their dress uniforms, gold epaulettes winking in the lamplight. They seemed almost like identical toy soldiers but for one thing – each carried his own distinctive rifle. Most were Sharps, but there were a couple of Remingtons, an Enfield and even some modified guns. The sharpshooters were the best marksmen on the islands, and it had always been army custom to allow these elite soldiers the weapon of their choice.

One of Isabella's aides passed a folded note to Declan. He read it quickly, then sighed, relieved that there was no emergency.

'Queen Victoria is tired,' he explained to his wife. 'But she would like to see the balloons before she retires to the royal yacht.'

Catherine smiled. '*Everyone* wants to see these balloons,

Declan. Fireworks balloons, what an ingenious idea. Nitro-glycerine bullets, I imagine.'

'You are right, as usual,' said Declan, thinking, *Conor would have adored this. It's just the kind of harebrained scheme he would have come up with himself.* 'It's a little early for the full effect. Not yet fully dark.'

Catherine pinched his shoulder. 'Away with you to your men, husband. This is not a day for disappointing queens.'

'Or wives for that matter,' said Declan, with a rare smile.

Declan moved easily across the square. Even the biggest braggarts and drunkards stepped smartly out of his path. It did not do to trifle with an officer of the Wall with a Saltee Sharphooters' badge on his shoulder. Especially Declan Broekhart, who didn't have much use for life since a rebel took his son.

His men were waiting on the Wall, faces sweating above stiff collars and below hard hats.

'Not long to go, boys,' said Declan, digging deep inside himself to find the spring of camaraderie that once flowed freely. 'A pint of Guinness for every man who finds the target.' He peered across the sound at the glowing balloons straining on their leashes, nearly a mile away in half darkness. 'Make that two pints of Guinness.'

'Now you're talking,' muttered one brave lieutenant, a skinny Kilmore man whose father had served on the Wall before him.

Captain Broekhart grunted. 'She's all yours, Bates.'

Bates leaned a modified Winchester on the battlements, flicking up his sights.

'Your own barrel?' asked his captain.

'Yessir,' said the sharpshooter. 'Had it bored special, and added three inches to the length. Keeps the bullet on the straight for another hundred yards or so.'

Declan was impressed. 'A neat trick, Lieutenant. Where did you pick that up?'

'You, sir,' said Bates, and pulled the trigger.

It was a long shot. Long enough that they heard the gunshot before the bullet hit its mark. The glowing globe exploded in a riotous ball of Chinese sparks.

'Two pints to me,' said Bates, grinning.

Declan groaned ruefully. 'I shall be a poor man before the night is out.'

He turned to wave across the square at Catherine. She was on her feet applauding, as was everyone on the dais, including the normally stern Queen Victoria. Isabella, who had not yet got the hang of royal decorum, was hooting with delight.

Declan turned to his men.

'It looks like you boyos are to be the heroes of the night. So, who will be the next to take beer from me?'

A dozen rifles were instantly cocked.

Conor flew up so fast, it felt as though he were falling down. None of his calculations could have prepared him for the sheer chaos of his flight. He'd entertained notions of a brisk elevation, but calm and steady, with time to collect his thoughts and observe his surroundings. In short, master of the situation.

But this was a waking nightmare. Of all the elements in this equation, Conor had least control. There was wind in his face, blasting across his eyeballs, stuffing into his ears. He was deafened and almost blind. His arm was strained to the limits of muscle and bone, and finally with a violent gust of wind, nature casually dislocated Conor's shoulder. The pain was a white-hot hammer blow that spread across his upper chest.

I have failed. I cannot escape alive. Just let me lose consciousness and wake in Paradise.

This class of fatalistic thought was not normal for Conor, but these were extraordinary circumstances.

It seemed as though his arm would be ripped away utterly, and when this did not happen, his keen senses sliced through the fog of pain and pandemonium which enveloped him.

The balloon was gaining height, but its acceleration had slowed, and the air currents were calmer at this particular altitude. Conor knew he had to make any observations he could during this lull.

Altitude? Perhaps fifteen hundred feet. Drifting towards Great Saltee.

The islands shone below him like diamonds in the foreboding sea. Hundreds of lamps bobbed on the decks of visiting crafts, anchored off Saltee Harbour. Stars above and below.

He must separate from the balloon now. He was lower than he would like, but the wind was taking him out to sea faster than he'd calculated, and with his injured shoulder, Conor would be pressed to keep himself afloat for any length of time.

It was vital that Conor disentangle his arm from the netting, but he found that even a simple act such as finding one hand with the other was almost impossible in this situation. Pain, disorientation and wind shear would make normal motor functions a challenge for a man at peak physical condition, not to mention an injured and exhausted convict.

He had no control over joints or fingers, and the pain now seemed to come from his heart. Conor had dropped the bayonet and was forced to tug at the netting with fumbling fingers. It was impossible. His arm was wrapped up snugger than a turkey in an ice box. Conor Finn was ocean bound. His only hope was that the balloon was badly made and would pop its seams in the next minute.

Below him, the second from last balloon exploded, turning a black sky gold and red for a moment before the darkness reclaimed the night.

Perfect, thought Conor, smiling numbly. *It worked perfectly. High-class fireworks. Holding their light for several seconds. What a pity I am not suspended below that balloon, instead of stranded in the night sky.*

In his original plan he would be suspended far below one of the balloons when the Sharpshooters shot it down. The balloon would lift him free from the prison, then a bullet would bring him back to earth.

He wondered absently if he was the first person to see fireworks from above. Probably not. No doubt some intrepid aeronaut had sent up a balloon on an anchor.

A thought struck Conor.

I am flying as no man has flown before. No basket, no ballast. Just a man and his balloon.

And, somehow, this thought gave him some comfort in spite of his dire situation. He was alone in the skies, the only man here. Breathing rarefied air, blue-black expanse on all sides. No walls. No prison door.

Where will they find me? Wales? France? Or, if the wind changes, Ireland? What will they make of the device on my chest? My innovations?

Conor felt a measure of triumph too.

I have defeated you, Bonvilain. You will not use me, or torture me at your leisure. I am free.

There was also regret.

Mother. Father. Never an opportunity to explain.

But even in this mortal danger, Conor harboured a touch of bitterness.

How could you believe Bonvilain, Father? Why haven't you saved me?

The Coronation Balloons were a tremendous success, drawing huge applause with every successful pop. The sharpshooters were putting on a great show, with only Keevers missing his mark, and even then only because his nitroglycerine bullet exploded in the barrel, buckling his weapon like a rye-grass drinking straw.

Those firework boys were clever blighters, Declan had to admit. Each balloon was a bigger bang than the last, all carefully sequenced. The last one had shaken the very Wall itself. If Queen Isabella wasn't careful she might lose her crown.

Catherine looked beautiful tonight, up there beside her queen. She looked beautiful every night, but he hadn't noticed for a while. For two years in fact.

Conor would want his mother to be happy, perhaps his father too.

'Excuse me, sir.'

It was Bates. No doubt looking for his Guinness.

'A minute, Bates. I'm having a moment here. Thinking about my wife. You should try it instead of harassing a superior officer for beer.'

'No, sir, it's not the Guinness, though I haven't forgotten it.'

'What then?' said Declan, trying to hold on to his good mood.

'The moving target. The big finale, sir. They've let 'er up too early. Not my fault is all I'm saying. No one could hit that target. Must be over a mile, and the sea breeze has got her.'

Declan gazed across the square at Catherine. Glowing she was, and he knew why. Maybe her husband was coming home, at last. She needed a sign.

He held out his hand to Bates. 'Give me your weapon, Sharpshooter.'

As soon as Declan's fingers wrapped around the stock, he knew he would make the shot. It was fate. Tonight was the night.

'Is she ready?'

'Yes sir. One in the saddle, ready for the off. Little jerky on the recoil – hope your shoulder hasn't gone soft. You being a captain and so forth.'

Declan grunted. Bates had a mouth on him and no denying it. Any other night and the young lieutenant would be slopping out the latrines.

'Target?'

'Big glowing ball in the sky, sir.'

'Your sense of self-preservation should be all a-tingle right now, Bates.'

Bates coughed. 'Yessir, I mean, target eleven o'clock high and right, sir, Captain, sir.'

Declan caught the balloon in his sights. It was barely more than a speck now. A pale moon in a sea of stars.

Holy God, he thought. *I hope this is a straight-shooting rifle.*

But he knew Bates, and the only thing sharper than his mouth was his aim.

Declan pulled the rifle's nose up a few inches to allow for the drop off, then a few to the left to compensate for the cross breeze. Marksmanship could be learned up to a point, but after that it was all natural talent.

Balloons and guns, thought Declan. *Just like Paris the day you were born, Conor. But that time you came down with the balloon.*

Declan felt his eyes blur and he blinked them clear, this was not the time for tears.

Conor, my son, your mother and brother need me now, but I will never forget you and what you did for the Saltees. Look down and see this as a sign.

Declan took a breath, held it, then caressed the trigger, leaning into his right foot to absorb the recoil. The nitro-glycerine bullet sped from the extended barrel towards its target.

That's for you, Conor, he thought, and the final Coronation Balloon exploded, brightly enough to be visible from heaven.

Behind him, the entire island roared in appreciation, except for Bonvilain, who seemed lost in thought, which was never good for the one being thought of.

Declan tossed the rifle to Bates. 'Nice weapon you have there, Lieutenant, nearly as dangerous as your mouth.'

Even Bates was awed by this impossible shot. 'Yes, sir. Thank you, sir. That was a historic hit, Captain. Where do we stand on the beer now?'

But Declan was not listening; he was staring across the square, over the heads of the cheering mob. Catherine met his gaze across the distance. Her hands covered her nose and mouth; all he could see of that beautiful face were her dark eyes. In the orange glow of electric orbs, Declan could see that his wife was crying.

Her husband has come home.

The balloon exploded, flames igniting the fireworks pack before the fuse ever had the chance. The concussion perforated one of Conor's eardrums and a riot of sparks peppered his skin like a million bee stings. He was engulfed in a cocoon of raging flame which ate his clothing and crisped the hairs on his arms and legs, singeing his beard back to the jawline. As serious as these injuries were, Conor had expected much worse.

Then gravity took hold, yanking him back to earth with invisible threads. Down he went, too shocked to cry out.

This had never been the plan. There was supposed to be ten fathoms of rope between him and the balloon, dangerous certainly, but a lot healthier than riding the balloon itself.

There was something he was supposed to do. The plan had a next stage surely.

Of course! The device!

Conor forced his good hand down against the airflow, pulling aside the smouldering remnants of his jacket.

My God! There were sparks on the device.

The device was, of course, a parachute. Aeronauts had been jumping out of balloons for almost a century with varying success. In America, dropping animals from balloons had become popular after the Civil War. But jumps had only been performed as entertainment, in perfect weather conditions. Rarely at night, hardly ever from an altitude under 6,000 feet and positively never with a flaming parachute.

Conor located the release cord and pulled. He'd been forced to pack his chute carefully into a flour bag then strap it across his chest. He could only pray that the lines would come out untangled, or else the parachute would not even open. As it was, at this low altitude it was quite possible that the parachute would not have time to spread at all, and would merely provide him with a shroud for his watery grave.

The release cord was sewn to the tip of a tiny parachute, much like those Victor and Conor had often used to sail wooden mannequins from the palace turrets. In theory, the drag on this parachute would be enough to pull out the larger one. This was one of the many new ideas Conor had scrawled in the mud at the back of his cell. He had hoped, at the time,

that all of his inventions would not have to be tested in such
outrageous circumstances.

Though Conor did not see it happen, his small parachute
performed perfectly, slipping from its niche like a baby marsu-
pial from the pouch. It shivered in the wind for a moment,
then popped its mouth open, catching the air. Its fall was
instantly slowed, while Conor's was not. The resulting tension
dragged the larger parachute into the night air. The silk rustled
past Conor's face, bouncing the wind in its folds.

No tangled lines. No snagged folds. Please, God.

His prayers were answered, and the white silk of the parachute sprang open to its limits cleanly, with a noise like cannon
shot. The severity of the deceleration caused the harness straps
to snap hard against Conor's back, leaving an x-shaped rope
burn that he would carry for the rest of his life.

Conor was largely beyond rational thought now and could
only wonder why the moon seemed to be following him.
Not only that, but it appeared to be on fire. Angry orange
sparks chewed away large sections, so that he could see the
stars through the holes.

Not the moon. My parachute.

It seemed to Conor then, that he was still in his cell, in
the planning stages and his imagination was throwing up
possible problems.

*If sparks from the balloon catch on the parachute silk, that will
indeed be a dire development, because it will mean that someone has
shot the balloon, in spite of me loosing it from the wall. If this
happens, I can only hope that my velocity has decreased sufficiently
to make a water landing survivable.*

Conor's descent was steady enough now that he could distinguish sea from sky. Below him the islands were rushing up fast. He could see Isabella's palace and of course the Great Saltee Wall, with its rows of electric lamps, that had been described by *The New York Times* as the *First Wonder of the Industrial World*.

If I could steer, Conor thought, *the lights would guide me in*.

The boats spun below him in a maelstrom of light. Quickly the largest of the boats filled his vision and he realized that he would land there. There was no avoiding the craft. It loomed from the black depths like one of Darwin's bioelectric jellyfish.

Conor felt no particular sadness, more the disappointment of a scientist whose experiment has failed.

Ten feet left and I might have survived, he thought. *Science is indeed a slave to nature*.

But chance had one more freakish card to play on this night of unlikely extremes. A heartbeat after his parachute dissolved into blackened embers, Conor crashed into the royal yacht *Victoria and Albert II* at a speed of some forty miles an hour. He hit the third starboard lifeboat, slicing a clean rent in the blue tarpaulin, which would not be noticed for two days. Below the tarpaulin was a bed of cork lifejackets, temporarily stored there until hooks could be hung to hold them.

Two days earlier and the recently requisitioned jackets would not have been on-board, three days later and they would have been distributed about the yacht.

Despite the parachute and tarpaulin, Conor's bulk and speed drove him through the cork to the deck. His dislocated shoulder punched through to the floorboards, where he bounced once then came to rest.

The bilges must be spotless, he thought dimly. *Nothing to smell but wood and paint.*

And then: *I do believe the impact righted my shoulder. What are the odds? Astronomical.*

This was his final thought before oblivion claimed him. Conor Broekhart did not move a muscle for the rest of the night. He dreamed vividly but in two colours only: crimson and gold.

PART 3:

AIRMAN

CHAPTER 12:

ANGEL OR DEVIL

Little Saltee, 1894

On the night Arthur Billtoe met the devil, he was indulging himself in one of his favourite pastimes. The prison guard was on the skive in a comfy spot near the cliffs on the island's seaward side. Billtoe had half a dozen such spots all over the island, places he could set down his head when prison life did for his nerves.

Dossing off was not a simple thing on a walled island with a fort perched on the south-eastern wedge and a dozen lookout towers along the wall itself.

Stupid electric lighting, Billtoe often thought. *How's a man supposed to grab a kip?*

This particular comfy spot was Billtoe's favourite, a shallow little dugout near the salsa garden, fifteen paces from the base of the wall. The floor was an ancient tarp the ferry boys were flinging, and the roof was one of the old doors from Wandering Heck's days, frame and all, still on the hinges. The entire thing was near invisible from the outside, covered as it was with mud, grass and scrub that had crept down over the door.

Billtoe felt a swell of pride every time he sneaked himself into its pungent, welcoming darkness. Of all his doss spots, this was his favourite. Dry as a bone come hell or high water, and he could uncork the spy-hole and use it as a chimney, which saved him revealing his embers to the watch.

One more smoke, thought Billtoe. *One more and then back on the job.*

Arthur Billtoe had been spending more and more time in his hidey-holes in the six months since Conor Finn had disappeared. He wasn't nursing a tender spot for the soldier boy, but he was fearful that Marshall Bonvilain had a plan for that young man, and him being dead was not part of that plan.

On the night of Finn's disappearance, Billtoe had stood in the chimney stack roaring for hours. When that had proved fruitless, he had fetched a twelve-year-old Cockney boy who was doing a dozen or so years for robbing toffs, and sent him up the stacks with a promise of a few years off his sentence. The boy came down empty-handed after half a day, and Billtoe sent him right back up again at gunpoint. Forty-eight more hours in the labyrinth and the boy came back down with bloody knees and no news. It was no use. Conor Finn was not up there. Somehow, Arthur Billtoe had been duped.

Then he began to wonder about the butcher who had become entangled in one of the coronation balloons.

Could that have been Finn? Could soldier boy have got above ground somehow?

Billtoe could never know for certain and this itched him like a beetle crawling under his skin. Maybe Finn was desiccated in the chimneys, or perhaps he had a lungful of brine in Saint George's Channel. Dead was dead and bones was bones. But that wouldn't be the end of it. Sooner or later Bonvilain would come looking for his special prisoner and then all hell would be brought down on Arthur Billtoe's head.

Unless. Unless . . .

Unless the marshall would be fooled by his deception. Billtoe had considered upping sticks and hopping a steamer to New York when Finn disappeared; one of his possible fathers was in New York, if he were still alive. Even if he weren't, then there could be some form of estate. But that was all eating rat and calling it turkey. He hadn't the money for the Atlantic, nor would he have with a year of saving. It was frustrating to have a fortune in stolen diamonds that he could not convert into hard cash.

Anyway, things were rosy on the island at the present moment. He was Bonvilain's boy, what with his coronation balloons being such a success. Pretty soon, he might find himself at one end of a promotion's handshake. Maybe then Arthur Billtoe might be in a position to smuggle some of his diamonds off the island, and then maybe he could travel first class on that steamer to New York.

Until then, he would have to pray to whatever god would have him that Marshall Bonvilain did not look too closely at the bearded youth he had slung into Conor Finn's cell. The boy was roughly the same age, build and colouring. After a few beatings he had the same haunted eyes and lopsided looks. It could be the same young man, if you didn't look too hard. Billtoe hoped that Conor Finn was a simple hostage job and not someone with facts in his skull, because if it was information that the marshall was after, then he'd best be looking up high and down low, because he wouldn't be finding it in Conor Finn's cell.

Billtoe had a sudden idea.

I should cut out the ringer's tongue. Say it happened in a fight with Malarkey. The marshall couldn't hold me responsible for that, as it was he who ordered me to set Malarkey on the boy.

That, as far as Billtoe was concerned, was a capital idea, far better than salsa gardens or coronation balloons. Or twelve-shot revolvers for that matter, which had turned out to be a pile of fool's gold. A Kilmore gunsmith friend of Billtoe's had nearly lost a finger trying to build that particular weapon.

I will slice that boy's tongue out as soon as I get back, thought Billtoe, tapping his boot to make sure his good knife was nestled there against his shin.

Mightily pleased with this notion, Billtoe blew a final flute of smoke through the peephole, then stubbed out his cigarette on a clamshell he kept in the hidey-hole for that purpose. He toed the door open a crack to release any lingering smoke or smells, then clambered up into the darkness like a corpse rising from its grave.

Not only will cutting that ringer's tongue out serve a purpose, vis-à-vis my plan, but it will also improve my mood.

Billtoe's general routine was to hug the wall until he reached a stairwell, then trot up as if he were simply taking the air. No one would challenge him, especially since the coronation. He was a big shot now, was Arthur Billtoe.

That's Mister Billtoe, to you, Pike.

As he had become fond of saying lately.

The night was overcast, with barely a star winking through the clouds. The Wall crenellations had an orange haze drawn above their blocks by the electric lighting. Billtoe used the orange line as a marker, easy to navigate by. He nipped across the springy rock grass under cover of darkness, a little sharpish as it turned out, because his boot heel slipped on a pat of moss and he went down on his back. The wind went out of him like dust from a beaten rug.

Billtoe lay there on his back, wheezing and gasping, when suddenly the clouds parted, letting a silver guinea moon shine through. When Billtoe recovered his wind, his lips spread in a plug-stained smile, because finally, after so many years, he could make out the man in the moon that everyone prattled on about. Must be the angle, because before this moment he had never seen anything but smudges.

I can see the face now for the first time. And I get to cut out a prisoner's tongue. Happy day.

Then, through the gap in the clouds came some kind of figure. A man with wings. Flying.

This kind of event was so strange, so impossible, that Billtoe was not even surprised initially.

A man with the wings of a bird. An angel in black.

The angel banked sharp starboard so as not to overshoot the island, then descended in a tight curl, spiralling down until Billtoe could hear the craft as well as see it. It creaked, flapped and fluttered and the human-looking creature fought it as though he were being borne away by a great eagle.

I know what is happening here, Billtoe realized.

Arthur Billtoe had in his life read two books. *London's Most Gruesome Murders* by Sy Cocillée, which he found most educational, and *The Noble Indian* by Captain George Toolee, which he had *hoped* would concern itself with settler massacres and scalping, but which actually turned out to be an in-depth study of the Indians' culture. Billtoe had almost tossed the book into the fire, but it had cost him a few shillings so he persevered. One chapter described a tent known as the sweat lodge, where the Indians got themselves good and smoked up until their spirit guide appeared.

My hidey-hole is like a sweat lodge. Now my spirit guide has appeared, and it's a swearing bird-man.

The bird-man contraption came down fast, wings cracking as the air filled their sails. It seemed as though the creature would break itself against the rocks, like a sparrow against the window – which Billtoe always found amusing – when at the last possible second the angel creature pulled up his nose, gliding in for a smooth landing.

His speed took him running for a dozen steps until he managed to halt himself.

Billtoe gazed up, terrified at this otherworldly creature who loomed above him, the moon haloing his head. It was close enough to stab. But what would be the point? There was no killing a creature like this.

The creature was dressed in black from the top of his leather cap to the tip of his knee-length riding boots. His face was concealed by a pair of glassed goggles and a scarf pulled tightly across the mouth. His breath was ragged though the scarf, and his chest heaved.

Something twinkled on the angel's chest. An insignia of some kind. Two golden wings, springing from a letter 'A'. Could it stand for Angel?

Arthur Billtoe wished with all his heart to remain still and silent. He felt once more like the seven-year-old boy he had been in a Dublin alley, hiding in a water barrel, being hunted by a drunken crone for the sixpence in his pocket. His life was worth no more now than it had been then. This creature would kill him with a glance. He longed to draw the grass and weeds around him like a blanket and sleep until this fearsome flying creature had departed.

Do not whimper, he told himself. Whimpering at times of danger had always been a failing of his, and had earned him bruises more than once in the past.

Hold it in, Arthur me boy. Suck it down to yer boots.

He might have managed it, had the creature not pulled a sabre from its scabbard at his belt and began plunging it into the ground, as though seeking to wound mother earth. Each thrust brought him closer to where Billtoe lay shuddering.

Finally he could absorb the fright no more.

I will die if I don't speak. My poor ticker will burst her spring.

'What are you?' he hissed, the power of his emotions lifting him to his feet. 'What do you want with Arthur Billtoe?'

The creature reared back, then steadied himself. Its glass

eyes flashed orange in the lamp glow, then blackened as they landed on the prison guard.

'Billtoe,' it growled. 'Arthur Billtoe!'

If Billtoe could have, he would have changed his name on the spot, such was the hatred in the creature's voice. These winged types must be hateful by nature.

While Billtoe was contemplating this, the airman darted forward, his curved wings rearing upwards from the sudden movement, lifting the black-clad stranger into the air. He dropped to earth like a giant snarling gargoyle within arm's length of Billtoe, a fact he put to good use by clasping the guard's windpipe in steel fingers.

'Billtoe,' he said again, laying his sabre blade flat along Billtoe's pale throat.

'A-are you angel or devil, sir?' stammered the guard. 'I needs to know. Are you taking me up the ways, or down?'

The glass circles studied him for a long second. Billtoe felt the blade slide along his Adam's apple, he felt the keen cut sing. Then the blade stopped its deadly arc and the creature spoke.

'I can be angel or devil, *monsieur*,' it said. 'But in your case, I will always be a devil.'

'Will you kill me now?' asked Billtoe, his voice almost a shriek.

'No, *monsieur*, not now. But you are making a lot of noise so . . .'

The devil lifted his sabre high, and brought the pommel down on Billtoe's brow. The guard collapsed like a dropped puppet.

He was not quite unconscious, but Billtoe thought it would be better to seek out the darkness, rather than open his eyes and incur the wrath of the airman. He kept his eyes closed and soon drifted away.

When Arthur Billtoe awoke, it was daybreak. His head felt like one giant wound, and the warden's dog walker, Poole, was standing over him, encouraging the little terrier to use Billtoe's boot as a piddling spot.

'Geddoff!' snarled Billtoe, kicking at the dog, then remembered the French devil, who could still be in the area.

He rolled himself from the marshy puddle in which he had lain, and scrambled to all fours, unable to go any higher because of the pain hammering his skull.

'Devil,' he panted. 'French. Big ruddy wings. Flying about like a nighthawk. Did you see it?'

Poole's response to this lunacy was to pretend he didn't hear. He coughed furiously to cover Billtoe's chatter, then chastised the terrier.

'Bad, Sir Percival, bad, making to piddle on *Mister* Billtoe like that, and he coming out of a dream, the details of which I have no desire to hear. I would kick you, Percy, if you weren't such a lovely lad.'

He picked up the dog and delivered the message he had been sent with.

'Warden is looking for you,' he said, unable to meet Billtoe's eyes. 'He says he's full fed up of you and your hidey-holes. And you can either fill 'em in yourself, or he'll fill 'em in with you inside. And that's what he said to me, word for word. I been repeating it to myself over and over.'

Billtoe was still wide-eyed, his gaze darting around the rocky area, a thin string of drool hanging from his lips.

'He found me. He found me. I was in the barrel with sixpence, and he found me.'

Poole decided to misunderstand. It was easier. 'Yes, sir. The warden finds everyone. He must have eyes in his backside.'

Poole chanced a flash of wit as he trotted after Sir Percival back to the guards' billet.

'Or maybe he has a set of wings and he flies over the island at night looking down on us.'

Billtoe sat himself down on a rock, prodded the goose-egg bump on his forehead and began to cry.

The sky

Conor Finn was flying, but it was not the gentle experience he had hoped for. The glider was a beast, and to conquer it meant constantly wrestling with the contraption as they soared through the air. Truth be told, it did not feel like soaring, rather a buffeting battle with the elements. The wings banged, cracked and jerked, threatening to snap their ribs with every gust of wind. The harness bit into his chest, restricting his breathing and even a collision with a sea bird would send him spiralling to the earth. Nevertheless, Conor would not have missed the experience.

I am the moon, he thought. *I am the stars.*

And then.

Look out. A seagull.

The glider was holding together as well as he could have hoped, though he would swear that the third rib to starboard was splintering. He would slip it from its sleeve later, and replace it with a new rod. The steering bar, one of his own innovations, was working perfectly, allowing him to shift his weight and exert a certain control over his trajectory. But it was a tenuous control, and one that could be contemptuously overruled by the smallest updraught or current.

The night sky was heavy with clouds, reflecting the lights of nearby Wexford and Kilmore on their underbellies. Every now and then, Conor passed below a hole in the clouds and the full moon would spotlight him with her silver rays. Conor hoped that from below his silhouette would be that of a large bird, but nevertheless he was glad of his decision to use black fabric for the wings. Dyed black not painted. Paint would be too weighty.

Up close and in broad daylight, it would be obvious that the glider was little more than a cleverly designed kite. Two elongated eight-foot curved ovals for wings, linked by a central circular space where the pilot hung suspended in his leather harness. A short-stemmed tail rudder with leg braces and a nudge pole that could be tipped by the feet, and a trapezoidal steering bar which was attached directly to the main wing strut. In theory, if one could successfully locate rising thermals, it was possible to fly forever, suspended below a glider like this. Of course, this was a very optimistic theory, which did not allow for wear and tear, bad science and the simple fact that thermals were only slightly less difficult to locate than unicorns.

Conor himself was outfitted in the sturdiest ballooning gear, leather chin-strapped cap, goggles and tight boots. His uniform was a convincing copy of that worn by the French Army's aeronauts, but all in black down to the trouser piping, and no insignia's apart from a mysterious winged 'A', which could possibly stand for *Aeronautique*.

If I do happen to crash on the Saltees, thought Conor, *I will look for all the world like a French airman, who does not want to be identified as such. In other words, a flying spy. That should stoke Bonvilain's mistrust of the French Army.*

It was a small comfort, but twisting a thorn of disquiet into Bonvilain's heart was better than dying and leaving nothing but a corpse.

His luck had held tonight. A good launch from the tunnel, with everything performing as it should. The steam fan had popped a few of the tunnel planks out of their grooves, but that was easily repaired, and there hadn't been any great loss of wind power. His mounting mechanism had worked a thousand times in suspension from a tower beam, but tonight it had worked in the open air and he had managed to lean forward in the body harness and ratchet his legs back into the stirrups. This was one of his major innovations, though there were a thousand small ones, from the steam shaping of the ribs, to the tail rudder.

The coastline approached, and the black sea – with the Saltee Islands glowing upon it like two nests of fireflies. The moment he cleared Saint Patrick's Bridge, the long bar of shingle that curved from the mainland to point like an arthritic finger towards Little Saltee, the thermal he had been riding disappeared and his gilder stalled, tilting forward at the nose.

Conor was prepared for this, but not ready. If the stall lasted more than a few moments, he would plummet to earth to a certain death.

In the event of a stall, hold the nose down and set loose the bands.

There were three ropes tied off to the steering bar and all three were linked to Conor's wrist. He released the bar, tugging sharply downwards, untying the hitches on all three ropes.

The central rope was connected to a hinged forward panel – the beak – which pulled the nose down. The other two slipped from the blades of two wooden propellers, which were immediately set whirring by the released energy of two stout rubber cords.

The rubber-band propellers would only work once per flight, and the amount of thrust they provided was minimal, but it might be enough to pull him out of a stall.

It was. The glider jumped forward barely a yard, but it righted itself and caught the sea breeze. Conor felt it running along the length of his body, smelled the salt in each gust.

Before him, the Wall lights of Little Saltee marked his target in the blackness.

Heart-shaped, he thought. *From up here, the island looks like a heart.*

And then. *I am returning to Little Saltee. God help me, I am going back.*

And he could not suppress a shudder that was more dread than cold.

On the night of his daring escape, Conor had spiralled flaming from the sky like Icarus of legend, crashing into a lifeboat on Victoria's royal yacht, which was a-bustle with preparations for departure.

Conor Finn lay undiscovered below a scattered dozen of cork life preservers for the duration of the overnight voyage, unable to move even if the rough hand of discovery landed on his shoulder. The hand never came, and Conor was able to sleep until the yacht blew its horn to alert a skiff in its path.

Fortune had smiled on him once more in London, where he had been able to slip overboard a couple of leagues out of harbour and swim to a slipway on the Thames.

Conor stole a jacket, which fortunately had some bread and cheese in the pocket, then spent the remainder of the day walking the docks, listening for an Irish accent. By dusk he had spotted a group of London Irish who had too few teeth and too many tattoos to be Customs spies.

If you ever do make it out of this hellhole, Malarkey had often said, *find my brother Zeb on the London docks. Show him the ink and he will look after you.*

Conor rolled up his sleeve for the dockworkers, revealing his Battering Ram tattoo, and spoke the magic word. *Malarkey.* Inside the hour, he was up to his neck in soapy water with a mug of coffee in one hand and a fine cigar in the other. Zeb Malarkey was a man of means, most of these *means* being fruits of his own personal import tax.

Zeb himself had arrived at the inn a couple of hours later, and without a word of greeting examined both Conor's tattoo and the Little Saltee brand.

How's Otto? he wanted to know. *How's his hair?*

Conor supplied the crime boss with as much information as he could. Hair silky, health fine. Nice little line in rackets going.

Zeb had already heard of Conor through a prison guard on Little Saltee who took bribes to pass on information.

Conor Finn? The soldier boy. Otto speaks highly of you. Says you put order on the Rams what is locked up. Fancy doing the same here?

It was tempting, simply to shed his old life completely, like a reptile shrugging off a brittle skin. But Conor knew enough of his own heart to recognize that being a waterfront enforcer was not for him. He may not be Conor Broekhart any more, but he was not entirely divorced from his mother's morals. He could hurt another person to survive, but not for payment.

He was an airman. That was his destiny. He needed to stick to the plan. Go to Ireland, build the means to reclaim his diamonds and then sail for America with the funds to equip his own laboratory.

So he told Zeb Malarkey thank you, but no. He had business on Little Saltee. Business that could make the Rams a lot of money. Perhaps Zeb had a few men in Ireland or perhaps on the Saltees who could help?

The Rams have men everywhere. What kind of business? Revenge?

*Not exactly. There are items on the prison grounds that belong
to me and your brother. I gave Otto my word that I would see him
free. My thanks for his friendship these past years.*

Zeb Malarkey tossed him a purse of guineas.

Go then, islander. Go and spread chaos.

Which was exactly what happened.

Little Saltee was suddenly below him. In less than three
minutes he had crossed the two-and-a-half-mile wide band
of ocean between the prison island and the mainland. If he
had been one of an army, the island would have been overrun
before they could sound the warning cannon.

Conor's body ached from the constant stress on his joints
and he was relieved to pull back on the bar and swing his
glider into a descending curve. In test flights, he had succeeded
in landing the glider inside the fences of a field far smaller
than this island. But that field had hedges instead of guards.
And the hedges were populated by badgers and squirrels,
none of whom were likely to aim a rifle at flying creatures.

Even at night, a bird's-eye view was very revealing. There
were three guards on the wall, all at the northern end in the
shelter of a tower. Conor could see the glowing bowls of
their pipes bobbing close together. They should be evenly
spaced and on the move, but centuries of quiet had bred
complacency in them.

There were actually two walls on Little Saltee. The main
outer ring, and an inner wall that circled the prison building.
In between the two was the work area where inmates took
exercise and toiled over their salsa gardens. This was where

Conor wished to land. Where the diamonds were buried.

A thermal suddenly took his craft, causing him to overshoot his preferred landing spot by a hundred yards. Conor kicked the nudge bar to extreme port, and pointed the nose down. This put him into a tail-spinning descent, but his alternative was to land in the ocean. It would be a pity to drown tonight, having flown further in a glider than any man before him.

Victor would be proud.

The thought unsettled him. In prison he had tried not to think of the family and friends from his old life, but since his escape he could think of little else.

I could simply go back. Explain. Father could challenge Bonvilain.

Yes. And be murdered for his pains. Mother too. Best to simply nail the door shut on the past and begin his new life.

Conor dropped quickly. Rocks and hillocks grew from what had been syrupy black space. The glider fought him all the way down, and he fought back, cursing at his infernal craft, refusing to allow it its head.

Once inside the wall's shelter, the turbulence disappeared and the glider grew docile and sweet, lifting her neck graceful as a swan. Conor's boot heels dug into soft earth, and he ploughed twin furrows for ten feet before he cranked the wings up behind him with a winch on his belt, and came to a halt.

There was no time to rejoice in his landing, or congratulate himself on the effectiveness of his collapsible wings, though at the moment they were technically only hoisted. To be fully collapsed, two struts had to be removed.

To work, to work.

The diamonds were buried one foot beyond the northernmost corner of each salsa patch. Seven patches, seven bags of diamonds. The nearest prison garden was virtually at his feet. If he worked quickly and was not discovered, he could possibly retrieve three bags tonight.

Conor drew a sabre from his belt, using it to dig into the sod, searching for diamonds, but was distracted from his labour by the sight of a dark and distraught figure rising from the earth.

A trap. I am trapped.

But that was not the truth of it. The shivering figure spoke. 'What are you? What do you want with Arthur Billtoe?'

Conor felt an anger so intense that it was physical. His brow burned and the sabre's leather-bound pommel creaked in his fist.

'Billtoe,' he growled, springing forward. 'Arthur Billtoe!'

The speed of his motion caught the air, and the wings jerked skywards. Conor was elevated briefly, but if Billtoe thought he could escape, he was wrong. Conor landed not two feet from the terrified guard, wrapping steel fingers round the man's gullet.

How the tables have turned. Who is the master now? Not twenty yards from where you bullied and humiliated me.

'Billtoe,' he said again, laying his sabre blade flat along Billtoe's pale throat.

'A-are you angel or devil, sir?' stammered the guard. 'I
needs to know. Are you taking me up the ways, or down?'

Conor considered killing him. The urge was strong. In all
likelihood, this wretch had murdered Linus Wynter. He
indulged this desire to the tune of a small cut on the guard's
neck. But he could not complete the motion.

Still not a killer, Linus might have said.

Stick to the plan. You are a French spy.

'I can be angel or devil, *monsieur*,' said Conor. 'But in your
case, I will always be a devil.'

'Will you kill me now?' cried Billtoe.

'No, *monsieur*, not now,' said Conor with more than
a touch of regret. 'But you are making a lot of noise
so . . .'

He struck Billtoe sharply on the temple with the sabre's
hilt, relishing the thump of contact. Funny, the guard did not
seem so threatening now, stretched in the grass. A coward
without his gun or the weight of authority behind him.

Get the diamonds. One bag at least.

Conor's plan to unearth three bags was shot. Billtoe could
wake at any moment, and, tempting as the notion might be,
he could not keep bashing the Billtoe's skull all night. Neither
could he bind and gag the man, as he did not have a rope or
cloth. Something to remember for his next visit, should he
survive this outing.

Conor returned to his digging, levering clods from the
earth with the sabre. It occurred to him then that Malarkey
could have lied, and secreted their booty in another spot,
but Conor thought it was unlikely. In spite of inauspicious

beginnings, Otto Malarkey had become his friend, and the Battering Rams had a strong sense of loyalty. They would mount the gallows' steps before betraying another man who bore the mark.

Conor's trust was warranted. His blade soon clinked against a clutch of diamonds. He put away the sabre and scrabbled in the dirt with his gloved fingers, pulling the pouch of diamonds from the earth.

One found. Six more to go.

He was tempted to try for another. With a second bag on his belt, his future would be secure and he could leave for America tomorrow.

Go now. Be prudent. Billtoe could wake at any second.

One more. Just one.

Conor ran to the second salsa bed, all the time imagining that Billtoe regained his senses.

Should I have killed him?

No. A dead guard would raise suspicions. There would be an investigation. Billtoe having conversations with a flying Frenchman on the other hand would be viewed as the ramblings of a drunkard, unless Bonvilain got wind of them.

Too late now. Fetch the second bag.

The salsa bed was further north along the wall's curve. Conor ran close to the plinth, avoiding the swirling currents that flowed over the island's hillocks, and also the salty mist that would weigh down his wings.

The glider needs to collapse further, he told himself. *The wings catch every breath of air.*

The second pouch was as easy to find as the first had been. Otto Malarkey had followed his instructions well. The bag slid from the earth, trailing clods and pebbles. It was the size and weight of a small rabbit.

Heavy enough. Two found.

Now it was most certainly time to fly. To attempt one more search was to invite disaster. Conor had a sudden image of passing the remainder of the night back in his old cell and a shudder rippled along his spine. He must be away.

The guards were doubtless huddled in the northern tower, filling their pipe bowls, so he would make his escape from the south. Conor returned to the base of the wall, and followed his nose until he found the garderobe, a privy hollowed into the base of the wall with a drain running through into the ocean. Garderobes were normally near the stairwell, so the guard would need as little time away from his post as possible.

And, just as he had hoped, the stairwell was a mere three paces past the garderobe, built as a stepped bulwark to the main wall. Conor crab-walked up, keeping his wings behind him, safe from damage, but open to gusts of wind. More than once he was forced to brace his legs against the efforts of his hoisted wings to drag him from the steps.

Not yet. Higher still.

There was neither sight nor sound of a sentry on the wall walk, though he himself would be visible plain enough as soon as he emerged from the stairwell. It was all exactly as planned, but for Billtoe. What in heaven's name had the man been doing? Sleeping in the outdoors?

Conor lay his body flat along the top steps, peering along the wall's curve at each side. The cobbles, worn smooth by centuries of patrol, shone orange in the electric light. The crenellated parapet was head high with rows of horizontal gun ports. The wind whistled through each one, sending up an eerie banshee howling.

An offshore wind. Still strong.

It would have been most fortuitous had the wind changed to a sea breeze, blowing back towards the mainland. But these were the kinds of odds that could not be relied upon. Take advantage when lady luck smiles, but do not plan for it. And so Conor's immediate destination was not Kilmore, but Great Saltee, for that was where the wind was going.

Conor gathered his feet under him, pushing his harness lower. He gripped the wing-hoist lever in one hand and the rudder bar in the other.

Once more into the air.

He stood and ran across the wall walk. His footsteps seemed absurdly loud as his boots clacked on the stone. Surely the sounds would march along the wall to the guards' tower.

Concentrate on your actions. The slightest slip could be the death of you.

It was curious, but sometimes the voice in Conor's mind sounded like Victor Vigny.

I have a guardian angel, and he is French.

This made him grin, and so in spite of the life-or-death situation, it was a smiling Conor Finn who hoisted himself on to the Little Saltee parapet, and launched himself into the night sky.

I am flying home.

Sebber Bridge, Great Saltee

Pike generally worked the early shift on Little Saltee, then spent sunlight hours and leisure days on the big island, nursing his one-legged mother and fixing the cottage wall, which he had been working on now for fifteen years. When he wasn't mixing mortar for the wall, Pike was making himself money hand over fist selling information to the Battering Rams.

Pike was never going to be in the gang's inner circle, but he was a useful man in any situation because in spite of his apparent lack of grey matter, he had an uncanny knack of accumulating information. The warden, a political man, appreciated this and granted Pike extra leave time to hook him any court gossip he could, while the Battering Rams paid him handsomely for any Customs information he was able to wheedle from his mates on the docks. Two bags of coin per week and neither party any the wiser.

As well as information, Pike ran the odd errand for the Rams. Nothing violent that could see him hanged, and also he was an inveterate coward. His latest job was simplicity itself, if a little puzzling. Until further notice, on any night there was a stiff breeze from the mainland he was to tow a skiff around to Sebber Bridge and leave it there. Simple as that. Beach the boat on the shale outcrop below Promontory Fort, then row back up the coast to the harbour. No lights, no whistling nor singing sea shanties, or the Saltee Sharpshooters would put a bullet in his behind. Simply beach the boat and go. The skiff would make its own way back to Saltee Harbour the next day.

Simple orders, but not to Pike's taste. Thanks to his double pay packet, he was well aware just how valuable good information was, and he felt certain that there were those who would pay to know what manner of person was picking up a skiff on Sebber Bridge in the wee hours. Not someone on the up and up, that was for certain. Honest citizens came and went through the harbour without the need for skulduggery like this.

The trick was how to sell the information without falling foul of the Battering Rams. But he could chew on that problem when he had some information to sell.

So Pike decided to delay his departure awhile, until the mystery sailor had set sail. Then he would know what kind of a nugget he had, and how much it was worth.

He concealed his own punt under a bank of weed, then crawled high into the rocks and settled in to wait.

After a couple of hours, he was regretting not bringing more tobacco along, and was considering stuffing his pipe with seaweed, when something whooshed overhead, causing him to drop his pipe altogether.

If that was a bat, then it was a big one. Low-flying gull more like, or a kestrel over from the mainland.

Pike had a vague sense of the creature's bigness.

There would be some eating in a bird like that. A pity I don't have my slingshot along. Even a gull can taste passable when you cook it right.

He wriggled forward out of his crevasse just in time to see a man with wings swoop in to land on Sebber Bridge, his heels dragging up arcs of shingle.

A flying man, he thought, flabbergasted. *A man that can fly.*

Pike knew instantly that this was the most valuable thing he would ever see. He pulled a pad from his pocket, licking the stub of a pencil that hung from a string on the binding.

A good tout never knows when a nugget will need recording. Keep your pencil close to your heart, and you'll never miss a trick.

So, with his heart rattling his ribs and his fingers shaking, Pike sketched the winged airman hanging on to the skiff's gunwale, lest the breeze carry him off to the moon.

He drew arrows pointing to the wings and above the arrows wrote *wings*, as if writing the word made what was before his eyes more believable. He noted it down when the airman pulled a lever and his wings were hoisted behind him. He drew a diagram of the harness and how it cradled the sky rider from shoulder to knee. He saw how the man took himself out of the harness like a lady from her bodice, and collapsed the whole contraption down by pulling out a few stays, till the wings folded up neater than a picnic blanket.

Perhaps I should just take those wings, thought Pike. *That airman don't look so big. I could part his ribs with my knife and present those wings to the warden. Perhaps that would be the best course of action.*

But then he noticed a sabre on the man's belt, and a revolver on his other hip. There was also the possibility that these airman types possessed strange mystical powers such as the evil eye, or the deathly hex.

Best leave it at pictures for today, he decided. *Next time I will be prepared, and he will be relaxed. A nice short-handled axe should do the trick.*

The airman stowed his gear neatly under the aft seat, then dug his toes into the shale, pushing off. The skiff slid sweetly into the dark water with no more of a splash than the waves were making on the north shore.

He's gone, thought Pike. *I am safe.*

But perhaps he thought his thoughts too loudly, because the airman froze and turned his glass-goggled eyes towards the rocks. His head was cocked like a puzzled deer, and he scanned the higher levels with twin orange circles.

His eyes are on fire, thought Pike. *He can see in the dark.*

But then the strange flying man turned, leaping neatly into the skiff, his landing sending her scudding out across the water, prow slapping the waves. In seconds the dark sail unfurled, and she tacked to starboard wide of the island.

Pike sighed in relief.

Perhaps a short-handled axe will not do the job, he decided. *Perhaps I need something with a long handle.*

CHAPTER 13:

THE SOLDIER'S RETURN

Kilmore Quay

Conor tacked wide, riding the offshore wind as far as possible, before dropping sail and rowing towards Kilmore Harbour. The clouds had thickened and a few spatters of rain knocked on the planking. The tide was on the rise, so he made good time in spite of the wind on his back.

Conor had expected to feel elated at this moment; he had been wishing for it long enough. There were diamonds at his belt and freedom in his future. Zeb Malarkey had sent him new papers so he could book passage to New York tomorrow if he so wished.

Enough to start a new life.

He did feel a certain satisfaction, but it was grim and muted. It seemed as though memories of his old life were reclaiming their place at the forefront of his mind now that he was out of prison.

Conor wondered if he could ever feel true joy again without his loved ones to share his accomplishments with. He allowed himself a brief daydream. He imagined landing his glider not on Little Saltee, but on the long mainland beach of Curracloe, which ran straight and flat for several miles. This was the spot where Victor had incessantly talked of testing their aeroplanes.

There would be crowds present, of course, and journalists from all over the world. Gaggles of sceptical scientists too. But Conor did not care a fig for any of them — he was on the lookout for his parents, and Victor too. They would be hugging each other with excitement and pride. His father would reach him first as he swooped in to land. Perhaps Isabella would attend.

His heart sank. *Isabella.*

She believes that I helped to kill her father. How could she believe that?

Instead of gliding on to the golden sands of Curracloe, he was alone in a boat, with no one to boast to. No one to celebrate with. The power of flight was no longer an achievement in itself — it was a way to aid him in his thievery.

I have flown further than any other man. I have flown over water at night. No one to tell but the stars. The only person who knows is a cruel prison guard. A buffoon who thinks that I am the devil. I am the world's first flying thief.

Conor shook his head to dislodge this disquieting daydream, then threw his back into the oars. He sculled skilfully, as his father had taught him. Bend forward, dip the blades but not too deep. Pull with the back and then arms. Develop a rhythm and let that rhythm calm you. A man can be truly at peace on the water in a small boat, even though only a plank of wood separates him from the cold, unforgiving ocean.

Can a thief be at peace? For a time perhaps.

Conor tied the skiff off at the quay, stuffed his hat and goggles into a jacket pocket then draped the coat over the folded glider. He hefted the nondescript package on to his back and climbed the ladder to the pier. The diamonds clinked like bags of marbles with each step he took along the quay wall. He hailed two boys patching a net on the slip and gave them two shillings.

One for the ferry back, and the other for yourselves.

It was common for visitors to the Saltee Islands to have one tankard too many and miss the last ferry. Common enough not to raise suspicions. There were always a couple of boys on the docks willing to return a borrowed boat, for a fee naturally.

I may have need of these boys a few nights more, thought Conor. *Then I leave this place forever.*

But there was no relish in the thought. As thoughts of his family grew stronger, his dream of America had paled. Nevertheless he would persevere, as staying here, close enough to home to see the kitchen light burning, would be intolerable.

I am Conor Finn now. I have no family.

Kilmore village was quiet enough due to the lateness of the hour, though there was still some argy-bargy emanating from the doorway of the Wooden House, the local pub built almost entirely from the deckhouse of a sunken Greek ship.

Conor was tempted to go inside and sit himself down with a bowl of stew, but the cargo on his back and belt was too valuable to stow under a tavern table, so he trudged on up the hill, leaving the village behind.

His new home was two miles past the village, off the old coast road. Conor climbed a stile and followed a worn path along the cliff edge to a set of late medieval gates, with eagles perched on their mossy pillars.

Eagles, thought Conor. *Victor's little joke.*

The wrought-iron gates were imposing enough, and might have deterred thieves had not the walls on either side been cannibalized by locals over the years to build their dwellings. Cut stone is not so cheap that it can be left piled high on a derelict estate. There were no more than odds and halves left now littering the grass.

Conor stepped over the broken wall, walking along an avenue that wound through a copse of willow trees. Behind this screen stood a Martello tower, a squat cylinder of stone with walls of a prodigious thickness, built by the British Army to keep an eye on the Saltee Islands. The single door was eight feet from the tower's base and could only be reached by ladder and the windows were letterbox gun ports that would allow the garrison stationed inside to pick off any poor unfortunates unlucky enough to be on the offensive.

Conor disentangled a ladder from the weeds at the base of the tower, propping it up against the tower wall, then, balancing the weight of the collapsed glider on his shoulder, he edged slowly up the rungs.

A pity to survive night flights over Saint George's Channel only to crack my skull falling from a ladder.

The door seemed flimsy, of dry, crumbling wood held together by rivets and steel bands, but there were many deceptive things about this tower. Conor had spent many hours working on the structure, almost exclusively on the inside. No need to advertise the renovations. A steel door lay behind the wooden one, housed in a reinforced frame. Conor threaded a key though the lock, and let himself in.

He sighed in almost unconscious relief as he locked the door behind him.

Home. Alive.

The inside was far more salubrious than the exterior suggested. On the first storey was a fully equipped laboratory for the study of aeronautics, with more advanced machinery than would be found in many a royal college. Charts were nailed to the walls. The theories and diagrams of da Vinci, Cayley, the Marquis de Bacqueville. Models of gliders to various scales hung from the ceiling beams. Tyres, tubes, wings, engines, oil drums, timber planks, frames and reams of fabric were stacked neatly around the walls. Baskets of reeds. Ball bearings, magnets, rivets and screws lay neatly in wooden bowls on the long bench. On a steam-winch platform to the roof sat rifles, revolvers, swords, two small-calibre cannon and a pyramid of cannonballs.

Victor was preparing for a battle. He knew Bonvilain wanted him dead.

A Corsican tower at Mortella Point had once withstood bombardment from two British warships for almost two days with the loss of only three men. The British had copied the design and misspelled the name, changing *Mortella* to

Martello. If Bonvilain wished to gain entry to Victor's laboratory, he would have to pay dearly for the privilege.

It had not been difficult to locate the tower Victor had told him about on the last day of his life. There were two Martello towers in the vicinity of Kilmore and one had been occupied for the past fifty years. That left the gloomily named *Forlorn Point*. The tower had originally been called simply *Saltee Watch*, but the men of the garrison stationed there had soon taken to calling the tower after the headland it stood on. A name more in tune with the unrelenting winds and typical leaden weather of the region than the almost cheery-sounding *Saltee Watch*. So *Forlorn Point* it became, made somewhat notorious by the folk singer Tam Riordan in his 'Lament of Forlorn Point', which began: ''Tis off I am to Forlorn Point for my sins.' The second line was no jollier. 'And if there's a tide, I aim to throw myself in . . .'

It was said that the tower was haunted by the ghosts of thirty-seven men who were burned alive inside its walls when the armoury caught fire. No wonder it slid to dereliction.

That is until Victor Vigny decided that it would make an ideal workshop and persuaded King Nicholas to fund the project. The Frenchman purchased the tower in his own name, to hide Nicholas's involvement, then had a series of shipments sent there from London, New York and even China.

The materials had been winched to the roof and then humped downstairs to the laboratory floor, and there they had lain for two years, undisturbed by the drunken local caretaker until Conor arrived to find a key waiting for him in the talons of the pillar's stone eagle.

Conor was not worried about the ghosts, indeed he was thankful for the legend as it kept the superstitious locals away. Once in a while a lad would bring his girl as far as the tower wall, so they could touch the clammy stones then run away squealing, but besides those minor intrusions he was left alone.

He was civil in the village, but did not invite friendship. He bought his supplies, paid with coin and went on his way. The locals were not sure what to make of the pale, blond young man living at Forlorn Point.

He walks like a fighter, some said. *Always ready to draw that sabre of his.*

Handsome but fierce, concluded the women.

One girl disagreed. *Not fierce*, she said. *Haunted.*

The innkeeper had chuckled. *Well, if it's haunted Mister Handsome-But-Fierce wants, he's in the right place.*

Conor's living quarters were underneath the laboratory at ground level, but he did not spend much time down there, as the gloomy enclosure reminded him of his cell on Little Saltee. Victor had equipped it luxuriously with four-poster bed, bureau and chaise longue. There was even a toilet plumbed down to the ocean, but when the lights went out and the walls juddered with every wave crash, Conor was transported back to Little Saltee. Each morning he was woken by the booming cannon shot from the prison and one night he found himself almost unconsciously scratching some calculations into the wall with a sharp stone. It was difficult enough living in such proximity to home, he decided, without recreating his prison cell here on the mainland.

And so he slept on the roof, or, rather, what had been the roof, but was now an extra level: Victor's pièce de résistance. Martello towers were constructed with completely flat roofs that could bear the weight of two cannon and the men to operate them. Victor had used this strength and flatness as a base for a powerful wind tunnel, driven by four steam-powered fans. For years, they had been forced to study the effects of wind over wing surfaces using a whirling arm device, but now lift, drag and relative air velocity could be accurately measured using the most powerful wind tunnel in the world. The device was unsophisticated, but effective. Twenty feet long and twenty-five feet square powered by a steam injection system that was capable of producing a flow velocity of sixty miles per hour.

With this tunnel, Conor had learned that many of his prison designs were flawed, and that many more showed promise. Four of his gliders made it past the model stage, and he was convinced that his engine-powered aeroplane would fly too, when he put it together.

There was another use for the wind tunnel. Conor used it to augment his launch from the tower roof. He would hitch himself up, spread his wings then duck obliquely into the wind stream, to be propelled into the sky as though shot from a cannon.

You are taking risks, Victor would have undoubtedly said.

Leapfrogging over several steps in the scientific process. And your records are vague and often coded. What manner of scientist are you?

I am no more a scientist, Conor would have replied. *I am an airborne thief.*

That morning he sat on the roof, back resting against the wind tunnel's planking, swaddled in a woollen blanket and eating from a can of beef. The rising sun cast a golden glow over the distant Saltee Islands, as though they were some kind of magical place. Mystical islands.

He thought of his parents and of Isabella, then in a fit of irritation sent his fork sparking across the stone roof and tramped down the stairs to the lower level.

I will sleep below and be reminded of my cell. I need strength of purpose.

Two days later, Conor had finished repairing the wind-tunnel planks and made the trip to Kilmore. He fancied a cooked meal, and to hear the voices of others even if they were not addressing him. It had come as something of a shock to him when he realized that his loneliness had intensified since escaping from prison. It was necessary for him to seek out the company of men for the sake of his own sanity.

It was market day in Kilmore and so the quay was lined with stalls, and for every stall a dozen beggars. There was great excitement over a humongous steam engine, painted green and red, which rumbled on metal wheels along the seafront, belching out great puffs of acrid smoke. A penny a ride.

Conor had a quick look at the engine, but quickly saw that there was nothing for him to learn here. This engine was twenty years old, a fairground workhorse, not at all the scientific marvel its owner claimed it to be.

He stepped inside the Wooden House, found himself a corner table and called for a bowl of stew.

Life was being lived in front of his eyes. He could see it and hear it and smell it. The scratch of elbows on tables, the knocking of wonky chairs. Sunlight through the pipe smoke. Yet there was a distance between him and the world. All he could feel was an intense irritation towards people in general. Everything upset him: the sound of chewing, the slurp of porter, the nasal whine of a drunkard's breathing. He could make allowances for nothing.

I have forgotten how to be human. I am a beast.

Then Conor's mood was lightened by music drifting through the tavern window, a gentle violin that rolled itself out like a fine carpet, playing overhead, riding the stale air and pipe smoke. It seemed to cut through the fog surrounding Conor's heart, warming it with its melody.

I know that music, thought Conor. *I have heard it before somewhere. But where?*

The landlord arrived with his stew, a rich soup of beef and pork with vegetable chunks floating on the surface.

'Generally I move the beggars on, young man,' he remarked. 'But this blind fella, the way he plays, reminds me of my childhood in the stables. Wonderful years.' He wiped a tear away with a tattooed knuckle. 'Onions in the stew,' he blubbered, then moved on.

Conor worked on the stew, savouring its flavours and textures, enjoying the strangely familiar music.

I will throw a shilling to the musician as I leave, he decided. *What is that tune?*

The more Conor listened, the more the puzzle vexed him, and then suddenly everything became clear.

I have heard this music and I have read it. 'This blind fella,' the landlord said.

Conor dropped a brimming spoon halfway to his open mouth, rose from his chair as though in a daze, and barged his way through the fair-day crowd. Outside the sudden sunlight blinded him after the tavern's smoky gloom.

Follow the music.

He ran on like a rat in thrall to the piper of Hamelin. To the side of the Wooden House, a small throng had gathered, swaying as one to a gentle adagio. A tall black-garbed figure at the crowd's centre led the sway with the tip of his violin bow, lulling the listeners.

Conor stopped in his tracks, completely flabbergasted. He could not decide whether to laugh aloud or weep, eventually settling on a hybrid of the two.

The musician was, of course, Linus Wynter.

'So, Billtoe did not lie. You actually were released?'

They sat at Conor's table in the tavern, enjoying a glass of porter after their stew. Linus Wynter's gangly limbs were too long for the furniture and he was forced to straighten his legs to fit them under the table. His crossed feet poked out the other end.

'Released I was,' he said, fiddling with pipe and tobacco pouch. 'Though I fully expected to be *released*, if you see what I mean. Nicholas had signed the order before he died and it took a few days to reach the island. And as Marshall Bonvilain had not expressly forbidden it, out I slipped. Free as a bird.' He rasped a match along the tabletop and played the flame over the pipe. 'I doubt you slipped out so easily.'

'Not quite,' confirmed Conor.

Wynter smiled, smoke leaking from between his teeth. 'I was playing in Dublin in a nice alehouse. Then I began to hear rumours of a baker, flying up to the moon on a balloon.'

'It was a butcher, and he never got anywhere near the moon, believe me.'

'So I thought to myself, all Victor ever talked about was balloons, and young Conor was his student. Coincidence? I think not. So, I began taking the train from Westland Row to Wexford once a week or so, hoping you would show yourself. I was beginning to think you hadn't survived.'

'I almost did not. It is a miracle that I sit here today.'

Linus patted his violin. 'You remember *The Soldier's Return*?'

'How could I forget? I committed large sections to memory.'

'Ah, you found my notes.'

'I used the space for my own diagrams. Did you know that the coral was luminous?'

Linus tapped his temple. 'No. Blind, don't you know. Dashed inconvenient in the area of luminous coral and such. It gave me comfort to trace the notes with my fingers, helped me to remember. There was also the danger that I would die in that place and my music would be lost forever.'

'Well, Linus, your notes shone. It was something to see.'

'My notes always shine, boy. A pity the rest of the world doesn't see it.' Wynter took a deep drag on his pipe. 'Now to business – do you have a plan? Or would you like to hear mine?'

'A plan to do what?'

Wynter's puzzlement showed in the lines between his ruined eyes. 'Why to ruin Bonvilain, naturally. He has robbed us of everything, and continues to destroy lives. We have a responsibility.'

'I have a responsibility to myself,' said Conor harshly. 'My plan is to collect all the diamonds buried on Little Saltee, then begin a new life in America.'

Wynter straightened his back. 'Hell's bells, boy. Bonvilain killed your king. He killed our friend, the incomparable Victor Vigny. He has torn your family apart, taken your sweetheart from you. And your answer to this is to run away?'

Conor's face was stony. 'I know what has happened, Mister Wynter. I know something of the real world now too. All I can hope for is to leave this continent alive, and even that is unlikely, but to attack a kingdom alone would be lunacy.'

'But you are not alone.'

'Of course, the boy and the blind man will attack Bonvilain together. This is not an operetta, Linus. Good people get shot and die. I have seen it happen.'

Conor's voice was loud, and attracting attention. Bonvilain was not a name to be bandied about even on the mainland. It was said that informers took the marshall's coin in every country from Ireland to China.

'I have seen it happen too,' said Wynter in hushed tones. 'But lately I have not seen it and have had to imagine it instead, which is far worse.'

Conor had imagined death many times in prison, and not just his own. He had imagined what Bonvilain would do to his family if they ever found out the truth of Nicholas's murder.

'If I fight, *he* will kill my parents. *He* will do it in the blink of an eye, and it will cost him not a moment's sleep.'

'Do you believe that your father would thank you for making him the marshall's puppet?'

'My father thinks that *I* had a hand in the king's murder. He denounced me for it.'

'All the more reason to tell him the truth.'

'No. I am done. I love my father and hate him too. All I can do is leave.'

'And your mother,' persisted Linus Wynter. 'And the queen?'

Conor felt his melancholia return. 'Linus, please. Let us enjoy our reunion. I know that we were only cellmates for a few days, but I see you as my only friend in the world. It is nice to have a friend, so let us avoid this topic for the moment.'

'Don't you want to clear your name, Conor?' persisted Linus. 'How can you let your father live with the idea that you have murdered his king?'

The idea would eat Declan Broekhart from the inside, Conor knew, but he couldn't see a solution.

'Of course I want to prove myself innocent. Of course I want to expose Bonvilain, but how can I do these things without endangering my family?'

'We can find a way. Two brains together.'

'I will think about it,' said Conor. 'That will have to be good enough for now.'

Linus raised his palms in surrender. 'Good enough.'

Wynter turned his face towards the window, feeling the sun on his face. 'Can you spy a clock, Conor? I can't read the sun from in here. I need to return to Wexford for the train.'

'Forget the train, Linus Wynter, you are coming home with me.'

Wynter stood, his hat brushing the ceiling beam. 'I was so hoping you would say that. I do hope the beds are comfortable. I stayed in the Savoy once, you know. Did I ever tell you?'

Conor took his elbow, leading him towards the door. 'Yes, you told me. Do you still dream of the water closets?'

'I do,' sighed Linus. 'Will we have privacy in this house?

We must have privacy if I am to hatch my schemes.'

'All the privacy in the world. Just you and I, and a small company of soldiers.'

'Soldiers?'

'Well, their ghosts.'

Linus plucked his violin strings in imitation of a music-hall suspense theme.

'Ghosts, indeed,' he drawled. 'It seems, Mister Finn, that once again we are destined to share *interesting* accommodation.'

CHAPTER 14:

HEADS TOGETHER

Linus quickly settled into his new digs, and Conor was happy to have him. Usually his thoughts stayed inside his head so it was a relief to let them out. They sat on the roof together, and while Conor tinkered with the skeleton of his latest flying machine Linus worked on his compositions.

'A lute here, I think,' Linus would say. 'Do you think a lute too pastoral? Too vulgar?'

And Conor would reply. 'I have two main problems. Engine weight and propeller efficiency. Everything else works; I have proven that. I think, I really think that this new petrol engine I have built will do the trick.'

So Linus would nod and say. 'Yes, you are right. Too vulgar. A piccolo, I think, boy.'

And Conor would continue. 'My engine needs to supply me with ten horsepower at least, without shaking the aeroplane to pieces. I need to build a housing that will absorb the vibration. Perhaps a willow basket.'

'So, you're saying a lute? You're right, the piccolo simply does not command the same respect.'

'You see,' Conor would say, chiselling his latest propeller, 'there is no problem we cannot solve if we put our heads together. *We need to bump skulls*, as Victor used to say.'

They were reasonably happy days. The spectre of Marshall

Bonvilain watched over them from the islands, but both man and youth felt a sense of camaraderie that they had not known in years.

Of course they argued, most notably when Conor set the steam fans whirling in preparation for his second flight. Linus Wynter climbed the ladder from his bedchamber, shouting over the steam engine's noise.

'Hell's bells, boy. What do you need engines for at this time of night?'

And so Conor told him, and the musician almost fainted.

'You are going to hurl yourself into a windstorm, so you can fly *into* a prison? Why don't you write that sentence down and read it? Then perhaps you would realize how insane you are.'

Conor settled his goggles. 'I have to do this, Linus. That island owes me. Five more bags and I leave – we leave – for America.'

'You *have* to hurl yourself into space for greed? For science I can understand, barely – that's what Nick and Victor dedicated their lives to.'

'It's more than greed. It's right.'

Linus barked a bitter laugh. 'Right? It would be right for you to rescue your parents and your queen from the madman who has deceived them.'

This gave Conor pause. Linus was speaking the truth. His loved ones were in danger and he had no idea how to save them without dooming them all. And, if he were honest with himself, he dreaded seeing that look of pure hatred in his father's eyes.

'There's nothing I can do,' he said finally. 'Nothing except take my diamonds.'

Linus raised his arms like a preacher. 'All of this. All of it for diamonds. It's beneath you.'

Conor ratcheted up his wings, ducking into the wind stream.

'Everything is beneath me,' he said, but his words were snatched away, as he was, into the night sky.

Great Saltee

Billtoe and Pike were in the Fulmar Bay Tavern, spending their evening off over a bucket of half-price slops as was their custom.

Pike followed a long swallow with a belch that shook his stool.

'Them's good slops,' he commented, smacking is lips. 'I'm getting wine, beer, brandy and a hint of carbolic soap, if I'm not mistaken.' Pike was rarely mistaken when it came to slops, for it was all he ever drank, even though with Battering Ram money in his pocket he could afford actual beer, rather than whatever ran off the bar into the slops' tray.

'What do you say, Mister Billtoe? You tasting soap? Goes down easy, but doesn't stay in long, eh?'

Billtoe was not in the mood for tavern chatter. He wanted nothing more than to drink himself into oblivion, but he was mightily afraid that when he *reached* oblivion, the French devil would be waiting there for him. Since that night on

Little Saltee one week ago, Arthur Billtoe had not been his usual cruel and cheerful self. He felt the presence of the flying demon looming over him, waiting to bring down his blade. Then there was the small matter of Marshall Bonvilain's dead prisoner. Billtoe lived each waking moment struggling with his panic. The effort was such that he had developed a shiver.

'I've been meaning to ask you, Mister Billtoe,' said Pike, 'if there's something wrong with you. You ain't been taking the usual care with your ruffled shirts, and they're your pride and joy. You been shaking a lot and mumbling too. And that's plague right there, or maybe Yellow Jack, though I never heard of that this far north.'

Billtoe's mood was darkened by the realization that Pike, the hairless simpleton, was his only friend. He never had much use for friends before now. When you had as many dark secrets as Arthur Billtoe, the last thing you needed was friends to wheedle them out of you. But tonight he was on the brink of utter despair and he needed words of comfort that came out of an actual mouth, and not just the imaginary voice of his favourite slipper to which he talked occasionally.

'Pikey, can I ask you something?'

'Of course you can, Mister Billtoe. I would appreciate nothing with numbers or directions though, cos they give me blinders.'

Billtoe took a deep, shaky breath. 'Do you believe in the devil?'

'Warden's the devil, if you ask me. I mean, why can't the

convicts eat each other? Two birds with one stone right there. Convicts get fed, and we don't have to bury the dead ones.'

'No!' snapped Billtoe. 'Not the warden, the man himself. Old horned head.' He turned on his barstool to face Pike. His face was gaunt and his eyes were wide and red-rimmed, and the ruffles of his pirate shirt did seem wilted. 'I've seen him, Pikey. I've seen him. With his wings and flaming eyes. He landed on the island last week, coming for me he was. Called me mon-sewer. The devil called my name, Pikey. He called my name.'

Billtoe buried his face in his forearms, and soon his back shook with sobbing.

Pike licked his palm, then smoothed back his one strand of hair. He had seen the devil too, except it wasn't your actual devil, it was a man with wings strapped to his back. Pike saw them taken off and folded up. It was a shame to see Arthur all broke up with his devil talk, but information like this was worth money, which Pike himself could collect as soon as the Rams sent their man for a parley.

Then again, if anyone knows how to make real money out of a situation, it's Arthur Billtoe. And won't he just love me when I take away his devil.

Pike wrestled his sketchpad from the pocket it was bent into, opened it to the sketches he had scratched at Sebber Bridge and slid the book across the bar.

'I seen him too, Mister Billtoe, your devil.'

Billtoe's bleary eyes peeked out from over his sleeves. For a moment he didn't understand what he was seeing, then he recognized the figure that Pike had drawn. And if Pike had seen the devil too, then Arthur Billtoe was not losing his mind. His eyes assumed their usual piggy cunning and one hand scuttled out crablike to grab the notepad.

'That's him, ain't it, Mister Billtoe?' said Pike. 'Only he ain't no devil – he's a man like you and me, except taller and better made than us. You being stumpy and me being, well, me. But that's him I'll bet, ain't it, Mister Billtoe?'

Billtoe straightened shrugging off his mood like a dog shaking water from its coat.

'Call me Arthur, Pikey my friend,' he said.

Pike smiled a gap-toothed smile. He was familiar with that look in Billtoe's beadies. It was the same look he got just before he searched a prisoner. Billtoe could smell guineas.

An offshore breeze blew constant and the moon was a silver shilling behind a veil of clouds. The perfect evening for clandestine flying. Conor Finn felt almost contented as he dipped the glider's nose, swooping in to land on Sebber Bridge. His control of the craft was much improved and there was no greater impact on his heels than if he had jumped from a low wall. The propeller bands were still fully wound as fortune had steered him clear of stalls. There was also the heartening fact that he had recovered three bags of Battering Ram diamonds from the salsa beds on Little Saltee without a sniff of a prison guard. He had worried that Billtoe might have swallowed a bottle or two of courage and come looking for his devil with a few cronies, but there had been neither sight nor smell of Arthur Billtoe.

I scared that rat for now. But he won't stay scared long.

One more trip. And I shall have all seven pouches.

Why do you need all seven? was a question that Linus might have asked, and now Conor asked himself.

I need seven as compensation for my imprisonment. It is a matter of honour.

This was the argument that had sustained him in prison. He would do what Billtoe could not: take his diamonds off the island. But now, this plan seemed flawed. Why expose himself to danger time and time again, when he should already be on the steamer to New York? It was true that Otto had been promised half of the diamonds, but even if he paid off the Malarkeys in full, he would still have more than enough diamonds to buy him a passage to America and a new life when he got there.

I do not wish to leave, he realized. *But I must.*

Staying was of no benefit to him or his family.

Seven pouches. Then America.

The skiff was beached high on the shale, with a single set of tracks heading back towards Fulmar Bay. Zeb Malarkey was keeping his end of the deal, and why wouldn't he, with half the diamonds in his coffers and more to come.

Conor sat on the boat's gunwale, unfastening the glider's harness. Not much flight damage tonight, but he would check every rib and panel tomorrow to make sure. Even the tiniest tear in the wing fabric could unravel an entire panel and drop him from the sky like a plugged pigeon.

One of the diamond pouches slipped from inside the harness, clinking on the shale. To Conor, the sound seemed louder than a gunshot. He squatted low in the skiff's shadow, then gathered the bag to his chest like a babe, scanning the Wall for movement. There was none, but the liquid shimmer of lamplight.

Take care, airman. One mistake could see you on the ferry back to Little Saltee.

He stowed the pouches under the aft bench and laid his collapsed glider gently on the deck. Then something happened that made him smile.

Conor stood straight, raising his palm to feel the breeze.

The wind has changed. I can sail directly to Kilmore.

He slid the skiff along the shale to the lapping water-line.

Still waters and a fair wind. Good omens.

Conor felt the water raise the skiff, and hopped on board, the deck shuddering under his weight. With one hand he untied the sail, shaking it loose of the mast, with the other he grasped the extended tiller, setting a course wide around the west coast of Little Saltee.

Home in an hour, he thought. *Perhaps Linus would play something. Music is a tonic for the soul.*

Conor's sail caught the breeze, pulling the small skiff across the waves.

A good boat. She skips along.

He sailed for his new home, forcing himself not to look back. Nothing behind but heartache.

From high in the rocks, Arthur Billtoe watched the strange airman depart. And though a sharp rock pressed into the guard's stomach, he would not so much as twitch until the man he had believed to be a demon had disappeared completely round the bend of Little Saltee's coastline.

Pike did not have the necessary concentration span for such caution; he had relieved himself and was skipping stones into the surf before Billtoe joined him at the groove sliced by the skiff's keel in the shale.

'Dunno why they call it Sebber *Bridge*,' muttered Pike. 'It's not a bridge is it? Just a spit of stones going out into the current.'

'It used to be a bridge, thousands of years ago,' said Billtoe, the words rattling nervously out of him. 'Before the sea washed it away. Went from here to Little Saltee, then from there on to Saint Patrick's Bridge on the mainland.'

'That airman really turns your backbone soft, don't he, Arthur?' said Pike, changing the subject.

'He had a sword at my neck. A ruddy big sword, none of your fencing namby-pamby pinprickers. This thing could take the top off an oak tree.'

'He's a *man*, though, Arthur. You seen it yourself. Those wings of his are some sort of kite. That's all.'

'That's all!' said Billtoe incredulously. 'You idiot! Don't you realize what we have just witnessed?'

'Idiot? Arthur, idiot?' said Pike, injured. 'I took away your devil, didn't I? You can sleep again because of my gift. Idiot seems a bit harsh.'

'Not harsh enough,' snapped Billtoe, who was fast forgetting his fear. 'That man has a flying device. Have you any idea how much the Battering Rams would pay for that? They could just drop into whatever port they pleased, and hang Customs. A device like that would change smuggling forever.'

Pike cleared his throat. 'As it happens, I knows a few gents who might have ties to the Rams. Possibly.'

Billtoe clamped a hand over Pike's mouth, as though the gents in question could somehow hear. 'No. No. We don't involve the Rams until we have those wings locked up safe somewhere. Otherwise those treacherous coves would nab the wings themselves and feed us to the sharks. What we want is to get ourselves into a strong bargaining position.'

Pike shrugged off Billtoe's hand, which stank of sweat and worse. It was clear to him that they were friends no more. It was business as usual for Arthur Billtoe, which meant that Pike was back to being a lackey to be abused.

'Whatever you say, Arthur.'

'That's –'

'I know, that's *Mister* Billtoe to me.'

He turned to the sea, skipping one of the stones in his hand across the surface.

Typical Arthur Billtoe. I took away his devil, and he forgets it with the first sniff of a payoff. I thought it was Pikey and Billtoe to the end. How wrong I was.

Throwing the stones calmed him, each successful skip reminding him of his childhood. He was reaching back for a big throw when Billtoe grabbed his arm, then wrestled the stone from his fingers.

'Where did you get this?' he demanded, excitement reddening his cheeks.

Pike wondered was this one of those questions that weren't really questions, and if he answered it, would he look stupid?

'It's a stone, Arthur . . . Mister Billtoe. I just picked it up.'

Billtoe dropped to his knees, scrabbling in the shale until he found half a dozen more stones that pleased him. He held them in his cupped palms, like a tramp guarding his egg breakfast.

'Arthur. Are you feeling ill? Would you like me to collect a few more stones for you? I saw a nice piece of wood further along.'

Billtoe was too happy to be annoyed. 'These are not just stones, Pikey. These are rough diamonds. That's why our airman was stopping off on Little Saltee. He's a diamond smuggler.'

He rubbed his hands together, clinking the diamonds like voodoo bones.

'Are you trying to tell the future with those things?' joked Pike, the naked greed in Billtoe's eyes making him nervous.

'I *know* the future,' said Billtoe. 'We round up a few of the boys, we ambush this airman, sell his wings and steal his diamonds.'

'What about the airman? We let him go free I suppose.'

Billtoe elbowed him good-naturedly. 'Nice one, Pikey. Let him go free. No, we kill him, cut him into little pieces and then burn the pieces. As far as the world is concerned, this airman never existed.'

Pike swallowed. All this talk of blood made him nervous. He resolved there and then never to invent anything useful, or Billtoe might orchestrate a gruesome end for him too.

CHAPTER 15:

HOME

There was almost perfect peace as Conor sailed the skiff north-north-east between the Jackeen and Murrock Rocks in the Saltee Straits. These rocks spent most of their lives submerged, but sometimes a trough dipped low, exposing their flattened peaks. When the five-year-old Conor had first seen these gnarled oblong shapes one evening on the patrol boat with his father, he was convinced they were crocodiles and would not be calm until Declan agreed to fire a warning shot. Sure enough, the crack of gunfire did the trick and the two crocodiles sank below the waters.

This little story had become one for the fireside, and it was dusted off whenever a friend visited for brandy or lemonade. It had always made Conor scowl, but now it near drove him to tears.

I cannot endure this. They are too close.

His mother's face seemed to hover before him, calling him home, and he could ignore her no longer. No doubt she suffered as much as he did, perhaps more. He needed to know.

If I could just see them. Look on their faces once more before I leave, to make sure they endure.

Conor nudged the tiller with his knee, and tightened the sail for a south-west tack. He was going home.

*

From a distance, Saltee Harbour seemed much as Conor remembered it. A grand tiara, points shining silver and orange. Inside the pincers of the sea walls, it was clear that some of the tiara's lustre had faded over the past few years. Sea slime crawled along the granite and the dock was clogged with haphazardly berthed boats, trussed together like tangled tops. The new outer-wall project had been abandoned, and the half-built structure trailed off into the sea like an eroded sand fort. The planned beacon tower was only half built and stood askew, a crumbling reminder of a past era, rather than the proud symbol of a new one. King Nicholas's loss was being keenly felt, even here on the waterfront.

Conor knotted the skiff's stern line to a mussel boat, and tossed the anchor into the half tide. It fizzed, bubbled, then sank quickly, bearing with it three securely fastened satchels of diamonds. Conor skipped across the prows of half a dozen bobbing fishing boats, before hauling himself to the quayside flagstones with the aid of a brass hitching ring.

He strolled nonchalantly along the quay, flicking his eyes upwards to the Wall guards. Whatever else grew slack and haphazard, Declan Broekhart would not allow his sharp-shooters to lower their standards. Four guards stood atop the Wall, their wind capes fluttering around them. Conor saw the glint of a barrel and he knew that at the first sign of belligerence a warning shot would kick up sparks and slivers at his feet, at the second sign he would be dead before his body hit the water. He moved slow and easy with both hands in plain sight.

The quayside walkway curled the length of the outer wall to a cobbled market area, which would be bustling with stalls during the day. Merchants, innkeepers and housewives converged on the market each morning to fill their baskets with mackerel, cod, pollock, mussels, lobster, crab, crayfish and salmon. Boats arrived empty from Kilmore and left full or vice versa, depending on which crew had the run of the waters that day.

By evening, the air was tangy with smells of turning fish and salt. Scrubbers pumped water from the harbour, hosing the blood and guts into the sea. Most young lads on the Saltees had done their time as scrubbers, armed with stout bristled brushes and the energy of youth, they scrubbed the grime from the flagstones, only for them to be splattered crimson once more the following day.

Conor walked beneath the Wall arch, past a Customs booth.

'Anything?' asked the guard.

Conor raised his empty palms. 'Just a raging thirst, sir, and a rendezvous with my sweetheart.'

The guard smiled. 'Ah, the beer and Bessies. Two good reasons to visit the Saltees. It's not your first time inside the Wall, then?'

Ahead, on the hill, the palace turrets poked into the night, blotting out patches of stars.

'No, sir. I've been here before.'

As a boy, Conor had not spent every minute lost in his studies. He'd passed his share of time up to his armpits in mud and seaweed. He'd climbed cliffs, built dams and on occasion stolen eggs from the puffins that waddled along the flat rocks like clockwork toys.

These manly endeavours sometimes caused him to miss his curfew, and when this happened Conor would spy through the windows of the Broekhart apartments to see whether or not his father was home or even what kind of mood his parents were in.

He occupied the same spot now, straddling a gargoyle drain, ten feet off the ground across the square from the Broekhart house. Water from the salt spray trickled from the gargoyle's mouth, painting white streaks on its twisted stone lips. Even climbing the wall brought pangs of longing for home.

My feet find the footholds in the stone. I climb this wall as though I had done it only yesterday.

The Broekhart home was quiet and dark, but for a single candle in the kitchen window. There was no sign of his parents.

It is late, I suppose.

Conor was greatly disappointed, but relieved too. The knot of nerves in his stomach was tighter now than it had been during his balloon flight from prison. He knew that if he had seen his parents in abject misery, it would have been almost impossible not to venture inside and reveal the truth.

They hate me now, Mother and Father both, but it is a false hate. Manufactured. Underneath there will still be love.

Inside the Broekhart dwelling, a shadow drifted into the

kitchen. Conor felt his pulse throb in his forehead.

Perhaps my mother cannot sleep; nightmares haunt her, as they do me.

It was his mother. Catherine Broekhart drifted past the window, her hair sleep dishevelled. Her eyes were half closed, and both hands waved the air, until her eyes adjusted to the sudden light.

Mother. Oh, Mother.

The simple sight of her tore down the barriers Conor had erected round his heart. It was time to end Bonvilain's cruel charade. The consequences were on the marshall's head, not Conor's.

He shifted his weight, to dismount the gargoyle, then froze. His father had entered the kitchen and he was not alone. There was a child in his arms, a tousled toddler, lower lip jutted with bad temper.

A child. My brother.

His father was not the broken man he imagined. Declan Broekhart wore a familiar smile as he coddled the little boy, wrapping him in the sleeve of his robe. He spoke, and through the open window Conor recognized his tone even if he couldn't quite make out the words.

My father is happy.

Catherine poured a mug of water for the little boy, and they fussed over him together, sitting by the fireplace while he had his drink. Gradually the child's temper softened, as the memory of his nightmare was replaced by the sight of two loving parents.

Outside on the gargoyle, Conor felt scalped, as though

the final remnants of Conor Broekhart had been cut away.

A child. A brother.

Things were not as he had imagined them. It seemed as though he was the only one suffering. His parents had rediscovered happiness with their new son.

The cold of the stone gargoyle spread through his thighs, creeping up into his chest. Salty spray fell in sheets over the Wall drenching his jacket, the chill soaking through to his shoulders.

They have a good life, thought Conor. *They are happy again.*

Conor knew that he could not reveal himself, or the truth.

Bonvilain would kill them without a second's hesitation. It would be my fault.

Conor turned his face away from the window and swung himself down from the gargoyle.

I am Conor Finn, he told himself, taking quick determined steps towards the harbour.

The airman flies one more time. Two bags of diamonds and then America.

Forlorn Point

Linus Wynter was busy when Conor reached the tower. He had completely rearranged the sleeping chamber to his personal preference. There was hot chocolate on the stove, along with a pot of bacon and potatoes and he was stitching a seam on the sleeve of his dress coat.

'It's the middle of the night,' said Conor, climbing through the elevated door.

Linus tapped his temple. 'It's always night for me, boy. I sleep when I am tired.'

Conor peered down into the cellar. 'Why do you bother to move the furniture? We leave in a few days, I told you this.'

'In a few days? Your precious flying machine is not finished.'

When Conor was not patching the wings on his glider, he spent every minute constructing the aeroplane he had designed in prison, complete with petrol engine and retractable landing gear.

'It is almost complete. Anyway, if needs be, I can ship it to America.'

'We're not tethered to one another,' said Linus, laying the needle against his finger to find the ripped seam. 'Maybe I'll stay behind and save your family myself.'

'My family don't need saving. They live in a palace with a new son.'

This gave Linus pause. He listened for Conor's breathing, then walked carefully towards him, feeling for his shoulders.

'You are so tall,' he said, surprised. 'Victor said you would be. Long bones, Frenchy always said. So you have yourself a little brother. That is wonderful news. Wouldn't you like to meet him before you leave?'

Conor felt tears film across his eyes. 'I . . . I, of course that is what *I* would like, but what would it mean for the child . . . My . . .'

'You can say it,' said Linus. 'He is your brother.'

'What would it mean for my brother?' blurted Conor. 'Bonvilain would murder him. If my father challenges the marshall, he will kill them all.'

Linus seemed to glare down at Conor, as though he could see through the silk scarf tied across his eyes. 'And what of Isabella? I hear talk in the village, she has already repealed taxes and abolished import duty. She is becoming a true queen. How do you think Bonvilain will respond to that?'

Conor wiped his eyes. 'She *is* the queen. She has people to protect her. She loved me, she said, and yet she believed that I helped to kill her father.'

'That's not what I hear. There is talk of Conor Broekhart in the village too. He was a hero, they say. He died trying to protect the king.'

Conor snorted. 'The official story. Bonvilain said that my *part* in the murder would be covered up to spare my family. That was his *gift* to the Broekharts.'

'And you are certain that Isabella was included in this deception.'

This was a startling thought. What if Isabella had not known? Imagine if she believed her young suitor to have perished that night.

Don't think about it. It is too painful, and it makes not a jot of difference.

Conor sat at his workbench, clenching both fists before his own face.

'Please, Linus, stop. I can't bear to explore possibilities. My connection with the Broekharts is severed. I cannot be responsible. Bonvilain is too big. I am Conor Finn.'

'The name Finn. Bonvilain's gift to you.'

Conor felt as though his forehead were collapsing, crushing his brain.

Love, family, happiness. They were luxuries. Life was the prize. Stay alive and keep your family alive.

'I am alive. I will stay alive.'

Linus barked a short laugh. 'Stay alive? Which is why you hurl yourself daily from a tower.'

'I made a promise to Otto Malarkey.'

'So, you would kill yourself for diamonds, but not for family or honour. I think Victor would be much disappointed in his student.'

Conor surged to his feet. 'Do not lecture me, old man. You are not my father.'

'Exactly right, boy,' said Linus softly, the anger draining from his face. 'I am not your father.'

Conor turned his back without another word, gathered the collapsed glider under his arm and climbed the ladder to the roof.

CHAPTER 16:

SNAKES IN THE GRASS

Conor and Linus barely spoke the following day, apart from a few grunted greetings. The American purposefully bashed himself against the furniture a few times, hoping to squeeze some concern from Conor, but without result. Either Conor didn't hear the groaning or he was ignoring it.

His heart may have been hardened by Little Saltee, thought Wynter, *but it was petrified by the sight of his little brother.*

Night came with little change in mood, but when Conor primed the engine for the wind tunnel, Linus felt he had to speak.

'You cannot fly tonight, Conor. The wind is wrong.'

Conor did not turn round. 'You are not my father, remember? And the wind is not wrong, it is a few degrees more to the south than I would like, but I can manoeuvre around it.'

'And the moon? There should be a harvest moon tonight.'

Conor buttoned his black jacket, scanning the panorama before him. There was barely a cloud in the sky. A glowing moon was reflected in dancing sections on the ocean's surface. As clear a night as he had ever seen.

'It's overcast,' he said brusquely, positioning himself below the glider, which hung from a gantry overhead. 'Lower the glider, would you?'

Linus, familiar now with the rooftop layout, counted the steps to a winch bolted to the wall.

'Ready?'

Conor raised his arms, ready to thread through the harness. 'Lower away. Five cranks of the handle.'

'I know. The same as yesterday. Will I bother with dinner?'

'Yes. Sorry about last night. I was in no mood for eating.'

'Nothing fresh, mind. I will reheat last night's fare.'

'The hot chocolate too? I regretted walking out on that. The roof is cold.'

Linus smiled. 'Sometimes a tantrum is expensive.'

The glider settled on to his back, and Conor buckled the harness across his chest, and drew the straps up between his legs. He reached down, curling his fingers around the harness winch handle, like a gunfighter checking the butt of his pistol.

'I wound the propellers,' said Linus.

Conor twanged one of the bands. 'Good and tight. Nicely done.'

'I have a heightened sense of tautness,' quipped Wynter, locking the winch. 'Can't you wait, Conor? The wind is wrong. I can smell the salt.'

Conor buttoned the flying jacket to his chin, then fixed his goggles. Once disguised, his entire demeanour changed. He stood taller and felt capable of more violence, no more a boy.

'I cannot wait, Linus. Not another night. I will have my

diamonds and be done with this life. America awaits. We can open a business together. I will fly my gliders and you can test the tautness of things.'

Wynter's smile was tinged with sadness. 'I am not ready to return home just yet, boy. Nicholas brought me here to do a job and I intend to see it through. At the risk of sounding melodramatic, I shall not rest while Bonvilain flourishes. He took the best men I have known away from me. Tonight, I fear, he may take another.'

Conor drew his sabre, balancing it on one wrist to test its weight. 'Do not fear for me, Linus. Fear for anyone who stands in my way this night.' He sheathed the sword, then checked the load in both revolvers.

'Oh, and would you turn off the wind tunnel before you go to bed?'

Conor ducked into the wind tunnel and was blasted into the night. Linus heard him go in a whoosh of air, creak of wood and trailing whoop.

Come back alive, boy, he thought. *You are their only hope.*

And then.

Perhaps I will make dinner from scratch. Some of my famous grits perhaps. An airman deserves to eat well. Fresh hot chocolate too.

Conor held his breath while the tunnel blast filled his wings and propelled him towards the stars. That first moment of tumult and force was as confusing as ever. He could not tell sea from sky, stars from their reflections. The air pummelled his torso with ghostly fists until the glider aligned itself with the wind's direction.

Then came the moment of pure flight when the wind lifted him, his glider creaked and took the strain and he was propelled bodily further from earth.

A moment of happiness. Nothing to do but be at peace.

Conor found that he relished this brief stretch more each time he flew. It was a calm before the storm, he knew, and yet while he flew with the wind at his back he could forget his troubles; they were as earthbound as most humans.

Rising thermals lifted him to an altitude higher than he had ever flown. The land spread out below him like a living map. He could see white tops stretching in lazy meanders for miles along the coast, like contour lines on a map. Several small boats bobbed gently on the silver black sea, fishermen taking advantage of the night tide and calm waters. Conor thought he heard a chorus of halloos from one boat. Had he been seen? It didn't matter – after this night the mysterious airman would fly no more. The next time he took to the air would be as a free American citizen with papers to prove it, thanks to Zeb Malarkey. He would ship the flying machine in parts to be assembled in Nebraska, or Wyoming or maybe California. Whichever was furthest from the Saltee Islands.

Conor moved hand over fist across the steering bar, turning the glider in a wide arc. Time to concentrate on his work or he would overshoot Little Saltee. Two more salsa beds, two more bags. Then Otto could buy his freedom and there would be plenty left for a secure life in America.

Great Saltee

Billtoe and Pike lay behind the ridge above Sebber Bridge, a series of soot-blackened blades arranged in the long grass around them.

'That cleaver is my special favourite,' said Pike fondly. 'Does for any sort of flesh. Fish, fowl or human. It will put a fair fracture in a bone too, it will.'

Billtoe begged to differ. 'Your common cleaver is clumsy, you gotter swing yer arm too high. Plenty of time for me to nip in and tickle a lung with this beauty.' He dinged a long and deadly ice pick with his nail.

'I favours my beloved sabre, name of Mary Ann,' said a husky Irish voice behind them.

'Quiet, you dolt,' hissed Billtoe. 'The airman could be here any moment.'

'*You* was talking,' said the man, wounded.

'*I* was *whispering*,' corrected Billtoe, and then to Pike. 'Why did you bring this scatterfool?'

'I could only shave three men from the prison guard,' said Pike. 'And you said it would take the half-dozen to knobble the airman. So I picked Rosy up in the pub. He hasn't had more than a quart of ale.'

Billtoe was not pleased. 'You *saw* the airman. He was a six footer at the very least and armed to the gills. We need sharp eyes and quick hands to take him, not drunken red-nosed Paddies.'

Rosy snorted. 'You is a Paddy yerself, Arthur. And I can chop down any man you point me at. Let's face it — this airman of yours, he's no more real than the banshee; he's just one of those yokeybobs, ain't he?'

Billtoe chewed his bottom lip, causing his chin stubble to quiver. 'A yokeybob?'

'You know. In yer brain. A phantom cos of you in that barrel.'

'You told him, Pikey,' said Billtoe reproachfully.

'You told me yourself in the tavern,' laughed Rosy. 'You told anyone who would listen all about the devil and poor little Billtoe in the barrel. There ain't no airman. I'm only here for the five shillings' payment. Why all the blades anywise? One bullet would do the trick.'

'We need the blades, you beer-brained beetroot face,' fumed Billtoe, 'because a gunshot would have the Wall guard on us like flies on a cow biscuit. And that would lose us any bounty our airman might be carrying.'

'If there was an airman.'

Billtoe wrapped his fingers around the hilt. 'Well, Rosy, if there ain't an airman, why don't you tell that there fellow in the sky above you that he's just a yokeybob sprung from my brain.'

Rosy glanced up fully expecting to see nothing but stars. What he did see had him pawing the grass for his beloved sabre.

'God preserve us,' he breathed, crossing himself with his weaponless hand. 'A man with wings.'

'Yokeybob, my eye,' snorted Billtoe, then talked no more as his teeth were clenched on a dagger blade.

*

Conor had succeeded in unearthing the final pouches, but they had cost him dearly. The silver moonbeams lit his wings like Chinese lanterns.

A guard had seen him glide over Little Saltee's outer wall, and being one of the few stout chaps on the island had decided to chase what he took for an albatross. He stalked his prey to the salsa beds where he realized his mistake and put a round through one of the glider's wings, just as the strange airman bent low to retrieve some kind of pouch. Only a slight nervous shake to the guard's hand spared Conor a bullet in the brain gourd.

The shot split a stone at Conor's feet, throwing up a shard that scored a lightning flash on the left lens of his goggles.

He reacted quickly, ditching the glider with two yanks on the harness belts, then spinning towards his attacker, pistols drawn.

'Yield or die, *monsieur*,' he called, cocking the revolvers.

The guard could not decide whether he wished to yield or die, or something in between. Yielding was not something he was comfortable with, but neither did he relish a midnight battle with a flying Frenchy. Those fellows were dangerous enough without wings, as his grandfather had learned at Waterloo.

By the time he had considered his options and thought to cock his firearm, the black-clad airman was upon him, leaping from rock to stone with the speed of a cat, the guard would later swear. And growling too, like a hungry wolf. A cat-dog Frenchy, twirling guns and with blades clanking on his thighs.

'*Bonsoir, monsieur,*' said the airman, then clocked the surprised guard on the crown.

Conor was examining his glider almost before the guard fell. The upper port section had been punctured, but there were no rips radiating from the hole and the heat of the bullet had sealed the edges well enough. It would hold to Sebber Bridge if he could get himself into the air.

Conor threaded his arms through the straps then rolled both shoulders into the harness, cinched it tight and ran for the nearest stairwell. His wingtips scraped the walls on both sides, and he chided himself for not binding them in leather. The stairwell funnelled wind from above and it rattled his wings, pushing him down, but Conor struggled against it, forcing his way head first to the top step.

The gunshot had woken every guard in the billet, and they converged on the stairwell in ragged formation, clutching at rifles and trousers, shaking dreams from their heads. The sight of Conor had half of them convinced that they still slept.

One loosed a shot, but it was wild and high. The rest stared stupidly, mindless of each other until they tangled and fell in a bundle. Conor took advantage of the confusion to mount the parapet and leap into the sky, catching as much air as he could.

A wind, he prayed. *One tiny draught.*

Jupiter heard his prayer and sent a gift. An uplifting breath that filled his wings and threw him high above the heads of the watching guards. They scowled and screamed and stared in silence. Two thought to aim their weapons but the one who might have hit the target was accidentally shot by the other who pulled his trigger too early. In the blink of a crow's eye, the airman had disappeared into the night. Swallowed by black, like a stone sinking in the night sea.

For a long moment, nobody on the wall uttered a syllable. Then they began to jabber furiously, each man telling his own version of what he had seen. Even the wounded man gabbed with the rest, mindless of the blood pooling at his foot. This was a story they would tell many times and it needed to be made solid now. Wrap words around the bone before daylight made the whole thing seem unlikely.

It was an airman, they decided. *The Airman. Hadn't there been a whisper of something like this on Great Saltee?*

We saw the Airman. Seven feet tall with fiery, circular eyes.

The story was started. The word was spreading.

Word spreading is not what a man wants when he is a smuggler and a thief.

Conor rode the fair wind to Great Saltee, heart pounding in his chest. His blood was up, and he knew that was dangerous.

A man takes risks when the battle fever controls him, Victor had once told him. *I have seen too many clever men die stupidly.*

Be calm. Calm.

There was not time for calm. The air grew suddenly choppy and Conor was forced to wrestle with his craft simply to stay aloft. Great Saltee loomed below him, as though the earth had revolved to meet him. Conor pointed the nose down, holding it there against the tug of air resistance. Wind pulled at his goggles and poked fingers through the bullet hole in his wing.

On a night like this one, Conor could almost believe that men were not supposed to fly.

He came down at a sharp angle, too fast and too steep.

I will be lucky if my ankles survive this, he thought, gritting his teeth against the impact.

Though his vision was impaired by a cracked lens and whirling elements, Conor saw the skiff on Sebber Bridge, and he also spotted the men lying in wait for him behind the ridge.

Snakes in the grass, he thought without a shred of fear, utterly ready for a fight. He shifted left on the steering bar in order to come down in their midst.

May as well have a soft landing.

Rosy was attempting to run when Conor crashed into him, driving both boots into the man's shoulders. He heard something snap and the man rolled howling down the rocky slope. The rest jumped to their feet and ranged about him in a ragged circle. None attacked, sizing up their opponent.

These men cannot understand the principles of my rig, thought Conor. *Therefore I am a ghost, or a creature. That will not last long. Soon enough they will see for themselves that my wings are fabric and my chest heaves with exertion. Then they will shoot me dead.*

Or perhaps not. No guns were drawn yet, though there were plenty of blades.

Of course. There will be no gunplay here. The reports would bring the Wall watch down on us, and these brigands are not here to arrest me.

One of the five remaining men stepped forward a pace, brandishing an ice pick.

'Gibbus de dymon,' he said, then removed the dagger from his mouth and spat. 'I said give us the diamonds, Airman.'

Diamonds. The dropped pouch! He had left a trail.

'Billtoe,' growled Conor, his voice coarsened by deep hatred.

The prison guard quailed. 'Who are you? Why me, personally? I never wronged no parlayvoo.'

Billtoe will be first to fall, thought Conor. *At least I will have that.*

His hands flashed to twin scabbards at his hips, drawing two battle sabres.

'*En garde,*' he said and lunged forward. A breeze caught the glider, elongating his stride, and Billtoe who had thought himself at a safe distance was suddenly face to face with the Airman.

He tried a move employed in a dozen bar fights – a sly dig with his ice pick – only to find the weapon batted aside.

'Shame on you, *monsieur,*' said the Airman. 'Bringing a kitchen tool to a sword fight.'

Conor slashed down and out, his blade biting deep into Billtoe's thigh. The guard squealed and grabbed the wound. He was no longer a threat. Both hands would be employed trying to keep the blood inside his leg.

Even now I do not wish to kill him, Conor realized. *There is only one man I could kill.*

He heard a rustling behind him as two men advanced.

They are too cautious. The strange uniform scares them.

A fortuitous breeze snapped his wings and Conor added to its force by leaping directly upwards. The two men passed below and the Airman descended on them with boots and blades. Both were soon dispatched. Neither dead, but certainly nursing a reluctance to participate in moonlight ambushes.

Two men left. One was quaking and the other circling warily, biding his time, watching for weakness. It was Pike, and he did not seem inclined to retreat.

'You go ahead, matey,' he said, propelling his comrade towards Conor.

The unfortunate man had barely time to squeak before Conor knocked him senseless with a casual blow from the sabre's guard.

'Jus' you and me, Airman,' said Pike, sporting a careless grin. He studied Conor, took in the stance and the muscle and the weapons dangling from fist and belt.

'To hell with this,' he said, reaching for his pistol. 'I'll take my chances with the Wall watch.'

Conor drew faster, exchanging the sword in his right hand for a revolver.

'The guards can hear my shot or none, *monsieur*. The choice is yours.'

Pike was already committed to his action, so Conor buzzed a shot past his ear to regain his attention. The guard fell, temporarily deafened, to his knees, gun tumbling from his fingers.

'A warning shot. The next one will put a hole in you.'

It was useless to speak. Pike could not hear and combed the grass with his fingers, till he found his weapon.

'Drop that pistol,' said Conor. 'I have the advantage over you.'

But Pike could not or *would* not hear and lifted the barrel, his intention clear.

Conor shot him in the shoulder, the copper-jacketed slug bowling the guard diagonally over the ridge, screeching like a barn owl.

Gunshot and screeching, and at night too. Noises certain to attract the attention of the Wall watch. Conor jumped over the ridge, squatting behind it. On the Wall above, three lights were extinguished. This was protocol. At the first sign of disturbance, the guards plunged themselves into darkness to avoid becoming targets. Next half a dozen flares came arcing over the Wall, painting the bay with harsh red light.

It was time to leave. Quickly now, before the flares dipped low enough to light the skiff. Conor collapsed his wings and ran doubled over to the small boat. There was no time for careful folding of the glider, and several of the craft's ribs snapped as he shoved it under the seat.

No matter. Wooden ribs by the stack in the tower. My own ribs are more difficult to replace should they be splintered by gunshot.

He pushed hard into the gunwale, scraping the keel across the stone and sand until the water took its weight.

Shouts behind him now as guards poured from a fortified gateway, hurrying along the coast path. Some on horseback. The baying of hunting dogs echoed across the flat sea.

Dogs! The watch wasted no time leashing their hounds.

Conor leaped into the skiff, his momentum pushing it to sea and safety. He tugged the mast from its bracket, laying it flat across the planks. Less of a profile from shore. Cold water splashed over the prow, spattering his face and he was glad of it. He could hear his heartbeat in his ears like great hollow drums in the distance.

I wish to be a scientist. Doing injury holds no pleasure for me.

Not even Billtoe? Did you not enjoy that cut?

Conor ignored the question. He would deal with the workings of his mind on another day.

You will be a scientist again. In America. A new life, new inventions, home, friends and perhaps another girl who does not remind you of Isabella.

Conor turned his mind to rowing. He could not even contemplate girls without a vision of Isabella blooming in his mind.

So, the ocean. Conor felt confident that he was safe now. The robust little craft bore him away on the current. The skiff had served him well. Already Great Saltee was little more than a dark wedged hump receding.

Billtoe had called him Airman. That will be a short-lived title.

The glider lay on the planks, its wings folded awkwardly like those of a broken bird.

No matter. It is over now. The mysterious Airman will fly no more.

The Martello tower was visible on the Irish coastline, a lantern burning in an upstairs window. A beacon to guide him home.

Conor smiled.

Linus has forgiven me, he thought.

And then.

I hope there is hot chocolate.

CHAPTER 17:

TANGLED WEB

Two hours later, Arthur Billtoe sat on a fruit box in Marshall Bonvilain's office trying to hold the flaps of his wound together. His trousers were soaked and small gouts of blood pumped between his fingers in time with his heartbeat.

Marshall Bonvilain entered the room, and the gouts pumped faster.

'Sorry about the fruit box, Arthur,' said Hugo Bonvilain, sitting behind his desk. 'But the brocade on my chairs is worth more to me than your life, you understand.'

'O-of course, Marshall,' stammered Billtoe. 'I am bleeding, sir. It is quite serious, I think.'

Bonvilain waved this information away. 'Yes, we will come to that later. For now, I wish to talk about this creature.'

He took a notepad from his desk drawer and spun it across the desk towards Billtoe. It was Pike's notebook, open to a dynamic sketch of the Airman.

'They are calling him the Airman and he can fly apparently.'

In cases like this, Billtoe had learned that it was always best to plead ignorance.

'We was taking a walk, and he sprung himself on us. Amazed I am.'

'Hmm. So it was all a coincidence? You just happened to

be at Sebber Bridge making yourselves a target for the Wall watch, when this Airman descended from the heavens?'

Billtoe nodded eagerly. 'That's it exactly. You have gone straight to the nub of the matter, as usual.'

'And did Mister Pike do his sketching before or after he was shot? I don't see how he could have done it at either time.' Bonvilain leaned forward, his bulk casting a shadow on Billtoe. 'Could it be that you are lying to me, Arthur Billtoe?'

Blood pulsed between the guard's fingers. 'No, sir, Marshall, never.'

Bonvilain sighed, obviously enjoying his game of cat and mouse.

'You are weaving yourself a tangled web. I think it's best if I tell you what I think you've been up to, and then when I am finished speaking, you colour in any details I might have missed. How about that, Arthur?'

Billtoe nodded, as if he really had a say in proceedings.

'So, firstly, there's *you* giving me ideas for flying and salsa beds. Then there are reports of a flying man digging up things in the salsa beds. Things which Pike tells me are diamonds.'

'Pike is raving,' objected Billtoe. 'Bullet fever.'

Bonvilain raised a finger. 'No time for lies, Arthur. You're bleeding, remember? And I have not finished speaking.'

'Sorry,' mumbled Billtoe.

'Now, you are far too ignorant and short-sighted to have thought up this diamond scheme yourself . . .'

'Exactly,' said Billtoe, relieved. 'Ignorant and short-sighted, that's me.'

'So you must have been manipulated by whoever supplied these ideas. Now I know of only one person on Little Saltee with a fascination for flying.' And here Bonvilain's easy manner was replaced by cold, hard danger. 'Be careful what you say here, Billtoe, because if your answer displeases me, you will not live long enough to die of that leg wound . . . Were these ideas Conor Broekhart's?'

'Who?' asked Billtoe, genuine confusion writ large on his features.

'Finn. Conor Finn.'

Whatever blood was left in Billtoe's face drained from it. He had always known this moment would come. Only one card left to play.

'Yes, Marshall,' he said, shamefacedly. 'He sold his ideas for blankets and such. It seemed a harmless deception.'

Bonvilain grunted. 'Until he escaped on that coronation balloon. With your help, I'll warrant.'

'No, sir,' said Billtoe, squeezing the flaps of his wound together. 'Finn is locked up in the mad wing, just as you ordered. No escaping for Conor Finn.' Billtoe paused guiltily. 'Though he may look a tad different than he did last time you saw him. The years have been hard on the poor lad. What with the bell work and the beatings that you ordered. I wouldn't be surprised if you didn't even recognize young Conor Finn.'

Bonvilain laced his fingers, squeezing them until the tips were white, then rolling the knuckles along his forehead. He knew what had happened, of course he knew. It was his own fault.

Conor Broekhart should have been tossed out of the window years ago, not kept alive on the off chance he would be needed to control his father. What tangled webs we weave . . .

Bonvilain admitted to himself that he had liked the idea of having a witness to his genius. How much more agonizing must Conor Broekhart's imprisonment have been, knowing his father believed him to be a murderer.

The marshall smiled tightly. No, it had been a good plan. Incredible circumstances had scuppered it. An Airman, if you please. How could a man prepare for eventualities that had not yet been invented.

Conor Broekhart may be a genius, but Hugo Bonvilain was ingenious. This situation was a test of his mettle. It would involve some quick thinking, but already the germ of a new plan was sprouting roots in the marshall's mind. There would be murder involved, but that was not really an issue, except it could very well be murder at a high level, and when indulging in such murders one must seem completely blameless. European royal families did not approve of commoners disposing of their monarchs. And royal disapproval generally took the form of approaching warships and annexation. Hugo Bonvilain did not intend to share *his* diamonds or *his* seat of power with anybody, especially not with Isabella's close friend, Queen Victoria of the British Empire.

The Bonvilains had been striving for too many centuries to reach the very position that he was in now for him to pack his satchel at the first sign of worthy opposition.

Bonvilain remembered the night his father died. He had been raving from the leprosy that he had picked up on a pilgrimage to Jerusalem, and much of what he had said was gibberish but there were moments when his eyes were as clear as they had ever been.

'We have been pruning,' he'd said to the young Bonvilain. 'Do you know what I'm saying to you, Hugo? For centuries we have been pruning the Trudeaus. They breed like rabbits, God blast them, but we have set the crown on the right head, keeping the Saltee Islands independent. You must finish the job. You are the last in the line of servants, and the first in a line of Bonvilain masters. Promise me, Hugo. Promise me.'

And the dying man had clutched at his son's forearm with bandaged hands.

'I promise,' Bonvilain had said, unable to look at the wasted remains of his father's face.

It occurred to Bonvilain that he had been rocking in his seat, knuckles to forehead for several moments now, which may appear strange. He leaned back, tugging straight the red-crossed, white Templar stole over his navy suit.

'That's my thinking position, Arthur. Any objections?'

'No, Marshall. Not a one.'

'Glad to hear it. Anything else you care to tell me about our Airman?'

Billtoe fished inside his head for some pertinence that the marshall would appreciate.

'Um . . . erm . . . Oh! He speaks French, calls a body mish-yoor.'

Bonvilain slammed the desk with both fists, bouncing his writing set into the air.

French. That clinched it. He had in a moment of miscalculation revealed his Francophobia to Conor Broekhart. It seemed as though the boy had a sense of humour. Best to dispose of him as soon as possible. The last thing he needed was a vindictive Airman flying around stealing his diamonds and undermining his plans.

'So, Arthur, you maintain that Conor Finn languishes in his cell?'

Billtoe swallowed hard, his Adam's apple bobbing. 'Apart from the *languishing* bit, which I am not certain on, yes. He is in his cell.'

'Good. I would like to speak to him.'

'What? Now?'

'Yes, now. Does this pose a problem for you?'

'No, there is no problem.' Billtoe's features were drawn with pain and desperation. 'Except that I'm bleeding, Marshall, quite badly. This wound needs closing or I might not survive the ferry to the prison.'

Bonvilain glanced at the fireplace. Flames crackled orange and blue in the hearth, and a model broadsword, used as a poker, hung from a hook by the coal scuttle.

'You're right, Arthur,' he said brightly. 'It is time to seal that wound.'

Bonvilain boarded the ferry with Captain Sultan Arif, his most trusted officer. Billtoe cowered in the stern, every now and then poking at the scar of fused flesh on his thigh, seeming surprised each time the contact caused him pain.

He passed out during the short trip and each time woke up blubbering like a babe and blurting the word *barrel*.

Bonvilain found that he was not in the least anxious now that he had considered the night's developments. In fact, he felt invigorated by the challenge of maintaining his position, or even improving it. After all, Conor Broekhart was a youth with a kite. Hugo Bonvilain was a military strategist with an army behind him. Apparently young Conor was reluctant to commit murder, whereas Bonvilain regarded murder as a time-honoured and valid political tool.

The marshall leaned close to Sultan Arif's ear.

'There may be some poisoning later. Ready your potions.'

Sultan nodded casually, toying with his splendid moustache. 'Yes, Marshall. May I ask who we *may be* poisoning?'

'Myself, I regret to say,' replied Sir Hugo.

Sultan seemed unsurprised. 'There will be others, I take it?'

'Oh, yes,' Bonvilain confirmed, his gaze distant. 'There will be others.'

Little Saltee

There was a prisoner in Conor Finn's cell, but it was not Conor Finn.

'And who, pray tell, is this?' asked Bonvilain, pointing to the terrified wretch huddled in the corner away from the lamplight.

Billtoe knew he was rumbled. 'Don't kill me, Your

Worship,' he begged, dropping to his knees, and grabbing the hem of Bonvilain's Templar stole.

'Please spare me. I don't know how the blighter escaped. One minute he was there, the next gone. Some form of magic. Perhaps he 'ypnotized me.'

Bonvilain did not kick him off immediately, enjoying the grovelling.

'What I don't know yet, Arthur, is if you were actually Finn's accomplice. *You* helped him escape, and *you* were his smuggling contact.'

'Oh no sir, Marshall,' gibbered Billtoe. 'I never done no colluding. I don't have the depth of thought for that.'

'I'm not so sure. This *substitute* scheme of yours might have worked with any other prisoner. You were unfortunate to lose this particular one.'

'That's all it was, sir. Bad blasted luck, not an ounce of co-operation with the prisoner in it.'

Bonvilain decided a display of anger was called for, after all Sultan was watching.

'You lied to me, Billtoe,' he shouted, his voice echoing in the tiny cell. 'You stole my diamonds!'

The marshall whipped his stole from Billtoe's fingers then delivered a mighty kick, which sent the guard tumbling over the bed and into the wall behind. A muck plate cracked and fell. Billtoe lay in a heap like a spilled sack of laundry.

'Well struck, Marshall,' said Sultan. 'On the point of the chin. He rolled like a cartwheel. Should I finish him off?'

'No,' replied Bonvilain. 'Something more poetic, I think.

Perhaps our friend Arthur needs some time to reflect on his shortcomings.'

He was distracted by a strange glow from the rear of the cell. Billtoe's forehead had knocked some mud from the wall, and strange ghostly scribblings shone behind.

Curious, Bonvilain stepped closer, bending to examine the markings.

'Coral, I imagine,' he mused. 'Old Wandering Heck would have loved this.'

But the markings were man-made. Diagrams and equations. Someone had tried to cover up these markings with mud, but the mud had not bonded completely with the damp surface below. A glider was plainly visible on the wall. Bonvilain tapped it with a gloved finger.

'Hello, Airman,' he whispered. 'It seems I provided you with your laboratory.'

He drew a pistol from his belt, rapping the wall with its grip. Another plate of mud cracked and fell, revealing that the glider had been launched from the roof of a tower.

'And you have left me your location. And more valuable secrets, I shouldn't wonder.'

On the floor, Billtoe moaned.

'Am I to be executed now, sir. Is that my fate?'

'Not at the present time,' said Bonvilain, stretching. 'I have use for you, Arthur Billtoe. Your immediate fate is to clean the dirt from these walls, then transcribe every mark you find underneath.'

'Oh thank you, sir,' said Billtoe, tears of relief dripping

from his nose. 'I shall have one of the inmates get to it immediately. Top of my list.'

'You misunderstand, Arthur,' said Bonvilain, catching the guard's lapels in his fist, wrenching the very coat from his back, tumbling Billtoe further to the back of the cell.

'You will not be supervising this task as prison guard, you will be performing it as inmate.'

Bonvilain turned to the young man who had occupied the cell for almost a year.

'What is your name, boy?'

'Claude deVille Montgomery, Yer Majesty,' answered the youth promptly. 'Though me nears 'n' dears call me Spog.'

Bonvilain blinked. Life never failed to surprise.

'Old Billtoe there said to answer Conor Finn if anyone, 'specially yerself, ever got around to asking, but that was only if he didn't get around to pulling me tongue out, and as you can see . . .' Spog opened his mouth wide to reveal two teeth and a grey tongue.

'Thank you, eh, Spog. Tell me, has Mister Billtoe been unkind to you?'

Spog's whole face frowned. 'Blinkin' nasty, the evil scut. With the hitting and spitting. Pulling hair too, which is hardly gentlemanly, is it now?'

'Well then, now is your chance for revenge,' said Bonvilain tossing him the guard's jacket. 'You are now the prison guard, and he is the prisoner. Do unto him and so forth. His life is yours, and yours his.'

Spog greeted this announcement with complete calm, as though his fortunes were reversed every day.

'I'm yer man, Yer Highness,' he said, approximating a salute. 'What're yer views on torturin' them what used to be guards?'

'I am all for it,' said Bonvilain. 'It builds character.'

Spog smiled, his teeth like gateposts in his mouth. 'I'll make you proud, Yer Worship.'

The marshall winced. 'Let's stick with *Marshall*, shall we?'

'Yessir, Yer Worship.'

Billtoe's senses were swirling around in his head like spirits in a witch's cauldron, but still he managed to get the gist of what had transpired.

'I'm . . . I'm an inmate now?' he gasped, hauling himself on to the bed.

Bonvilain patted Spog's shoulder. 'Handle your prisoner, Mister Montgomery,' he said. 'I don't deal directly with criminals.'

Spog's eyes glowed with vengeful malice. 'Yessir . . . Yer Worship. My pleasure – you might want to avert yer eyes.'

Bonvilain folded his arms. 'Perhaps. But not right away.'

Billtoe backed away from his new gaoler, deeper and deeper into the cell till his elbows knocked mud from the walls, revealing blocks of diagrams and calculations.

The coral's green glow traced the dawning horror on Arthur Billtoe's face. The misery he had visited on so many others was now to be his.

Bonvilain winked at Sultan. 'As I said. Poetic.'

Forlorn Point

Due to the night's activity, not one fight but two, Conor got no more than an hour's sleep. And that sleep was filled with dreams of prison guards with blades for hands and diamonds for eyes. There was something else, though, leaping up and down in the background, seeking attention. A small memory of Conor and his father rowing across Fulmar Bay when he was nine.

Watch the oar's blade, Declan Broekhart had said. *See how it cuts the water. You want to scoop the water, not slide through it.*

Then in the dream Declan said something that he had never said in real life.

The same theory applies to the blades of a propeller. That might get your aeroplane off the ground.

Conor sat up in bed, instantly awake. What was it? What had he been thinking? Already the dream was fragmenting. The oar. Something about the oars. How could an oar help to fly an aeroplane?

It was obvious really. The oar had a blade, just like the propeller.

See how it cuts the water . . .

Of course! The oar was not bashed flat into the water, it was presented at an angle to reduce drag and maximize thrust. The same ancient principle must be applied to the propeller. After all, the propeller was really a rotating wing. When the aeroplane eventually flew, the propeller would have to absorb the engine's power and overcome the flying machine's drag. It must be treated like a wing, and shaped accordingly.

Flat propellers are of no use, thought Conor, hurriedly pulling on his clothes. *They must be angled and the blades shaped to provide lift.*

By the time Linus negotiated the stairs with bacon, soda bread and hot coffee, Conor was chiselling the second blade on his new propeller.

'Ah,' said Linus. 'A new propeller.'

This pronouncement stopped Conor in mid-motion. 'You are blind, are you not? How can you possibly know what I'm doing.'

Linus laid the breakfast tray on a bench. 'I have mystical powers, boy. And also you've been talking to yourself this past hour. Lift, drag, propulsion, all that interesting stuff. We blind folk ain't necessarily deaf you know.'

The scientist in Conor wished to continue to work, but the ravenous young man dragged him away from his precious propeller to the delicious breakfast.

Linus listened to him tuck in with a cook's satisfaction.

'I picked up the bread fresh in the village. The folk down there are all a-frenzy over stories about this Airman creature. Apparently he slew twenty men on the island last night.'

'I hear he's ten feet tall,' said Conor, around a mouthful of bread.

Linus sat beside him at the bench.

'This is no joke, Conor. You are in danger now.'

'No need to fret, Linus. The Airman's short career is over.

No more night flying for me. From this day on, scientific flights only.'

Linus stole a strip of bacon. 'Perhaps you might think of finding yourself a girl. You are of an age, you know.'

Conor could not help but think of Isabella. 'Once, there was a girl, or could have been. I will think of females again when we reach America.'

'When *you* reach America. I plan to stay here and conspire against Bonvilain. There are others who think like I do.'

'You mean it,' realized Conor sadly. 'I had hoped you would change your mind.'

'No. I lost friends. We both did.'

Conor had no desire to rake over the coals of this familiar argument.

'Very well,' he said, pushing away his plate. 'The tower is yours, and there will be abundant funds too. But I am going. In America there are airmen like me, eager for the sky.'

'I see. And when will you go?'

'I had planned to leave today, but now I am impatient to test this new propeller. She is a thing of beauty, don't you think?'

Linus Wynter tapped the velvet sleep mask that he now wore over his ruined eyes.

'I'll take your word for it. I had this mask sent from the Savoy. Did I ever tell you that I once stayed there?'

'Let us make a bargain,' said Conor. 'Today I transport my aeroplane to Curracloe beach. It will take two days to assemble and another to test. When I return we will ship my equipment to New York and go by ferry and train to London. We will live like kings for one week in the Savoy, with no talk of revolution or science, then review our situation.'

'That is a tempting offer,' admitted Linus. 'Some of the suites have pianos. My fingers twitch at the thought.'

'Let us agree then. One week for ourselves, then back into the world. Separately perhaps, but I pray that we will be together.'

'I pray for that too.'

'Then we are agreed. The Savoy.'

Linus extended a hand. 'The Savoy.'

They shook on it.

Bonvilain and Sultan came ashore incognito, faces shadowed by broad-rimmed toquilla hats. Their Saltee uniforms lent them no authority on the mainland and they were unlikely to attract attention dressed in civilian clothes. Local rowdies are far less likely to trouble dangerous-looking strangers than they are soldiers off their patch. In fact, some of the Kilmore lads knocked huge sport from taunting Saltee Army boys who were under strict orders not to retaliate. Bonvilain and Sultan were restrained by no such orders. They made no overtly hostile gestures and were the very definition of gentility, but still the local harbour boys got the impression that to trifle with this odd pair would lead to immediate and lasting discomfort.

They strolled down the quayside and into the smoky depths of the Wooden House.

'I have visited taverns all over the world,' confided Hugo Bonvilain, ducking under the lintel. 'And they all have one thing in common.'

'Drunks?' said Sultan Arif, toppling a sleeping sailor from his path.

'That too. Information for sale is the common factor I had in mind. That wretch for example . . .'

The marshall pointed to a solitary man, elbows on the bar, staring at an empty glass.

'A prime candidate. He would sell his soul for another drink.'

He sidled up beside the man, and called to the innkeeper for a bottle of whiskey.

'Do I know you?' asked the innkeeper.

'No, you don't,' replied Bonvilain cheerfully. 'And I recommend you keep it that way. Now leave the bottle and make yourself busy elsewhere.'

Most good innkeepers develop an instinct about their customers and their capabilities. The proprietor was no exception. He would ask no more questions, but he would check the load in his shotgun just in case the oddly familiar broad-beamed customer and his grinning companion unleashed the trouble that they were surely capable of.

Bonvilain opened the bottle, turning to the solitary, glass-gazing man.

'Now, good sir, you look like a gent that could use a drink. I certainly hope so, because I have no intention of imbibing one drop of this ripe spirit, which by the smell of it has already been passed through the stomachs of several cats.'

The man pushed his glass along the bar with one finger. 'I'll do you a favour and take it off your hands.'

'Very noble of you, friend,' said Bonvilain, filling the glass to the rim.

'We ain't friends,' said the man, grumpy in spite of his sudden good fortune. 'Not yet.'

Half a bottle later they were friends and Bonvilain steered the conversation as though the man had a rudder fixed to the back of his head.

'Stupid gas lamps,' said the man. 'What's wrong with candles? A candle never ruptured and exploded. I hear a gas explosion destroyed an entire city in China, 'cept for the cats what are immune to gas.'

Bonvilain nodded sympathetically. 'Gas. Dreadful stuff. And as for foreigners buying our buildings . . .'

'Stupid foreigners,' blurted the man vehemently. 'Buying our buildings. With the big smug heads on them. Do you know the English own one hundred per cent of the big houses around here? If not more.'

'And don't they just love living in towers, lording it over the rest of us.'

'That they do,' agreed the now-sozzled man. 'We got us a right scatterfool at Forlorn Point. Takes on a blind musician to cook and clean for him.'

Bonvilain was extremely interested in this scatterfool. 'A boy like that shouldn't even own a *tower*,' he prompted.

More whiskey was slopped into the glass. 'No! Blast it. No, he shouldn't. Boy like that. Should be out cutting hay

356

like the rest of us at that age. But what does he do? Buys
reams of material. Sends off for all sorts of mechanical
parts. What's he building up there? Who knows. Like Doctor
Frankenstein he is. Whatever he's doing, the noise coming
out of that tower at night is enough to waken a dead
pig.'

The man downed his drink in one, its harshness shocking
his system from stomach to eyeballs.

'And don't tell me lobsters aren't getting smarter. I caught
a lobster last month and I swear he was trying to
communicate. With the clicking claws and the pointy head
yokes.'

The landlord rapped the bar with a knuckle. 'You can
shut up now, Ern. They've gone.'

'Don't matter,' said Ern, clutching the bottle protectively
to his chest. 'I don't like fellows with hats anyways. Never
trust a hatter.'

The landlord was tactful enough not to point out that
Ern himself sported a jaunty cap.

It took mere minutes for Bonvilain and Sultan Arif to find
Forlorn Point. The old British Army marker stone by the
roadside helped quite a bit.

'The place is well named,' noted Arif, placing his shoulder
satchel on a tree stump. From inside he selected twin
revolvers and a selection of knives, which he arranged on
his belt.

'I presume we are not sending for help.'

'As is occasionally the case, Sultan, you are correct,' said

Bonvilain. 'This is a Martello tower; we could have a battleship off the coast and still not gain entry. We proceed cautiously. Diplomacy first, then guile, and finally violence should it become necessary.'

They stepped over the ruined remains of the wall and across the yard, careful not to snag their boots on treacherous creepers that snaked from the rocky soil.

'It doesn't look much,' said Sultan, picking moss from the tower wall.

Bonvilain nodded. 'I know. Clever, isn't it?'

A quick circuit of the tower confirmed that there was indeed only one doorway, above head height and plugged with a wooden door.

'I'll wager that door is not as flimsy as it looks,' muttered Bonvilain.

Sultan placed his cheek against the wall. 'The stones vibrate from a generator, Marshall,' he noted. 'I can hear classical music. It sounds as though there is an entire orchestra in there.'

'A phonograph,' said Bonvilain sourly. 'How very modern. Conor Broekhart always liked his toys.'

'So, how do we get in? Throw stones at the doorway?'

This is the Airman's tower, thought Bonvilain. *He enters and leaves from the roof.*

'I throw stones,' he said to his captain.

'You always had a good arm for stone throwing. What can I do?'

'You can search in that bag of yours and see if you brought your crossbow.'

Sultan's eyes glittered. 'No need to search. I always bring my crossbow.'

Linus Wynter was enjoying Beethoven's *Ode to Joy* while he fried up some traditional Southern grits on the pan. His secret ingredient was cayenne pepper – of course, Conor's limited galley did not have any pepper so he was forced to use a pinch of curry powder instead. It may not be quite up to his normal culinary standards, but it was unlikely that Conor would complain after two years of Little Saltee food. At any rate, Conor had left for Curracloe beach not more than five minutes previously, and by the time he returned the grits would be no more than a distant memory.

That phonograph was a scientific wonder. Conor had explained how an orchestra could be transferred to a wax cylinder, but in all honesty Linus hadn't made much of an effort to understand. The sound was scratchy and the cylinder had to be changed every few minutes, but it was sweet music all the same.

In spite of the crackling music and the sizzling grits, Linus heard the muffled voices outside. At first he assumed it was the local lads poking about, but then he heard the word *Marshall*, and his mild curiosity turned to a ball of dread in his stomach.

Bonvilain had found them.

Wynter had never been much of a marksman, but all the same he felt a little comforted once his thin fingers closed round the stock of the repeater rifle concealed beneath the worktop.

Just let Bonvilain open his mouth and I will do my utmost to close it forever.

Seconds later, a rock thumped against the door, followed in quick succession by three more. The last ringing against a steel band.

'I thought as much,' said a voice. 'A reinforced door.'

Linus checked the breech with his thumb, then shouldered his way along the wall to a gun port.

Loaded and ready. Say something else, Marshall.

Bonvilain did. 'Conor Broekhart. Why don't you come down so I can finally kill you. May as well be blunt.'

Linus sent six shots winging towards the voice.

Perhaps God will favour the virtuous, he thought as the gunshots echoed around the tower's curved walls and the discharge smoke sent his windpipe into spasms.

'So,' called Bonvilain. 'Conor is not at home and the blind servant pulls the trigger. Just so you know, blind man, you just grievously wounded the pillar I was sheltering behind.'

Or perhaps the devil looks after his own, Linus concluded, covering his nose and mouth with a wet cloth from the sink.

I must warn Conor. He must not be taken. I will fire the emergency flares.

Conor was worried about Linus alone in the tower, in spite of the fact that the American had survived wars and prison for fifty years without his help, and so he had rigged a series of emergency flares to the roof. The fuses trailed down to various spots throughout the tower and were capped with sulphur sleeves. It was only necessary to yank off the sleeve to light the fuse. The fuses were linked so if one sparked, they all sparked.

The nearest fuse was in what they jokingly referred to as the lounge, a collection of chairs clustered around the fireplace, which Linus was using as a gin still.

Fifteen steps from the rifle slot to the lounge. One step down. A bench by the wall. Nothing I don't pass by a hundred times a day.

Linus coughed the last of the rifle smoke from his lungs and began his short walk carefully. What a shame it would be to come unstuck from a twisted ankle. There was plenty of time. Bonvilain would be reluctant to enter through the front door, as there could be any number of guns pointed at that target.

Walk slowly but surely.

Linus was thrown into turmoil by a series of gunshots, each one clanging against the door, setting the metal ringing like a bell.

Wynter dropped to all fours, puzzled.

Has the marshall grown stupid? The door is reinforced; he said it himself. Why shoot at it?

The answer was obvious, and occurred to Linus almost immediately.

He is not trying to kill me, he is trying to distract me. The marshall is not alone . . .

Something cold, sharp and metallic pressed against Linus's neck.

'You left the roof door open, old man,' said a voice in

heavily accented English. Linus knew immediately who it was. Sultan Arif, Bonvilain's deadly second in command.

'You of all people should know,' continued Sultan, 'that sometimes trouble comes from above.'

The fuse. I must ignite it.

Linus made a lunge for the lounge, suffering the blade at his neck to gouge deeply, but there was no escaping Sultan Arif. The captain grabbed him as though he were a struggling pup and hoisted him to his feet.

Keep your bearings. Know where you are.

It was a difficult task with such distractions to his senses. There was pain in his neck and wet blood down his back. The gunshot echo had not yet faded and Sultan swung him around. Linus was utterly disorientated.

Concentrate. Where are you?

In the end, Sultan made it easy for him.

'Let's go down and meet our master, shall we?' he said, pushing Linus across the room. Wynter heard the door bolts scrape back and the gush of cool air against his face.

I am in the doorway, he thought, fingers questing for the frame.

Sultan's voice was loud by his ear. 'I have him, Marshall,' he called. 'The blind man is alone. There is a rope ladder here, I shall tie it off.'

'Don't be so tiresome, Sultan, throw him down,' said Bonvilain. 'Nothing is more amusing than watching a blind man fall.'

Sultan sighed, this was a task without honour, but honour was not a quality greatly prized by the marshall.

'Relax, old man. Tight bones are broken bones.'

The leather in his coat creaked as he bent his arm to push. Linus waited for the right moment, and as Sultan propelled him into space he screamed. Loudly enough to mask the sound of a sulphur sleeve being ripped from a fuse running along the doorframe.

Linus cried as he regained consciousness, for as his head had struck the earth he had seen something. A flash of light – just for a moment – now all was dark again. His breathing was restricted by the weight of a boot on his chest.

'I remember you,' said Bonvilain. 'You played piano for the king. Very clever, a blind spy. Well, old boy, your piano-playing days are over. Your spying days too, come to think of it.'

'Damn you, Hugo Bonvilain,' rasped Linus valiantly. 'There is a special pit in Hell reserved for your ilk.'

The marshall laughed. 'I have no doubt of it, which is why I intend to delay my departure from this life as long as possible. Your departure, however, is imminent, unless you answer my questions promptly.'

Linus's own laugh was bitter. 'Just kill me, Bonvilain. Your prison couldn't break me, and neither can you.'

'Do you know, I think you're right. I believe that you would resist me with your final breath. I shall never understand you principled people. Sultan has a few principles, but he can ignore their berating voices when the situation calls for it. I don't really need you at any rate. Broekhart will be back and I will be waiting, simple as that.'

'Perhaps not so simple,' said Linus.

At that moment, the linked fuses sent half a dozen flares rocketing into the sky. They exploded pink and red, their light reflected on the bellies of dark clouds.

Bonvilain watched their slow descent with catty dismay.

'Warning flares. How this young Broekhart wriggles. I swear, sometimes it seems I have been trying to bury him for his entire life.'

'Help is on the way,' gasped Linus. 'The fire brigade will be called.'

Bonvilain thought briefly, knocking his knuckles on his forehead, then called to Sultan. 'Fetch me pen and paper from the tower. I will nail a special invitation to this man's head.'

'I am not eager to murder a blind man, Marshall,' said Sultan calmly.

'We have talked about this, Captain,' hissed Bonvilain, in the tone of a parent who does not wish his children to hear. 'In your soldiering days you had no such morals.'

'That was war. They were soldiers. This is a blind old man.'

'Fetch me the pen,' insisted Bonvilain.

'I did not unfurl the ladder.'

'Unfurl? *Unfurl?* Are you William Shakespeare now? Fire *another* bolt then, climb up *another* rope.'

Sultan nodded towards the village. 'That will take several minutes. I do not believe there is time.'

Bonvilain scowled petulantly. 'This is really too much, Sultan. I fervently hope this old man is the one who puts a knife between your ribs. I will lean over your dying body just to say I told you so.'

Sultan bowed low, to show his continued loyalty.

'Too late for bowing now, my good man. I am very disappointed in you.'

'My apologies, Marshall.'

'Yes, of course, apologies. How useful. At least do me the kindness of tying this spy to the pillar.'

'Of course, Marshall.'

Linus was hoisted upright and thrust roughly against the gate pillar. Bands of rope crossed his legs and torso, cinching tight enough to burn. Sultan's footsteps circled round, making him dizzy.

Dizziness without sight. Darned unfair.

But at least it seemed he was to live, though with Bonvilain involved there would definitely be a condition.

'Very well, blind man,' said the marshall's voice to his left, low and mocking. 'You have earned yourself a reprieve. Deliver this message to the Airman. Tell him that I am hosting a gathering tomorrow night. A small dinner to celebrate the life of Conor Broekhart, which I find amusingly ironic. It will be the third anniversary of his death. Family and friends only. Wine will be served for a special toast, a potent vintage. *Very* potent. It will seem as though the rebels have managed to infiltrate the kitchen. Tragic.'

Linus did not have the breath for insults.

'Be sure to tell Conor that I am going to all this trouble because of him,' continued Bonvilain, fingers digging into Linus's shoulder. 'If he had remained where I left him, then none of this would be necessary, but because he escaped and then stole from me, his brother becomes an orphan. You know, perhaps I will make the infant my ward. Raise him as my own. A little marshall.'

Bonvilain chuckled, enjoying his own twisted sense of humour.

'How the people would love me. Noble Bonvilain adopts another man's child.'

Linus managed a short sentence. 'No one loves you, Bonvilain.'

'You're right,' said the marshall. 'And you would think that might bother me, but no, I seem to find all the fulfilment I need in material wealth.'

Sultan moved, bowing, into Bonvilain's line of sight. 'Marshall, those flares could attract attention.'

Bonvilain was disappointed. No doubt the villagers would come to investigate the flares. No more time for gloating. A pity – he enjoyed it so, and there were all too few occasions. Ah well, poisoning the queen and the Broekharts was something to look forward to. And with any luck Conor would throw himself into the pot too. And, even if he did not, Bonvilain would soon be prime minister and nothing anyone said would be able to change that.

Time for one last word with the blind man.

'I suppose the Irish will untie you,' he said. 'But, even so, do not run away. Remain here and deliver my message, or your master will not have the chance to kill himself attempting to foil my plans.'

Bonvilain slapped Linus hard across the cheek. 'After that,

spend the rest of your life wondering when I will kill you. As we know, *you* will not see me coming.'

Linus kept his lip stiff and his frown in place, but he was breathing hard through his nose, and had the ropes not held him he would surely have collapsed.

I hate myself for feeling this terror. I have seen war and plague. I have lived in darkness with the ever-present fear of pain. But terror? Never before, until now.

'Damn you, Marshall,' he sobbed defiantly. 'The devil take you.'

But he knew by the hollowness of the air and the drift of his voice that he was alone. Bonvilain had gone to make preparations for his celebration.

I should be happy, Conor Finn thought. *My plan has succeeded and I am a scientist again, with funds to continue my experiments far into the future. I should be at least content.*

But he could not escape the knowledge that this was not his life. He was skirting the borders of it as though banned from entering. And somewhere, just beyond his reach, another true life was waiting.

Further away will be better. How can I start again when every time I raise my eyes I see the Saltees on the horizon.

Conor was steering his horse and cart down the coast road to Wexford, and from there to Curracloe beach, five miles on the other side. It was already noon, as it had taken longer than expected to winch the wings down the side of the tower. He would have to sleep on the beach for an extra night, perhaps two, depending on conditions.

The journey too would take longer than expected. They had travelled less than a mile from Kilmore, and already the horse tired from such a load. Wings, engine, tail, body and of course his new propeller. It was a heavy burden for an old horse. He would see about trading the beast in on the Wexford docks.

He thought of Linus, and laughed aloud.

My mind compares Linus to an old beast. He would not be happy to hear that.

With Linus Wynter on his mind, he glanced over his shoulder to check for flares, as he had a dozen times already on this trip.

As if Linus needs me. As if Linus needs a . . .

The flares were up. All of them it seemed. Pirouetting to earth, leaving pink trails like the spokes of a ghostly umbrella.

Linus was in trouble.

It must have something to do with last night's encounter. It could not be coincidence.

Conor pulled the cart off the road, driving it deep into a wooden copse. The horse complained, shying away from low branches, but Conor drove her on, wedging the cart tight between two trunks. The trees shook raining pine needles down on man and horse.

In seconds, Conor had unhitched the horse and was urging her back along the coast road. With this animal there were two choices. He could run her short and fast, or slow and long. Conor chose fast, something told him that long would be too late.

*

Conor arrived at the tower to find his only friend tied to the pillar, his face and neck rent with contusions. His first thought was, *Dead. I have lost him again.* But then the old man coughed.

'Linus!' he said, taking the American's weight. 'You're alive.'

Wynter seemed surprised. 'Conor. I didn't hear a horse.'

'She collapsed outside the village. Her heart I imagine.'

He quickly sliced through the rope, sliding his friend down along the pillar.

'You won't die today,' said Conor, conducting a quick check for broken bones. 'But there's not a piece of skin on you that isn't bruised. Your blood is blue, you'll be delighted to know. I always suspected you were royalty.'

'Listen to me, Conor,' said Linus, his throat raw and rope-burned. 'It was Bonvilain.'

Conor actually fell backwards to the grass. 'The marshall himself? Here?'

'Him and his bloodhound, Arif. I left the roof door open, to clear the cooking fumes. Stupid old man. They only left because they thought the villagers would come to investigate the flares. I could've told them that you've been firing up flares and God knows what for weeks now and the locals are bored rigid watching them. I could've told them that, but I didn't.'

'What did he say?' Conor demanded. 'Tell me, Linus.'

Linus sighed deeply. His face scarred by pain and sadness. 'He knows you are the Airman, Conor. He plans to murder your family, Isabella too. Poison most likely, at a dinner tomorrow night. A dinner for Conor Broekhart.'

Conor squatted on the grass, dumbstruck by these tidings. It was the worst possible turn of events.

He plans to murder your family.

What can I do? What can be done?

Linus read his mind. 'You must forget America now, Conor. It is time for action.'

'I know. Of course. But what must I do?' asked Conor.

'It's a puzzle,' replied Linus. 'Bonvilain knows you are coming. Exactly when and where. They will be watching sea and sky, waiting for the Airman.'

'I could surrender myself,' blurted Conor, desperation large on his features. 'Then the marshall would have no need to kill anyone. His secrets would be safe.'

Linus disagreed vehemently. 'No! It's too late for that, Conor. Bonvilain doesn't know who you have spoken to or what army you may have gathered with your stolen diamonds.'

'But why does he tell me about the dinner? To torment me?'

'To ensnare you,' corrected Linus. 'All of his enemies die in one night and the Airman is their murderer. Blaming you for murder is a tried-and-trusted method for Hugo Bonvilain.'

Conor sat still as a statue, staring at the stones as though they would yield up the solution to his terrible dilemma. A breeze funnelled through his fingers, and sunshine warmed his crown, but what could these normal things mean to him. Would a *normal* life ever be his?

'Conor?' said Wynter, crawling forward, one hand reaching ahead, patting the air. 'Conor? Are you all right?'

Conor made no sound but shallow breathing and Linus realized that he would have to take charge.

'We must leave the tower,' he said, attempting to sound brisk and businesslike. 'We load what we can on to the cart and leave here tonight. Even if Bonvilain sends soldiers to hunt for you, they may not know to look for Conor Finn.'

There was a rustle of grass and cloth as Conor climbed to his feet. If Linus could have seen his young friend's eyes, he would have been struck by the sudden determination burning there.

'Conor Finn?' said the Airman. 'Conor Finn is dead. My name is Conor Broekhart and I need to speak to my father.'

CHAPTER 18:

HEAVIER THAN AIR

It was clear to Conor that there was only one way to end this nightmare. He must expose the marshall as a murderer. Running away was no longer an option now that Bonvilain was threatening his loved ones. Confronting the marshall would at least give the Broekharts and the monarchy a fighting chance to survive.

That is how my father would wish it. He may hate me, but surely the truth will change that.

Conor knew now that he should have made himself known that night on Great Saltee, when he had seen his young brother, but his parents had seemed so happy without him. So safe. To embrace him as part of the family would have put them all in danger.

False reasoning. Weak logic.

Making contact now would be close to impossible. Bonvilain was expecting him and would have every man on the Wall with orders to shoot on sight, as often as possible. They knew he travelled by glider and boat and so would be expecting those crafts, but there may be a third option.

Conor purchased a fresh horse in the village for an exorbitant amount, and rode it hard back to where he had hastily concealed the laden cart. Not a moment too soon, as there were half a dozen local boys perched atop the tarpaulin, picking at the ropes like curious monkeys. Conor considered hunting the lads off, but decided to employ them instead. Each boy was offered the staggering sum of a rough diamond for his strength and silence. Needless to say, the offers were accepted, as a single stone was worth a year of a grown man's wages.

Even with the help of his new apprentices, it took sweaty hours of heaves and grunts to free the cart from within the tree trunks, and almost as long to back it on to the road.

'Now, buckos,' Conor said to his troops, once the horse was hitched and ready. 'Hot chocolate for all if we make it to Saint Patrick's Bridge before dark.'

The boys put their shoulders to the cart with gusto. Hot chocolate, diamonds and mysterious cargo! They felt like princes on a quest.

Saint Patrick's Bridge was a long shingled bar, curving from the mainland towards the Saltees. Legend had it that when Saint Patrick was chasing the devil from Ireland, he finally managed to trap him in the Galtee Mountains. The devil took two huge bites from the slopes to clear himself a path, and off he scarpered into County Wexford with Saint Patrick in hot pursuit, hurling rocks and boulders gathered in the fields.

Old Nick was forced into the water at Kilmore, and swam hard for the open sea, stones peppering the water around him. These stones were to form Saint Patrick's Bridge. A couple struck the devil on the noggin, knocking the chunks of mountain from his gob and into the ocean. The smaller became Little Saltee, the larger Great Saltee.

Conor had never believed these stories, putting his faith in coastline erosion and ocean currents, but today, glancing out to sea at the dark, jagged islands, it was easy to believe that they were the devil's work.

Conor and his crew arrived at the field above Saint Patrick's Bridge with an hour of sunlight still left in the day. A winding path led down to the bridge itself, but it was too treacherous to be negotiated by horse and cart. Everything would have to be carried.

Conor stood on the cart and issued instructions like a general commanding his troops.

Carry the lot down. Lay the pieces high on the bridge, above the waterline. Everything was breakable and secret. So care and silence were the orders of the day.

The moment Conor stripped back the tarpaulin it became obvious what the secret cargo was. Wings, engine, propeller.

One boy, the leader of the small pack, stepped forward, half-terrified, half-incredulous.

'Sir, would you be the Airman what stuck it to those prison guards?'

Conor noted the gleam in their eyes, the lust for extraordinary adventure. 'I am indeed the Airman, and I need your help. What say you, boys?'

The leader mulled it over on behalf of the group.

'Well, Mister Airman,' he said, 'I have a brother on Little Saltee for life, didn't do more than rob a few guineas and perhaps break a few bones. So I say, let's get to carrying.'

The rest cheered and rushed to the cart, eager to be first down the lane.

I hope their enthusiasm lasts, thought Conor. *A long night of work lies ahead.*

Boys are fickle creatures, and by midnight three had been distracted by hunger or mischief or parents calling them home. Three stayed, though, and finished the lugging of aeroplane parts down to Saint Patrick's Bridge. Whether they negotiated with their parents or were there without permission, Conor did not know and had not time to find out.

He sent one with a message for Linus, and a while later the American arrived with food and oil lamps, picking his way down the steep path. Seeming uncertain on his own lanky legs, like a beginner on stilts.

The boys gathered firewood and they lit fires around the workspace where Conor laboured among engine parts, tubs of grease, crank handles, springs, pistons, lengths of unsealed muslin, rolls of wire, pots of glue, stiff brown paper, a strange curved propeller. And slowly the aeroplane was assembled.

The boys' leader, who went by the unlikely name *Uncle*, displayed a surprising aptitude for mechanics and was invaluable when it came to fetching tools, and even predicting which tools were needed.

'I need a wrench, Uncle. The medium.'

'I think prob'ly the small, Airman.'

Of course Uncle was proved correct, and lit himself a celebratory smoke.

Conor took to explaining his innovations to keep his mind on his work and off his family.

'Steam engines are too heavy for aeroplanes. To lift a steam engine you need a bigger steam engine. So, Victor, my teacher, suggested a compressed gas engine, or gasoline, which is better but still too heavy. But then I remembered aluminium.'

'Isn't that rare? Like gold.'

'It was. Fifty years ago, aluminium was so hard to produce that bars of it were exhibited at fairs. But now the Bayer Process makes it and, if not plentiful, then it is at least obtainable. So my crankcase and water jacket are made completely from aluminium. This engine is light enough to lift itself and the aeroplane, and it will give me at least ten horsepower in the air.'

'You hope,' said young Uncle.

'Yes. I really do hope. And Uncle?'

'Yes, Airman?'

'I hate to say it, but you smell rank. Don't you wash?'

Uncle stubbed out his cigarette on a boot heel. 'No, Airman. I follow the Egyptians on washing. Bad for the soul.'

The sun rose on a new day, to find the five workers huddled around a brazier sharing a pot of chocolate. All were exhausted, but none were in a mood to quit. By mid-morning, the little band was back to full strength, as the boys who had taken off the night before happily played hookey for a chance to see the Airman fly.

'Pick any large rocks from the bridge and toss them aside. I need a smooth runway.'

This was a simple task, and Uncle set the slower boys to it.

'Pointless asking the dullards to help with mechanics,' he explained. 'Stone clearing is exactly the work for those ones. All you need are open eyes and a strong back. Every ten minutes or so, I assures them of their genius.'

Conor nodded with exaggerated gravity. Uncle was proving invaluable.

While the others cleared the sky road, Conor bolted on the wings, which were constructed from steam-curved ash ribs covered with unsealed muslin.

The craft's shape was clear now. Single wing set, thirty feet across. A long thin body resembling a river punt, with the aluminium four-inch-bore engine centre mounted behind Conor's new-shaped propeller.

'I ain't never seen a propeller like that,' commented Uncle, who was apparently an expert on everything. 'How'd she go in tests?'

'What tests?' grunted Conor, tightening the last nut on the propeller.

Linus kept the food and drink coming and when the boys flagged he pulled a tin whistle from his pocket, playing a jig or a reel, and without knowing it the boys would pick up their pace again.

The labour consumed the better part of the day, but

finally the aeroplane was ready, sitting on the spit of shale on three wheels like a great sleeping bird. It was a marvel, and for long minutes the little band was silent, simply gazing at the craft, absorbing its every curve and strut.

There was fear too and none of the workers would lay a finger on the material for fear of waking the bird. Only Linus Wynter was not awestruck. He had Conor lead him to the aeroplane's propeller, then gave the craft a thorough examination.

'Victor would have been proud,' he said.

'I hope so,' said Conor. 'The theory is as much his as mine, which is why I did this . . .'

Conor pulled a strip of paper from the nose and laid Linus's hand on what lay beneath. The American felt flaky lines of dried paint under his fingers. The paint spelled out two words.

La Brosse.

Wynter smiled sadly. 'He would like this, that French peacock. I declare, if my tear ducts were working I would cry.' He wiped his nose, and pulled the lapels of his dinner suit together. 'I should have written something special. An aria to speed you on your way.'

'There's still time. I need at least a hundred feet to take off, so I cannot leave until low tide.'

Uncle overheard this comment, mainly because he was standing at Conor's elbow listening.

'Tell me something, Airman. If you need a hundred feet to take off, how many do you need to land?'

It was a pertinent question but not one that Conor seemed

inclined to answer. He turned and strode towards the flat rocks, avoiding the enquiring gazes following him.

'It's complicated,' he mumbled. 'Technical. I still have some calculations to complete.' And then, as though that was the end of the matter, 'Anyway, where are those ash ribs? I have a few repairs to make.'

Uncle lit himself another cigarette. 'I know Great Saltee well enough. If Airman needs the same to land as he did to take off, he's not going to find it on that island. Anything flat on Great Saltee has a house on it. The only place he could possibly land would be outside the Palace Gates in Promontory Square.' Uncle laughed at the lunacy of this notion. 'Promontory Square. Imagine. If Marshall Bonvilain were a spider, that would be his web. Which would make Airman . . .'

'The fly,' breathed Linus.

Great Saltee

Marshall Hugo Bonvilain was uncommonly excited, after all this day was to be a momentous day, not just for him but for every Bonvilain who had ever been forced to toady to an idiot king. Today all their sacrifice would be made righteous. Hundreds of years it had taken to accomplish the task, but finally the Bonvilains were about to supplant the Trudeaus.

And so, when Sultan Arif had arrived in Bonvilain's office that afternoon, he'd found the marshall almost giddy with anticipation. Bonvilain stood at the office window, clapping his hands rapidly in time to the Strauss waltz being played by a lone violinist in the corner.

Sultan cleared his throat for attention.

'Ah, Captain, you've come,' said Bonvilain delightedly. 'What a day, eh? Historic and all that. I love Strauss, don't you? People take me for a Wagner man, but I say just because my duties are sometimes gloomy it doesn't mean I have to be. No, Strauss is the man if you've had a trying day. I think I shall have an Austrian orchestra brought over for my swearing in as prime minister.'

Sultan was surprised by this lack of discretion, and it showed in his face.

'Oh, don't worry about him,' said Bonvilain, jerking a thumb at the musician. 'Poor chap was run over by a horse and carriage a few years ago, left him deaf and blind. He plays from memory. I got him from Kaiser Wilhelm, only arrived this morning. It's an omen I said to myself. How can anything go wrong today.'

Sultan began to feel nervous. Things always went wrong around the marshall, usually for other people.

'God willing, all will proceed well.'

'How can it not?' asked Bonvilain, stepping in from the balcony. 'The queen and her loyal supporters will soon be dead. There are no heirs and so I will be sworn in as prime minister. This Broekhart boy, this Airman, will no doubt attempt some form of rescue, and then we will have him too. And even if he does not come, once Isabella is gone he will be nothing more than a disgruntled fugitive.'

The marshall sat at his desk, smoothing the felt surface with one palm. 'Now, let us talk about poison.'

Sultan Arif placed a corked ink bottle on the desk. It was half-filled with a pale yellow powder.

'This is wolfsbane from the Alps,' he explained. 'A thimble of this can be mixed with a glass of wine or sprinkled over food. Several minutes later the victim will experience a strange tingling in the hands, followed by chest pain, extreme anxiety, accelerated heartbeat, nausea, vomiting and eventually death due to respiratory arrest.'

'Eventually,' purred Bonvilain. 'I like that.' He picked up the bottle, holding it to the light as if its deadly qualities would become more apparent. 'Now, Sultan, you know how vital it is that I appear blameless in all of this. I must suffer with the rest, and only my strength shall save me. It cannot be sham. The queen's own physician must confirm that I am at death's door.'

'Then you must only drink half of your glass,' said Sultan. 'That is half a thimble of wolfsbane. You will suffer as wretchedly as the others, but without the respiratory arrest.'

Bonvilain poured a glass of brandy from a crystal decanter. 'Half a thimble you say? Are you certain? You would wager my life on it?'

'Reluctantly,' replied Sultan.

'I have an idea,' declared Bonvilain, tapping a pinch of powder into his glass. 'Why not test the measure on the musician.' He pulled a sad face. 'But you are so fond of blind men, and I am eager to hear more of his repertoire.'

Sultan felt a bead of sweat run down his back. 'There is no need to test it, Marshall. We have used this method before.'

'But not on me. I want *you* to take it, that would reassure me.'

'But it will take hours to recover,' protested Sultan weakly. 'I am needed today.'

'You *are* needed, Captain,' said Bonvilain, proffering the tumbler. 'And this is what you are needed for.'

'But if the Airman arrives?'

'If the Air*boy* arrives I will deal with him. I have been on a few campaigns, Sultan. I do know how to swing a sword. I am asking you to drink this, Captain. Will you refuse me again?'

Sultan felt trapped in this opulent cage. The portraits of Bonvilain marshalls though the ages glared down at him, daring him to disobey.

I could kill him, he thought. *At least I could try.*

But it was a battle of the mind and Sultan had already lost. He had been doing the marshall's bidding for years now.

I have done worse than this. Much worse.

Sultan Arif thought of the damage he had done in the name of the Saltees, the lives he had ruined. The men who suffered in prison still.

He reached out, took the glass and threw the liquid into the back of his own throat.

'Bravo,' cried Bonvilain. 'Careful with that glass now, it's crystal.'

Sultan plonked the glass on the table and waited for the poison to take effect. Numbing of the extremities was the first symptom of wolfsbane. When his fingers bean to tingle, Sultan stared at them as though they belonged to a stranger.

'Numb,' he said.

'Capital,' cried Bonvilain. 'It begins.'

Sultan was all too aware of the misery the coming hours contained. He would suffer the pain of the damned and if he was lucky live to forget it.

'Play something doleful,' Bonvilain called to the violinist, though the man could not hear him. 'The Captain needs cheering up.'

An hour later, when Sultan was clawing at the carpet, his lungs aflame, each breath like a dagger wound, Bonvilain squatted before him, clicking his fingers for attention.

'Now, Captain,' he said genially. 'The next time I tell you to kill a blind man, you do it. Understood?'

Sultan may have nodded, or he may have lapsed into spasm. Either way, Bonvilain felt certain that the lesson had been learned.

Saint Patrick's Bridge

The time had come to fly. Sundown and low tide. The shale bridge was as smooth as it could ever be and the engine was primed for take-off. There was nothing to hold Conor back but his own anxieties.

He sat on the flat rocks watching the sky for birds.

'Do you hear any bats?' he asked Linus, who reclined

beside him, long skinny legs stretching down to the sand.

'Bats?'

'Yes. If this is a haunt for bats, they could gum up the propeller.'

Linus was silent for a long moment. 'No. No bats. But something is lurking on the ridge. I hear shuffling. A lot of shuffling.'

Conor stood, craning his neck backwards for the view. The villagers lined the ridge like teeth in a vast mouth, more arriving every second to fill the gaps. They peered down to catch a squint of the Airman.

'All of Kilmore is here,' he groaned.

'What? Did you expect to give away diamonds, build a heavier-than-air flying machine on the beach and stay a secret? You are the Airman, come to fight Bonvilain. He is not a popular man.'

'Look, they're lighting torches now. They have lamps.'

Linus tapped his temple. 'I can't look, boy. Blind remember. And, anyway, couldn't you use a few lights?'

'My God!' exclaimed Conor. 'Of course. Lights would be most helpful.'

'Well then, invite those good folk to come down. After all, in a few hours none of this will matter. The queen will know the truth, Bonvilain will be banished and you will once again be Sir Conor of the Saltee Islands.'

'Not necessarily,' said Conor. 'There is an alternative ending.'

Linus stood, brushing off the seat of his pants. 'Not tonight, my young friend. The planets are aligned, the runes have been thrown, I found a four-leaf clover in the grass. Tonight, after three years, Conor Broekhart comes back from the dead.'

'Perhaps,' said Conor. 'But for how long?'

Great Saltee

Two-year-old Sean Broekhart lay in his bed, but he was not sleepy.

'I think he has a fever,' said Catherine, touching the back of her hand to the young boy's forehead. 'Perhaps we should stay at home.'

'Stay home,' agreed the smiling Sean.

Declan stood in the doorway, shoulders broad in his dress uniform. 'Sean is fine, darling. He thrives. Were he any stronger I would enlist him right now. If you don't want to go, just say the words. No need to drag little Sean into your schemes.'

Catherine straightened a row of medals on her husband's chest. 'I have been saying the words since the invitation arrived. It's so strange, don't you think? This sudden desire of the marshall's to celebrate Conor?'

Declan's brow creased. A lot had changed in these past weeks. He felt more himself than he had in years, three years to be exact. And while he still felt gratitude for what Hugo Bonvilain had done for Conor and the family, he had concerns about the man's methods, especially the tight rein he held over Little Saltee. Recently his men had begun to tell him horror stories about the prison.

'It's not strange, it's natural. Hugo feels some guilt too. After all, his men were supposed to be guarding the king. That was always the problem with Nicholas, he did not want to live his life under guard. He was too trusting by far.'

'Talk to Isabella, Declan. She is expecting it.'

'You have already spoken to the queen about this?'

Catherine took her husband's arm. 'She spoke to me. Isabella has concerns too. She needs an ally that the men will listen to. You are the only one who can challenge Bonvilain.'

Declan did not want this burden. 'The marshall is my superior officer and he has been very good to us.'

'I don't wish to wound you, Declan, but your mind has been elsewhere these past years. You have been blind to the injustices that grow commonplace on the Saltees. Nicholas's dream was to create a Utopia for the people. That has become Isabella's dream too. It is not Hugo Bonvilain's. He wishes to be prime minister; he has always wished it.'

Declan admitted the facts like shafts of light through chinks in a heavy curtain. 'I have heard things. Perhaps I can investigate.'

Catherine's grip tightened on his arm. 'One more thing, perhaps this is not the night to say it, but Victor Vigny, a traitor?'

'They found letters in his apartment detailing the island's defences. My own men were with Bonvilain when he found the bodies.'

'I know all about the evidence, but I knew Victor too. He saved us, remember?'

'He saved himself,' countered Declan, then gently, 'Victor was a spy, Catherine. They are a cold breed. We saw of him what he wished us to see.'

There were tears in Catherine's eyes now. 'Just promise me you will stand by Isabella, whatever she decides to do. Your first loyalty is to her.'

'Of course, she is my queen.'

'Very well,' said Catherine, drying her eyes. 'Now I must ready myself again. Why don't you tell your son a story, put him off to sleep before the nanny arrives.'

Little Sean seized on the word. 'Story, Daddy,' he called. 'Story, story, story.'

Declan squeezed his wife's hand before she left the room. 'I am here now, Catherine. I will take care of us all, including the queen.'

He sat on Sean's bed, and as usual he could not gaze upon one son without thinking of the other, but he forced the melancholy look from his features and smiled down at the boy.

'Well, Sean Broekhart, not feeling sleepy tonight?'

'No sleep,' replied Sean belligerently, tugging his father's sleeves with small fingers.

So small, thought Declan. *So fragile.*

'I think one of my stories might do the trick. Which one would you like? Captain Crow's army?'

'No Crow,' said Sean, his lip jutting. 'Conor. Tell me Conor story. Sean's budder.'

Declan was taken aback. Sean had never asked about

Conor before and for some reason, Declan had never anticipated this moment.

'Conor story,' insisted Sean, pummelling his daddy's leg.

Declan sighed. 'Very well, little one. A Conor story. There are many tales about your brother, for he was a special person who did many amazing things in his life. But his most famous deed, the one for which he earned the gold medal in the cabinet, was the rescue of Queen Isabella. Of course, she wasn't a queen in those days, merely a princess.'

'Princess,' said Sean contentedly.

'On this particular summer afternoon, Conor and Isabella had exhausted the fun to be had tracking an unused chimney to its source and decided to launch a surprise pirate attack on the king's apartment . . .'

And so Declan Broekhart told the story of the burning tower, and when it was over and the princess saved, he kissed his sleeping boy and left the bedchamber with a heart that felt strangely lighter.

Saint Patrick's Bridge

This is madness, thought Conor. *Lunacy. There are so many things that can go wrong.*

The engine could prove too weighty in spite of the aluminium casing. The propeller has not even been tested in a wind tunnel and could rip the nose apart as easily as propel the craft. The untreated muslin was lighter than the treated variety but may not deflect the air currents sufficiently to give lift. The steering was rudimentary at best and would allow no more than a twenty-degree turn and even that could pull the wings off. The wing tips may not provide enough balance for a take-off.

So many things.

Saint Patrick's Bridge had become a cathedral of sorts. The villagers had made the trek down the steep path for the spectacle, and most were crowded into the natural amphitheatre above the shale outcrop. They wiggled into comfortable positions, opened baskets of food and chatted amicably while they waited. The rest lined both sides of Saint Patrick's Bridge, holding their lanterns aloft, lighting a path for the Airman.

More expectations, thought Conor. *As if overthrowing a military leader were not enough, now I must entertain a village into the bargain.*

He made a final tour of *La Brosse*, holding an oil lamp close to the underside of each wing, searching for tears, smoothing down bumps. No more need for delay.

'That's your fourth *final* inspection, if my ears serve me correctly,' said Linus from the shadows. 'Go now, Conor, or you will miss the tide.'

'Yes, of course, you are right. I should leave, immediately. It must seem silly to everyone. All this preparation for such a small journey.'

Linus stepped into the lamp's glow. The light caught him from below, casting ghostly shadows along his thin face.

'You are wrong, boy. This is a momentous journey. Historic.'

Conor buttoned his aeronaut's jacket. 'Not historic, I am afraid. There will be no official record, no photographs. Nothing is acknowledged without at the very least a fellow of the Royal Society. Every week a new crackpot appears claiming to have flown.'

Linus raised his arms high to the watchers, like a conductor acknowledging his audience.

'Every man, woman and child here will remember what is about to happen on this beach for the rest of their lives, no matter what the history books say. The truth will never die.'

Conor strapped on his goggles and hat. 'Linus, if something happens – something unfortunate – will you find a safe way to contact my father? He must know the truth.'

Linus nodded. 'I will find a way, boy. This old spy has a few tricks up his sleeve, but I have faith in you.'

Conor climbed the short ladder to the pilot's seat, positioning himself carefully on the driver's bench.

Something on his jacket clinked against the frame. It was the winged 'A' symbol.

'I don't suppose I need this any more,' said Conor, unfastening it. 'Bonvilain knows exactly who I am.' He tossed it twinkling over Linus's head to the boy known as Uncle.

'A keepsake for you, so that when people tell you that this never happened, at least you will know different.'

Uncle polished the winged 'A' on his shirt. 'Thanks, Airman. I was hoping for the goggles, but I suppose you'll be needing those.'

'Unfortunately, yes. But you can have this pair if I come back, in return for one last favour.'

'Anything,' cried the boy, already imagining strutting along Kilmore quay, goggles at a jaunty angle on his crown. 'So long as it doesn't involve bathing.'

'No. No bathing. I need two of your tallest boys to stand at the wing tips. They must be strong, and they must be quick on their toes.'

Uncle summoned his two tallest boys and positioned them as Conor had asked.

'These two are so thick they make the village idiot look like Sherlock Holmes,' Uncle confided to Conor. 'They'll run straight into the sea if you want.' Then to the two lads: 'Run fast, won't ye, buckos. Hold the wings level and I'll swap those diamonds for two bars of toffee.'

'Righto, Uncle,' said one.

'Toffee,' said the other, who looked a lot like the first.

'They can stop before the water,' said Conor, fixing his goggles. 'I need them to run alongside and keep the wings balanced. As soon as I lift off, they let go. Can they do that?'

'Of course they can, they're not thick,' said Uncle. 'Sorry, they *are* thick. But not *that* thick.'

Conor nodded. 'Good, Uncle, if things go badly for me tonight, I want you to stay with Mister Wynter, he will pay you a decent wage.'

'Will he make me bathe?'

'No, he will debate the matter with you until you decide to wash.'

'Ah. One of those. Very well – for you, Airman. Though I may have to murder him in his sleep.'

'Fair enough.'

I waste time talking with this boy. Time to be off.

Conor braced his feet against two wooden blocks and stood, leaning forward to grasp the engine's crank. The engine had always run well enough on a block in the tower, but that was the way of things. Engines ran well until they were needed.

The engine caught on the second revolution, coughing like a sick dog then spluttering forth a roar. The crowd cheered, and Conor felt like doing the same. Stage one complete, now if he had done his calculations correctly, the vibrations would not tear his aeroplane apart for a while at least.

After an initial burst of enthusiasm, the engine settled to about ten horsepower, spinning Conor's revolutionary propeller and sending the exhaust fumes streaming over his shoulder. The aeroplane bounced and reared, eager to be off, a wild beast on a tether.

This can never work. I have no speed control. This frame cannot last for more than five minutes.

Too late for doubts now. Too late.

Conor strapped on his harness, then released the brake lever and the plane leaped forward, bumping over the shale surface.

In his peripheral vision, Conor saw Uncle urging one of the runners on with strokes from a switch. With one hand, he buckled his harness across his chest, while the other struggled to keep the tiller straight.

You should have buckled your harness before releasing the brake. Idiot.

The ocean was approaching fast, and he had not sufficient speed. He urged the craft forward with jerks of his torso, and tried to ignore the smoke and oil spattering on his face and goggles.

You should have fixed an exhaust pipe to the body. What were you thinking?

Lanterns sped past on either side, speed trails blurring one into the next. It was all he could do to keep the aeroplane between the lines. The vibration was terrible, rattling his backbone, clicking his teeth, rolling his eyes in their sockets.

Some form of absorbance is needed. Cloth padding, or springs.

This was not the time for ideas. The aeroplane, though just brought to life, was already dying. Rivets popped, material ripped and ribs groaned. It had minutes left before the engine shook it to pieces like a dog shaking a rag doll.

Conor's feet found the pedals on the floor and he pushed forward, angling the wings. The aeroplane lifted a fraction, then dropped to earth. He pushed again and this time the lift was greater and the vibration decreased. No longer could he feel the bump over each stone transmitted through the wood into his rear end, which was a relief.

The water loomed black before him and then underneath.
Conor vaguely registered his two runners splashing into the
ocean, then he was airborne and away.

I am flying a machine, he thought. *Can you see me, Victor? We
did it.*

Great Saltee

Marshall Bonvilain had arranged for the dinner to be held
in his own apartments, which was very unusual. None of
the guests had ever been in the marshall's rooms before this
night, and they had never heard of him extending an
invitation.

Bonvilain's tower was separate from the main palace,
further south along the Wall, and had been occupied by his
family since its construction. It had the distinction of being
the tallest structure on Great Saltee, and sat grey and
imposing on the skyline like a reminder of the marshall's
power. He could often be seen on his balcony, brass telescope
screwed to his eye, keeping a watch on everything, making
the entire island feel guilty.

The dining room was sumptuous, decorated with swathes
of Oriental silk and painted paper screens. The table itself
was circular and low to the ground, surrounded by thick
cushions.

When Queen Isabella and the Broekharts were ushered
into the area, it felt as though they had stepped into another
world.

Catherine was especially amazed. 'It's so . . . It's so . . .'

'Cultured?' said Hugo Bonvilain, stepping from behind a screen. In place of his usual sternly cut blue suit and Templar stole, he wore a Japanese robe.

Bonvilain could not help but notice his guests' surprised faces. 'This is a Yukata Tatsu robe. Tatsu is the Japanese word for dragon, embodying the powerful and turbulent elements of nature. I spent a year in Japan in sixty-nine, as personal bodyguard to Emperor Meiji, before my father died and I was called back. Emperor Meiji insisted I take some of Japan home with me. I rarely have it taken out of storage, but this is a special occasion and I thought you might like to see a more relaxed marshall.'

Catherine was the first of the small group to recover from her surprise. 'You look striking, Marshall.'

'Why thank you, Catherine. No one minds sitting on cushions, I hope.'

No one objected, though cushions are not the most comfortable of seats for those with ceremonial swords at their belts, nor for that matter for those in fashionable dresses.

'Thank goodness bustles are no longer fashionable,' Catherine commented to the queen, 'or we should be rolling about like skittles.'

The meal was mostly fish and rice, served by a single wizened servant.

'Coco is also the chef,' said Bonvilain. 'I lured him away from a restaurant in London with the promise of a decent kitchen. He is Portuguese, but can cook any meal you wish. Japanese is one of his specialities.'

An hour passed slowly, in spite of several cultural lectures from the marshall. Eventually Catherine's patience reached its limit. She made a small snuffling sound and twisted her napkin as if to strangle it.

Declan winced. He knew that snuffling sound well. Trouble was brewing.

'The meal is lovely, Marshall,' said Catherine. 'But I am sure we did not come here just for food and small talk. Your invitation was vague, and so I would like know – how do you propose to celebrate Conor's life?'

Bonvilain's face was a mask of regret and understanding. 'You are right, Catherine. I have been shying away from tonight's *raison d'être*. Conor. Your son. The hero of the Saltee Islands. I thought we could share our memories of that brave young man, and then perhaps raise a toast. I have been saving a special bottle of wine.' It was a good performance and the marshall felt that, if needed, he could produce a tear.

'But why now?' prodded Catherine. 'I admit to being a little puzzled, Marshall.'

He was spared the need to answer by the sound of a bugle piping from the Wall.

Declan leaped instantly to his feet.

'That's the call to arms!' King Nicholas had insisted that the Saltee buglers learn US Army signals.

'No need for panic,' said Bonvilain, hurrying to the balcony. 'I was warned he might show up.'

'Who?' asked the queen.

'An enemy of the state, Your Majesty,' explained Bonvilain,

fixing his eye to a brass telescope. 'This one calls himself the Airman.'

'Airman,' said Declan. 'I've heard rumours about him. You mean he's a real threat?'

'Real? Yes,' said Bonvilain, squinting into the eyepiece. 'A threat? Absolutely not. Simply a Frenchman with a kite. Come and look. The lenses in this thing are quite fabulous.'

Catherine grasped Declan's arm to stop herself shaking. All this talk of flying and Frenchmen had put Victor Vigny in mind.

'A Frenchman in a kite?' she said, voice strained.

'Oh, dear God, of course,' said Bonvilain, feigning shock. 'Exactly like Vigny the murderer. I believe this Airman could be one of his acolytes. A curious hybrid of crazed revolutionary and scientist. I should not have even mentioned him; how insensitive of me. Please remain indoors. The Wall guard will shoot him down.'

Declan took Bonvilain's arm, leading him to one side. 'Shoot him down, Marshall? But you said he posed no threat.'

Bonvilain bent his head, spoke in a low voice. 'Not a realistic one, though my men have found a grenade workshop.'

Declan blanched. 'Grenades! Marshall, I am Captain of the Wall watch. Why do I not know all of this?'

'Captain. Declan. My informants on the mainland reported to me barely two hours ago. I fully intended to broach the subject after dinner, but, in all honesty . . . a

Frenchman, in a glider, dropping grenades? It seemed ludicrous. Something from a penny dreadful. At any rate, the wind is *towards* the mainland tonight, so how could this madman possibly glide here?'

At that moment a clunking mechanical noise echoed across the channel. It thrummed from a low register to a high one, spluttering alarmingly.

'Perhaps this Airman does not rely on the wind,' said Declan, snatching the telescope from its stand. 'Conor always said that one day man would build an engine-powered aeroplane.'

'Engine-powered,' said Bonvilain, through gritted teeth. 'A clever one that Conor, eh?'

Declan glanced down at the Wall. The watch had extinguished their lights and gathered in a cluster at the third tower. Several had climbed the parapet and were pointing skywards. Two held telescopes pointed thirty degrees skywards north-east. Declan raised the marshall's telescope to his eye and followed their line. For a moment he saw nothing but night sky and stars, but then something flashed across his field. Not a bird. Too big to be a bird.

Declan zigzagged the telescope, trapping the object in his circle of vision. What he saw took his breath away.

It was a flying machine. Conor's dream come alive in front of his eyes.

The aeroplane could not be called graceful, but it was flying, lurching through the air, trailing billowing streams of smoke. In the moonlight, Declan saw the Airman seated behind the engine, shoulders hunched as he wrestled with the controls, face obscured by goggles and soot, gritted teeth white against the blackness.

'I see him,' he gasped. 'The Airman. He's flying.'

Catherine rushed to the balcony, leaning over the rail, peering skywards.

'Oh my goodness. If only Conor could have seen this.' She turned to her husband. 'This cannot be coincidence. You need to talk with this sky pilot.'

Behind them a shrill whistle blew twice, and immediately the Wall watch stripped off their cloaks, twirling them like bullfighters. Three Gatling-gun teams hoisted their weapons on to custom wall mounts. Whoever this Airman was, he was headed straight for a hail of fire.

Bonvilain still had the whistle to his lips. 'The order is given. I had no choice, Catherine. He may be carrying grenades. My first duty is to the queen. Declan, surely you understand?'

Catherine turned to her husband, eyes blazing, fully expecting his support, but it was not forthcoming.

'The marshall is correct,' admitted Declan, though it pained him to say it. 'There is an unidentified craft approaching the island. The pilot may be armed. There is no option but to open fire.'

'He is flying a motorized kite,' said Catherine, her eyes stung by Declan's betrayal. 'The walls are four feet thick. Had he a brace of cannon on his wings, he could not penetrate the tower.'

Declan would not be swayed from his duty. 'This man has conquered the skies so perhaps he can conquer our walls too. I hear rumours of grenades filled with poison gas. We must not expose the queen.' He took Catherine's hands in his. 'The queen cannot die, do you understand?'

Catherine searched her husband's face for a deeper meaning to his words, and she found it.

The queen cannot die because if she does Bonvilain becomes prime minister.

'Very well, Declan. I understand,' said Catherine dully. 'The queen must live, so the Airman must die.' She dropped her husband's hand and stepped across the threshold. 'I have no stomach for this murder. Enjoy your victory, Marshall.'

Absolutely, thought Bonvilain, but aloud he said, 'One never enjoys the death of another, madam. I have been involved in many battles, but no matter how righteous the cause I have always concluded they could have been avoided. This time, sadly, there is no alternative.'

And with a regretful half-smile on his lips, the marshall raised his whistle and blew one final blast.

Below, on the Great Saltee Wall, the Gatling operators cranked their handles, pouring a thousand rounds a minute into the sky through their revolving barrel system. The bullets sped towards the Airman trailing grey smoke tails.

No one can survive that, thought Declan. *No one.*

Bonvilain was thinking exactly the same thing.

It was a battle of vectors and gravity. The Gatling cradles would only allow for a certain elevation, and even though they had a level range of 6,000 feet the Airman was as yet too high to be struck. But gravity was his enemy too. His fragile craft could not stay aloft forever, and when it dropped the bullets would shred it to confetti.

The noise and sheer concussion from the guns were shocking. It seemed as though the very island shook. It was easy to imagine the Wall being pounded to dust under repeated recoil. The chambers belched long cylinders of smoke, and steam rose in clouds as the water boys cooled the barrels by dousing them from buckets.

Declan had never seen Gatling guns at work on a battlefield, but he had heard that a single round could tear a man apart. There was enough lead in the air now to defeat an entire army. The sky was thick with their buzzing, like a dense swarm of metal hornets determined to find the same target.

Declan raised the telescope for one last look at the Airman. Even from this distance, it was clear that he was in dire straits. Hot oil bubbled on his face and goggles. Both hands were locked in struggle with a vertical rudder, and strips were coming loose from his wings, flapping behind the aeroplane like May Day ribbons.

Declan lowered the telescope.

He is gone. We will never know his true purpose.

Seconds later, the Airman lost his battle for control and altitude. His engine spasmed, growled and died. It seemed then as though there was a moment of echoes, as the craft spiralled down and the marksmen held their ammunition. Waiting.

It was not a long wait. Mere seconds. A short command was barked from the Wall, and the Gatling cranks were turning once more. Eighteen barrels spat fire and a fresh blizzard of rounds rocketed into the night sky. Spent cases clinked on the parapet like coins thrown to a beggar.

The bullets tore through the craft's wings and body, almost halting its descent. The impact was terrible, splintering the fragile body and tearing the wings to nothing. Round after round slammed into the engine until it exploded in a tight orange burst. Tendrils of flame shot along ribs and ropes, tracing the remains of the aeroplane against the night sky.

They did not hear a splash.

The night sky

Conor flew his machine through the sky above Great Saltee. A savage crosswind sheared across his bow, tilting him to starboard and he noticed a congregation of lights by the third tower. Lights meant guards.

The lights below winked out one by one, and Conor's stomach heaved with dread.

I am the target now.

For a moment there was nothing but shadowed activity from the third tower, then dots of fire flashed and a hail of shot erupted towards the heavens. A second later Conor heard the scream of the bullets and their frustrated cry as they passed below.

Pure panic bubbled in Conor's chest, and he almost jumped bodily from the machine.

Wait. Wait. I must pass Bonvilain's tower.

The engine was stuttering, missing beats like a failing

heart, losing its battle with the skies. Both wings were in tatters now, the wind's claws ripping strips of muslin from the frame. Below Conor's toes, the pedal had broken free from its stanchions and jiggled uselessly.

Almost in position. A few more yards.

A second swarm of bullets blasted towards him, and Conor felt the highest missiles tugging at the landing gear, sending the wheels spinning. He was in range now. Time to say goodbye to *La Brosse*. All evidence of his flight would soon be destroyed.

Conor knew that the marshall would never have allowed him to reach Great Saltee alive, so the trick was to persuade Bonvilain that the Airman was finally dead. This was a challenge. As a master of deception, Bonvilain was not an easy man to deceive.

But he knows nothing about flight. In the heavens, I am the master.

Conor wore his glider harness with one extra strap that connected him to his flying machine. The rest were, as usual, buckling him to his glider, which lay folded across his back, ribs slapping against his flying jacket, ripples running along the fabric. Linus had repaired it for him and it was stronger now than it had ever been.

One more flight, old friend.

It was difficult reaching down in all the confusion, it was *difficult* figuring which way was down, so Conor ran his hand along his own body, finding the strap at his waist. He yanked it upwards freeing the buckle and the aeroplane rocked loosely around his torso, but did not fall away as they were still bound together by momentum and gravity. The bullets were splintering the wood around his legs now – if he did not separate, his invention would become his coffin.

With a practised motion, Conor reached for the spring-loaded lever at his side. One swift tug, and the glider's wings deployed. They spread themselves wide against the stars like some great night bird, acting like a powerful brake, lifting Conor clear of the doomed aeroplane.

He watched it go, dipping into the shoal of glinting bullets. His historic invention was obliterated completely. Nothing left but burning fragments and a crushed metal heart.

The engine exploded, blew itself into fist-sized pieces, which spun into the darkness.

Gone. No place in history for La Brosse.

Far below on Great Saltee, a haze of gun smoke shrouded the Wall and through it Conor saw the muted glow of electric globes.

They turn the lights back on because they believe themselves safe.

Conor hung in the sky, finding his bearings. Bonvilain's tower was marked out by the rectangular glow of an open door. Isabella and his parents were inside that tower, in mortal danger. It could be that he was already too late.

Into the lion's den, thought Conor, then dipped the glider's nose, aiming for the light.

Bonvilain's tower

Marshall Bonvilain stepped over the threshold into the dining room, his face an exaggerated picture of regret. Behind him the last flames of destruction flickered out in the sky. From below on the Wall came the sounds of high-spirited congratulation, and the hiss of steam rising from glowing gun barrels.

'A great pity,' he said, chin low. 'That man had so much to teach the world.'

The gathering had been morose before, now the humour had switched to irate. Bonvilain took one look at the mood writ on his guests' faces and realized that a crisis was fast approaching.

'There was no other way, ladies . . . Declan. As marshall, I could not permit an assault on the Wall.'

Isabella stood by the fireplace, flushed cheeks contrasting with a high-collared ivory dress.

Bonvilain was unsettled by her expression, as he had not seen this look before. Ever since the coronation Isabella's confidence had been growing; now she had the temerity to glare at him. And just after he had supposedly saved her life.

I sincerely prefer the old Isabella, he thought. *Confused and grief-stricken is how I like my monarch.*

No one was talking, and they were all treating Bonvilain to the same disgusted stare.

They have been conferring, Bonvilain thought. *While I was on the balcony.*

'Are we all distressed?' he asked innocently. 'Shall I close the window?'

And still no one spoke. Bonvilain saw that the queen was working up the courage to deliver a lecture.

'I think I shall sit for this,' said the marshall calmly, dropping cross-legged to a cushion. 'Else my legs may give way. You have something to say, Majesty?'

Isabella took a step forward. Her dress almost disguising the shake in her legs.

'The sweep found something, Marshall. In my father's chamber.' These were her first words of the evening.

'Oh really?' said Bonvilain brightly, but inside he was discomfited. In his position, there was no such thing as a good surprise.

'Yes, Marshall, really.' Isabella took a small leather-bound book from her bag, and held it close to her heart. 'This is my father's diary.'

Bonvilain decided to brazen it out. 'Why, that's wonderful, Majesty. Something to connect you to King Nicholas.'

'Not so wonderful for you, Marshall,' continued Isabella, clutching Catherine's hand for support. 'My father was very suspicious of your activities. He wrote how you abuse your power to build a personal fortune. How you cultivate a network of spies on the mainland. How you are suspected of complicity in dozens of murders. The list goes on.'

'I see,' said Bonvilain, while in his head plotting.

It will be difficult to make them take the poisoned wine now. Already they do not trust me.

Isabella's legs were no longer shaking, and her tone was regal. 'Do you see? I think not, Marshall. Did you know that my father planned to see you in prison? Did you know that he planned to completely revise the power structure on the Saltee Islands? To inaugurate a parliament?'

Bonvilain managed to maintain his bland expression, but he knew that a crisis was upon him.

Typical, he thought. *Murder one enemy and three more spring up in his place.*

'May I read something for you?' asked Isabella.

Bonvilain nodded. 'It is not my place to allow or forbid, Majesty.'

'I shall take that as a yes,' said Isabella, with a curt smile. She released Catherine's hand to open her father's diary. '"Hugo Bonvilain is a scourge,"' she read. '"His power is formidable and he abuses it at every opportunity. When I have proof of his crimes, he will spend the rest of his life staring at the same cell walls he has condemned so many to suffer within. But I must be careful: nothing is below the marshall and I believe if he knew of my plans then he would take whatever steps necessary to thwart them. I do not fear for my own life, but Isabella must be kept safe. She is my heart."'

Isabella's voice almost broke at the end, but she reached for Catherine's hand and finished strong.

Bonvilain clapped both palms on his knees. 'Well, that's damning stuff,' said Bonvilain. 'Obviously the text is a forgery, planted by one of my enemies.'

I must make them drink. How to do it? How?

'I know my father's hand,' said Isabella firmly.

'I have no doubt of it, but an expert forger can deceive sharper eyes than ours. Have the book verified by an expert of your choice. I insist on it. This book is a grave insult to my life's work, and I will have my name cleared.'

'I have not finished,' declared Isabella. 'You are removed from office immediately. Declan . . . Captain Broekhart will take your place.'

Bonvilain kept the rage inside him corked up tight. 'Declan would certainly make a fine marshall. I thoroughly approve, but surely I deserve an opportunity to . . .'

'Enough!' ordered the queen, in a tone that brooked no argument. 'You will remain here under house arrest until your affairs can be investigated.'

Bonvilain silently cursed himself. He had provided the queen with the perfect forum to launch her attack. He had some men hidden in a secret compartment behind the wall, but it was difficult to reach behind a tapestry and pull a hidden lever under such scrutiny.

Everything rests on the poisoned wine. If it were just the queen I could force it down her gullet, but Declan Broekhart would run me through with that darned ceremonial sword, and if his wife's stares were daggers I would be dead already.

A great relief shone in Isabella's eyes, and shoulders dipped as the tension drained from her body. The prospect of this confrontation had terrified her since the diary's discovery. She had planned every word in her speech and, finally, victory was hers, and her father's.

'And now, Hugo Bonvilain,' she said, 'I think we should conclude what we are here to do. We should raise a toast to our beloved Conor Broekhart.'

Bonvilain bit his lip.

Oh, thank you, spirits of irony. The gods have a sense of humour after all.

Bonvilain's expression was peevish. 'I hardly think . . . Under the circumstances . . .'

Catherine stepped forward, plucking the special bottle from the ice bucket.

'I realize that you invited us here in a transparent attempt to toady to Isabella and Declan, but we wish to honour our son and you will raise a glass with us.'

'This is ridiculous,' grumbled Bonvilain. 'But I, of course, will not cause my queen displeasure.'

He stood and slouched while Declan opened and poured, Bonvilain muttered under his breath and threw hateful stares. The picture of a beaten bully, and certainly not a schemer on the verge of his greatest coup.

They held their crystal glasses aloft, Bonvilain's at half-mast. With Catherine's smile of approval, Isabella gave the toast.

'To Conor, my best friend. My prince and saviour. Look after my father.'

Tears sparkled in Catherine's eyes, and Declan actually moaned. Bonvilain tried not to laugh, but it was difficult.

Look after my father? You can look after him yourself if I have my way.

Bonvilain waited for his guests to drink, but they did not. He abandoned his surly expression for a moment to glance at their faces. Each one regarded their twinkling glass with dawning suspicion.

Perhaps this wine is poisoned. Perhaps this is why Bonvilain invited us here.

There was only one way for Bonvilain to allay this suspicion.

Ah well, there goes my evening. It's the water closet for me until morning.

'To the Broekhart boy, how I miss him,' he said, quaffing half of his glass in a single swallow.

'To Conor, my son,' said Declan. 'Heaven is lucky to have him.' And raised the glass to his mouth.

But before he could do more than wet his lips something dark detached itself from the night outside and pounced on Hugo Bonvilain. Something dark with wings.

Conor hurtled through the window, a creature of the night, crashing into Bonvilain, tumbling them on to the low table. Crockery and cutlery flew, and both men were instantly entangled in swathes of gold embroidered tablecloth. Only Conor's wings remained exposed and he must have resembled a giant moth, attracted to the cloth's bright pattern.

Declan reacted quickly, throwing his glass aside and wrapping his fingers round the grip of his ceremonial sword. Ceremonial, but razor sharp nonetheless.

It is the Airman, he thought. *Come to kill the queen.*

The situation with Bonvilain must be set aside until this common enemy was dealt with. He grabbed a hank of tablecloth, bent low and used his weight and strength to spin the warring pair from the table. They rolled across the floor, still battling, though Bonvilain's blows were growing weak and ineffective. The Airman drove his fist repeatedly into his enemy's face, until Bonvilain's eyes lost their focus.

Declan reached for the collar of the intruder's jacket

but was too slow. The Airman spun around, speaking urgently.

'Did you drink? Have you raised the toast?'

A strange question for an assassin to pose, thought Declan. *But no time for distractions; put him down then ponder his questions.*

He swung his sword, intending to render the Airman unconscious with the flat of his blade, only to find it almost causally batted aside by his enemy's forearm.

'The toast. Did you drink?'

Something in the man's attitude unsettled Declan, as though he were about to make a terrible mistake. The face or perhaps the voice. Something. He held back from striking, uncertain now of his strength of purpose.

Catherine had no such doubts. She saw nothing of the Airman's face. From her angle there was only her husband and the man attacking him. She hitched up her skirt and planted a solid kick square in the Airman's side, following it with a dashing blow from a handy flower vase.

Conor staggered sideways, dripping water and wearing daffodils.

'Wait,' he gasped, shrugging off his harness and wings. 'Don't . . .'

But he was given no respite. Isabella pulled a samurai sword from its presentation case, and adopted a fencing stance before him.

'*En garde, monsieur*,' she said, then launched a blistering attack. Conor's sabre barely cleared its scabbard in time to parry the first thrust.

'Isabella,' he gasped, completely disorientated. 'You must stop.'

The queen was in no mood to stop anything.

'I will stop when you are dead, assassin.'

Conor managed a lucky counter riposte, which bought him the second he needed to find his balance.

Isabella had improved as a fencer since their lessons with Victor, but Conor could still see the bones of his teachings.

'You have studied Marozzo well,' he gasped. 'Victor would be proud.'

Isabella's blade quivered, then froze.

What did this mean? Who was this man to invoke Victor's name?

Declan gathered his wife and the queen behind him, sword raised for battle.

'You will show your face, sir?' he demanded. 'I grant you five seconds before we duel to the death. And that death will be yours.'

Conor slowly reversed his grip, then buried the tip of his sword in the floorboards.

'Very well. But, before I do, tell me if you drank a toast.'

'There was no toast,' snapped Declan. 'Now, off with those goggles, sir.'

Conor's shoulders slumped and he seemed on the verge of collapse, but he drew himself erect and pulled the collar down from his chin, then pushed the goggles up to his forehead. His face was blasted black from soot and oil, but his eyes were clear, and a lock of blond hair had come loose from his leather cap.

The watchers were confused. What they were seeing was not possible.

'Father, I know you vowed to kill me should we meet again,' said Conor slowly. 'But there are things you do not know. Victor did not kill the king, nor was I involved. It was Bonvilain.'

'Conor,' breathed his mother. 'You live?'

Declan sank to his knees as though gut punched. His breath was laboured and tears streamed down his face.

'My son lives. How is it possible?'

And suddenly Conor understood the scale of Bonvilain's deception.

My parents genuinely believed me dead. Bonvilain spun a different lie for each party.

Isabella was the first to reach him, hugging him tightly, kissing his cheek. Her tears mingling with his.

'Oh, Conor. Conor, where have you been?'

Conor held her tightly, reeling from the strength of emotions aimed at him. He had been expecting mistrust and anger. Not love.

'That was you in the cell,' moaned Declan. 'I said I would kill you. I sent you to hell.'

Catherine rubbed her husband's back, but then couldn't keep herself away from her son. She rushed to him, taking his face in her hands.

'Oh, Conor. You are a man now,' she said. 'Grown as tall as your father at seventeen.'

Conor was vaguely surprised to remember that he *was* only seventeen. Conor Finn had been more than twenty.

Declan Broekhart's face was suddenly terrible with rage.

'Bonvilain did this. All of it and by God I will make him pay.'

Bonvilain!

In the swirl of emotions, Conor had forgotten about Hugo Bonvilain. He turned clumsily in the embrace of his mother and queen, to find only a puddle of blood where Bonvilain had fallen. He plucked his sabre from the floorboards and scanned the chamber to find his old enemy sliding along the wall, quietly making for the door.

'Father,' called Conor, pointing with his sword. 'We must secure Bonvilain.'

Finding that his escape was thwarted, Bonvilain reached behind a tapestry and pulled his hidden lever. The fireplace slid aside on a pulley mechanism, revealing a tightly packed group of Holy Cross guards.

Bonvilain smiled, his mouth a bloody mess, more than one gap in his teeth.

'My last line of defence,' he said, spitting crimson. And to the soldiers. 'Kill the women. They are impostors.'

It was a cunning order, diverting Conor and Declan from their path in order to defend Isabella and Catherine. The soldiers tumbled from their confined space, drawing daggers and swords. No guns – guns would bring the Wall watch running.

Luckily the secret space was cramped, and so the men

were stiff and light dazzled, which gave the Broekharts a second's advantage.

They used it well, bundling the half-dozen Holy Cross guardsmen back towards their hiding place.

'Watch the marshall,' Conor called to Isabella.

'He is no longer the marshall,' said the queen, raising the samurai sword.

'I have been taught how to slice a man into three pieces,' she said to Bonvilain. 'Take one step towards us and I will demonstrate those strokes for you.'

Bonvilain pinched the bridge of his nose. Ordinarily he would rush this silly girl and crush the hands that held the sword, but the poison in his wine was beginning to affect him. Already his fingers were tingling and a volcano bubbled in his innards. He needed to be away from here before the more extreme symptoms.

The path to the door was blocked by the Broekharts. His secret passage was a melee of flailing limbs and blades and the only other exit was the balcony.

Bonvilain tripped over Conor's discarded wings and on to the balcony, searching furiously below for something to rescue him.

Imagine. Hugo Bonvilain needs rescuing. How embarrassing.

Below, the Wall watch stripped down the Gatling guns, apparently oblivious to the commotion sixty feet above their heads. They had obviously not noticed the giant bird-like creature crashing into their marshall's apartments.

Bonvilain felt his stomach lurch as the poison twisted his guts.

I must escape. I need a way down.

There! Crossing the courtyard below was Sultan Arif, a duffle bag in his hand and another slung across his back.

Where the devil is that fool going?

'Sultan!' he shouted. 'Captain Arif. I need you, now!'

Sultan missed a step, but he did not stop.

'I am going home, Hugo,' he called, without turning. 'I have many sins to atone for.'

For the first time in many a year, Bonvilain experienced real rage. 'Get back here!' he demanded, pounding the railing. 'I don't have time for your sulking. Send me a rope on a crossbow bolt.'

Arif disobeyed yet again. 'If you have drunk the toast then I would advise you stay calm, Marshall,' he advised, quickening his pace towards the gate. 'A speeding heart moves the poison more quickly through your veins.'

'Traitorous wretch,' roared Bonvilain. 'Do not doubt that we shall meet again!'

'And I know where we shall meet,' whispered Sultan, his back turned on Bonvilain once and for all.

A speeding heart moves the poison more quickly.

Bonvilain realized the truth of those words as a spasm hit him and he vomited bile over the balcony.

Calm yourself, Hugo. There is still time.

With one last shake of his fist in Sultan Arif's direction, Bonvilain went back into his own apartment . . .

. . . Where Declan and Conor Broekhart were battling furiously with three of the Holy Cross guard. Three were already down, unconscious or clutching their wounds. At that moment, Declan Broekhart took a blade in the shoulder, leaving his son to fight alone.

Catherine dragged her husband clear, and Queen Isabella kept her sword levelled at Bonvilain.

That girl is really becoming quite irksome. Why did I let her live this long?

Bonvilain realized that he had allowed his schemes to become too elaborate.

I need these people dead, but, more than that, I need to be in a safe place where I can regain my strength. I have funds and supporters on the mainland.

Conor drove the three Holy Cross guards back with a wide swing, then drew a pistol from his belt, firing off two low rounds. A couple of soldiers collapsed with shattered shins.

Gunfire! thought Bonvilain. *That and the word 'poison' from the courtyard will have the Wall watch running. I must away.*

The poison was in his legs now, sticking needles in his toes, cramping his muscles.

Across the room, Conor Broekhart struggled with the final guard, a huge Scotsman wielding a shortened broadsword. This was one of Bonvilain's mercenaries and a veteran killer. For a moment Bonvilain nurtured a glimmer of hope, then Conor stepped under the big Scotsman's swing and knocked him flat with the sabre's finger guard.

The Airman tumbled the final guard back inside the cavity then reached behind the tapestry and sealed them inside. Their moaning could be heard through the grate.

'Behind you, son,' said Declan, through gritted teeth. 'The marshall.'

Conor rounded on Bonvilain with three years of hatred glowing in his eyes. He was a figure from children's nightmares. A man in black, wielding a bloody weapon, lips pulled back in a snarl.

'Bonvilain,' he said, with a strange calmness.

Generally Bonvilain would have relished the opportunity for some choice remarks, followed by swift mortal combat with this whelp, but now his system was afire with wolfsbane. His tongue felt strange and swollen in his mouth and his legs bent under the weight of his torso.

Soon my judgement will be gone. I must escape now.

Isabella stepped forward. 'You will answer for your crimes, Hugo Bonvilain. Your reign is over. There is no escape.'

Bonvilain bent low, grunting like a wild boar. He grasped Conor's harness, dragging the glider on to the balcony.

'Escape,' he muttered, drool dripping from his slack lip. 'Fly away, Airman.'

Conor followed him, cocking his pistol. 'I'm warning you, Bonvilain.'

Bonvilain managed a dry laugh. 'Conor Broekhart. Always in my way. In Paris when I ordered your father's balloon shot down. When I set the king's tower alight. Even now. Perhaps you are magical, as people believe.'

It was difficult to understand what Hugo Bonvilain said, his loose lips bubbled with spittle and blood. The marshall rolled his body up on to the balcony's parapet.

'Keep away, or you will never know my secrets.'

Conor ached to finish Bonvilain, but Isabella's light touch prevented it.

'Don't, Conor. I need to know everything he has done. There is so much to be set right.' Isabella turned to the marshall. 'Come down from there,' ordered Isabella. 'Your queen commands it.'

Bonvilain struggled to his feet, clumsily pulling the harness round his shoulders.

'I have no queen, no god, no country,' he mumbled, cinching the chest belt with rubbery fingers. That would have to do, he did not have the dexterity for the remaining buckles. 'All I have is cunning.'

And with a focus born of hatred, Bonvilain reached inside his dragon robe to a dagger at his belt, with the intention of flicking it from the waist. Conor saw the gleam of the blade as it cleared the silk.

Isabella! Even now he tries to kill Isabella.

Conor swung his pistol, but Declan Broekhart was quicker, even though his shoulder was wounded. He hurled his sword, spear-like, with such force that it pierced Bonvilain's vest of chain mail and lodged in his heart.

Bonvilain sighed, as though disappointed with the book he was reading, then stepped backwards off the parapet, into the night. An updraught filled the glider's wings, floating Bonvilain over the courtyard past the disbelieving eyes of the Wall watch and hundreds of Saltee islanders raised from their beds by the Gatling guns.

Bonvilain hung there for several moments, his dripping blood painting swirls on the flagstones, before a crosswind flipped the glider about, urging it out to sea.

Conor watched him go, dropping closer and closer to

the cold ocean, the silhouetted sword protruding from his lifeless heart, and with him went the nightmare that his life had become.

None could tear their eyes from Bonvilain's corpse, arresting even in death. Further from land he drifted, and lower too until his toes skimmed the ocean. Conor wished to see him go down, to be certain that it was over, but he did not. Bonvilain was lost to sight before the ocean claimed him.

Below was consternation. The watch were hammering on the Wall access door, and the people surged against the foot of the tower.

Declan Broekhart took Isabella by the hand, leading her to the parapet.

'The queen is safe,' he called, raising her hand. 'Long live the queen.'

The cry that came back was relieved and heartfelt.

'Long live the queen.'

CHAPTER 19:

TIME APART

Great Saltee. One month later

Queen Isabella had taken to walking the Wall every morning at sunrise. She believed that it gave her subjects heart to see her there. Before too many sunrises, she could call to everyone she saw by name.

Conor often joined his queen on her morning strolls, and on the morning before his planned departure to study for a science degree at Glasgow University, they met below what had been Bonvilain's tower.

Isabella stood with her elbows on the parapet, watching a cluster of fishing boats half a mile offshore, the small crafts bobbing in the choppy channel currents.

'They will never find him, you know,' said Conor. 'Bonvilain's mail vest has taken him straight to the bottom. He is food for the crabs now.'

Isabella nodded. 'Without a body, he becomes the bogeyman. They say he has been seen in Paris, and Dublin. I read in the London *Times* that Bonvilain survives as a killer for hire in Whitechapel.'

They were both silent for a minute, convincing themselves that they had actually seen Hugo Bonvilain die.

'What will you do with this place?' Conor asked finally, slapping the tower wall.

'A diamond market, I think,' replied Isabella. 'It seems ludicrous that the diamonds are here, and yet we trade in London.'

'You're making big changes.'

'There are many things to be changed. Little Saltee, for one. Did you know that only fourteen of the prisoners are from the Saltee Islands? The majority of the other poor souls are from Ireland or Great Britain. Well, no more. I will shut the prison down and contract the mining to a professional firm.'

Conor glanced at the *S* branded into his hand.

Little Saltee will always be with me. It has marked my body and mind.

'What will happen to the prisoners?' he asked.

'Every case will be reviewed by a judge. I suspect most have served their sentences and more besides. Reparations will have to be made.'

'I would be grateful if you could look kindly on a certain Otto Malarkey. He is not as fearsome as he seems.'

'Of course, Sir Conor.'

'You will make a fine queen.'

'My father was the scientist; I am a businesswoman. You can be my royal scientist . . . on your return.'

'Mother told you?'

Isabella took his arm, and they promenaded along the Wall. 'Catherine told me about Glasgow. I am supposed to talk you out of it.'

'And how would you do that?'

'I could always have you hanged.'

Conor smiled. 'Like the old days. Sometimes I wish the old days were here still.'

Isabella stopped at one of her favourite spots on the Wall. A dip facing the mainland where centuries ago masons had built a lovers' seat. From this vantage point, at various times during the morning, it was possible to view morning sun illuminating the church tower's stained-glass window. As the sun moved, it seemed as though the Saint Christopher figure in the window moved a little too.

Isabella sat on the stone seat, pulling Conor down beside her.

'I miss the old days too. But it's not too late for us is it, Conor?'

'I hope that it is not,' replied Conor.

'Then I shall wait,' said Isabella. And her playful side surfaced. 'Shall you fly home to see me, Sir Airman?'

'I am merely a *sir*. Is that not too common for a queen?'

'That is easily fixed. With one prick of my hat pin, you can become a prince.'

'Hat pin? Is that legal?'

'It doesn't have to be a hat pin, so long as there is blood and you are in great pain.'

Conor took her hand in his. 'I think now that I shall be in great pain until I return.'

'Then study hard, earn your paper, and come home quickly. Your queen needs you. I need you.'

And they kissed for the first time, with the stained-glass sun painting rainbows on their faces and the hubbub of morning trade rising from the square below.

All the goodbyes had been said. He had kissed his mother and dangled his little brother upside down. All that was left was to leave.

Conor strolled down to the port on a sunny morning, keeping one eye on the barrow boy bobbing down the hill with his luggage. The sea was calm and a small passenger steamship chugged on its ropes in the outside dock.

A small crowd had gathered on the deck and Conor smiled when he saw the attraction. Linus Wynter was treating the passengers to an impromptu rendition of an aria from *The Soldier's Return*.

He stopped singing when he heard Conor's footsteps on the planks.

'It's about time you showed up, boy. I had to sing just to stop the captain casting off.'

'Any excuse, Linus,' said Conor, flipping the barrow boy a shilling. 'You have secured the laboratory?'

'Our tower is in good hands. Uncle has moved in with a couple of his *dullards* as he calls them.'

'How does Uncle smell?'

'Not so good. All we can hope for is that he will fall into the ocean with a bar of soap in his pocket.'

Conor leaped across a yard of sea on to the steamship.

'Do you think Scotland is ready for your genius?'

Linus smiled broadly, adjusting his tinted eyeglasses, which

Conor had fashioned for him. 'The Scots are famous for their appreciation of music. Robert Burns was a poet of the people, like myself. Glasgow will take me to its bosom, I feel sure of it. In six months we will be the toast of the city.'

'You can see into the future now, old friend?'

Linus searched the air until his hand found Conor's shoulder. 'Other men look up and down, left and right,' he said. 'But men like us are different. We are visionaries.'

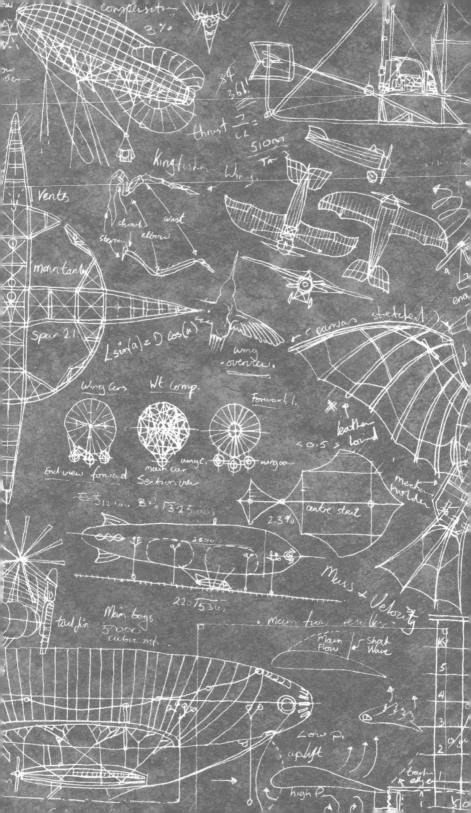